THE FOREST
OF
DAMNED
SOULS

THE FOREST OF DAMNED SOULS

—— by The Sinister Mind of Tully

CHAPTER 1

The whisky-bile cocktail smacked the concrete with a violent splatter. The man composed himself. Until another curious glimpse at his neighbour's exposed ribcage induced more hot vomit.

Helpless, he could no longer stomach kneeling next to the goulash of bloody intestines stewing in the warm evening air. His hands were lathered in the sticky wax of his friend's blood, the same blood that slithered across the concrete, soaking his jeans; blackcurrant knees sticking to his skin.

Climbing the porch steps of his static caravan, the man stumbled, partially due to shock, partially because of the bottle of Ardbeg he had glugged that evening. He left a bloody handprint on the wooden beam as he attempted to steady himself.

A shrill cry from a grieving mother diverted his attention back to the cul-de-sac corner of the caravan site. Quivering as he took a deep breath, the man scanned the horror show from right to left.

His dead neighbour's wife was entombed within the collapsed roof of their porch. The support beams buckled under the impact of the assailant as easily as a sledgehammer colliding with a shinbone. Whether she was slain by the killer or crushed by the roof, death was the outcome.

The man burped whisky molecules, which were spiralling within his mouth like fireballs. He regained focus, following the carnage trail to the roundabout at the end of the cul-de-sac. A new resident, one he did not know, lay dead with his shotgun aside. The first shot did not hit its mark, and the attacker moved swiftly to maul the unknown neighbour as he flustered reloading the gun.

Next to the swing set, the hysterical mother was attending to her unconscious daughter, who fainted upon seeing her brother being swiped from the swing and transported into the forest behind. A splintered gap in the flimsy wooden fence, the size of a compact car, showed the attacker's escape route from the caravan site to the forest.

The man shivered while staring into the deep black abyss, imagining that the attacker was lurking, waiting to pounce again. He never believed the rumours that Bannock forest is cursed. It may boast a deadly history, but he never believed it was the forest manifesting the violence, malevolently luring victims into its wooden tentacles. Now, he believed. He believed in the forest of damned souls.

Staggering into his caravan, the man paused. His head was spinning. Booze and horror twirled his cognition into a cocktail of confusion. He dialled the police on his mobile. The call failed. He had fumbled a wrong digit. He tried again.

'Hello, emergency services. How can I help?'

'We need help.'

'Okay. Can you…'

'There's been an attack. Folk are dead.'

'Are you at the crime scene now?'

'Aye.'

'Are you in a safe place, away from any danger?'

'No one is safe.'

'Please move to a safer location, sir.'

'I'm in my caravan. I'm okay for now.'

'What's your name?'

'Henry Burke.'

'Okay, Henry. You said there's been an attack. Is the attacker still in the area?'

'I don't think so.'

'How many people are injured?'

'None. They are all dead.'

'How many are deceased, Henry?'

'Four, well three definitely, one maybe. The wee lad was taken away. I suppose I don't know if he's dead, but I guess he probably is. If only the wee ones had gone inside when the attack started.'

'I can see you are calling from Dalmally caravan site, Henry. The police and ambulance services are on their way. They won't be long. Stay in your caravan until they arrive, okay?'

'You'll need the fucking army, love.'

4

'I'm going to ask you a few questions about the incident, so I can provide a more detailed update to the inbound officers.'

'Okay.'

'Do you know who the victims are?'

'Yes, well, I know Jim and Mags across the road. They visit their caravan three or four times a year. I don't know the guy at the end of our street. I know the wee lad, though. He was with his family. They only visit once a year. If only they came a different week.'

Burke whimpered as if starting to cry, but the call handler maintained his focus.

'Do you know the person who attacked these people? Did you see the incident?'

'Person? This was no person.'

'Oh, was it an animal?'

'Animal?'

Burke stumbled. His mouth moved further away from the phone. To the call handler, he sounded like he was whispering from a deep well, and all she could discern was the faintest word: wolf.

'Can I confirm it was a wolf that attacked these people?'

'Naw, wolfs dinny attack humans. This was something bigger, deadlier.'

'Could it have been a large wolf?'

'You dinny get wolves like this in Caledonia, love. This was something we've never seen before.'

'Can you describe the animal to me?'

'It was a werewolf.'

CHAPTER 2

Detective Nikki Achebe assessed herself in the dull reflection of the glass trophy cabinet, tugging nervously on the lapels of her purple-tipped blazer. Detective trilbies and bravery awards for her superiors, Premier Detective Tom Dargo and Senior Detective Xander Bullock, glinted back at her. As a newly promoted detective in Caledonia's Major Crimes Unit, she fantasised that one day she could match their brilliance.

Standing outside the Major Crimes office, she was preparing to address an impatient task force of constables - or peace officers, as their uniforms stated. Her stomach roiled with nerves. She had presented to the same peace officers hundreds of times, providing updates on cases and delegating tasks. But that was always as a High Constable, and always at the command of Dargo and Bullock. Now that she was a detective in her own right, she held superior rank and status, which given she was only twenty-eight-years-old, spread a viral resentment throughout the other high constables and peace officers.

Her new title soured their personalities, bitter judgement clouding their ability to be pleased for her. She did not expect everyone to be thrilled with her appointment, but friendships had regressed to co-worker status, inclusion in the coffee runs had evaporated, and her social significance took a final blow when they removed her from the constables and officers' group chat within minutes of her promotion announcement, absent of any

6

parting congratulations. While Achebe initially baulked at their pettiness, she could not deny their behaviour stabbed her deep.

Pulling her shoulders back, Achebe took a deep breath, and entered the Major Crimes office.

The volume fizzled out as the officers noticed her entrance, but an unnerving whisper remained. She felt the eyes of the room upon her, which only increased her stomach-churning. Their contempt was compounded by a crabbiness at being dragged out of their beds to form an urgent response team.

Achebe hopped onto an elevated platform at the front of the office.

'Can I have everyone's attention, please?'

She glimpsed Dargo and Bullock's shadowy movements between the blinds to their private office, separate from the open-plan Major Crimes workplace. Their absence was deliberate to ensure the officers knew Achebe was firmly in charge of the investigation. While she appreciated their approach, she felt vulnerable to the officers' judgemental gazes. Their resentment hovered in the air like smoke in an old pub. It was suffocating, and she missed the rhythm of her next breath, causing a mini gasp to explode from her mouth as she spoke.

'High Constable Gardyne?'

'Here.'

Some officers sniggered at her obvious nerves as Giovanni Gardyne shuffled his muscular physique to the front of the group. He was of Caledonian-Italian heritage and was called the "stripper" amongst the officers for appearing too handsome in his uniform. However, when he laughed the nickname off with a deflective quip, his unpolished Caledonian accent exposed his rugged roots. It was this breezy, easy-going nature that meant Achebe got on so well with Gardyne, but he too had given her the cold shoulder since she became a detective.

'Any word from the zoos?'

'The zoo and safari park are checking their inventory, but no animals reported missing yet.'

Achebe contemplated lightening the mood with a joke about having a safari in the miserable Caledonian climate, but her nerves decided against it.

'Thanks. High Constable Robinson?'

It felt fraudulent to state Jen Robinson's rank before her name, having operated at the same level only three weeks ago. They were inseparable in the office, laughing and joking and pushing each other to better themselves. But even such a strong relationship with Jen had become fractured. Achebe was slightly younger, and they always assumed Jen would become a detective first.

'Yes, boss.'

Achebe internalised a smile at Jen's professionalism and support in calling her boss, even if she didn't look happy about it.

'I need you to contact Wildlife Rescue and get a list of all institutions and individuals that own big cats and exotic animals. They must have a blacklist of individuals who previously held wild animals illegally as well. Can you pull a list of names together and start investigating them one by one to make sure no one has lost Tony the tiger.'

'Grrreat.'

Jen never put much gusto into the joke, but it made some officers chuckle and indicated to Achebe that she was on board despite her promotion disappointment.

'You do not need to investigate Jim McAllister. I am going to see him tomorrow once the zoos and safari park confirm no animal has escaped from their premises. He was notorious for holding big cats and bears illegally in the past, so he is my first port of call.'

'Okay, boss.'

A slightly more composed Achebe addressed the room.

'Okay, as you know, an animal attacked Dalmally caravan park. It dragged one boy, seven years old, into Bannock forest. That's roughly two hundred square miles of dense woodland. The Special Response Unit is on site, and forensics will analyse paw prints found at the scene. We do not know what type of animal it is yet, if it even is an animal. It could be someone's sick idea of a hoax.'

'You're not in an episode of Scooby-Doo, honey?'

The comment broke Achebe's flow. Her cheeks flushed with a mixture of rage and embarrassment. Constable Edmunds' follicles were thinning as fast as he was approaching forty. He stood confidently with his arms folded as a group of his posse stood behind him like a boxer's support team, laughing at his jibe. His comment was not banter. It was demeaning; an attempt to chop a sapling detective before she got too big for her roots.

'All I'm saying is to keep an open mind and rule nothing out.'

'So, should we be working on the basis that we are searching for a human or an animal?' Edmunds retorted while shaking his head.

'An animal.'

'You just said it might be a hoax.'

'We don't know all the facts yet. Our best guess is the animal is a wolf, but wolves rarely attack humans unless provoked, and never to the extent of this attack. I'm just trying to make sure we keep an open mind.'

8

'Talking shite more like.'

The posse erupted with laughter. Achebe's body burned with fury.

'Okay, Edmunds. You're coming with me to meet Jim McAllister tomorrow. That way, I can keep an eye on you and make sure you're committed to this task force. If not, you're more than welcome to act like a wanker in traffic control.'

Edmunds flinched; the same flummoxed expression people display when surprised by the first spots of rain landing on their forehead. His senior years turned juvenile as his face blushed and his head lowered into his neck.

'But I'm meant to be helping High Constable Robinson.'

'I'm sure High Constable Robinson doesn't mind you spending half a day with me.'

Achebe glanced at Robinson, pleading for her to join in. She shrugged nonchalantly to show her indifference to Edmunds' whereabouts.

'There you go,' Achebe said. 'And make sure you polish your shoes before we see a suspect.'

Edmunds looked down to his feet, along with every other officer. His face turned beetroot as Achebe exposed the childish grey scuff marks on his toes.

'Have you been playing football at break time with those?' Achebe said, removing the stab to the gut he inflicted seconds ago and twisting the knife into Edmunds.

One of his posse nudged him on the arm while laughing. Edmund's stare told him to fuck off.

Achebe maintained a composed exterior as she cut Edmunds off at the knees, but the clingy armpit sweat hidden beneath her blazer meant the ordeal was more taxing than her demeanour suggested.

She tugged the bottom of her blazer as Senior Detective Bullock exited his office upon hearing Achebe raise her voice. He glared towards the group of officers like a lion deciding which zebra he wanted to eat first. He rested his six-foot-three frame against the wall. His wavy brown hair shimmered like a movie star, and his sharp facial features poked at the room underneath his permanently furrowed brow. As he folded his arms, his brown leather biker jacket squeezed with a choked squeak.

'Everything alright, Detective Achebe?'

He gazed into the group of officers while stroking the fine hairs of his goatee. The officers were suddenly more amused with their shuffling feet than Bullock's eye line.

'Yes, sir. Everything is fine.'

9

'Nothing you can't handle, I'm sure. But if you encounter any more annoying little problems, you can always send them my way.'

Bullock winked at Achebe, but it wasn't for her benefit. It was a signal to the officers that he was ready for them should anyone step out of line. Achebe continued with her briefing.

'As I was saying, the Special Response Unit is searching the forest for our missing child. We have already deployed rescue helicopters to search the area. However, our helicopters do not have infrared capabilities, so we've sourced one from down south, which is mildly embarrassing, and as you can imagine, we are being charged a fortune for it, but it is what it is. We have warned locals from conducting their own search parties for the boy until we understand exactly what we are dealing with. It would be too dangerous to let them walk into the forest unarmed, and far more dangerous if they were to arm themselves. As I said, forensics will take samples of the paw prints, so we should learn what we are dealing with within twenty-four hours.'

Achebe pointed to a map on the board behind her.

'You are probably wondering why I dragged you out of your beds if the Special Response Unit is conducting the search instead of us? It's all about effective communication and reassuring the public. As you can see here, the caravan site sits on the fringes of the southernmost point of Bannock forest. High Constable Gardyne, I want your team to visit every property on the caravan site, patrol Dalmally town as well, and warn anyone you see of the ongoing situation. For now, the rhetoric is there is a dangerous animal on the loose and to stay indoors if possible, only travelling by car if they need to leave their homes. It goes without saying that you are not to use the word werewolf, despite what the witnesses say.'

The officers nodded obsequiously.

'If residents use the word werewolf, then please deny this and state that the animal is not a mythical creature, but *is* highly dangerous. If the public hears the term werewolf, they won't take our warnings seriously. We are trying to appease them, but we need to leave enough fear in their minds to keep them indoors until we've caught whatever is out there.'

'We'll start right away, boss.' said Gardyne.

'Thanks. High Constable Robinson, there's a forestry company twenty miles northeast of the caravan site. I need you to visit there, inform them of the situation and inquire about any potential sightings.'

'Yes, boss.'

A desk phone demanded attention. Achebe nodded to a junior officer, giving him permission to answer it. She returned to the map and pointed to a spot roughly ten miles north of the crime scene.

'High Constable Robinson, I also need one of your team to look into Bannock Manor. Find out what's going on there and if we need to warn anyone who lives or works on the land.'

'Bannock Manor has been derelict for at least fifteen years.' Robinson responded. 'It was owned by a guy called Hamish Stewart. I'm sure he died while trying to perform a magic trick underwater. An unusual death, that's why I remember it. I'll do some more digging, though.'

'Thanks, and what about this quarry a few miles away from the manor?'

'I believe it's just a skeleton crew that works up there, but I'll confirm and reach out to them if needed.'

'Thanks. The Chief will issue a statement later this morning about these events, warning the public to avoid Bannock forest, but I feel we need officers on the ground now to make sure those living closest to Bannock forest feel as safe as possible, and ensure they don't travel anywhere on foot.'

The officers nodded in agreement. Achebe was pleased with how attentive they were, but she knew that was because of Bullock's sniper gaze. She glanced in his direction, surprised to find him gone.

'What about the central and northern areas of Bannock forest?' asked Robinson. 'It's the height of summer, and we have all that woodland in the middle that people can camp and ramble in. Then at the top, there are the Cairngorm hills and lochs, all of which attract thousands of tourists every day.'

'The Chief will include warnings for these areas in his press communication. Our focus is on the immediate area for now. Until we find out what animal we are dealing with, it is hard to understand how vast an area to cover. Is this an animal that travels several miles every day? Does it create a den and roam close to its home? We don't know at this point. Local police will be deployed to deliver a message of caution in their respective areas. The entire forest is open to the public, so we are not at liberty to ban people from it, but hopefully the Chief's statement deters most from attending the area. In the meantime, we can only do our best to catch this thing as quickly as possible.'

'Yes, boss.'

'Okay, let's get to work. You know where I am if you need to speak to me.'

The officers dispersed like worker ants attending to their small, but significant, role in the grander plan. Achebe heard a whisper between two officers.

'The forest of damned souls lives on.'

The junior officer placed the phone down with a quivering hand. His throat croaked on his first attempt to attract Achebe's attention.

'Excuse me, boss.'

'Yes.'

'They found part of the boy.'

'Part of the boy?' Achebe asked as the pit of her stomach sunk in anticipation of the officer's reply.

'The boy's father entered the woods despite our advice and found the boy's left arm; hacked clean off. I think it's safe to assume that the boy is dead.'

CHAPTER 3

The mugshots of three missing teenagers were pinned to the corkboard; their smiling profiles contradicting the seriousness with which Premier Detective Dargo was inspecting the information beneath them. Another corkboard displayed a family photo, all of whom were also missing.

'Two unrelated missing persons cases occur at exactly the same time.' Senior Detective Bullock said. 'It's a strange auld time in Caledonia.'

Achebe entered Dargo and Bullock's the office feeling exhausted after a briefing which had tested her emotional range.

'Sorry to disturb you, guys.'

'Not a problem, Nikki,' Bullock said.

Achebe shut the door with a dainty push to avoid distracting the great mind of the Premier. She longed to swap brains, just for five minutes, to gain an insight into how Dargo analysed a case and interpreted evidence to form his conclusions. Of course, he was far more experienced, but raw instinct and intuition make the best detectives, something she figured Dargo always held in abundance. He turned to give Achebe his full attention.

'Nikki, how are you getting on?'

His voice was soothing, wrapping a cloak of calmness around her. He was not quite fifty, but at least a decade older than Bullock, and their age difference was starting to show. Dark heavy bags pulled under Dargo's eyes and his hair displayed equal smatterings of salt and pepper. But despite his evident ageing, Dargo was a restless hound when he had a case to chew on. His devotion to the job was still as unquenchable as the day he started. There was no talk of early retirement, no moaning about the late hours interrupting quality time with his family. He was a model professional.

'I'm not bad, sir.'

'Sounded like an interesting briefing.'

Dargo's wry smile forced one upon Achebe.

'Was only Edmunds being a cheeky shite as usual.'

'He's a wanker.' Bullock said. 'Don't be afraid to give him a bollocking. Put the dickhead in his place.'

Achebe grinned at Bullock's brashness. Most officers crumbled with fear in his presence, but Achebe always felt relaxed in his company. They had both supported her since she was a young officer, and they were the main advocates for her promotion to detective.

'I didn't realise being a detective made you the most hated person in the office.'

Dargo swivelled in his chair with a knowing smile.

'The police force can be a hostile working environment. You'd think fighting crime would unify us, but the individuals in that office are just as ambitious and jealous of success as Wall Street brokers. I'm afraid that's just what happens when you move up the ladder, Nikki. Don't expect invites to the Friday night drinks. Don't expect to be privy to the office gossip, because now you are the gossip. You are part of the hierarchy now. It's just the way it is.'

'I hear what you say, but I feel there's something more to it than that.'

'What do you mean?' Bullock asked.

'I've been around long enough to witness other internal appointments, some more questionable than others, but I've never seen or felt disrespect as publicly as this. They think I'm a tick-box appointment. I suppose I fill the diversity quota nicely. Black and female. Just need to come out of the closet and I'm poster-perfect for the force. Do you think Edmunds would make snide comments if I was a newly qualified male detective? Or someone older than him, rather than younger?'

Dargo leaned forward on his desk.

'You are a tick-box appointment, Nikki, but it's nothing to do with your physical appearance. You tick all the boxes to be a brilliant detective. Some of those people in there think they are ready to make the step up, but if they are, then we are yet to see it. You have the right balance of skill and potential.'

14

'They don't see that. They see inexperience.'

'As I told you when we gave you the job, experience is not always necessary. An opportunity should be afforded when all the other boxes are ticked. Without mentioning any names, I question the resilience of some of the other candidates. You have a natural instinct for investigative work. You are analytical, hardworking, and you're a leader. Don't let their jealousy obstruct you from performing at your best. Xander and I will always have your back.'

While reassuring, the faith of Dargo and Bullock induced further nerves, as Achebe did not want to let them down.

'Thanks again to you both. I do appreciate it. I will definitely need your help during the investigation.'

'We expect you will, but we are leaving it for you to come to us. We don't want to be sticking our noses in and for your team to think we are the chairman of the football club who tells the manager which players and formation to play.'

Achebe acknowledged with a nod.

'You also need a private office of your own.' Bullock said. 'I'll speak to the Chief about getting contractors in to partition off part of the main office for you. It'll be similar to this space.' Bullock said while darting his eyes around his and Dargo's shared room. 'It won't be anything special. And has your detective trilby arrived yet?'

'No trilby yet. It's in the post, apparently. I'm not sure I need my own room, though. I'm happy with my desk out there.'

'No, Nikki. I know the latest corporate trend is for everyone to work in an open plan office. But sometimes, especially in the police force, it's good for people to see the hierarchy.'

Achebe conceded with a nod, but was keen to move the conversation onto her investigation.

'So, the witnesses are saying a werewolf attacked Dalmally caravan park.'

'We heard.' Bullock scoffed before realising Achebe did not share his dismissive reaction.

'I mean fair enough if one looney was claiming it was a werewolf, but all five eyewitnesses have said the same.'

Dargo massaged the tram track wrinkles on his forehead as he listened to Achebe. Bullock stroked his goatee as he perched on a filing cabinet.

'How reliable are the witnesses?' Dargo asked.

'One's a drunk, and the others are in shock, so hardly the most credible, but it's still weird.'

15

'What's the vibe of the people at this caravan site?' Bullock asked.

'What do you mean?'

'Are they a cult, sacrificing certain members of the group to a werewolf as part of some fucked up belief system?'

'Not getting a cult vibe at all. The mother of the missing child is inconsolable, and the other witnesses are in severe shock. This is not something they were expecting as part of a ceremonial offering.'

'What are the zoos and the safari park saying to it?'

'They are checking their inventory, but no animals are reported missing yet. I think we would know by now if they were short of a lion. I'm going to see Jim McAllister tomorrow. Well, later this morning.' Achebe said as she watched the clock tick closer to one in the morning. 'He lives an isolated life to the west of the forest, so it's not inconceivable that a wild animal could roam south towards the caravan site.'

'I remember him.' Dargo said. 'He was always housing some animal or other in his barn. He should be on the Wildlife Rescue's blacklist.'

'Jen is getting that list as we speak.'

'Seems like you're on top of things.'

Achebe reclined in Bullock's chair, deep in thought.

'Something's bothering you, Nikki. Spit it out.' Bullock said.

'One witness was harping on about the forest of damned souls, and I just overheard an officer mention it. I've lived in this country for eighteen years now, but I've never given the stories much consideration because I don't believe in silly old fables.'

'The cross around your neck suggests otherwise.'

'Oh, this.' Achebe said while fiddling with the gold crucifix necklace. 'I just wear this to appease my mum. I don't actually believe in any of that religious shite.'

'Fair enough.'

'Where does the forest of damned souls story stem from then?'

'I guess, like all myths, no one really knows how it started,' Bullock said. 'I suppose it goes back to the fifteenth century. They used to drown witches in the lochs. Then over the years there's been many disappearances, accidents, and deaths in Bannock forest which have all contributed to the theory that a dark spirit governs the area.'

'It's just classic human behaviour to overhype the negatives and underplay the positives.' said Dargo. 'Every time a disaster happens, it feeds into the myth, but what no one talks about is the fact that millions of people have entered the forest and millions have walked out alive. People live by the lochs, hike the trails, and work in the forest every day.

It's a hive of activity all the time with no adversity, but that gets overlooked when a situation like the one we have now comes to the fore.'

Achebe let the forest's reputation infiltrate her mind. Despite stating she was a non-believer of religion and mythologies, the statements from the witnesses threatened her resolve. They all claimed to have seen something that has never been seen before: a werewolf. It was so specific, and they had all said it. No one said a bear. No one said a wolf, of which there were plenty roaming in the highlands of Caledonia. When questioned whether it could be an unusually large wolf, or a rabid wolf, they all flat-out refused the suggestions. They were all clear. It was a werewolf.

Achebe stared at the corkboards detailing Dargo and Bullock's case.

'Enough about me. You guys are in late as well. Any luck with your investigation? Missing teenagers and a missing family. Are the two linked?'

Dargo stood once more, turning his back to Achebe as he observed the corkboards.

'I don't think so. Two very different modus operandi as far as I can tell. The teenagers all went missing after being in nightclubs and the families while at their holiday homes up north.'

'Families? Another is missing. I thought the first family had gone missing on a hike. The conditions on a mountain can turn ugly fast.'

'We thought that might be the case initially, but now a second family has gone missing. We have camera footage of a van heading towards the second family's holiday home on the day their friends and family lost contact with them. It was last registered to a Mr Bob Huskins. The weird thing is he is a man with no history of violence and works as a mechanic in a small town five miles from where they were staying.'

'Mechanics do call-outs, don't they?'

'They do, but we have been unable to locate the van or Bob Huskins since.'

'Seems like Huskins is your man, then.'

'Indeed, but with no apparent ties to either family, I am struggling to understand why he would abduct them or what his plans would be once he has them.'

'Some psychos don't need a reason.' Bullock grumbled.

Achebe got up and leaned towards the door handle.

'Before I leave you to it, I got a text from Sam Stone at the Thistle magazine. She wants to meet me about my case. Is this something I should be accepting or rejecting?'

Dargo's smile stretched the wrinkles around his eyes.

'You've met Sam before, right?'

'Briefly. Her message was blunt. I'm not sure if she has information to share or if she will try to extract information from me to publish in the magazine.'

Dargo shook his head politely.

'Sam won't do that. As you are aware, since Caledonia became independent, the governance over the police force has been pretty lax compared to what it used to be. We can dish out some brute force and bend the rules in ways we couldn't before. That being said, though, there are still limitations to how we can operate, and Sam has become a useful ally in finding ways around these limitations. We keep our working relationship with Sam hidden from the high constables and peace officers, so you won't know this, but she was instrumental in helping Xander and I stop that paedophile ring a few years back. Like you, she is young and ambitious, and she is not afraid to venture on the wrong side of the law in order to get the information she needs. In return for sharing information with us, we turn a blind eye to the illegal means by which she obtains the information.'

'Such as?'

'Petty crime like breaking and entering, trespassing, theft. Don't worry, she isn't a vigilante taking out criminals when the police can't convict them. She's not an assassin, not in the physical sense, anyway. She'll take someone down with her words in the Thistle magazine. The information she gathers is often enough for us to put whoever her target is behind bars. We have a good relationship. She is formidable, so tread carefully, and if you don't feel comfortable with the conversation, then you can always walk away.'

'Okay, I'll see what she has to say, then.'

As Achebe left Dargo and Bullock's office, she stewed over the eyewitness accounts once again. The prospect of a werewolf was preposterous, and yet she could not help but give some credence to their stories, so much so that she chastised herself for doing so. If Dargo and Bullock heard someone cry werewolf, they would ruthlessly dismiss it and focus on the facts. Being a detective meant making key decisions to eradicate unnecessary distractions that delay getting to the truth. Disregarding the notion of a werewolf should be a simple decision to make, and yet she could not do it. She attributed her hesitance to incompetence. But gut instinct was important, and her gut was telling her that the stories of a creature never witnessed before were not entirely untrue.

June 6th

CHAPTER 4

The road to Jim McAllister's isolated home on the outskirts of the Highlands was so peaceful that Achebe forgot an awkward tension dangled within the car. Constable Edmunds was the ringleader of the office dissidents, so Achebe decided it was best to kill the virus before it spread too far. In the thirty miles from the city of Edin, they had barely spoken a word to each other. Her foot lifted ever so slightly off the accelerator as she concentrated on addressing the petulant adult.

'Do you know why I chose you to join me on this inquiry?'

Edmunds fidgeted with the plastic section of his police bunnet, alternating between staring out the window or down at his feet. Anywhere but towards Achebe's eyeline.

'Stop playing with your hat. You'll bend it.'

Achebe noticed a sheen on his hands. All the confidence he displayed in front of his peers drained as quickly as the sweat flowing off his knuckles. You fucking wimp, she thought.

'You thought it was appropriate to undermine me in front of everyone?'

'You embarrassed me.' he retorted.

'For your manky shoes? I wouldn't have done that had you acted professionally. Would you have behaved like that if Dargo or Bullock were giving the team talk?'

Edmunds closed his eyes as if summoning the strength to apologise.

'I'm sorry. I guess it's hard for me to see you get promoted in such a short space of time. What age are you, thirty?'

'I don't think it's relevant, but I'm twenty-eight.'

'Fuck! I'm thirty-nine and not even a high constable yet. Trust me, age is relevant when you're nearly forty and haven't achieved what you wanted.'

'Life experience can be crucial, but it's not the be-all and end-all, or at least it shouldn't be. I like to think I was promoted because I've displayed the necessary skill set when working on past investigations. If you don't believe I'm good enough to be a detective, then that's fine, but I ask that you don't discredit or undermine me in front of the other officers again. That's my team now. I need them motivated to work for me and that's hard to do if they think I'm not fit for purpose. That's why I was so harsh on you. Do you understand?'

Edmunds' fingertips pressed harder into the plastic ring of his bunnet. The guilt of his actions was written all over his face in capital quivers.

'I'm sorry. It's just hard to take orders from someone so young.'

'As I said, age shouldn't be an issue. We are both police officers, and we share a common goal to protect the citizens of Caledonia. That should be enough to unify us.'

Achebe paused, watching a lonely car wave frantic windscreen wipers as it drove in the opposite direction.

'So, we share a mutual objective.' Achebe continued. 'But I realise everyone has their own personal agenda and desires as well. So why don't we align those?'

'What do you mean?'

'You want to move to the next level, become a high constable?'

'Yes'

'Well, let me help you get there. If that's what you really want and that's the real reason you're upset with me, then let me help you.'

Edmund's cheeks blushed with embarrassment, cowered by Achebe's kindness.

'How will you do that?'

The question was clunky, pushing the responsibility back on Achebe as if it were her job to hand him a promotion on a plate. She forgave the question, putting it down to Edmund's anxiousness.

'You need to prove you can lead tasks and take ownership of parts of the investigation. I can give you certain tasks to head up. You manage four or five officers and report back to me and High Constables Gardyne and Robinson.'

'That would be great.'

'It would be great, but you've given me a real issue. How is it going to look if the other officers see me giving you extra responsibility? They'll think, "oh, Edmunds verbally attacked Detective Achebe at the team meeting, maybe that's what I need to do to get my own way". They'll think they can bully me into doing whatever they want, and let me tell you, Edmunds, I will not be viewed as a pushover by my own team. Do you hear me?'

Edmund's shoulders slumped. He spotted a lonesome sheep adrift from the rest of the flock, exposed to the wind and rain, battered by the elements with no shelter or comfort, yet having a better time than him. So uncomfortable in his own skin, he almost wished he could trade places with the animal that was bred for slaughter.

'Also, I would be doing those who *do* behave a disservice if I single you out to support me. Why should I do that? Is that fair to the other officers?'

The consequences of Edmunds' big-man antics were beginning to sink in. His career would remain stilted with no hope of progression.

'You can start with an apology to everyone when we return to the office. I will not instigate it. I'll let you do it in your own time if you wish to do it at all, but it's a condition of the support I'm offering you.'

Achebe suppressed the flicker of a grin as she read Edmunds' mind. He would be wondering how an apology would look in front of his peers; the macho man falling on his sword. Edmunds contemplated for longer than Achebe had anticipated. I'll fucking retract the offer if you don't like it, she thought.

'I'll do it.'

Edmunds stumbled over his next words.

'I'm so sorry, boss. I was a fucking idiot, a complete fucking idiot. I do respect you. I think you will be a great detective. I guess I'm just, just jealous. I've sat on my hands for so many years, and I took that frustration out on you. You definitely didn't deserve that and believe me when I say I'm right behind you on this investigation.'

'Yes, something along those lines should suffice.'

After another laconic thirty miles, the sat nav instructed Achebe to turn right onto a slither of road winding down into the expanse of the valley. The rain turned the mountainside foliage a deeper green, which Achebe thought made the landscape taller, each peak a dark giant watching over their kingdom.

The car slid down a sloping, muddy driveway to Jim McAllister's bungalow. He had built his house from scratch, as well as the chicken coop and the large barn at the back of the property.

'That barn is where Mr McAllister housed lynx, cougars, bears, mountain lions and who knows what else, unbeknown to the authorities for years.' said Achebe. 'We don't have a warrant, but we need to check that barn before we leave.'

Achebe paused after shutting the car door, drinking in the view while inhaling the fresh, moist dirt smell. She could easily imagine a wild cat roaming the land undetected, hunting deer and rabbits before returning to Jim's barn for rest, never meeting another human because the nearest hamlet was over thirty miles away. Achebe also reckoned that if a wild animal *was* living with Jim McAllister, it wouldn't be hard for it to flee his control.

A skinny river collected the rainwater beyond the barn, but as the water flowed down the slope, it mixed with the dirt to cover the ground with a thick coating of sludge. They squelched through the front yard on their way to McAllister's house. Achebe made a mental note to keep a pair of wellies in the boot for occasions such as this.

A small, burly man wearing a blue woolly hat answered the door. Achebe noticed he had two jumpers on, one orange and one green, as well as fingerless gloves. He had a three-day stubble and unwelcoming eyes. There was no awning over the door, so Achebe and Edmunds were left battered by the rain. McAllister showed no signs of offering a reprieve.

'You're the police.' he said.

'How could you tell?' Achebe asked.

''Cause you look very uppity, and he looks like a massive wanker.'

Edmunds gritted his teeth and was about to bark back, but Achebe chimed in before he got the chance.

'Let's start over and pretend you didn't just insult two police officers. I'm Detective Achebe and this is Constable Edmunds. We're here regarding a very serious matter, and you can choose to cooperate with us now, or you can come down to the station with us and we can ask you a few questions there. We don't mind driving you thirty miles to the nearest station, but it would be a helluva long bus journey back for you. Where's the nearest bus stop?'

Achebe turned as if properly searching, knowing fine well there were no bus stops for miles. McAllister groaned and turned back into his house, leaving the door open for them to enter.

If it was respite from the elements Achebe and Edmunds sought, they were not granted it. The house was a fridge and felt colder than the mild summer temperature outside, which explained why McAllister was so wrapped up.

Although chilly, the house was beautifully maintained for a man who lived independently with no visitors to impress. Only a few plates and mugs lying by the kitchen sink waited to be washed. Edmunds expelled a pronounced shiver.

'Do you not get cold in here?'

Achebe sighed internally at the thoughtless comment.

'No, no, no. I don't want you here, so you don't get to ask me questions about the way I live. I'm not gonna entertain any small talk and you'll no be getting offered coffee and biscuits either. Just ask me what you need to. I'll answer your questions, and then you'll fuck off.'

'There's been an attack at Dalmally caravan park,' Achebe said as she led the conversation to the matter at hand.

'Saw it on the news. Werewolf, isn't it?' McAllister formed a wry smile and chuckled ironically. 'You want my help to catch it?' he asked boastfully.

'No. We want to speak to you about your wee hobby of hoarding wild animals here.'

McAllister's face drooped with offence upon realising he was being questioned as a suspect, not an expert.

'That was fucking years ago. You took my black puma away. Not even to a zoo, either. You fuckers just put her down. Killed her. Fucking bastards.'

'The puma wasn't the only animal you kept, was it?'

'Naw. I had a few bear cubs. At least you found alternative homes for them. They were so well trained. They used to pull fish out of that river with ease. Intelligent creatures, so they are. I had other wild cats, but they were all taken away to live in poorer conditions than I offered here.'

McAllister looked out the kitchen window towards the river, reminiscing. Achebe's shoulders shook involuntarily under the unhomely chill, so she cut to the chase.

'We're here to check you don't have any animals on site that could have caused the attack.'

'And how the fuck am I supposed to smuggle an animal here these days? The black market has become too expensive. I don't know what animal caused the attack, but I'll tell you one thing, there's certainly not as many sheep and cattle in the fields as there used to be ten years ago. Whatever is out there has been here a while. The farmers have cried about it for years, but no one gives a fuck about farmers, do they? You should speak to a man called Duncan Weir, works on an estate for some auld lady, manages the garden and her livestock. He'll have some stories for ye. Better be quick, though. He's about to pop his clogs. Cancer's a bastard.'

'Thanks. We will follow that up. For now, can we check your barn?'

McAllister paused before answering.

'Do you have to?'

'Yes.'

'I only keep chickens in that coop there. There's nothing in the barn.'

'Should be a quick visit then.'

'You'll need your wellies for the backyard. You got a pair?'

'No.'

'What a shame.'

McAllister sat on a wooden stool to put on his wellies before leading them out the backdoor. Achebe noticed three other pairs of wellies that McAllister failed to offer them.

The backyard was a bigger swamp than the front. McAllister walked through it with ease, leaving Achebe and Edmunds behind. Their steps were more deliberate, and each one threatened a filthy ending. Planting their feet pressed the sludge over the top of their shoes, daubing the hems of their suit trousers. To compound the misery, the rain drove at them from an angle, pelting their rain jackets with the same pitter-patter effect as if hitting the top of a tent.

McAllister looked unimpressed as the two officers ambled their way towards the chicken coop. The mahogany structure was eight feet tall with immaculate joinery. He pulled open a latch. No need for locks when you live in the middle of nowhere.

The chickens clucked and flapped as they entered, six or seven all jumping on top of each other with fright. The smell of animals, hay, feed, and scat would be unpleasant to most, but to Achebe, it evoked wonderful memories of her early childhood in Botswana when her family kept chickens.

'It's more like a chicken massacre than a chicken coop in here.' Edmunds said, referring to the feather and blood flooring.

'The heavy rain meant the ground underneath gave way and the coop started sagging. The foxes got through a weak section of the flooring in the corner. Lost a fair number of chickens. That's why there's blood everywhere.'

McAllister paused.

'That, and sometimes if I get angry, I just kill one of the fuckers for my dinner.'

The coop went silent. Even the chickens shut their beaks as if they understood the callous remark. McAllister's smirk returned.

'Unless you're looking for a chicken killer, shall we leave?'

'Onto the barn.' Achebe said to make sure McAllister was taking them there next.

McAllister's jaw clenched.

'There's fuck all in there.'

'Fine. We just need to see it for ourselves.'

McAllister mumbled moody mutterings as he let the coop door slam with the force of the wind before applying the latch.

More sludge-walking was required to the barn, which was another immaculately built structure with two stories and bitumen roof sheets. Achebe wondered why the barn needed a new shiny padlock when the chicken coop required none.

Inside, the barn split into three holding pens on the ground floor, similar to horse stables. One was substantially bigger than the other two and had fresh hay on the floor. Achebe spotted a mould within the hay, recently imprinted by an animal as they slept.

'As you can see, there's nothing here.'

'Not at this very moment, but which animal was lying in that hay?'

'None.'

Achebe tilted her head to show McAllister she was not an idiot. He turned in disgust while shaking his head.

'I've been hunting badgers, okay? Not to kill them. I hunt them and try to train them. If I canny get my hands on any bears or big cats, then I'll have to make do with what I've got out here.'

'That's illegal, Mr McAllister, you know that?'

'I'm hardly endangering the species. I just want to be around them.'

McAllister raised his voice, miffed that he was being reprimanded and questioned. Achebe noticed grey hairs on the ground. Wearing a forensic glove, she stuffed a clump into an evidence bag.

'Checking that for werewolf DNA?' McAllister shook his head while chuckling. 'Fucking useless. You're as headless as the chickens I choose to eat.'

'Oi, have some respect.' Edmunds jibed.

'Time for you to get off my property, Cuntstable.'

'Maybe you'd like a reminder of who's in charge here.'

Edmunds hovered a threatening hand over his baton. Achebe stepped in front of him.

'We're leaving Mr McAllister. But know that I may be in touch with you again.'

'Whatever. You can walk around the side of the house to your car. You ain't getting inside with those muddy feet.'

McAllister locked the barn and was outside his back door before Achebe and Edmunds had waddled halfway across the boggy terrain. Achebe had trudged to drier dirt when she heard a yelp from behind. She turned to see Edmunds' foot slipping forward uncontrollably, his back knee lowering into the mud. His hands became lost under the sludge as he attempted to regain a standing position, but his body kept spreading to perform an inflexible version of the splits. Then his right hand slipped, causing his hip and elbow to splat into the sludge.

McAllister bellowed a guttural laugh from his back step.

'Oh cuntstable, it's bad enough slipping in the mud, even worse when there's a big pile of sheep shit mixed in right where your hand is.'

Achebe pursed her lips to conceal a smile that was desperately trying to burst through.

'Hey detective, you've brought a *bog-standard* officer with you today.'

McAllister shut the door and left Edmunds scrambling in the mud like a spider trapped in syrup.

'You need to strip before you get in my car. Put your clothes in the boot.'

Edmunds mumbled expletives as he hopped into the passenger seat wearing only pants and a plain white t-shirt, looking like a naughty wartime schoolboy ready to be caned in front of his class.

'Oh, pipe down. I'm not going to tell anyone in the office, so don't worry.'

Edmunds looked relieved, but once again, Achebe was unimpressed by his behaviour.

'I appreciate it is common these days to apply a little muscle to get quick answers from suspects, but that doesn't mean we have to always act that way. Sometimes you need to give concessions to a suspect to get what you want from them. The wellies, for example. We could have asked to borrow the numerous pairs that were lying at the backdoor, but cantankerous Mr McAllister saw that as a mini victory to have us struggling through the mud.'

'I never saw any wellies.'

'Are you listening to me? If you push too hard or anger people like McAllister, he will become more defensive and shut us out. We'll get more out of him if you make him feel a little more in control and at ease. We always have the backup tactic of threatening to bring him into the station or coming back with a warrant, which, let's be honest, we can't be arsed with as much as him, but he doesn't know that. What I'm saying is, aggression is rarely necessary. I've never seen Dargo use any physical force on anyone other than a criminal.'

'That's cause Xander does it for him.'

'Detective Bullock's violent reputation is simply not true. He is the master at knowing the right time to apply a bit of force and aggression, but more importantly, he knows when not to use it.'

Edmunds turned on the heating to warm up his legs, which possessed the same complexion as one of McAllister's plucked chickens.

'Do you think he's only keeping badgers in there?' Edmunds asked.

'Probably. If a big cat or a bear were living there, we would have spotted an imprint in that mud. It would be hard to conceal in that terrain. Did you see any paw prints?'

'No.'

Edmunds jerked his neck nervously, which told Achebe he had not thought to look for any.

'He seemed to take particular glee when he thought we were seeking his help to catch the animal.' said Achebe.

'You think he let an animal loose knowing we would soon come to his door? Or as revenge for taking animals away from him previously?'

'It's a possibility, but he's not the attention-seeking type. If he was holding an animal, I think he'd rather keep it than release it to get back at the authorities. We can't rule anything out, though.'

Achebe played a voicemail from High Constable Robinson over the car speakers.

'Hi Nikki, it's Jen. Just a quick update to say that forensics has analysed the hair found at the scene, and it has matched that of a timber wolf.'

Timber wolves were not native to Caledonia, but Achebe was relieved to hear the animal was not a figment of mythology.

'However,' Jen's voice was suddenly ominous. 'The paw prints found at the caravan park are not immediately identifiable. They don't belong to a timber wolf. We are sending the prints to niche specialists in the hope of finding some answers. I can explain more when you come back to the office, but for now, I have been dragged into an emergency response team for Tom and Xander's investigation. They are hightailing it to a location where the van suspected of kidnapping the families has been sighted. I'll explain more when I see you.'

CHAPTER 5

The van sat like a jalopy amongst the weeds stemming from the cracked concrete. It wore a cloudy grey coat mottled with blood rust; a grimy conduit to transport the kidnapped family to the dilapidated tin tomb; an old factory not merely abandoned, but forgotten on the outskirts of Edin.

Dargo stopped short of the gated entrance to the disused industrial estate so the kidnapper would not hear the car engine. Stealth was the preferred approach as they exited the vehicle without shutting the doors.

There was a scream, instantly muted by the sound of a passenger train running behind the factory. When it passed, only the distant sounds of the city could be heard.

All Dargo and Bullock could see were floating apparitions flickering behind the factory's cloudy fenestration. Dargo crouched in front of the door at the far left of the rusty building. Peering through the door's paint-stained window panel, he saw five family members hanging roughly eight metres above the ground, metal harnesses strapped around their waists. A father, mother, son, daughter, and auntie gripped onto metal chains which extended to the ceiling as if they were preparing to bungee jump. Near the roof of the building, a man paced along a metal gantry. He was talking, but Dargo could not hear him over the screaming mother.

Bullock flicked away strands of hair that fell over his eyes as he crouched next to Dargo by the door, taking a peek into the factory for himself.

'Did you see the cunt up the top?' asked Bullock.

'Yip. I'm not sure what's going on, but I'll go in and distract him while you find a way to get up to the gantry and stop him from initiating whatever he plans to do.'

'Agreed. We don't have time to wait for back-up.'

Bullock remained crouched as he scoped the side of the factory. A vertical ladder led to the roof, its black enamel peeled to its original metal. It was a relic of old fire safety measures that would never pass inspection in the modern era. One slip would result in severe casualty or fatality. Bullock tugged the ladder to test its rigidity, and despite being unconvinced it was safe, began climbing; the ladder shoogling under each careful step.

Dargo entered through the factory door, his cheeks burning under an instant heat. The family stopped screaming, and the man on the gantry stopped bellowing illegible nonsense.

The moment of hesitancy gave Dargo time to assess his environment. Each family member hovered over a different fate of death. The father dangled above a large jacuzzi of boiling water, the jet streams swirling with fury. The mother dangled precariously over a pallet trolley with metal spikes hammered across its surface, ready to impale the fallen victim. The aunt twisted in her shackles over an industrial meat grinder, the mouth of which was big enough to catch her with one crunching bite. The boy, not even a teenager, was suspended over an incinerator. The open hatch blew dark smoke around his twiggy arms and legs. He coughed violently within its gaseous grasp. The girl, the youngest of the group, was hanging upside-down a few metres higher than the rest, poised for a deadly head-first drop onto the concrete floor.

Canvas sheets were piled underneath a set of metal stairs which clung to the left side of the factory, eventually reaching the gantry upon which the six-foot-seven behemoth stood. Dargo was sure the man was Bob Huskins, but from afar, the behemoth's scraggly beard darkened the lower half of his face to obscure definitive identification.

The behemoth's expression changed from confusion at Dargo's appearance to a satisfied grin, pleased to have an audience for his macabre puppet show.

'I'm Premier Detective Tom Dargo. You need to stop what you are doing and let these people go.'

The mother started screaming for help and shouted to *get them out of here* as if Dargo was not already attempting to soothe the situation to her desired outcome.

'Here that folks, the Premier is here to see you die.' echoed the deep voice from above. His throat crackled from cigarette abuse. He wore off-white dungarees atop a bulky physique shaped by years of hard labour and alcoholism; so heavy that the metal lattice platform shuddered as he paced.

'Whatever it is you are planning to do to this family, you have not done it yet. There's still time for you to do the right thing and let them go.'

'You mean I will only be charged for abduction rather than murder?'

Dargo knew the question was insincere.

'Yes.'

The behemoth coughed out laughter.

'Too late. This family will suffer just like that one did.'

The behemoth pointed proudly to the corner of the factory. Dargo jumped when he saw the pile of bodies, if they could even be classed as such: one boiled, one chopped, one minced, one fried, one bone shattered.

Dargo suppressed his nausea, turning back to the hanging family, their helpless, terrified eyes resting all their hope on him. He knew talking the behemoth out of murder was not going to work. He was merely stalling until Bullock reached the roof and found a way onto the gantry.

'Why are you doing this?' Dargo asked.

'For fun.'

The behemoth pressed a button on a device he was holding. The harnesses were clipped into a metal girder on the ceiling with ballpoints moving each family member across the girder like the production line in an abattoir. A metallic clicking sound echoed in the factory as the family moved in a circle. Dargo lunged forward into nothing, hopelessly terrified at what might occur. He counted eight seconds for the family members to drift and stop over a different method of death.

'Do you like my contraption, Premier?'

Dargo chose not to answer while he assessed how to prevent each death.

'Every time I press this button, they will move over to the next station. I can drop any of them at any point with this button here.'

The family screamed harder as they felt their lifespans decrease from minutes to seconds. The behemoth grimaced at their panicked wriggles within the chains before continuing.

31

'Each time I press the button, they will lower closer to each contraption, apart from the head-first drop, of course. Whoever lands on this lucky station will be raised high above the ground.'

The behemoth pressed the button again. Dargo watched as the boy dipped closer to the boiling water, the girl over the spikes, the father over the meat grinder, the mother over the incinerator, and the aunt was twisted upside-down in anticipation of the drop.

'Adding to the excitement is the fact that each harness will release at predetermined heights above each contraption.' The behemoth started laughing. 'And I can't even remember what I programmed those heights to be, so anyone could fall at any time. Can you feel the anticipation, Premier? What a time to be alive.'

The behemoth pressed the button again. Dargo moved towards the family, but he was helpless, praying that none of them dropped to their death on this iteration.

'Where the fuck are you, Xander.' Dargo whispered.

None of the family members fell. Dargo's heart raced, his mind equally pulsing for a brainwave to stall the behemoth.

'Before you go any further, I think these people at least deserve to know why you are doing this? Why did you pick them?'

The family stopped screaming, as if curious about the answer.

'Why does there have to be a reason? Life is meaningless. Therefore, taking lives is also meaningless. We all die eventually. Whether it is now or after a few more years is irrelevant.'

'Their lives are not meaningless to them, though. They may be to you, but they are not to them, and they are not to me.'

'Pathetic.'

The behemoth went to press the button again, but the murky glass windows at the back of the factory smashed as Bullock swung feet first from the roof onto the gantry. The behemoth flinched, turning his back to Dargo due to the unexpected visitor.

Dargo moved fast, switching the incinerator off and pulling the lever to close the hatch. Using his toe, he lifted the brake on the pallet trolley of spikes and pushed it into the corner away from the family.

The behemoth looked from Bullock, who was shedding glass fragments as he steadied his feet on the gantry, back down to Dargo. He pressed a button on his device, which triggered the family members to rotate between the deadly apparatus. He left it on a continuous cycle, meaning the mechanics would keep moving until every family member died.

Bullock identified the behemoth as Bob Huskins as he speared his waist, knocking Huskins and his device to the floor. The behemoth's hand gripped Bullock's face and pierced his nails across his cheek. Bullock hammered Huskin's face with his fists in response until they grabbed each other's arms and rolled in a judo grapple.

The family rotated again, four victims lowering while the other was raised high. Dargo turned off the meat grinder and wheeled it away so no one could fall in it.

A set of shackles snapped.

Dargo's heart stopped.

The auntie dropped with a scream.

Dargo choked on his next breath, but was relieved to see the auntie was above where the meat grinder had been. Her fall was heavy but low enough not to be life-threatening. Dargo ignored her whining as he concentrated on saving the others. His focus was on the drum of boiling water. It was not on wheels and he could not immediately see a switch to turn it off, and even if he did, it would stay deadly hot for a while yet.

Clinking metal announced another spin on the metal girders.

The father's shackles released. His hands slipped from the chains, but there was no pallet of spikes below to pierce him. Dargo pulled him to his feet.

'Help me.' Dargo shouted.

He dragged the father to a rolled-up canvas that lay underneath the metal stairs.

'Hold that edge.'

The father did as he was told while Dargo unfurled the canvas and tied a knot around one of the solid support beams that stretched the height of the factory. The father shifted his position as he cottoned onto Dargo's plan. Between the pillar, Dargo, and the father, they held the canvas in a triangle underneath the boy, who was poised to drop head-first to his death.

Huskins smashed Bullock's cheekbone. The skin under his eye burned and grew instantly puffy, but he never had time to dwell on the pain as he dodged a left-hand jab. The behemoth smiled to reveal teeth like splintered wood chips. His breathing was wheezy. Normally, Bullock possessed greater strength over any assailant, but on this occasion, stamina would be his advantage, stamina and intelligence.

He dropped his boxer stance as he took off his leather jacket. Before Huskins could react, he opened the jacket and threw it towards him like an eagle using its wings to land softly. As the distracting jacket was mid-flight, obscuring Huskins' vision, Bullock cracked the killer's kneecap with his steel-toed boot.

Three more movements around the circle of death went by without another fall. The boiling water was the only station Dargo could not solve for.

Another rotation started.

A shackle clinked open.

The boiling water sizzled.

The mother screamed.

Her body kissed the exterior of the incinerator with a sizzle. She wailed in pain on the concrete floor as her jeans singed into the broiling red wounds on her leg.

The father let the canvas drop out of one hand as he motioned to go help his wife.

'No!' Dargo snarled. 'Keep hold of the canvas.'

The father obeyed.

The apparatus clicked.

Another shackle released.

There was a loud, prolonged scream as the girl fell head-first into the safe centre of the canvas.

'You. Hold this,' Dargo shouted to the aunt who had stumbled to her feet, having finally recovered from her fall. She delicately held the canvas. 'Tighter!' Dargo growled, her knuckles whitening as she gripped harder.

The only method of death not utilised was the boiling water preparing to fry the boy. There were two more rotations to go before the boy hovered over the hot tub, giving Dargo time to run up the stairs. He stopped when he reached the same height as the boy. Steadying himself on the edge of the railing, he leapt with his hands outstretched, gripping a metal shackle and using his momentum to swing towards the boy like an industrial monkey. He gripped the boy without letting go of the original shackle he was holding, which began rotating to where the meat grinder was initially situated.

'Put your arms around my neck and hold on tight.'

The boy obeyed. His arm was so skinny that Dargo's hand wrapped around his flimsy bicep, gripping so tight that the boy screwed up his face in pain. Dargo did not care. He was too focused on his sweaty palm, which was struggling to keep hold of the greasy shackle. He slid down the chain; the boy screaming as they disconnected.

Dargo's weight meant he swung away from the boy, who now hung alone, drifting agonisingly around the apparatus.

Dargo pulled himself up the shackle and used his momentum to swing back towards the boy. He stretched out his arm, but his oily fingertips aquaplaned off the boy's shackle.

'No!' Dargo shouted.

Terror adorned the boy's face as he watched his saviour fly away.

The metal girders clinked again. The swirling white tips of the boiling water were directly below the boy, the steam teasing his toes, ushering him in.

Dargo pulled on the shackle and pushed his legs through the air to generate momentum, as if on a child's swing. The increased propulsion clattered him into the boy's shackles.

The boy's harness released.

He dropped towards the boiling water.

The boy failed to grip Dargo's shoes, but the detective grasped the boy's fatless arm.

Letting go of the boy's shackle, they swung to the area where Dargo's metal vine had rotated. He released the boy, who fell safely onto the canvas to the delight of his family.

On the gantry, Huskins knelt on his unharmed knee. He caught the next kick from Bullock within his bear paws and threw him backwards. He rose to his feet and Bullock stood to meet him. Huskins stepped forward to land a punch, but as his weight shifted onto his shattered knee, his body fell sideways into the brittle gantry railings, bending the flimsy metal, causing him to tip over the edge.

Bullock stood over the lip of the gantry. Huskins clung to the railing, which whined under the strain of his weight, threatening to separate from the gantry with each passing second. Bullock considered offering his hand for support, but feared the maniac would pull him over the edge. Instead, he watched Huskins' wooden smile appear once more.

'Life's one big experiment. It's all meaningless.'

Huskins deliberately let go, his body falling into the drum of boiling water. His shin bones cracked off the side of the jacuzzi before sliding into the water like softened spaghetti.

Dargo waited to slide down the shackle as he was currently hovering above the incinerator. Through the black smog, he watched a red figure flail in the water, his face curdling and popping as skin and tissue melted away layer by layer. The family screamed as they witnessed the howling monster boil to death; a motion picture that would give them eternal nightmares as their potential fate played out in front of them.

Dargo slid down the shackle like a fireman's pole when it was safe to do so. Bullock galloped down the stairs, blood trickling from his

35

blueberry cheek. He hugged his partner, who was trying to catch his breath. In the background, they could hear the sirens of the backup squad approaching the industrial estate.

'Well done, Tom. Well done.'

'You too, Xander.' Dargo said through a series of coughs. 'How the fuck does a mechanic with no criminal history suddenly commit a crime as monstrous as this?'

CHAPTER 6

The dance floor was an echo chamber of orgasmic vibrations. A thumping pulse projected from the monolithic speakers, bouncing off the walls and surging through the dancing feet as the nightclub tingled in a unified heartbeat. A technicolour laser show painted the room with temporary illustrations, intermittently highlighting sweaty foreheads while shrouding other dancers' shape-cutting into deserved darkness.

Squinting through the alternating lightscapes, the man thought he glimpsed the girl smiling in his direction. He maintained a nonchalant dance while glancing at her, making sure her smiling advances were not the flickering lights applying an illusionary curl at the side of her mouth.

The lasers exposed the girl's face once more and this time he saw the innocuous flick of her hair, the inviting eyes and the seductive smile. It was time to make his move. Time to indulge his cravings.

As he brushed his way past inconsiderate elbows and belly flab, he began profiling his target. He marvelled at the athleticism of her legs. Her thigh muscles were strong but sleek, lightly tensing as she grooved in a short black dress. He imagined rolling his tongue along her calves, round the bend of her knee and up the inside of her thigh to the elixir of excitement. His fist clenched as he eyed her squeezable definition. He fantasised about how rough he could be with her body.

As he moved closer, the girl's hair swayed to expose her neck. His eyes were drawn to the skin; fangs wet with lust. Bite. Bruise. Blood. Grab. Squeeze. Choke.

A splash of gin and tonic disrupted his musings, his nipple now perky atop his muscular pec. The man glowered at the excitable clubber who had hopped into him.

'Sorry, bud.'

'I'm not your bud. Fuck off.'

The man's words were drowned out from the girl's earshot because of the brain-thumping noise. As he shuffled past the inconsiderate runt, he could not resist the urge to use his superior strength, subtly barging the boy into a group of drunken dancers who all raised their arms in *what the fuck* motions. The girl saw this but did not seem to care. He approached her.

'Some people can't handle their drink,' he said.

'Can you?'

'Want to find out?'

'You buying?'

The girl looked furtively to the floor. He recognised the behaviour, feigned bashfulness. This would undoubtedly be the millionth time a guy had hit on her. This was not a new, overwhelming experience, but she acted as if it was.

'I'll buy you as many as you want.'

She leaned into his ear.

'Vodka lemonade. Make it a double if you think you can handle it.'

He put a soft arm around her as they glided to the bar.

'Can I get two triple vodka lemonades, please.'

The girl flinched, attracted by his boldness. When the triple vodka arrived, she downed it in one, grimacing as the liquid burned her throat.

'I'm going to dance. Down that if you want to join me.'

The man drank the vodka so fast, a little tipped out the glass before it reached his lips. He dabbed his wet chin before leading her into the noise.

They danced on the perimeter of an ebullient crowd who screamed when the first chords of a pop remix began to play. Movement was impossible without bumping into bodies, and when they did, the girl pushed closer to him, deliberately resting her hand on his chest. As she barged into him for a fourth time, her breasts pressed into his abdomen. He wanted to hold her there, squish her tits some more, but pull her in too close and she would feel the contour of his erect penis pressing against her.

They danced for over an hour, the triple vodka providing ample fuel. The man grew in confidence with each song: touching her hand, clasping her hand, touching her waist, rubbing her back, and then diving his head down to kiss her. His approach was formulaic. This is how he had seduced the other girls, three in the last two weeks. She was going to make an excellent addition to his collection.

Their tongues twisted in a vodka eddy with saliva chaser, juicy and moreish. He gently bit on her lip, clamping slightly to pull her further against the wall. The girl recoiled, shyly looking to the floor. The man cursed himself. He had been too rough too early and spooked her. Now she had the chance to flee to her friends and escape. His chances of luring her to his place were slim unless he acted fast. He leaned into her ear.

'Sorry, I got carried away. You're just so irresistible.'

'Not here,' the girl replied. 'I'm not a fan of public displays of affection.'

'Let's leave then.'

'Okay.'

'Do you want to tell your friends first?'

'No, I'll message them. Do you want to tell yours?'

'No, they'll figure out that I'm having a much better time,' the man said, grinning.

The summer midnight temperature was mild, but compared to the microwave nightclub, it was cool. While initially refreshing, sweat beads quickly chilled on their bodies like snow pellets.

'No jacket?' the man asked.

'Nope. A gentleman would offer me his.'

'I don't have one either.'

'Then a gentleman would do the next best thing and hug a girl until a taxi arrives.'

The man gently palmed the back of her head into him, consciously keeping her nose away from his sweaty pits. She was so light compared to him. He would dominate her in the same way he had with the others. But in this instance, he would enjoy lengthy, tortuous foreplay before making a definitive move.

'I'll order one. I've got the Cabbie app,' he said.

'Don't bother with that. Taxi drivers can't refuse a helpless girl in the cold.'

She flung out an arm to a passing cab. The taxi slammed the brakes as if practising an emergency stop. She curtseyed on the spin to celebrate her triumph.

'Back to mine then,' the man suggested.

'No, I was thinking my place.'

'I'm only five minutes away.'

'I'm about fifteen minutes, but I'd feel much more comfortable at my place.'

The man took a breath, smiling to hide his disappointment. This was not part of his plan, but if he insisted too much, she might become unnerved. He would have to improvise, but first, he needed to know the environment he was walking into. His next question was risky. It sounded sinister, but dressed in the right way, it might not sound too creepy.

'I wouldn't want to disturb any of your flatmates. I live alone, so we'll have the place to ourselves.'

'I'm in a flat of four, but we won't be disturbed, either. I really would feel more comfortable at my place,' the girl said with puppy dog eyes.

The boy forced a smile and ceded to the girl's request.

'No problem. Whatever you wish.'

The girl poked her head in the passenger window to tell the driver her address, then climbed into the backseat where they coorie in until they arrived at their destination.

A lingering smell of incense caused the man's nostrils to flare as he entered the flat, a mixture of lavender and pinecones. The hall opened straight into the living room, decorated with ornate wooden artefacts; beautifully handcrafted animal sculptures were displayed with museum level showcasing. A flick of the switch lit up a blend of soothing oranges to supplement the room's warmth. A Turkish rug of assorted reds and yellows hung on the wall to the left of the balcony doors. Behind the wall, he could hear the faint moaning sounds of a TV. He didn't like thin walls. He wanted to make the girl scream.

'I'm going to tidy myself up in my bathroom,' the girl said, pointing to the bedroom, which had an en suite. 'There's another toilet there if you want to do the same. Help yourself to a drink from the kitchen as well.'

'Cheers.'

Under the toilet light, the man's sweat rings were visible in the mirror.

'Fuck!'

There was a shower, but he refused to use it. The noisy water flow would announce to the girl that he was a sweaty man; not very sexy. Instead, he took off his shirt, ran water over a bar of soap, and started washing under his arms. He soaked in the soap by leaning over the sink and scooping handfuls of water into his armpits. He dried them with a towel before moving on to his next problem; his cock and balls.

40

Caressing his genitals, his palm became sticky with a sweaty lather, as if his penis was already smothered with lube. The shower was still not an option. He stretched onto his tiptoes and dunked his genitalia into the sink, but could not reach the tap. He began splashing tepid water over his balls, pulling the foreskin back to give his penis a proper clean. It tingled as he massaged around the tip. Just wait till you force her wet little mouth around it, he thought.

He became semi-erect, so he stopped. He pulled his trousers up, but remained shirtless. As he entered the living room, he heard her voice from the bedroom.

'Are you coming in?'

He threw his shirt on the sofa. Fuck it, he thought, whipping his trousers off as well.

In the bedroom, the girl was lying in black lace underwear. Her legs were pressed together as she rubbed the open space on the bed invitingly. He ignored the space and leaned over her, forcing her legs to spread so their bodies came together. She wrapped her legs around his waist as they kissed violently, biting each other's lips, testing their pain thresholds.

He tilted his head and bit into her neck. The girl gasped in painful delight as he sucked on her skin. She retaliated by sucking his ear and biting his lobe, then dragging his head back to a central position so they could kiss again.

Although he had recognised her muscular thighs, he was still surprised she was able to use them to flip him over. Now she was on top, feeling his penis grow against her crotch.

She unclipped her bra to expose perfectly round breasts. The man sat up and sucked on her nipple, licking a route from one to the other. She pressed his head into her, groaning as his tongue tickled her teats.

She pushed him onto his back and leaned in to kiss him, but as he pouted, she recoiled, teasing him. Grinning, she bit his neck. It was his turn to gasp. She continued down his body, kissing his chest and abs, then stopping at the band of his boxers. She pulled on the fabric like a dog with a blanket. He craned his neck as the girl tickled his balls underneath the cotton. He arched his back, allowing the girl to pull off his boxers to reveal his unfathomably hard penis.

'What the fuck is that?'

The girl jumped off the bed.

'What the fuck am I supposed to do with that?'

She pointed to his penis. He turned red with embarrassment.

'What do you mean?'

'What do you mean *what do I mean*? Your fully erect penis looks like a pig without the blanket.'

'Fuck you.'

The man burned with hot humiliation. He wanted to grab her by the neck, throw her on the bed and force the fuck she craved mere seconds ago. The girl began dressing, but he spun her round to continue his enquiry.

'We're still having sex, right?'

'Not only will I not fuck you, but you won't be staying here. Leave now.'

The girl wriggled out of his grasp, but he gripped on stronger.

'Who the fuck do you think you are?'

'Get off me.'

'You think it's okay to just humiliate me like that?'

The girl twisted his nipple, causing him to release his grip as he recoiled back to the bed. It gave her enough time to flee to the bathroom and click the lock shut.

'Leave now.' she barked from behind the door.

'I'm not going anywhere till I get an explanation. Dancing all night, I paid for your drinks, paid for the taxi, and now in your bed you just decide you won't fuck me.'

'What is there to explain? You have the body of an athlete but a penis the size of a prawn, and not the king-sized ones. I wouldn't even feel it, so I can't deal with you.'

He turned away from the door. His breathing was heavy and prolonged, his intoxicated mind a hotbed of aggressive thoughts.

He could hear the girl shuffling in the bathroom.

'Doors can easily be kicked down, you know.'

The lock on the bathroom door clicked open. Before he turned to look at her, a thick black rope slashed at his body, tearing his skin as if an octopus' tentacle had gripped and ripped the flesh on his chest. He fell back to the foot of the bed. The girl raised the whip back and aimed at him again. The crack echoed as another ugly gash formed across his abdomen.

'What the fuck are you doing?' his voice squealing into a scream mid-sentence.

'I asked you to leave.'

The whip was raised once more, but before she swung in his direction, she paused, waiting for their eyes to meet. He could have sworn they were a soothing, seductive blue in the nightclub, but now they were beady black shark eyes. He never moved, so the girl slashed at his legs, scything a ligature across both shins.

'I told you to leave.'

The man scampered out of the bedroom without his boxers. His bearings were lost underneath the searing pain bursting from each gash. Rather than collect his clothes from the living room, he stumbled into the kitchen. Lost and limping on his left foot, he wafted away beads hanging from an archway. The beads obscured the entrance to a pitch-black room.

Sensing he had taken a wrong turn, he turned back, but the beads were gone, replaced by the girl's haunting silhouette in the archway. The whip writhed like an agitated snake by her side. He stumbled upon seeing her and landed in an oil drum of water. His left buttock and thigh were soaking. As he tried to push himself up, his left arm also plunged clumsily into the liquid.

Eventually, he stood, begging to the girl.

'I'm leaving. I'm leaving. Don't hit me.'

The girl silently moved from the archway, allowing him to exit the dark room. Too horrified to gather his clothes, he fled the flat naked.

The girl picked up his phone from the sofa. She leaned over the balcony, and as the man stumbled naked across the courtyard toward the city centre, she threw his phone. She did not watch it land, but heard the satisfying plastic crash as it smashed off the concrete path below.

Closing the balcony doors, the girl gritted her teeth. Her evening had not gone to plan. She wanted someone new, something fresh, a different physique to play with. But if she could not find it, she would resort to the backup option lying waiting for her. She lifted the bottom of the Turkish rug and stepped through the hidden gap in the wall.

CHAPTER 7

Spin!
Cherry, Seven, Diamond.
Spin!
Cherry, Bell, Bell.
Spin!
Diamond, Lemon, Seven.
Nudge.
    'Could've used the nudge on the last spin. Typical machine.'
Spin!
Seven, Lemon, Seven.
Nudge, nudge.
    'Nothing.'
Spin!
Seven, Diamond, Bar.
Spin!
Bell, Bar, Bell.
Nudge.
    'Now we're talking.'
Nudge, nudge.
    'C'mon! It's right there. Give me another nudge. Fucking machine.'
Spin!
Seven, Cherry, Cherry.

Spin!

Diamond, Seven, Bar.

Spin!

Bell, Seven, Bell.

Nudge.

Bell, Bell, Bell.

'Ya dancer! What a cracking wee machine you are.'

Dargo patted the top of the slot machine like an obedient dog. Tens of Caledonian merk clinked one after the other into the winner's bowl and his smile widened. That was until he spotted a replay of the day's big football match on the TV above the casino bar. A last-minute goal scuppered his two-all prediction and the chance to claim three-and-a-half grand from a three hundred merk bet.

Dargo scooped his prize money and faced the casino floor. The vivid red carpets and faux gold drapes were desperately trying to evoke an image of grandeur. The roulette tables, slot machines, and croupiers displayed weary attempts to replicate Monte Carlo. But like a knock-off Gucci handbag being flogged at a market stall, the location ruined any illusion of authenticity. No high-net-worth individuals were flying to the unlit streets of Leith docks for a high-stakes poker match. No million-pound jackpots were on offer. This was a strictly no-frills casino. You come in, lose your money, and leave.

Dargo recognised a few familiar faces throughout the casino. More than their faces, he recognised the type of characters that occupied the seats. The casino was filled with Jovials. They were easy to spot because they smiled regardless of winning or losing, only attending on special occasions. Tonight, there was a stag party; twelve drunken loudmouths with accents from down south huddled around one roulette table. They would cheer if they won money and cheer when their mates lost. No bet was played in tranquillity.

Then there were the Blunders. Casinos always contained a few. Blunders were individuals who spent beyond their means. Lifestyles were being gambled in the blink of an eye. The difference between dining at fancy restaurants or dining-in with a bowl of plain rice all rested on whether the ball fell on red or black. Blunders wore an expression of despair, and with each loss, their face either paled or reddened depending on their propensity to rage. Dargo recalled a time a man became so angry he collapsed and was taken to the hospital, later learning the man passed away. The lucky bastard avoided having to tell his wife that he blew thirty grand quicker than his journey time to the emergency room.

45

Dargo smiled as he spotted the third category of gamblers, the Habituals. These were the usual suspects of the casino floor, the ones who made the spin of the roulette wheel an everyday occurrence. They were small chip gamblers, and like the pub regulars who attended every day to nurse their pints, these resident gamblers were not enticed by chasing wins. Instead, their attendance was an escape from the misery of life and a means of socialising with someone other than a delivery driver.

Dargo did not fit into any category. The casino was an opportunity to momentarily dispel the strains of the job. He did not attend nearly enough to be classed as a Habitual, did not spend enough to be classed as a Blunder, and certainly did not smile enough to be a Jovial.

Dargo approached the usual roulette table surrounded by two Habituals and one Blunder hunched on barstools. A young lad in his early twenties with dark hair, wearing a blindingly white tracksuit, greeted Dargo.

'Tom, you've decided to join us. The gang's together once again.'

'It certainly is. How are you doing, Connor?'

'I'm good. Yourself?'

'Not bad. The slot machines improved my finances for once. Didn't see you guys come in, otherwise I would have joined you earlier.'

'Aye, I saw you over there. Didn't wanna disturb ye. Ye were in the zone. Those bastard slots sucker you in.'

'That they do.'

Bert's hunchback was unmoved by Dargo's presence.

'How you doing, Bert?'

Bert briefly nodded in Dargo's direction, no hint of a smile.

'Shite as always.'

Bert fidgeted with his chips while staring at the roulette wheel as if capable of manipulating where the ball landed. But, alas, in his decades-long stint as a casino regular, he had not developed the telekinetic ability to influence the outcome. He was in his late sixties with deep canyon wrinkles etched into his battle-weary expression. The skin sacks under his eyes pulled at his face, giving him a permanent look of despondency, supplemented by a personality devoid of charm. Even his clothes were always a dreary shade of grey, with the occasional black.

Dargo never got to the root of what led Bert to become so bereft of life, but in fairness, he had never probed. It was an unwritten rule of the Midnight Club not to ask Bert too many questions, and Bert liked it that way. But despite his demeanour, Dargo sensed he enjoyed their company. Otherwise, he would have undoubtedly changed roulette tables to shake off their presence.

'Are you up tonight at least?' Dargo asked Bert.

'Up two hundred.'

'Amazing!'

Bert flashed a momentary glance of disapproval.

'When you've played the game as long as me, son, winning two hundred doesn't do much for you.'

'You could buy some eccies off me,' said Connor. 'You might crack a smile.'

Connor laughed while looking cautiously from Dargo to Bert, then back to Dargo. Out of all the banter enjoyed by the informal Midnight Club members, Bert was normally exempt from being the butt of the joke, and he duly sighed to show how unamused he was.

Dargo turned his attention to the final member, the Blunder. Ronan's cantankerous temperament was complemented with an intimidating frame that dominated the aura of any room he entered.

'And what about you, Ronan? How are you?'

Dargo imagined that if you pointed a remote at Bert and rewound twenty years, you would land on Ronan. He was once a hotshot banker with a wife and three kids living in a mansion house with the world as his playground. He lost his job the day after independence was announced, when all major financial institutions relocated their operations down south. Unfortunately, rather than reinvent himself and find a new job, he jumped on the slide of destruction after winning a free online bet. His wife divorced him when she discovered he had the aimlessly frittered away most of their savings, a figure Dargo pegged to be just shy of a million pounds based on Ronan's drunken memoirs.

Since then, he had seesawed in and out of rehab. Each time for a new addiction, and each time was ineffective. Bert had taken him under his wing and taught him how to gamble consistently on lower stakes to prevent ripping through all his money in a matter of months. His teachings largely had the desired effect, but they all knew Ronan's life was built on a fault line, ready to crumble at any moment without prior warning.

'I'm doing well. Saw the kids this weekend.'

'Good. What did you do with them?'

'We had a really amazing day. I took them for ice cream at the new place, Scoopz, up the west end. Then I took them to the soft play centre around the corner from it. You should have seen their faces, loving it, so they were.'

Dargo pictured Scoopz. It was next door to a bookies. The soft play was part of an entertainment centre, including an arcade with puggy machines and coin pushers.

'Nice to hear that, Ronan. You deserve it.'

'Thanks, Tom.'

Ronan looked chuffed, but Dargo struggled to ignore the pity he felt for them. He was conscious never to flaunt his stable lifestyle. He was in a loving relationship with his wife and two kids and had a job that he loved. His relatively low stake gambling was merely a method of freeing his mind from the stresses of the day job. The same way others relaxed by watching a movie, attending a football match, or playing a round of golf, he attended the casino.

He had tried other methods of escapology. Tennis and squash achieved the mental liberation he sought, however as courts needed to be booked in advance, he often cancelled matches at the last minute when developments at work or at home had to be prioritised. Gambling was accessible, required no prior arrangements, and the casino was on his route home from work. He could play for as long or as short as he wanted and bet as much or as little as he wished to. It always slotted into his schedule and proved a convenient retreat when he needed to cut the investigative umbilical cord.

Compounding its cheeky appeal was the fact that no one in Dargo's life knew he was part of the Midnight Club. It was not deceit, but canny evasiveness to maintain a necessary separation between work and pleasure. Dargo had found the jacuzzi away from the busy swimming pool, and if anyone found him, the peace would evaporate, and the strains of his life would dispense through the jet streams to muddy the waters once more.

Another cheer erupted from the stag party.

'Rowdy twats' Ronan mumbled.

Dargo detected a slither of envy due to the fact Ronan was not winning this evening.

'I've got something that could chill them out a bit.' Connor opened his pocket to stealthily reveal a bag of weed.

'Fuck sake, that batch is pungent. Put it away before someone calls security.'

Bert was stern with his words, so Connor put the weed away like a moody child who had just been harangued for misbehaving.

'You know I'm a police officer, and you still decided to flaunt that?' said Dargo.

'Weeds decriminalised now. You can't arrest me for it.'

'Just because it's decriminalised doesn't mean you can flaunt it in a public setting. Keep it in your house or go to a cake shop. It's still illegal to sell on the streets.'

'Right you are. I'm still learning the new ways. Might start my own cake shop.'

'I'd encourage you to. The government has dedicated a lot of time and money putting the appropriate infrastructure in place for controlled marijuana consumption, so they will deal with street-sellers harshly.'

'Cheers Tom. You're a sound guy.'

Dargo wasn't sure if he was sound, but he was certainly sympathetic. Connor was raised solely by his drug-addicted mother and had dropped out of school when he was fourteen. After his mum fatally overdosed, his only means of income was to perform odd jobs for people, including selling the same drugs that had taken his mother's life. Dargo decided not to meddle in Connor's affairs, turning a blind eye to the sale of drugs, especially those as harmless as marijuana.

The croupier's eyes kept flicking between Connor and his pocket, unsure how to respond. Bert noticed.

'Don't worry, son. The management knows us, and they know he sells this stuff. You might not like it, but your bosses are happy for anything to be sold if it results in guests losing their inhibitions. What you smell there is no worse than what you've presented us with on trays all night.'

Bert stopped fiddling with his chips and pointed to his pint. Ronan lost the sixth spin in a row. Another cheer from the stag party table erupted.

'Fuck sake.' Ronan muttered.

A waiter approached the table as he spotted their empty glasses.

'Tom, you want a pint?' Bert asked

'No, I'll have a gin and tonic, please.'

'Make mine a double,' said Ronan.

Dargo's phone buzzed in his pocket. It was a message from his wife, Sally. Dargo wondered what she was doing up in the middle of the night, then realised it was six in the morning. Sally would be getting ready for work and making sure the kids had breakfast before school and nursery.

'Are you seriously pulling an all-nighter after dealing with that awful murderer, or is there a mystery woman I should be worried about...? Seriously though, you need to rest at some point. I know it's breakfast time, but your body clock must be all over the place, so there's some of last night's lasagne in the fridge. Just heat it up again in the oven (if you remember how it works...). Try not to work late tomorrow night. We all want to see you. Love you, Sally.'

June 7th

CHAPTER 8

Even to the untrained eye, the paw prints looked alien. Achebe stood next to a series of them, the creature's giant gait bounding into obscurity within the forest. The armed Special Response Unit had followed the trail, but it ended abruptly as the summer rain turned the prints into slurry.

Achebe photographed several angles of the paw prints with her phone. As she examined them, the patter of the rain bounced off her hooded cagoule and lulled her into a soothing daydream. Entranced by the imprint closest to her, Achebe wilted.

'Careful!' shouted a voice.

It was Viti Chandra who snapped Achebe out of her trance. Viti was the wise sage of forensic pathology. She was a small, rotund individual who managed crime scenes with military control. Her team had spent the past forty-eight hours examining Dalmally caravan park, protected by armed soldiers who patrolled the immediate area. Viti expelled an age-revealing groan as she rose from her kneeling position.

'I sent the fur sample you collected from Jim McAllister's barn away for forensic examination, by the way. We should get an answer in the next day or so.'

'Thanks. So, it was timber wolf fur found at the attack site?'

'Yes.' Viti was shaking her head despite the confirmation. 'It's strange though, Nikki. Come and see this footprint.'

Achebe counted three human steps between the animal's strides. She knelt next to Viti. A murky pool of rain had collected within the mystifying indent they were examining.

'It's different.' Viti said. 'The one you were looking at has five digits and appears to resemble a foot. This one has four digits, but one looks like a thumb, and it doesn't belong to any wolf the zoology world is aware of.'

'It's an animal that can stand on hind legs and on all fours, then?'

'It seems that way.'

'More like a bear rather than a wolf, then.'

'The trail shows the animal travels mostly on all fours.'

'Could the tests on the fur be wrong? If the experts can't identify which animal these prints belong to, then we cannot be dealing with a timber wolf.'

'Highly unlikely for the tests to be wrong, almost impossible actually. I've shared photos of the prints with more zoologists. Some of whom are very niche in their fields, so we'll see if they can come up with an answer.'

'When did you send out the photos?'

'Yesterday afternoon.'

'That's roughly twenty-four hours. We would have an answer by now if it was obvious.' Achebe said.

'Patience, Nikki. We'll get there. Although, I've been thinking this animal could be something we haven't encountered before. There have been countless sightings of big cats in the highlands over the years, especially around the Dornoch area, some as recent as five years ago.'

'As unlikely as it seems, I've been thinking the same. We like to think we have conquered every nook and cranny on this earth, but we discover new species all the time. I was doing some research last night. A new species of Leopard, the Sunda clouded leopard, was only caught on camera in Malaysia for the first time in two thousand and ten. There have also been several alleged sightings of a Thylacine in Australia, an animal long believed to be extinct. In an area as vast as Bannock forest and the highlands, it's possible something we haven't come across before exists. Although, it feels like I'm clutching at hope rather than informed reasoning.'

Achebe rose to her feet, staring into Bannock forest, pondering what mysteries lay within. The rain had stopped, but the moisture was still trapped in a grey hue. The forest was silent, as if mourning the victims from the caravan site.

'Do you feel safe working here?' asked Achebe.

'I'm more scared of the Neanderthals holding the guns than the werewolf.'

Viti said werewolf with a cheeky grin.

'You can tell I've already told them off for contaminating the crime scene. They're keeping their distance now.'

Startled birds fluttered against the leaves.

The soldiers turned east with their guns poised. One instructed the others with hand gestures as they moved towards the rustling sound.

Achebe saw movement in the trees. It was fast, nimble, but no clear sighting. Instead, a deep, echoing groan shuddered her bones and choked her movement. She glanced to an equally concerned Viti as they huddled closer together.

The soldiers moved in formation, darting momentarily out of sight as they zig-zagged through the trees. Branches snapped underneath their feet.

There was another flurry of birds, and then Achebe saw the animal bounding between trees as it moved to attack. A clear visual was unattainable amid the dense forestation.

Flickers of fur.

A snout.

Four limbs.

Then came the gunfire that froze Achebe stiff.

Shadowy movements.

Glimpses of fur.

More gunshots.

'Don't shoot.'

The cry came from a soldier. Achebe saw the animal in the clearing.

'Just a fucking stag', she sighed to Viti as they exchanged relieved glances. 'We were a tad jittery there.'

'If only us city folk knew what a bloody deer sounded like. I take back what I said. I am glad to have the Neanderthals with guns.'

'Even though after spraying two dozen bullets, they failed to shoot a fucking deer?'

'How about we get out of here?' Viti suggested. 'I have a team of people examining Bannock Manor. There's something there that will spook you more than that deer.'

CHAPTER 9

The trees cleared as Achebe approached the dilapidated Bannock Manor, grateful she was finished navigating the snaking, pothole-ridden driveway. Nature had reclaimed the land; varicose vines gripped the exterior of house and weeds extended higher than the glassless windows on the ground floor. The roots of nearby trees injected a devastating bout of subsidence, meaning the house drooped on its right side.

Armed soldiers were dotted around a crumbling wall encircling the manor, protecting Viti's team as they scavenged the house for evidence of the beast.

'The animal's trail ends a few miles from here.' Viti said. 'We thought there might be a chance that it uses this house as a den. While there's no evidence of a den as such, the animal has definitely been here on several occasions.'

'How do you know that?'

'You'll see.'

Achebe parked the car on the gravel inside the walled perimeter.

'You'll need these.' Viti said, throwing a protective white suit and mask to Achebe. 'This place is riddled with asbestos.'

Achebe removed her waterproofs and pulled the protective white onesie over the top of her suit.

'They used to host raves here about ten years ago, maybe longer actually.' Viti said as their feet crunched towards the front door. 'Illegal, of course. They had no idea about the asbestos risk, but putting that aside, you can see the attraction of coming out here to party with no dissenting adults for miles. The house wasn't nearly as dilapidated as it is now. In fact, the kids probably caused a lot of the damage.'

'Why did the raves stop?'

'There were about a dozen raves over two or three years, but it all went horribly wrong when a few kids went missing.'

'Missing?'

'Yes, at least five or six. The raves ended when four kids went missing in one night. They broke off from the party, presumably to get down and dirty in the woods. Unfortunately, their bodies were consumed by the forest of damned souls.' Viti said in an overly dramatic tone.

'Their bodies were never found?'

'Nope.'

'Why have I not heard of this?'

'A bit before your time, I suppose. Some of the older heads in the office will remember it. Tom and Xander will for sure.'

'It must have been investigated at the time?'

'As I remember, the news coverage seemed to report the rebellious nature of the rave parties rather than highlight the tragedy of the missing teenagers. Their presumed deaths were attributed to irresponsible drug-taking, and the incidents were used as a lesson on the dangers of substance abuse. The search parties were not that extensive as far as I can remember.'

'The forest is vast, but I don't imagine the kids would've travelled far from the manor. You'd have thought they would find something during the searches. What do they think happened to them?'

'Drowned in the loch or fell into the quarry. It's only a couple of miles away.'

Achebe never asked any more questions as they approached the manor. She allowed Viti to enter while typing a message to High Constable Robinson requesting that she provide her with a briefing on the raves.

Achebe stepped through the fractured brick doorway. With no functioning electricity, the house was doused in an ominous gloom. The hallway plaster was ripped to expose the underlying brick, and the floorboards were littered with ankle-snapping holes.

Three of Viti's team, wearing identical protective attire, were working in the deserted dining room on the ground floor. Tripod lamps illuminated their immediate operating area.

'Brian!' Viti called.

A small geeky man looked up through his glasses as he entered the hall.

'Any joy?' asked Viti.

'Of sorts. The animal has definitely been here, and I believe, rested here for some time.'

'How do you know?' Achebe asked.

Brian walked back into the dining room to retrieve a torch.

'There's no glass in the windows, so as you can probably feel, the wind has blown away any fur samples. What we have found are scratch marks on the flooring. Then there's this.'

Brian pointed the torch towards the stairs, illuminating an image so horrifying Achebe forgot how to breathe. Four scraggily, inch-deep depressions trailed the length of the staircase wall.

Eventually coughing out a breath, Achebe examined the wall the same way she would a painting in an art gallery. A masterpiece could make her feel the emotion of the artist. Similarly, Achebe felt the ire of a tormented, flesh-hungry beast in the scratched wall.

Brian continued.

'What's strange about the scratches is after examining them all morning, we cannot find any nail fragments. They are not fresh markings, but I would still expect to find minuscule nail fragments. Unfortunately, there's nothing, absolutely nothing.'

'So, what are you telling me? Its nails are super strong and don't break?' asked Achebe.

'I'm not sure what it means, but it's unusual.'

'Big cats have retractable claws.' Achebe said. 'They preserve them for climbing, fighting or hunting. I wonder if a creature could create these scratches without using the tips of their claws. In other words, the part most likely to break off.'

'I'm not sure how that would work,' said Viti.

'Neither do I,' admitted Achebe. 'I'm talking out loud, trying to make sense of this madness. The scratches lead upstairs. Have you checked up there?'

'Not yet,' Brian said. 'We are working downstairs today. Start up there tomorrow.'

'We can have a gander, Nikki.' Viti said.

Achebe and Viti were deliberate with each step on the brittle staircase. The house maintained an unwelcoming aura as they ascended. Like wandering the dim halls of a hotel at midnight, the upstairs landing lacked soul. The wilderness wallpaper crept through the ruptured brickwork. The house was no longer in control. It would never be homely again.

Achebe battled with the cold underneath her paper-thin suit. She walked past a small bedroom, the door frame crooked due to subsidence. More claw marks decorated the walls in a swirl of erraticism. Achebe ran her fingers along the grooves, sensing rage in the depths of the cuts.

Viti ventured into a room as Achebe poked her head into what would have been the master bedroom looking out the front of the house. There was no bed, no paintings, no furniture of any kind. She imagined a DJ's boombox in the corner while a crash of teenagers bounced on the dimpled floor.

Achebe noticed the bottom right side of the far wall was torn. Faint blue shapes drawn on the underlying white plaster were exposed. Achebe would have passed it off as the mindless scribbles of drunken teenagers had the shapes not looked geometrically neat and part of something larger beneath the forest green walls.

Stepping into the room, away from the inaudible mutterings from under Viti's mask, the ground creaked and tremored as if an earthquake were brewing. The world slowed, and Achebe grappled for balance as the ground sucked her into the middle of the room like a black hole collecting all the surrounding matter. She turned to exit the room, but the angle of the floor was so acute she slid down the collapsing floorboards.

'Fuck!'

Achebe dropped with a thud into the lounge below. Dust surrounded her as if someone clapped flour in her face.

'Get out, get out, get out.'

Viti was shouting with the sternness of a headmaster from the doorframe of the bedroom above. She rushed down the stairs while Achebe sat like a baby amongst all her toys in a rubble. Her mask was askew across her cheek, and the protective white overalls ripped to expose her suit underneath.

Viti arrived at the lounge room door.

'Nikki, get outta here. The asbestos will get in your system. Mask on and move it.'

Achebe adjusted the mask back over her mouth and obediently left the room while dusting herself off. Viti backed away from her as if she was infectious.

'Take your clothes off.'

'What?'

'The suit is compromised and your clothes are likely riddled with asbestos now. Clothes off!'

Achebe took her suit jacket off, foolishly believing it would be enough to appease Viti.

'Chuck it over there. We'll bin it.'

'Bin it, cost me a...'

'Don't care. It could cost you your life if you take it away. Trousers off as well.'

'What? No. There are soldiers out there.'

'They'll perform a twenty-one-gun salute at your funeral if you don't listen to me. Off!'

'You want my bra and pants as well?'

'No, you can keep them on.'

'That wasn't a genuine question.'

The air hit Achebe's bare body with a mocking chill as she walked to the car, covering as much surface area with her skinny arms. A few soldiers glanced at her, then darted their eyes away as if they were never looking in the first place.

Viti stripped out of her protective suit and shadowed Achebe to the car, partially covering her from the soldiers' view.

'Shower straight away when you get home.'

Achebe had laughed at Edmunds having to strip down to his pants the previous day, and now here she was in the exact same position.

She composed herself in the car, watching Viti gesticulate to her team at the manor door. When her initial embarrassment faded, her mind returned to the case. The Chief's press release had struck the right chord with the public as local police had reported reduced footfall in Bannock forest. However, the anxiety-inducing part of the Chief's statement was how assured he was that the police were in control of the situation, a feeling she did not share. The paw prints and fur samples did not correspond to the same animal, and the scratch marks were absent of any nail fragments. Even the helicopter with infrared capability had arrived but found nothing, meaning the beast remained elusive and unidentifiable.

Dejected, Achebe exited the woods onto the main road. The branches waved sarcastic goodbyes in the rearview mirror as the forest of damned souls laughed mockingly behind her back.

CHAPTER 10

The only sign that Bert had gone home since Dargo left the Midnight Club that morning was the fact his unironed shirt was a different shade of grey. Connor appeared slightly more refreshed.

'Awrite Tom, how's things?'

'Same old.'

Bert chimed in as if he were waiting for the monotonous pleasantries to subside before he joined the conversation.

'I saw you on the news. The things that murderer did to that family…'

Bert left the sentence open-ended, and Dargo had to agree there were no words to describe the horrifying way Bob Huskins had murdered an innocent family.

'Any closer to finding what happened to the missing lads?' Connor asked. 'I might be next.'

Dargo shifted for comfort on the stool. He always shied away from discussing his work with the Midnight Club. The casino was his escape from the job. The clattering chips and whirring slot machines settled his mind like torrential rain cleansing the air with serene freshness.

'Not yet. If I'm honest. There's not a lot to go on.'

'You'll get there, I'm sure,' said Connor.

Dargo nodded to appreciate the sentiment.

'No Ronan tonight?' Dargo asked, keen to change the subject.

'He was, ah, let's say, a little disheveled by the time he left this morning.'

Dargo noticed Connor's glance towards Bert. There was something deeper to his words, and Dargo guessed Connor was understating the state Ronan was in.

'Is he okay?'

Bert hovered his chips over number fifteen. He paused before retreating the chips back to his pile as he considered whether to answer Dargo's question or continue betting. The croupier spun the wheel and set the ball in motion. Bert sighed, reluctant to become embroiled in a sentimental conversation.

'I've been coming to this casino for seventeen years. I've witnessed many people come and go, and when I say go, I don't mean they just walk out the door and happily get on with their lives. You catch my drift? Ronan is experiencing a breakdown, one I'm not sure he'll recover from.'

The ball landed on fifteen. Bert was unmoved, numb to disappointment.

'Is there anything we can do to help him?'

Bert's hunched posture was his trademark. Tonight, it resembled the dejection of Ronan's situation. A tepid shake of his head completed the answer.

'He's been on the slide for a while. The only way we could've helped him is if we stopped him at the door four years ago when he first set foot in this place.'

Dargo placed money on red.

Black fifteen.

He doubled his stake on red.

Black twenty-seven.

Dargo quadrupled his stake on red.

Red eighteen.

'Ya dancer. Knew my luck would change, eventually.'

A roar exploded from the casino entrance. Dargo turned just in time to witness Ronan tumbling down the stairs like a clumsy panda stumbling over its feet. At the bottom, he was surrounded by four shocked staff members, all eager to help him. They were confused when Ronan erupted with a guttural laugh that quickly transformed into a wheezy tobacco cough. Dargo saw the desperate man Connor alluded to.

Bert remained facing away from the commotion. Dargo assumed it was because he had seen it all before, but Bert's face was too sombre. Perhaps, despite his dispassionate persona, he cared enough that he could not bear to watch.

Ronan wore a smile of drunken glee as he flicked away the helping hands.

'And for my next act, a backflip off the slot machines.' Ronan said, followed up with more wheezy laughter.

'Oh sir, please don't. Take a seat and we will bring you some water.'

'Ah, fuck off. I'm only having a laugh. I'm not actually gonna do it. And you can use that glass of water to wash your mouth out after that suggestion. I want a real drink.'

The chips on the table bounced as Ronan slapped his paws down to steady himself on the stool, his backside almost missing the seat. Up close, Dargo saw his face was not red from the stairway tumble, but from the stale-smelling booze that effused from his body like an alki diffuser.

The croupier looked to his manager, who quickly substituted him for a more experienced colleague.

Ronan lay down a slab of notes. The three other members of the Midnight Club reclined to exchange worried glances. Even Bert threatened to sit up straight.

'That'll be ten grand,' shouted Ronan.

Dargo was used to interrogating killers, child molesters, even terrorists. In those scenarios, his questioning was justified. Questioning other people's life choices was a different matter, however. It evoked snootiness, a condescendence Dargo was unwilling to purport. He was relieved when Connor addressed the issue with a probing joke.

'You better not have been dealing on my patch to get that cash.'

Ronan laughed at a level that was overzealous for the tameness of the quip. He slapped Connor on the back with an accidental firmness that forced his young friend off the stool onto his feet.

'Na, I sold the car. Got twenty grand for it.'

'That's good.' Connor said.

'Is it fuck! Paid thirty-eight for the thing five months ago.'

Ronan received his chips in a rack. He put five hundred on black. Black twenty-one.

'Get in! Right, we having a drink?'

'How much have you had so far?' Dargo asked.

'No. That's not happening, Tom. I'm not your suspect. I'm not up for questioning, only partying.'

Ronan waved an obnoxious hand to summon a waiter to the table; a ginger lad with round glasses.

'Oi, Elton John. Four pints, four vodka cokes, four shots of absinthe.'

Ronan exhaled the word absinthe like a snake as he squirmed his hand across the table to place fifteen hundred on black.

'I won't drink the absinthe.' Dargo said.

'You ungrateful bastard.' Ronan said, staring Dargo down with a stern expression before whipping into a playful smile. 'Only joking, Tom. It's fine. I'll have it.'

Red twenty.

Ronan's behaviour was erratic. He scattered chips across the table, hoping one would strike gold. The ball landed on a number, clear of any bets.

'Luck's got to come at some point.'

He threw two grand on black.

Red four.

'Red I go.'

Black nine.

'Canny catch a break.'

Ronan slammed the side of his fist off the table. Dargo had the same feeling in his gut as he did when replaying footage of horrific car accidents at work. He knew an explosive event was imminent and there was nothing he could do about it. He would brace in his office chair while watching the impact, and now he found his arm outstretched on the table as if readying himself. The rest of the Midnight Club could barely watch. They were relieved when the drinks arrived to distract Ronan from the next two roulette spins. He serenaded the waiter with Tiny Dancer, which he, and he alone, found hilarious. It was not long before he was back in the game, slapping a grand on red.

Black thirteen.

'You're a robbing wee bastard the night.'

'I'm only spinning the wheel,' said the croupier. 'I'm on your side. I want to see you win.'

'I'm only having a laugh. No need to give a ro-bo-tic ans-wer. What is it with folk the night? Canny have a bit of banter.'

Dargo thought he could defuse Ronan's gambling by mentioning his children.

'How are the wee ones, Ronan?'

'Aye, fine.' The question had its desired effect, and Ronan soothed temporarily.

'You going on any trips away with them? You normally have something planned over the summer months.'

'Aye, we went camping last year, and I'm hoping to do the same again this year, but the cow is making me out to be a monster. She's trying to reduce the time I get to spend with them. I barely see them as it is. Fucking bint.'

Ronan chucked a grand on black and scattered more chips across the table. He won something, but Dargo was not sure it even covered his bet, considering the number of chips he had in play. Ronan did not seem to know or care as his mind wandered to his family.

'It's fine for her. Women always move on quicker than guys. They get attention from men and quickly find someone to fill the void we left behind. Guys have to work harder to move on. No woman wants me at my age. The only thing I have going for me is my kids, and I see them once a fortnight, once a frickin' fortnight. The two weeks that pass between my visits are unbearable. That's why I drink and gamble. That's why I'm fucking broke and fat and miserable.'

Ronan chucked two grand across random numbers.

Black twenty-seven.

Ronan gave the croupier a steely glare, as if he had purposefully placed the ball on a losing number. Bert kept his head bowed, flicking the chips between his fingers. Dargo noticed Connor's anticipatory glances at Ronan, like a terrified child, unsure of what their abusive father might do next.

'Last scatter.'

The ball landed on zero.

The muscles in Ronan's jaw rippled with rage.

'PRICK!'

He smashed the table with the bottom of his fist. His stool bundled toward the blackjack tables as he stood. Security guards approached. Ronan spotted them.

'Aw aye, you wait till I've spent my cash and then move in to kick me out. Ten grand in half an hour, then you tell me to fuck off.'

One security guard put his hand on Ronan's shoulder, but Ronan was bigger than them both. He removed the guard's hand and cracked him in the nose, causing the guard to retreat, cupping blood in his hands as he fell.

'Fuck off. Just paid your wages for four months, ya mutant.'

The other guard moved in, but Ronan threw a stool at his shins.

'I'm fucking going, you couple of amateurs.'

Ronan made to leave before turning back to the scrambling bouncers.

'A wee tip for you boys.'

Ronan waved a bundle of tens and twenties he retrieved from his wallet.

'Don't fuck with me.'

He put the money back in his wallet and walked to the stairs, but by the time he got there, four members of security had grappled him and were pushing him out the door with his hands behind his back.

'I'll make sure he gets home safely.' Dargo said.

'Don't bother.' Bert said, looking more forlorn than usual.

'We need to help him.'

'He's a lost cause, too far gone.'

'Bullshit! You heard how lonely he is. He needs us.'

'I agree.' Connor chimed in.

Dargo's phone buzzed in his pocket. He looked at the message.

'Shit! I need to go.'

'I'll drive Ronan home. My car's outside,' said Connor.

'You were drinking.'

'Just four beers. I didn't drink any that Ronan ordered.'

Like so many crimes Dargo heard Connor discuss at the roulette table, he let it slide. He read the text from Achebe again. There was a far bigger incident to worry about.

CHAPTER 11

Before the beef stew even touched her mouth, Achebe knew it was rich in flavour. The heavy aroma tingled her olfactory senses and dabbed her tongue with gourmet foreplay. No matter how basic the meal, her mum turned it into a masterpiece worthy of a Michelin star, making the cooking process appear infuriatingly effortless.

Post-meal, Mr Chill sat in his famous crimson armchair. It was a nickname given to Achebe's father by her schoolmates because of his cool, calm demeanour. If Achebe got in trouble at school, her friends would joke that Mr Chill would be so angry his heart rate might exceed forty beats per minute. So proud of the nickname, Mr Chill forced his friends and colleagues at the zoo to use it.

Synonymous with Mr Chill's style, the living room decor had undergone three grand makeovers, yet the well-worn armchair always remained, despite Achebe's mum's best efforts to dispose of it. In a rare show of surrender, she had painted one wall light red and bought two cream leather sofas to complement his crimson throne. The armchair was from Botswana, but the traditional African pattern on the cotton seat had faded long ago, not that any visitors noticed because Mr Chill was permanently perched atop.

He reached over the arm and picked up his ukulele.

'Have you been practising much?' Achebe asked.

Mr. Chill nodded to the TV and began playing the nagging jingle of the car insurance advert. He winked after he finished and smiled to expose a golden molar; another characteristic that had made him so cool among her friends.

'Not bad, huh?'

'Can you play a proper song?'

'Don't encourage him, Nikki.' Achebe's mother said as she entered with hot chocolate and biscuits. Achebe would normally baulk at any snack after such a filling meal, but the slack in her loungewear meant she could accommodate such an indulgence.

'How do you make the sauce so good? It's always the sauce that makes a meal taste delicious.'

'I gave you the recipe ages ago. Have you not been following it?'

'Yes.' Achebe lied.

'Are you even cooking, Nikki?'

'I cook a lot, but work gets in the way sometimes.'

'You mean all the time?'

Her mother's eyebrow raised like a taught catapult ready to fire, a technique that forced Achebe to obey throughout her childhood.

'You need to make time for yourself, Nikki. Exercise, eat well, find yourself a man. You should be settled now. Even your younger sister is engaged.'

Nikki rolled her eyes, unsurprised that a conversation about food with her mother had diverted to one about her love life.

'My path is different, mum. We've spoken about this before.'

'I'm not getting any younger. I want to be able to dance at your wedding, not pushed in on a wheelchair wearing nappies.'

Mr Chill continued eating and watching TV as if no conversation was happening.

'I've not found the right guy.'

'Are you even looking?'

'Not really. If I actively search for a man, then I'll end up forcing myself to be with someone who is not right for me, and that's how you end up in a miserable marriage.'

'So not looking at all.'

'I came round here for a relaxing meal. I left the interrogations at work.'

Mr. Cool tuned back into the conversation, darting a stare towards his wife to tell her to stop pestering their daughter.

'How's the case going?' he asked.

'Difficult.'

'Who would've thought hunting a mythical creature would prove impossible?'

Mr. Cool burst into his infectious chuckle, which forced a smile from Achebe. He had a knack for making a comedy out of a dire situation.

'I want to show you these,' Achebe said, selecting images of the beast's paw print on her phone. 'Do they resemble anything you came across while working in Chobe national park or at the zoo?'

Mr Chill pinched the temple of his glasses as he examined the pictures.

'Four digits are not uncommon in the animal kingdom. Lions have four on the back paw, but five on the front.'

'Could it be a lion's print?'

'No. The number of digits is not out of the ordinary, but the size and spacing between each one is unusual, very unusual. Not something I have seen before. The fingers are long and skinnier than a conventional big cat paw, and big cats tend to retract their claws when they walk, so the claw marks in these photos suggest another animal, but I don't know which. I can share these with my friends at work if you think that will help.'

'No thanks, I would get in trouble if I shared evidence with civilians. You are not meant to see these, so don't tell anyone you have. Similar pictures have been sent to expert zoologists, but it's been thirty-six hours now with no response. Surely, if they knew what it was, they would report back quickly? It obviously isn't a werewolf, but even I can't deny the evidence seems to point towards a wolf we haven't witnessed before.'

'That's not out of the question. I worked in Chobe for twenty-seven years, every day, all hours and do you know how many times I saw a pangolin during that time?'

'Three times.' Achebe said, already knowing the answer.

'Three times. Can you believe that? Three times in twenty-seven years. Each sighting was only achievable because we know pangolins exist. We know what dung to look out for, we know its habitat, and we know the markings it leaves in the sand. Without any of that knowledge, a creature such as a pangolin could go decades, maybe even a hundred years, without detection. Who's to say there isn't a creature, big or small, out there in the world that has evaded us all this time? Perhaps it has hunted its usual prey to extinction, within its local habitat I mean, and we are only seeing this creature now because it has had to venture further to find a food source.'

Achebe set her phone back in her bag and massaged her forehead.

'Are you getting enough support, Nikki?' her mum asked. 'This is your first case as a proper detective. If you need help, don't be afraid to ask for it.'

'Tom and Xander are so supportive. Do you remember them? You've met them at a couple of dinners and work events.'

'Yes, good guys.' Mr. Chill said.

'I remember them,' her mum said. 'Very nice gentlemen. I remember the longer-haired one being quite handsome actually, in a rugged sort of way.'

'Xander?'

'Yes.'

'He has a wife, and I wouldn't date anyone from work, and just, no, I'm not interested.'

'I wasn't suggesting anything.'

'I knew where you were heading.'

'Well, I'm proud of you, despite your lack of a man.'

Achebe rolled her eyes again, but this time she knew her mum was joking. She kissed Achebe on the cheek before lying across the other cream sofa as they enjoyed two hours of light-hearted TV entertainment.

The home renovation programme was building up to the big reveal when Achebe's phone vibrated so loud it was effectively a ringtone. When she realised it was from her work phone, she walked to the kitchen.

Two missed calls, a voicemail and a text message from Gio so close to midnight was never going to mean good news. Her nerves needed a calming glass of water, but no refreshment would prevent her mum's beef sauce from reintroducing itself after reading the message.

Nikki, there's been an attack at the Torridon forestry plant. At least two dead, one unaccounted for, and the only witness is claiming it was a werewolf.

CHAPTER 12

The teeth were sharp and robust, glistening through the fog towards Achebe with hypnotic, murderous intent. She imagined becoming caught within its fatal trap. Bones crushed to powder. Heavy machinery always made Achebe uncomfortable, and the grinding blades of the woodchipper were no different.

Standing atop the plateau of a grassy mound, Achebe scanned the entire forestry plant. Tree trunks were piled twenty feet high on the opposite side of a dimly lit yard; the floodlights straining to illuminate the miry terrain. On a clear night, the forecourt lit up like a gladiator's arena, and tonight, it was littered with fallen warriors.

Despite the hazy conditions, the beast's paw prints were visible from Achebe's elevated vantage point. The trail arrowed from the woodchipper at the edge of Bannock forest to the faint outline of a man lying face down in the sludge. His crushed skull lay inside his safety helmet like a broken vase, the hard plastic dented from the creature's stomp.

Achebe moved round the bend of the mound to witness the beast's next victim. His torso was gutted like a fish; organs and intestines sprawled across the mud like melted chocolate strawberries.

Beyond the body was a portable cabin, where Dargo sat with the sole witness. He recounted the attack while sitting in front of an unnerving claw mark which had pierced the side of the cabin. He had been inches from death. His survival coming at the expense of his injured colleague, whose cries for help distracted the beast at the other end of the yard. Through the gaping claw marks, the witness watched the animal puncture the fog as it ran and dragged his maimed colleague into the woods.

The witness was adamant it was a werewolf. But given the poor visibility, Achebe questioned how clear an image of the beast the man truly witnessed, surmising that he only referred to it as a werewolf because that is what he read about the previous attack. Yellow eyes and black fur; his description did not match the orange-eyed beast with brown fur that terrorised the caravan park.

As Achebe rubbed her arms for warmth, she suddenly felt vulnerable, assessing her distance from the car and wondering if the beast showed itself now, would she make it back safely?

'Nikki, get back inside.'

It was Dargo shouting from the cabin, concerned that the beast was still in the vicinity, lurking amongst the darkness. Achebe almost wished it to be true. Her desire to witness the beast superseded the danger.

'Nikki, come on. The Chief wants us back at HQ for an update.'

The ambulance lights flashed across Achebe's cheeks, but she remained staring at the shadowy trees. The forest was feasting on yet another damned soul and, despite not placing much credence on the eyewitness' description of a black, yellow-eyed beast, Achebe feared the possibility that two malevolent creatures were running wild, capable of killing again.

June 8th

June 8th

CHAPTER 13

The only creases to be found on Caledonia's Chief of Police, Vincent Thorne, were the crow's feet at the corner of his eyes, darkened by a permanent schedule of reduced sleep since taking on the role two years ago. His face wore the tiredness of being awoken by a midnight phone call, but the suit covering the rest of his totem pole figure was immaculate.

Dargo took a seat across from his desk. Achebe remained standing.

'Take a seat, Nikki.' said the Chief as he leaned into the slack of his brown leather chair. 'Three dead and one survivor, am I right?'

'Two dead, one missing and one survivor.' said Achebe, anxious that she had corrected the top boss.

Chief Thorne looked down at her over the top of his glasses.

'I think we can assume the individual taken into Bannock forest is dead, just like the boy from the previous attack.'

Achebe felt her pores open up, sweat sticking to her shirt.

'We need to get control of the situation,' said the Chief.

'The Special Response Unit has set a perimeter around the yard, and forensics are..'

The Chief waved a hand to stop Achebe from saying anything more.

'I'm not just talking about this incident. I mean the entire investigation. Are we any closer to catching this animal? Do we even know what animal we are trying to catch?'

'The SRU has set a trap near Bannock Manor using piles of chicken meat. We chose that location because there's evidence the animal has frequented that area and it is far enough away from any civilians.'

'No, is the answer to my question, then? I'm hearing a lot about what Maynard's SRU is doing, but what are you doing? Have we just shirked all responsibility to people with guns?'

'I have been working on it, sir. We have ruled out Jim McAllister as a suspect. Analysis of hair I found in his barn belongs to a badger, but nothing more sinister than that. Analysis of the hairs found at Dalmally caravan park belong to a timber wolf. The issue we have is we cannot match the paw prints to a specific animal. They do not match a timber wolf, or any wolf, for that matter. We may be looking at a new subspecies of wolf, or even a new species entirely, something we've never come across before.'

'We're not the fucking Ghostbusters. I've got a press conference about the latest attack in two hours. I need something substantial to tell the media.'

Dargo lifted his head from its resting position in his left hand. He blinked twice in quick succession, a sign that he was also lacking sleep, something Achebe recognised was an enduring sleepless stint rather than a one-off night.

'Nikki is doing everything she can. It's pretty difficult to catch an unidentifiable animal. I'm sure you can sympathise with what we are up against here, Chief.'

Chief Thorne nodded in response, but Achebe knew he did not accept Dargo's assessment.

'We need to control the press coverage.' said the Chief. 'They've been salivating over the term werewolf, and the hysteria on the back of it has been ridiculous. We should tell the press we have evidence of a bear or a big cat. Let's squash this werewolf nonsense.'

Achebe looked at Dargo. She thought he was displaying another pronounced blink, but this time he kept his eyes shut as if summoning the energy to counter the Chief's idea. Achebe spoke first.

'You want me to lie to the press, to the public? I can't do that.'

'It's not you that's speaking to the press, it's me. I'm doing you a favour by saving you from the firing line. And it's not lying, Nikki. It's managing the situation. Once the press loses the werewolf mantra, things will calm down and you can do your job with a little more peace.'

'I have no problem telling a white lie or concealing the full extent of the truth when it's necessary to do so, but I don't see how this could be of any benefit.'

'I've just told you the benefit. It manages the media and takes the pressure off us.'

'I don't mind the pressure. No one puts more pressure on myself than me.'

The Chief leaned forward.

'You've yet to feel pressure.'

Dargo opened his eyes again after his power nap.

'I agree with Nikki. We can't lie, because when Nikki catches the animal, and she will catch the animal, if it's not a bear or a big cat, we just look daft and lose any integrity in future press statements. I agree that sometimes a lie is necessary, but it's better to be honest in this situation, and the honest answer is we don't know what we're up against.'

The Chief raised his hand, signalling he wanted to intervene, but Dargo leaned forward, placing a delicate hand on the Chief's table.

'Give us a bit more time, Chief. Let the dust settle on this latest incident and let us assess the situation before we go to the media with the details you're suggesting. Another press release to avoid Bannock forest will suffice for now.'

The Chief took a deep breath.

'Fine! But I want progress on your case as well, Tom. Stopping Bob Huskins from killing another family was impressive work, but I've not heard any progress on the missing teenagers.'

'It's proving difficult, Chief.'

'Everything seems to be proving difficult. Next time we speak, I want to hear progress from both of you.'

The Chief's private office had two exits, one leading to the main corridor of police headquarters, the other filtering out to the Major Crimes office, to which Achebe and Dargo exited.

'Well done, Nikki.'

'For what?'

'You held your own in there. Others buckle under his pressure.'

'I don't feel I strengthened his opinion of me.'

Dargo motioned his head to indicate he wanted a word away from prying ears. Even in his office, Dargo lowered his voice.

'Amongst the high constables and peace officers, Xander and I have kept the fact we don't rate the Chief too highly a secret. He's a nice guy, or at least he used to be before he became Chief. But the job is too big for him. You got a glimpse of it just now. He faffs. Rather than staying calm and creating the best environment for you and me to succeed, he transfers the pressure he feels from the government and the media onto those around him.'

74

'I see.'

'He's a bright guy, but his faffing clouds rational thinking. Lying to the press.' Dargo shook his head. 'I understand where he's coming from. He wants the public and the media to take this threat seriously. But long term, lying always comes back to haunt you. As I say, you did well to stand your ground.'

Dargo checked his watch.

'Five a.m. It's probably worth going home to get four or five hours of sleep. Better than continuing on none at all. Gio's in the office already. He can manage the crime scene in the meantime.'

'I'm not sure I'll get any sleep.' Achebe said, reading a message on her phone. 'What's a cryp... cryptozoologist?'

'Bigfoot hunters,' said Dargo. 'They hunt for mythical beings. Obviously, they don't believe what they're looking for is mythical. With rumours of a werewolf, I suppose it was only a matter of time before those loonies got involved. What's happening?'

'Sam Stone sent me a message saying they've set up camp in Bannock forest, on the grounds where the posh lodges were going to be built. Under Caledonian law, they are free to camp on the land, but I better ask them to leave, even if our warnings fall on deaf ears.'

Dargo looked to the ceiling, praying for some respite.

'I'll come with you,' he muttered.

'You don't have to if you'd rather get some rest.'

'No, no. It's fine. I'll come. That was good of Sam to inform us of their presence. Did you end up speaking with her in the end?'

'Not had the chance to.'

As they exited, Bullock entered the main office wearing protective biker clothing and his helmet gripped in his left hand.

An officer finishing up his night shift called Dargo. 'See the football last night, sir. Won four hundred on a five-team accumulator, each game over two-point-five goals.'

'Really! Who did you have on?'

Achebe tuned out of their conversation as she waited for Bullock to reach her.

'Morning.'

'Morning, Nikki.'

'Wow, that's a shiner right enough.'

'Have a feel.' Bullock said, prodding the purple golf ball under his bloodshot eye, a remnant of Bob Huskins' right hook. 'It's entertainingly squidgy.'

'I'll pass, thanks. Is it sore?'

'Aye, made even worse cause Amy shouldered it in her sleep last night. I'm not convinced it was an accident. She's always moaning about my snoring.'

'Not gonna lie, it looks really bad.'

'You should see the other guy. Not only did he take a hammering from me, but he's now deep-fried. Cooked to perfection, the meat slid right off the bone.'

'That's disgusting.'

'*He* was disgusting,' Bullock said, scurrying into his office.

High Constable Gardyne called Achebe to his desk.

'I've been doing some research into what this animal could be. Given that most witnesses are claiming a werewolf, I thought it might be this.'

Achebe leaned in to view an image so incredulous she did not believe it was real.

'It's called a maned wolf. They live in South America.' Gardyne said. 'I'd never heard of it. I don't think many people have. It's unique in the sense that it's neither fox nor wolf, which may be the reason our experts could not identify the paw print.'

The animal on the screen had the menacing snout of a wolf, but its legs were disproportionately long.

'Is it real?' Achebe asked. 'There're loads of fake animal photos out there.'

'No, this is legit.'

'Why are its legs so long?'

'It says here they hunt in tall grass, so the long legs help to see its prey.'

'How tall do they get?'

'Only three feet tall, but I was thinking if this thing ran and jumped at you, it could look a lot taller. If the witnesses only caught a glimpse of this animal, then I can understand how they could confuse it for something supernatural. I think this could be our killer.'

'Can you pull up a photo of its paw print?'

Gardyne searched for an image, but for once the internet did not boast many options.

'Given the lack of images on the internet, I would say this animal is under-researched.' Achebe said. 'Who's to say there isn't a subspecies we are unaware of? Also, the witness from last night's attack claimed the creature had black fur and yellow eyes. From the pictures you are showing me, it seems the maned wolf has both brown and black fur, and if you flash a light in an animal's eye at night, they can appear yellowish. Is the maned wolf known to attack humans?'

'Not necessarily. Apparently, they are shy creatures, but will attack if provoked.'

'Okay, but let's say this animal has been illegally transported to Caledonia from abroad and dropped into a new habitat with no instinct for what it should and shouldn't hunt. It's plausible it could view humans as a food source.'

'I suppose so.'

'Good work, Gio. Send what you've found to Viti and ask her to share it with the zoology experts. See if they can re-run tests on the fur samples found at Dalmally caravan site against a maned wolf.'

Achebe sighed mid-yawn.

'I'm off to speak to some cryptozoologists who have placed themselves at the epicentre of the danger.'

CHAPTER 14

The sun was still deciding whether to bother waking up. Achebe swigged another gulp of coffee from her portable mug, desperately trying to stay alert while driving. Vigilance was made more difficult by the monotonous road to the cryptozoologist camp; no junctions, no roundabouts, and no other drivers to contend with in the sleepy hours of the morning.

The bigfoot hunters, as Dargo had so eloquently described them, had chosen a clear expanse on the fringes of Bannock forest as their base camp. The trees were felled for the construction of a luxurious housing estate, a site destined to become a soulless holiday village where the uber-rich convince themselves they are at one with nature, all while relaxing in their centrally heated homes. Fervent public opposition to the development fell on deaf ears. However, much to the delight of the Caledonians, the housing developer went bust, and no other developer wanted to take on the reputational risk of the job. The land's appeal had no doubt diminished further now that a deadly beast paraded through the forest.

Achebe turned beyond the last of the trees before the clearing.

'Jesus Christ.'

Achebe's astonishment woke Dargo. She was expecting an amateur operation with a handful of individuals. Instead, five large camper vans sat within a perimeter of cameras on stilts facing towards the forest.

78

Two dozen people were milling around a campfire or walking in and out of an enormous canvas tent used for communal gatherings.

'Didn't expect this many of them,' said Achebe.

'Reminds me of the opening scenes of Jurassic Park.' Dargo said. 'When the underprepared hunters are full of excitement before being picked off by the raptors.'

The car bobbled the two passengers as it drove over the rugged terrain towards the camp. Achebe and Dargo shut the car doors in unison. A pigeon-chested member strode towards the detectives.

'I'm Detective Achebe. This is Premier Detective Dargo. Are you in charge here?'

'I am. Ed Meldrew DSc.'

Ed Meldrew, wanker, Achebe thought. Meldrew was dressed in khaki attire, which included the god-awful trousers which zip off to form shorts. He removed a pair of glasses from his chest pocket to examine Achebe and Dargo's identification cards.

'How can I help you, Nikki?' asked Meldrew, his American accent bellowing like a megaphone.

'Detective Achebe, if you don't mind. What is it you hope to gain from being here?'

'I'm the head of Unmythical. We are here to gather evidence, sightings, and potentially capture the werewolf that has been reported in this area.'

'Paranormal investigators,' said Dargo.

Meldrew kinked his neck as if trying to crack it. Dargo's comment evidently irked him.

'Not paranormal. We are here to enlighten those who don't believe there are creatures on this planet that modern-day humans have not discovered yet.'

'Well, I'm here to ask if you can please leave this site.' Nikki said. 'The animal you are trying to interact with is extremely dangerous and you are putting all these people in danger by bringing them here.'

'The great thing about Caledonia is the land is free, and we are well within our rights to be here. I appreciate your concern, but you don't need to worry about anyone in our group. They are all here of their own volition. They know the risks involved.'

Meldrew raised his voice so the group cupping coffee mugs around the campfire could hear. Some looked over and politely nodded in agreement.

'Do you mind if we have a look around?' Nikki asked.

'Why?' said Meldrew, his chest puffed out further now that he was on the defensive.

'We just want to make sure there are no illegal weapons on-site,' said Dargo.

'We have licences for all our guns.'

Achebe lightly scraped her toe in the dirt as if embarrassed.

'We need to check your weaponry, but if I'm honest, I'm actually quite fascinated by your operation. I grew up in Botswana. We lived in a small village called Kasane on the fringes of Chobe national park. In fact, our backyard *was* Chobe national park, so occasionally we had to fend off lions and other animals to stop them from eating our chickens and livestock. I know what it takes to interact with predators, so I'm interested to see what equipment you are hoping to catch this creature with.'

Meldrew's shoulders softened.

'I was in South Africa recently searching for a lion that belonged to an extinct strand of the species. The one we were searching for is two times bigger than any lion you saw in Chobe.'

'Oh, you're talking about the Cape lion.' Achebe said.

'Yes.' said Meldrew with a grin spanning the width of his chubby face. 'Let me show you.'

Meldrew turned to start the tour, which blinded him from Dargo's eye-roll towards Achebe, mocking her ability to charm her way into the camp.

As they walked closer to the campfire, Achebe's stomach rumbled upon smelling fresh porridge bubbling in a pot. Meldrew began explaining the key aspects of the camp.

'As you can see, we have placed bait at several points on the edges of the forest. We hope to lure the werewolf out to the open to give our cameras the best chance of capturing it. We have state-of-the-art motion sensors set up around each bait station, so we will be alerted once the werewolf arrives. Our cameras have night vision and infrared capabilities, naturally.'

Better gear than the Caledonian police, Achebe thought.

Meldrew stopped outside the entrance of the main tent.

'You'll see we have surrounded the camp with wolfsbane.'

Only after mentioning the wolfsbane did Achebe notice subtle purple flowers winding around the legs of the camera stands. Meldrew opened the flap entrance to the huge canvas tent and continued explaining their capture strategy.

'Here we have tranquilliser darts as well as guns with silver bullets. All licenced, as I said.'

'Didn't know you could licence bullshit.' Dargo whispered for Achebe's benefit only.

Meldrew continued.

'They have a one hundred metre range, so we want the werewolf to come close to the camp. We will be perfectly secure because the wolfsbane will maintain the werewolf's proximity to a safe distance. We have some highly skilled shooters in the group that will hit the target.'

'Wolfsbane and silver bullets, you can't believe that folklore sh- stuff will actually work?' Dargo said.

'There's a reason these items are so embedded within folklore, as you call it. It's because it is based on the truth, based on human experiences in the past.'

Meldrew was not interested in conversing with Dargo, so he moved on to the next area of the tent.

'This is the motivation wall.'

The pinboard contained pictures of blurry blobs and green outlines of canine creatures, which were definitely just dogs caught on night vision.

'These hunts can last days, weeks, maybe even months, with no progress or activity. This wall reminds us of why we are doing this and helps the group keep focused. It reminds us of our past successes. Here are two photos of the Cape lion we found in South Africa and two of the yeti in Bhutan.'

Achebe grimaced at the black splodge, pictured about two hundred metres from whoever was holding the camera. It could easily have been a regular lion. She thought it best to keep her opinions to herself.

'Wow, that's amazing.'

Dargo massaged his eyelids.

'How do you fund all this?' Achebe asked.

'We have benefactors from all over the world, and some of us in the team are pretty wealthy, including me.'

'Any mandate to search for the Loch Ness monster while you're here?' Achebe joked.

'Yes, we will make a small jaunt up to Loch Ness once we are finished here,' Meldrew answered without noticing Achebe's sarcasm.

'You do know that even the tourist attractions at Loch Ness don't pretend the monster actually exists?'

'Such a shame that even the locals don't believe. So, what do you think of our set-up?' Meldrew asked, desperate for Achebe's approval after learning of her upbringing.

'It's certainly more sophisticated than the tools I had growing up. You seem well prepared, but not enough for the monster that's out there, and I have to urge you and your group to leave.'

'I'm sure you already know we won't be doing that, but I certainly appreciate your concern, Detective Achebe.'

Walking back to the car, Achebe wondered how many of the group were social members, content just being part of a team that travelled the world experiencing new countries and cultures rather than truly believing what they are hunting exists.

'Is that story about the Cape lion true? It's genetically bigger than a normal lion?' asked Dargo, while turning up the heating in Achebe's car.

'I've heard of sightings, but nothing has been caught on camera, certainly not by Meldrew and his team. They have to be deluded if those black smudges are their trophies.'

'Surely someone would have captured an image of the Cape lion by now if it exists?'

'Living in Africa, you realise the earth is far bigger than our minds can comprehend. Caledonia is a tiny country with a killer animal, possibly more than one killer animal, that we cannot catch even though we know it operates within a confined forest relatively close to human settlements. The helicopters with infrared capabilities have tried and failed to locate the beast from the air. So, if we can't find this creature, imagine trying to find one lion over an area seven times larger than all of Caledonia.'

Dargo nodded.

'Do you miss living near Chobe safari park?'

'It's not a safari park. It's a national park where safaris happen to take place. I miss it in some ways. Growing up, watching my dad fight against poachers was inspiring and definitely influenced my decision to join the police and stop any sort of crime.'

'Do you think you'll go back?'

'Maybe one day. As bizarre as it sounds with a rampaging beast on the loose, Bob Huskins kidnapping and killing families, and teenage boys going missing, it's safer over here. Out in Botswana, there are a million ways to die. Poor orienteering can lead to dehydration and starvation. There are apex predators, and even the more docile animals like elephants can charge you if they feel threatened. Then you have the free health service over here that we all take for granted. Over there, unless you're rich or know someone with medical training, training that is not to the standard of doctors and nurses over here, you fend for yourself. So, if you are seriously injured or sick, good luck to you.'

Achebe reached to switch on the ignition, but stopped before turning the key.

'You should see some of the crime prevention tactics adopted by the park rangers, though. They are even more brutal than the beatings some of our officers like to dish out over here.'

'Like what?'

'Well, there's a shoot-on-sight policy within the national park if any poachers are found. But if there's a large group of poachers, rather than shoot them all, they arrest them. The rangers then take them up in a helicopter and drop them one by one over a pride of lions until they disclose who sanctioned the hunt. I reckon we'd get a few more confessions if we were allowed to dangle criminals over the lion's enclosure at the zoo.'

Dargo smiled.

'You need to tell Xander that story. He'll love that.'

'The only issue I have with that story is the poachers are normally desperate people promised big money by a cowardly fat cat. Money that could see their families fed for a year or more. Unfortunately, these individuals are the ones caught and thrown to the lions, but the real poachers are the ones sitting in their gated mansion sipping wine with their trophy wife.'

Achebe switched on the engine. As she swivelled the car around, she glanced at some of the reluctant poachers huddled around the campfire, vulnerable to the beast, secured only by folly fables.

CHAPTER 15

The girl writhed with agitation underneath her wetsuit; desperate for a victim; desperate for a kill. Staring at a group of twelve-year-olds, throttling thoughts of murder threatened to demolish her thespian display of normality.

Splash!

The slap against the water mimicked the crack of her whip; the aqua spray portraying the blood. She watched a boy struggle, water gargling in his mouth, blocking any air. His choking triggered a blissful memory of asphyxiation from four nights ago.

'Leave your kayaks on the beach. I'll tidy them away,' the girl said while lifting the boy by his life jacket; his struggle made even more pathetic by the fact he was next to the shore in knee-high water.

She thumped his back to eject the loch water from his mouth, then discarded him on the beach while the rest of his classmates clambered to shore with their kayaks. He was a few years away from her target market, but he had potential if he developed some muscle.

'Please take your oars back to the cabin and place them in the rack next to the entrance. Give your wetsuits and helmets to Nick at the equipment shed. Your teachers have told me the bus leaves at half-past three, so you have thirty minutes to get showered and changed. Lastly, I just want to say a big thank you to all of you. You have been an amazing class to teach. You were all brilliant at kayaking and I hope you all decide to join us again in the near future.'

The high school children meandered from the loch-side beach to the equipment shed.

'Eh, what do we say, class?' said their teacher.

A concerted thank you emanated from the children, who competitively grabbed their oars and ran to the cabin, desperate to be first in the showers.

An anticipatory buzz developed within the girl's stomach. Her kayak lesson was over, and after a refreshing shower, she would be free to search for another arrogant hunk to add to her collection.

One girl ignored her peers' race and made her way to the kayak instructor. She was too shy to express further gratitude, so the instructor started the conversation for her.

'Hello! You were especially great today. Kate, is that right?'

The girl nodded.

'Thank you, Miss. I really enjoyed it.'

'You know we run a summer camp here? Starts in three weeks. I'll give your teacher some leaflets about it and she can share them with your class. If you sign-up for the summer camp, I'll give you a special discount. That's just for you though, so don't tell anybody.'

Kate smiled bashfully.

'Okay, thank you.'

Kate ran off and the instructor smiled as she watched her feet struggle in the thick sand.

The smile was short-lived. Diamond droplets shimmered across her wetsuit as she pulled the kayaks behind her two at a time to the storage shed, quietly devising her plan for the evening. She was left disappointed with her latest effort, but how was she to know the target did not possess the required dimensions to satisfy her? She would not let that deter her from trying again. She knew the place to go and the time to be there. All she needed was a fit and proper victim.

CHAPTER 16

Achebe eyed the world-famous investigative journalist as she unashamedly slurped her tonkotsu ramen. A thread of blonde hair dangled dangerously over the steaming bowl before Sam Stone tilted her head back and curled the loose strand around her ear mid-slurp.

'How's the case going?' Sam asked in between a spoonful.

'We are ruling out more leads than we are ruling in.'

'That's a skill in itself, to disregard distracting leads. I'm sure you are doing just fine.'

'I never said I wasn't.'

'It was implied in your tone.'

Sam lay her spoon in the bowl and dabbed her lips with a napkin. The restaurant's empty rooftop conservatory boasted a serene view over Edin, which breathed gently in the calm weather; its famous castle perched majestically on the crag.

Achebe shifted in her seat. Sam equally inspired and intimidated her. Working at the Thistle magazine, Sam had uncovered paedophile rings, interviewed the most feared criminals, antagonised and exposed corrupt politicians. She pioneered a fresh wave of social media journalism as she broadcast her stories in podcasts and short video episodes as well as print, something the new generation of media consumers found more digestible. It garnered her more online followers than most influencers.

Despite the inferiority complex, Achebe scratched her head in irritation that she had been summoned to the restaurant only to watch the famous journo slurp ramen.

'Your followers might be inclined to watch you eat noodles, but I've got better stuff to be getting on with.' Achebe said.

'Sorry, I was so hungry. I haven't eaten all day. Don't worry, though. I am hopefully going to give you some food for thought. I was wondering if you had investigated Strathaven Science Centre as part of your investigation?'

'I can't divulge information on the...'

Achebe stopped mid-sentence as Sam tilted her head and smiled condescendingly.

'Come on, Nikki. You know I can help you. I've worked closely with Tom and Xander before.'

'I'm not Tom and Xander. Case information is confidential and the last thing I need is you releasing an article detailing my investigation.'

'Okay, okay. I understand your reservations. Let me explain how I operate. I am not a tabloid hyena seeking to publish crude stories and outlandish headlines as your case progresses. I know how detrimental that is to any investigation, let alone one as high profile as this. The Thistle magazine has not earned its global status using such methods. We publish well-researched, evidence-based articles. I mainly focus on corruption committed by public figures and high-net-worth individuals. This means I spend months, maybe even years, researching a subject before I get anywhere close to writing a piece for the magazine. We are not controlled and coerced by the state like the standard news agencies.'

'I'll give you ten thousand merks for a five percent stake in the Thistle.'

Sam smiled, recognising she had gone overboard with the pitch.

'All I want to get across is that anything you disclose now will not be in an article tomorrow. Tom and Xander will vouch for me. I work closely with them and only write an article once their investigation is largely complete. I even run certain aspects of my stories past them to make sure they are happy with it, and I definitely omit a lot of juicy details on how cases are solved from my articles. God knows Xander would be jailed if I exposed his methods.'

Sam chuckled, but Achebe remained stoic.

'That's a joke, Nikki. Xander Bullock is an outstanding detective.'

'I'm well aware.'

'Look, my only goal is to ensure killers, corrupt politicians, or in this case, a werewolf, are stopped.'

'It's not a werewolf.'

'I wouldn't be so sure about that.'

Achebe squinted in bemusement, glancing over her shoulder in case anybody was eavesdropping, but there was no one there. The sliding doors separating them from the other diners in the main restaurant area were closed.

'Don't worry, I pulled a favour and asked for this space to remain private.' Sam said, replacing her smile with a frown before continuing. 'I implore you to investigate the Strathaven research facility, Nikki.'

'Why are you so adamant Strathaven has something to do with the attacks?'

'Do you remember Alba the rabbit?'

'It's not ringing any bells.'

Sam picked up her chopsticks, but rather than eat, she played with the small chunks of vegetables lying in a miso puddle.

'Years ago, a farmer was awoken during the night when he heard his horses neighing restlessly in their stables. When he went to investigate, he found a rabbit hopping through the stable. An illuminous rabbit. Of course, the farmer was so baffled by what he saw he questioned his own sanity. Was he dreaming, sleepwalking, hallucinating? He never told his wife or anyone about the rabbit, scared they would think he was insane. Instead, he set a trap and, sure enough, the very next night, there was a glow-in-the-dark rabbit in his trap. He informed the police and the press, but I would say it got fairly mild coverage for how incredulous the animal was, which is probably why you haven't heard about it.'

'When did this happen?'

'We would've been quite young. This was over a decade ago.'

'Why such a mild press coverage?'

'The farm was located near the Strathaven facility. They took responsibility for the animal, and being a government-backed institution, they held significant influence in the media, so the story was largely unreported. This was the days before social media or the Thistle. It was easier to bury unwanted stories back then.'

'So, they experiment on animals at Strathaven?'

'They vowed to stop animal experiments when the rabbit was found. Animal welfare groups put a bit of pressure on Rockwell to stop the experiments and resign. It's debatable if he did the former, but he definitely avoided the latter.'

'Is he still there now?'

'Rockwell? Dr Torion Rockwell, the Caledonian cunt? Please tell me you know who I mean?'

'I know of him, but...'

'Oh, Nikki. You need an education on where the bodies are buried in Caledonia now you are a detective. Forgive me if I start telling you things you're already aware of.'

Sam sipped water before resuming.

'Strathaven was built pre-independence. It was an expensive gimmick in a way. Build a facility in the Trossachs mountain range which, from a bird's-eye-view, is shaped like a leaf with the sole purpose of investing in Caledonia's sustainability. The facility employs thousands and set up a pretence that the Caledonian National Party had a vision for the country. Its construction was a major influence on voters during the independence vote. But like many claims that politicians pedal, the reality is far from their description. Yes, Strathaven has four research and development sectors that appear commendable endeavours: biological disease, renewable energy, transportation and cultured meats.'

'What's cultured meat?'

'Lab-produced meat. Means we won't have to breed and slaughter so much livestock and have fewer cows farting us to extinction.'

'I see.'

'Notwithstanding those research divisions, Strathaven has a dark side. An extremely dark side. One that caused Angus Mintoff to quit in his capacity as Minister of Business and Trade.'

'Angus Mintoff, the CEO of Pangea International?'

'Yip. We were a bit young to remember, but Mintoff only championed independence on the basis he would become Minster of Business and Trade. He believed, quite rightly, that politicians are not the most business savvy and efficient operators. They go into politics because their egos seek power, and the fact they probably wouldn't earn the same salary in the private sector where more intelligent, capable individuals would muscle them out of the way.'

'Harsh.'

'But not untrue. Anyway, being the successful serial entrepreneur that Mintoff is, he was vocal about the state of the economy, and had a track record of predicting economic headwinds before they arose. He was an important catalyst to achieving independence.'

'Popular with voters then.'

'Extremely popular. It was a shame he couldn't fill four roles at the head of the government. Many wanted him to become Caledonia's first prime minister.'

'What didn't he?'

'He's a normal, intelligent person who knew that becoming PM would be a distraction from delivering the trade deals Caledonia needed to boost their independence and actually achieve a sustainable pathway. He hired competent people from Pangea International to negotiate lucrative trade deals in sectors such as renewable energy, whisky, fish. Any pillar of commerce Caledonia has today can be traced back to his four years in government.'

'So why did he leave?'

'Now you're asking the sensible questions. He left because of Strathaven's infamous Sector Five.'

'Sector Five is the Department of National Defence, isn't it?'

'Well, that's the thing, Nikki. No one knows. Rockwell claims it's a defence division, but wee Alba the rabbit is our one and only insight into Sector Five, and everyone was a bit confused at how a glow-in-the-dark rabbit helps protect Caledonia. The other research divisions are open to journalists and the public for site tours. Students can gain work placements and world-renowned conferences are hosted on the grounds. But no one ever gets into Sector Five.'

'What about Sector Five made Mintoff quit?'

'No one knows that either. But the rumours are rife. This is years after Alba the rabbit was found, so many people surmised that Mintoff found out animal experiments were still occurring and quit. Some even suggest he discovered human experiments, but I don't believe those.'

'What do you believe?'

'I believe the department is used for defence purposes, but I don't think the methods and experiments in Sector Five are always legal. Mintoff wouldn't leave if it was merely weapons development. As nature-loving as he is, I don't think he would even leave if certain animal experiments were still taking place. He saw something he could not live with.'

'Mintoff hasn't come out publicly about what he saw then?'

'He can't. Legally, I imagine he is bound by a non-disclosure agreement. Informally, he's scared if he talks Rockwell would deal with him in his own way.'

'You don't mean.'

'Yes. If anyone discloses what goes on there, they will be disposed of. Mintoff and Rockwell have been like two rams butting heads ever since. Both Strathaven and Pangea International focus on creating a better world, a more sustainable world. Rockwell wants Strathaven's four publicly known units to crush any success Pangea International has, and vice versa. They tend to do their dirty washing in the press, constantly taking swipes at each other. But that's all timid foreplay. They're never going to truly fuck each other over. Deep down, Rockwell knows Mintoff is aware of the dark secrets of Strathaven, and Mintoff knows Rockwell is prepared to silence anyone to protect Sector Five.'

'How do you know all this? You sound like a mad conspiracy theorist.'

'I have my sources, but think about it. Why does a research facility like Strathaven need to be built in such a remote location? The only facilities located remotely are ones which require natural resources from the land, like whisky distilleries, or handle dangerous chemicals, like nuclear power plants, or something clandestine, like Area 51.'

'So Strathaven is in the Trossachs to keep the public away from Sector Five.'

'More like keeping Sector Five, and whatever experiments they are conducting, away from the public.'

'You think this creature is a Sector Five experiment?'

'I think if you've explored the obvious avenues: the zoos, safari park, animal smugglers, and you have a paw print no zoologist can match, then Sector Five is where this monster was born, and I'm going to find out if my theory is true.'

'How?'

'I'm going to break into Strathaven.'

'Woah, woah, woah. You're openly telling me you're going to commit a crime and expect me to accept it.'

'Yes.'

'Look, I'm grateful you text me about the cryptozoologists and giving me a background on Strathaven, but…'

'Nikki, I've worked with Tom and Xander for a long time. I know how it works inside the police. The Chief is a wanker. He'll be putting pressure on you to get results and he'll sooner throw you under a bus to cover his arse. At the moment, you have an investigation that's a bit rudderless, given the paw print. I think that's fair to say.'

'Hold on, what makes you think we haven't matched the paw prints to an animal?'

Sam tilted her head at the naïve detective.

'Nikki, c'mon. The police is like a sieve, but forget about that just now. I'm not a clickbait journalist. I haven't jumped on the werewolf bandwagon for cheap social media traction, have I? I want to discover the truth and right now you need my help to do that, so I'm hoping you'll reciprocate with support.'

Sam slid a black screen across the table.

'This burner phone only has one number in it. The number to my burner phone. My burner has two numbers: your burner phone and a burner that I'm giving to my boss, Leigh. Have you met Leigh?'

Achebe shook her head.

'I'll introduce you in good time.'

'What are the phones for?'

'I've broken into many places, Nikki. Places with higher security control than Strathaven.'

'Even higher than Sector Five?'

'Not sure, but I have a little help from the inside on this occasion that will make things easier.'

'You have a contact in Sector Five?'

'Sort of.'

'Who?'

Sam tilted her head and smiled.

'You're not going to give up your source.' Achebe sighed.

'Exactly. It's of no consequence to you in any case. Going back to your question, though. Of all the places I have trespassed or broken into, Strathaven has one thing that scares me above all else.'

'Don't you dare say a werewolf.'

'No.' Sam smirked.

'Rockwell.'

'Exactly. These phones are my protection if I get into deep trouble while inside. If I get caught, I don't think Rockwell will phone the police, if you get what I mean.'

'What do you think he'll do?'

'Lock me up, torture me, kill me.'

'Surely not. I find it hard to believe the head of a government facility would resort to that level of criminality and remain in charge.'

'Speak to Angus Mintoff, Nikki. He won't tell me anything about Rockwell or why he left his government role so abruptly, but he might tell you, a detective. He knows as well as I that Rockwell controls the government. He has a stranglehold on the media. Everyone fears him, and there is a short, yet significant list of Sector Five personnel who have died over the years. All accidents. All largely unreported. I don't think that's a coincidence. If Rockwell detects a rat, he exterminates it.'

CHAPTER 17

The singer sipped a glass of water as she waited for the appreciative applause to fade before introducing the next song. The jazz bar was a clandestine haunt tucked away in a cosey basement. Those who were privileged enough to descend the steep stairs were captivated by the magic of the brass sorcerers. They marveled at the calibre of talent, mystified that it was hidden beneath street level, wondering why the talents were not jamming on a grander stage, or why the owners had not spiced up the unassuming veneer. For the musicians, the only thing that mattered was the splendid acoustics the exposed brickwork of the windowless speakeasy boasted. Attracting custom was no issue. There was no entrance fee. No financial obligation to stay. The bar was merely another that guests could swing in and out of as they wished. Most nights, however, the guests all stayed, and tonight was no different. The keyboard tingled their enthusiasm. The saxophone ripped apart their stresses, and the singer hugged the room with soothing vocals in a deep crimson dress that glided beyond her ankles.

'Many artists have covered this next song, but my favourite version is by one of my musical heroes, Aretha Franklin. It's called "You're All I Need to Get By". An excellent song to sing to your partner, or perhaps like me, you can sing it to your glass of Scotch at the end of a long day.'

The audience gave a polite laugh to the cheap joke. Those on the dancefloor swayed to the opening bars of the intro. Those on seats marked their territory by sprawling a jacket over their chairs like pandas pissing on a bamboo tree. They made the awkward walk-dance transition to the postage stamp dancefloor while a collection of thirsty bodies by the bar tapped their feet.

The song was performed with perfect popularity as the ebullient crowd clapped while the band seamlessly transitioned into Jill Scott's 'Golden' to round off the first half of their set.

As the song ended with drawn-out sax notes, the audience cheered. Some clapped on the move as they scurried back to their seats, hoping not to find a brazen punter, ignoring the unwritten jacket rule.

With the help of a fellow band member, the singer stepped down from the stage to the no service area at the side of the bar.

'Jerry, can we get the usual, please?'

'Coming right up. Pitch perfect again tonight, Nikki.'

'Did you expect anything less?'

'Never.'

The pianist remained playing Oscar Peterson to maintain an ambient mood during the interval. Despite telling herself not to look at her phone, Achebe battled with the hide-and-seek interior of her handbag to find the device. Singing in the jazz bar was her one moment of the week to shut out the stresses of the job, but both attacks occurred at night, and with the Special Response Unit still set up in the forest, she was hoping for positive news.

Achebe plucked her phone from her bag, but before checking any messages, she was distracted by a compliment.

'You're an amazing singer.'

'Oh, thank you, I do try.'

Achebe looked down at her phone, keen not to get caught in a conversation with someone at the bar. She was not interested if someone was in a band of their own or used to sing in similar establishments back in their youth. It was staggering the number of people who thought her two hours a week show meant she would be interested in hearing about their amateur music career.

The individual remained lurking in her peripheral vision. Achebe glanced at them and failed to hide her shock at the handsome man who stared back. Embarrassed, she imitated her mum's favourite tactic by raising an authoritative eyebrow to elicit a response from the gawker. He smiled.

'I'm sorry. I had planned to ask you if I could buy you a drink, but I see you are already getting one, and most likely on the house, so I realised that would be a foolish thing to ask.'

'As foolish as staring at me in silence for an uncomfortable length of time?'

'I'm sorry. I guess I got lost for words pretty quickly. I just wanted to say you are even more beautiful up close as you look from the back of the room.'

'How many guys do you think have successfully seduced a girl after apologising twice in the opening thirty seconds of meeting them?'

'I'm hoping to be the first, I reckon.'

'Very good.'

Achebe smiled while shaking her head in feigned disapproval as she attempted not to dwell on his chiselled cheekbones.

Jerry placed two drinks on the bar and turned to make the other two.

'Perhaps I can take you for dinner sometime?'

'I'm not very good with dates, relationships, or commitments of any kind.'

'Wow, it wasn't a proposal. I only asked you to dinner.'

'Just a short-term piece of meat, then. Is that how you see me?' Achebe jibed.

'That's not what I meant, and I think you know that. I'm definitely not going to apologise for a third time.'

Fair play, Achebe thought. He had wriggled out of that tight corner impressively.

'Why do you not think you're good with dates?' he asked.

'My job can be overwhelming.'

'What do...'

'I'm a detective.' Achebe answered, tingled by the fact she could call herself such.

'Oh, wow.'

'Not what you expected?'

'No, it's just I've never met a detective before, even though I feel like I know what your job is all about, given the number of crime dramas I watch.'

'Well, it's not how it's portrayed on TV, let me tell you. It's even more insane. Anyway, I never came to the bar to talk about work. This is my downtime. What do you do? What is your name even? That's normally a good start when getting to know someone.'

'I would've asked your name, but it's on a big poster at the front door. You are Nikki from Nikki and the Jazz Hands?'

'The very one.'

'I'm Ash and I'm a PhD student.'

'Oh.'

'Not what you expected? Disappointing, isn't it?'

'Why would I be disappointed?'

'Most girls like a settled man with a career trajectory, not an academic who refuses to get a proper job.'

'That's quite an assumption. What do you study?'

'Medical research, mostly dementia-related work.'

'There you go. That's a noble endeavour. I'm sure you'll find yourself a girl, no problem.'

'Well, I'm asking you.'

Jerry handed two more drinks to Achebe. She turned and passed them to the guitarist on stage, who gave her the two-minute warning before the restart. Not even had a chance to piss, she thought.

'Looks like I need to go, so you better find your friends.'

'I'm just waiting for my girlfriend, actually. She's in the toilet.'

Achebe's neck recoiled. Startled, if not a little disappointed, that there was another girl involved. She thought it amazing how attraction could evaporate in a second. Here he is chatting her up while his poor girl is squatting on the bog. What a dickhead.

Ash grinned as Achebe waited for her bandmate to distribute the drinks and return to give her a helping hand back onto the stage.

'Better get back to her then before she catches you talking to me.'

'I thought detectives were good at spotting liars?'

'What?'

'I don't have a girlfriend. I just said I did so I could see your reaction. I was trying to gauge whether you are genuinely uninterested in me before I asked you, for a second time, if I could take you to dinner. There's only so much rejection a man can take, so I had to be sure, and I think I detected a little disappointment when you thought I had a girlfriend.'

Achebe slid her card across the bar but refused to admit his advances were smooth.

'Why did you choose the Jazz Bar tonight? And if you say because of me, I'll slide that card back in my bag.'

'I came in to catch some good music for fifteen minutes before I met up with friends, but I've been here for just under an hour now.'

She thought it amazing how attraction could materialize in a second.

'Hope you enjoy the second half, although if you have somewhere to go, I won't be offended if you leave. The date will still go ahead.'

'And if your work gets in the way, we can always rearrange. I won't be offended either.'

Four blinding flashes of light dazzled Achebe as she approached the mic. Jerry's voice projected over every other noise.

'Oi! Get that fucking flash off!'

Jerry gestured to a bouncer to deal with the person with the camera.

Achebe had no idea who had taken the pictures as her eyes readjusted to the warm glow of the room.

'Now that I can see again, shall we continue?' Achebe said to the guests.

The audience cheered and whistled.

'This one is Lovely Day by Bill Withers, and I hope you've all had a lovely day and will continue to have a lovely evening.'

June 9th

CHAPTER 18

Achebe's smile dimpled her cheeks. She appreciated the gushing audience and was buoyed by the conversation with the handsome man at the bar. Her smile evoked the personal pride of delivering a quality performance. A picture paints a thousand words, but the tabloid only used seven:

Who's Afraid of the Big Bad Wolf?

The longer Achebe stared at her expression on the front page, the more the image morphed from an elated singer to a naïve wee detective who thought she could have a personal life while a flesh-hungry beast still roamed Bannock forest. Shame cloaked her as she read the article in Dargo and Bullock's office.

Not Detective Nikki Achebe, it would seem. The newly appointed detective let her hair down in the jazz bar while five victims of the "werewolf" lie dead in the morgue and two remain unaccounted for. With many more injured and the killer animal still on the loose, is this young detective focused on the job? Or has the Chief of Police failed in his role by assigning a fledgling detective to such a high-profile case?

'You scrub up well, Nikki.' Bullock said.
'I'm so embarrassed.'
'Don't worry about it. This story will huff and puff and blow over in a couple of days.'
'You should work for the paper with that sort of creativity.'

Achebe resented Dargo and Bullock's calmness. They were enjoying watching her experience her first bout of public trauma, like parents giggling when their toddler stumbles on the carpet, having just learned to walk. The whole ordeal brought colour to Dargo's cheeks after weeks of sleepless translucence. Slumped in his chair with his hands behind his head like a misbehaving school child, he attempted to appease Achebe.

'Listen, they'll discuss it on the news today, commentators will make ill-informed comments, and keyboard warriors will make even less informed opinions until something else happens and their focus is diverted elsewhere. Just keep your head low, stay off social media and do not watch the news.'

A pale-faced Chief entered without knocking.

'Morning everyone. I'm not going to bother hiding my frustration, Detective Achebe. I can't believe you thought it was acceptable to have a night out while such a high-profile case is ongoing.'

'I was performing, sir. It wasn't a night out.'

'Even worse.'

No one knew why it was worse, but they let Chief Thorne continue venting.

'How could you think a public show was appropriate when you are the detective leading an investigation which has failed to catch a killer animal?'

Achebe's eyes grew pregnant with tears, but she resisted letting them loose.

'It's her hobby, sir,' Dargo said.

'I was at the football at the weekend.' Bullock added. 'It's an escape from all the shit we have to put up with here. Was I not meant to be there? Are we not allowed some relief from our work?'

'Going to the football is discreet. You weren't fucking playing, were you?'

'If I were playing, I wouldn't be slaving my arse in here every day.'

Dargo piled in further.

'Nikki performs a two-hour show every week in a bar that holds between eighty to a hundred people. Just because some wee prick from a rag snaps a photo doesn't mean it's worth our attention.'

'Are you telling me your social life is currently on hold because of this case, sir?' Bullock asked.

Bullock and Thorne shared a knowing stare. The Chief's attendance at a recent whisky tasting event with big-wig government officials was laced within the undertones of the rhetorical question.

Achebe took a deep breath. If there was one thing better than having Dargo fighting for you, it was having Bullock in your corner as well.

'Regardless, this is too much attention on us, and we need to respond. Detective Achebe, with regret, I am taking you off the case.'

Dargo rubbed his eyes, half in despair at the Chief's words, half because of tiredness.

'You take Nikki off the case, then you are effectively throwing her to the dogs and accusing her of doing something wrong when she hasn't. Support us. Tell them your staff are allowed some downtime amongst the late hours we put in on a daily basis, weekends included.'

'She got caught, and it looks bad. My authority is being questioned.'

'Then show some authority and nip it in the bud and don't make it worse.'

Achebe was witnessing the frenzied ineptitude Dargo had previously described. She was now enlightened to the Chief's weaknesses, like peeling a yellow banana, only to find it is mushy on the inside. The contrasting perceptions of the Chief between the peace officers and the detectives was disheartening. It did not make Achebe feel safer knowing Thorne was the highest ranked person in Caledonia's police force.

'We've all been subject to the media spotlight for apparent incompetence in the past, even yourself, sir,' said Dargo.

'That was different.' The Chief said, alluding to an event of which Achebe was none-the-wiser.

'I agree. It was much worse than this.'

The Chief scowled, but before he could speak, Achebe interjected, compelled to defend herself after Dargo and Bullock had softened his knee-jerk tendencies.

'Sir, I realise it might not look good, but those two hours were the only two hours I haven't thought about the case, and even then, I was checking my phone during the interval in case there was an emergency. This case stays with me all the time. I don't relax. I don't sleep. We have Maynard's Special Response Unit set up in the forest. I've got forensic teams analysing fur samples, zoologists reviewing paw prints, a team researching the history of Bannock forest and the manor. My team is also looking into the history of Strathaven's animal experiments, and I have sent a formal request to visit Sector Five so I can speak with Dr Rockwell himself. No one is more motivated to stop this beast than me. Trust me when I say I am not sitting on my hands waiting for the animal to magically appear.'

The Chief pointed his chin up, as if pondering Achebe's plea. He refused to directly acknowledge that she could stay on the case.

'Why do you want to visit Sector Five?'

'They have experimented with animals in the past. Who says they aren't doing the same now, with something bigger and deadlier than Alba the rabbit? I would appreciate if you could sponsor my request to access Sector Five. It needs your sign-off before it goes to the government for the final approval. I assume by Rockwell himself.'

'Dr Rockwell would've informed me if he knew what was causing the attacks.'

'Then it should be a routine visit to close off another lead.'

The Chief squinted at the young detective. Achebe detected he wanted to block her request, but could find no logical reason to do so other than Rockwell was his pal.

'I'll think about it. This is your last chance, though. Find this animal.'

The Chief swivelled out the door without saying another word.

In the main office, Achebe's cheeks still flushed with rage at the Chief's reluctance, both in letting her remain leading the case and in approving her request to visit Sector Five. She had to divert her attention onto the investigation or risk allowing the Chief's incompetence to consume her thoughts.

High Constable Robinson was sitting studiously at her desk.

'Jen, any update on the background of Bannock Manor?'

'Yes, I was…'

'Great! Grab your laptop. We'll discuss your findings over coffee.'

When Robinson did not immediately look as though she was preparing to leave the office, Achebe hurried her.

'Quicker the better, Jen. I need out of here.'

*

The coffee shop window looked out to Edin's main shopping thoroughfare, the sun-streaked castle shimmering in the background. Inside, a blended aroma of coffee and caramel warmed the cafe. Commuters stood glumly in a snaking queue awaiting their morning stimulants, but the booths were deserted.

The table oscillated because of Robinson's jangling leg. Jen had softened since the initial cold shoulder treatment after Achebe's promotion, but a lingering niggle still obstructed their usual chemistry.

'What have you found then?' Achebe asked.

102

'Nothing you can't find online, to be honest. Bannock Manor has a grisly history you'd never believe. Dating all the way back to the eighteenth century, there's been family feuds, murders, incest, beheadings.'

'Fucking hell.'

'Most recently, however, the manor belonged to Hamish Stewart. He inherited the property from his parents when they died in the late nineties.'

'How'd they die?'

'Murder-suicide by the mother. She poisoned the soup.'

'Was Hamish Stewart suspected? Seems pretty convenient for both of them to die if he wanted the estate.'

'I imagine he would've been suspected, but in his defence, the grief seemed to send him off the rails.'

'Grief or guilt?'

'According to reports, he couldn't cope with his parents' deaths and turned to the usual muses of drink, drugs and parties to take his mind off things. The closest he came to murder was when he fired a shotgun in the direction of two guests at a shooting party, thankfully missing.'

'Attempted murder?'

'No, it was an accident. I pulled the case file from the archives. He was on a four-day acid trip, so his head was scrambled. The guests pressed charges, but they settled before it got to court. It was after that incident that Hamish was institutionalised at Morven Asylum. He was released twelve months later and became reclusive, the polar opposite of the party animal reputation he gained before attending the asylum. No one saw him for years, but he became obsessed with magic. He even attempted to join the Magic Circle. I suppose magic became his new addiction after all the bad habits.'

'You mentioned previously that he died performing a magic trick.'

'Yes. He died while attempting an escapology trick on Loch Bannock.'

'What was the trick?'

'He was attempting to escape from a metal box weighed down in the middle of the loch. Inside the metal box, his hands and feet were bound with rope. He drowned trying to escape.'

Achebe paused from taking a sip of her coffee.

'When magicians do that kind of stunt, there's usually a team of people monitoring their safety, or an assistant with a failsafe method should the trick go sideways.'

'Let's be clear, he wasn't a magician. He was a wannabe. Delusional after years of drug abuse. The only person in attendance on the day of his death was the groundsman, Mr Ulrich Lundstrom. He alerted the police when Hamish never resurfaced.'

'How many years ago was this?'

'Seventeen. Strange thing is, the Bannock estate was left to Ulrich Lundstrom.'

'To the groundsman? There was no heir to the estate?'

'None. No siblings, cousins, or partner. Lundstrom had worked on the estate since he was a teenager. He knew Hamish's parents and served Hamish after their death.'

'Do you think he killed Hamish?'

'You've become even more sceptical since your promotion.' Jen said with a smile.

Achebe acknowledged with a chuffed head tilt.

'Well, it actually gets weirder.' Jen said.

'Go on.'

'Ulrich Lundstrom is now institutionalised at Morven Asylum.'

'Fucking hell. What for?'

'He was involved in a horrific accident with one of the industrial lawnmowers he used on the estate. According to reports, a lawnmower crashed into some stones on the property, flipping it on its side, and the razor spun off the axis and sliced his skull. He suffered permanent brain damage, which unfortunately means he's a permanent resident at the asylum.'

'A permanent resident who owns a multimillion-pound overgrown estate.'

'The forest of damned souls claims yet another tragedy into its mythology.'

'I'm starting to think there might be some truth to the myth,' said Achebe. 'This investigation feels like a cursed conquest.'

'You'll get there, Nikki. I know you will.'

'Thanks.'

Robinson swivelled the laptop on the table so they both could see the screen.

'This is the only picture I could find of Hamish Stewart and Ulrich Lundstrom. It's a bit grainy.'

'A bit.'

The image was a wide-angle shot. Hamish Stewart waved from the doorway of Bannock Manor while Lundstrom, wearing a sleeveless top, rested his foot on the perimeter wall before it became the crumbled ruin of today. Their faces were dark, expressionless shadows.

'Well, very grainy.' Robinson continued. 'Cameras have improved a lot since the nineties. I couldn't find any other photos.'

'None?' Achebe asked in astonishment.

'Hamish was famous for his partying in the late nineties, early noughties. Before mobile phones with cameras. His guests included the offspring of high-net-worth individuals who would not want any press stories of excessive drug-taking, hence no photographers.'

'Thanks for looking into all of this. It's maybe worth going up to Morven Asylum to see Mr Lundstrom.'

'I phoned Morven Asylum and spoke to his carer. His brain damage is severe. He doesn't talk or engage with anyone.'

'Maybe not then. Instead, let's go and speak to a Mr...'

Achebe checked her notepad.

'Duncan Weir. When I spoke to Jim McAllister about the attacks, he suggested a creature has been living in Bannock forest for a while, and that we should speak to Duncan Weir about it. He works for Lady Cameron, doing gardening and managing a small number of animals on her estate. It might not come to much, but my face is all over the morning headlines, so I need to get out of Edin for a while.'

CHAPTER 19

The house was quaint and the garden modest for an estate; the lawn stripes only stretching the size of a football pitch with gigantic hedges marking the perimeter. Smoke billowed from the brick chimney, clouding the lush mountains in the backdrop.

Duncan Weir was kneeling on a cushioned mat next to a sprawling, curved flowerbed containing all the colours of the rainbow. He did not hear Achebe and Robinson approach, so continued digging his trowel into the earth.

'Excuse me.'

The gardener's movements were stiff. Rather than crane his neck, Weir turned his whole body to look at the two police officers. He exhaled a painful growl as he pushed a fist into the ground to stand up. Removing his cap with shovel hands exposed ghostly, bald skin. Achebe thought it strange he did not possess the faintest hint of a tan, given he worked outdoors. But his gaunt complexion and grey eyes suggested an illness outfought the benefits of vitamin D. This was not a man capable of maintaining Lady Cameron's estate for much longer.

'Are you Duncan Weir?'

'I am. Who's asking?'

The man's voice was coarse and inoffensive, and he wore an expression long absent of any joy. An exhausted hunch made him appear small, but Achebe reckoned if he stretched his crooked spine, he would fetch over six feet with ease.

'I am Detective Nikki Achebe and this is High Constable Robinson.'

'Good day to you both.'

'Good day to you, too. We are investigating the recent animal attacks around Bannock forest and we want to ask you a few questions. I was told by Jim McAllister that you have been complaining about animal attacks for a while. Is that right?'

'I don't know any Jim.'

'Really? He seems to know you. He lives on the west side of Bannock forest. He used to keep big cats and bears at his home there.'

'Oh aye, Jim.'

Robinson and Achebe shared a pitiful look. Weir was approaching fifty, but he behaved like an eighty-year-old in the dementia ward.

'He was saying you've complained about animal attacks for years. You keep livestock here, don't you? Were any of them attacked in the past?'

Weir walked ten paces to a wooden bench. Thinking and standing was too much effort for him. He fell into the seat with a relieved sigh.

'I work here for Lady Cameron. She's got dementia and I humour her when she forgets things or repeats herself for the fourth time. As you can probably tell, though, my body is failing me as well. Arthritis and cancer — what a lethal combination. She's eighty-nine, but something tells me she'll outlive me. My memory is pretty poor, but there have been a few attacks on the animals over the years. I've complained to the police before, but they always said it was just a wolf.'

'You think it was something else that attacked the animals?'

'No, I know it is something different.'

Weir rose to his feet, wincing with each extension of his limbs.

'You don't need to get up for us, Mr Weir.'

'I've got something to show you.'

Weir hobbled to a stable next to the side of the house. He opened the latch on the gate, his movements laboured and arduous. Achebe noticed an array of motorised equipment, which probably did most of the work for the ailing gardener.

Weir clapped the head of a horse, pressing his face into its nose. The well-groomed mare reciprocated with a sombre bow, her eyes glistening, as if sensing the interaction may be one of their last.

'Beautiful creatures, aren't they?' Weir said.

'Gorgeous.' Robinson replied, stroking another mare at the neck as it leaned over its stall door.

'They are so intelligent, so innocent. Makes it even more tragic when you see this.'

Weir opened a stall door. The other horses became restless, hopping and neighing in distress. They knew what lay behind the wooden gate.

Achebe and Robinson walked behind Weir. The smell of hay and horse scat disappeared, replaced by rotting meat. They gasped at the sight in the stall.

The hay was red. Flies buzzed around a fallen horse; blood dried into its fur. A slash to its ribs inflicted the initial incapacitating damage. The severing of its head occurring once it was maimed, unable to retaliate.

'Must be some size of wolf you're after.' Weir said, his eyes dark, laced with the ire of a man who had not been taken seriously over the years.

'I can't look any longer,' Robinson said, quickly shimmying out of the stall.

Achebe remained analysing the headless horse, unnerved by the fact that whatever beast had caused the attack had done so for enjoyment, rather than a meal. There was no evidence of the beast feasting on the horse. It was a cold-blooded attack.

'What are you going to do with this?'

'I'm not strong enough to chop it up and move it. The safari park is coming to pick it up. They will feed it to the lions.'

'If you can please delay that pickup, Mr Weir. I'm going to ask our forensics team to come and have a look at this first.'

'Can they be quick? I don't want this around the other horses. It's distressing for them, and for me.'

'Certainly.'

'Thanks.'

'Are you at all surprised that there's an animal in these woods capable of such attacks?'

Weir paused.

'I don't believe in the forest of damned souls nonsense, but I do believe we are ignorant in thinking we know everything about this world, or even this forest. I've worked outdoors all my life, in woodlands and gardens. Quite often I've come across bizarre insects and I wonder, does anyone else know this species exists? This animal you are chasing is obviously larger, but to think that means we should be able to find it is to underestimate the intelligence of the creature.'

Achebe thanked the gardener and left him assuaging the other horses. In the car, Robinson spoke first.

'That was awful. That horse. It's easy to mock the witnesses calling this creature a werewolf from the comfort of the office, but when you come out and see something like that.' Robinson paused, shaking her head. 'You're much more knowledgeable than me about animals, but did that attack not seem overly brutal?'

'Yes.'

'And Duncan Weir is a poor soul. I feel really sorry for him. He's not got long left.'

'It was a shame.' Achebe said with little sincerity as she focused on what Weir had said. 'This beast has been around a lot longer than we think, Jen. This is not something that's just landed on our shores. People like Weir live and breathe this forest. They understand its nature. If he isn't surprised by the presence of an unknown wild predator, then we should take heed.'

The digital clock on the dashboard sneaked towards two o'clock. Achebe turned the radio off to avoid the hourly news bulletin in case she was a feature.

'What about the missing ravers at Bannock Manor?' asked Achebe, keeping her mind far from any media coverage.

'Ah yes, I looked into this for you. The raves started a few years after Ulrich Lundstrom had his horrible accident with the lawnmower blade. Someone obviously caught wind that there was a mansion lying empty, miles from any neighbourhood, and too secluded for the police to patrol regularly. The first kid went missing during the fourth rave, about a year after they started. He was never found. Then a girl went missing two years later. The site seemed to gain notoriety after that. If anything, the mystery spurred even more teenagers to attend the next party. I suppose the disappearances added extra excitement to the event.'

'The police must have taken an active interest after those incidents.'

'They did, but you know what it's like. Two years pass with no more parties and the police stop checking the site. The raves eventually stopped when four teenagers went missing at the same party. That was enough to spook even the most avid party animal.'

'A bit of a mood killer.'

'Just a tad.'

'None of the four were found?'

'Nope.'

'How do you go missing at a party in a mansion house?'

'Reading some old interviews from attendees, it was common for the ravers to venture into the foggy woods to smoke weed in a tree, have an acid trip in the wilderness, or get some alone time for a good old-fashioned shag.'

'I'm assuming all are now presumed dead.'

'There were heavy rumours that the first boy used the opportunity to do a runner. Tough home life, apparently.'

'What's the most likely cause of death, then?'

'The loch is a mile or so beyond Bannock Manor, so some assumed they drowned.'

'Their bodies would wash up eventually, though.'

'That's why others believe they died at the quarry. It's a couple of miles from the house, and the site has many pools of water and deep slurry.'

'Nasty way to go. Preserved like the bodies in the peat bogs up north.'

The next two minutes were driven in silence. Delegating Robinson to research Bannock Manor was less about uncovering key evidence for the case and more about assessing Robinson's commitment, having gained a promotion ahead of her. Achebe contemplated letting the relationship continue to re-emerge organically before deciding that any awkwardness could not linger any longer.

'Thanks for looking into Bannock Manor, Jen. I know you were disappointed when I got the detective role, so I appreciate the diligence and effort you are putting in. I sure need the help.'

'I am not disappointed that you got the detective role. I'm delighted for you. I'm disappointed because I never got it. That's an important distinction. I'm sorry I haven't been more supportive since your promotion. I just needed a few weeks to clear my head to regain my motivation after the setback.'

'That's understandable.'

'I'm behind you a hundred percent, Nikki. I want to stop this beast and I want you to succeed. And of course, I'm going to be diligent. Are you questioning my integrity?' Robinson said with a smile.

'Never.' Achebe said, giving Robinson's hand a gratifying squeeze as she drove back to the pressure cooker city.

CHAPTER 20

The easel was split into four quadrants, each containing a wheel with a central clock dial, ready to be flicked by the girl's finger. The top left wheel determined which victim the girl would play with that evening. Standing in front of the easel in her lacy red underwear, the girl spun the first dial. It landed on the name of her latest victim and she danced with excitement. He was the freshest, the most untouched, the most fearful.

The second wheel contained five options to decide the main weapon she would use. It landed on the whip, her favourite. She unhooked it from the wall and flicked her wrist to practice her technique, the clacking sound warming her blood with excitement.

She spun the dial on the next wheel to establish her secondary weapon. It was the choker. She grinned, her body tingling as she struggled to contain herself, desperate to begin.

The wheels had landed in her favour thus far, but the next wheel was the most vital. One quadrant was labelled "tantric torture", her least favourite because of the less intense nature of the activity. Another was called "sexy sadism", a style which empowered her but did not always fully satisfy her libido. The penultimate option was "rough and rowdy" with the final segment of the wheel labelled "violent rape", the most desired category.

The girl rolled her tongue along her lips as she twiddled the dial in her fingers. The spin was agonisingly long, threatening to stop on sexy sadism before edging into the violent rape section, her eyebrows raising in euphoria before flattening as the dial landed on tantric torture.

'No!' she moaned, staring at the wheel as if she could burn it with her vision.

Slouched on the sofa, devastated by the wheel's final decision, the girl considered disobeying its orders, but then remembered the other wheels had been kind to her, granting her the victim and weaponry she desired.

She bowed to the wheels, thanking them for their choices.

The girl then flicked the whip while holding the choker in her other hand; playtime.

CHAPTER 21

The tribulations of the day showed in Achebe's lumbering posture as she sleepwalked into her mother's embrace. Her stubborn independence succumbed to the cradling cuddle - safe and warm - shielded from the media spotlight and the judgmental eyes in the office. She was grateful until her mum let out a pitying moan.

'Don't condescend me, mum.'

'I'm not. I just hope you are okay.'

'I'm fine. I've not read or watched the news, but I can imagine what they are saying. I don't want your sympathy. I just want to ignore it as much as I can.'

Even Mr Chill exited his armchair to welcome his daughter into the house. She cushioned her head into his flabby chest.

'I'm fine, dad. Nothing to worry about. Just a bit drained, that's all.'

Achebe was too mentally disseminated to focus on the news stories. The pressure from the Chief and her fight to prove herself to the peace officers occupied her thoughts, invaded unpredictably by gory apparitions of the deceased; grisly reminders of future consequences if the beast was not stopped soon. The news reports were nothing more than a distraction, a thunder and lightning display gripping inconscient minds away from the fact their house was flooding from the stormy rain. Amongst the accusations of police carelessness and the tangential debates they sparked about police competence and funding, or a lack thereof, the alleged werewolf had morphed into a stalking horse to beat the police with, rather than treated as the dangerous and imminent threat that it was.

Achebe snuggled in a ball on her parent's sofa, ignoring the game show host who was shouting desperate entertainment. Reading Ash's text message made her warm. He either lived under a rock or was foolish for still wanting to meet up despite the news coverage. Whatever the reason, he had failed to mention anything about her face being plastered all over the press.

Achebe returned her gaze to the television, but her attention followed the leads of the case. The fur samples of the first attack belonged to a timber wolf, but which animal the paw prints belonged to was unknown. The horse that Duncan Weir had shown them was attacked by something vicious, something big, far bigger than any wolf the experts were aware of. Weir also thought it was plausible that something undiscovered could be living in Bannock forest, and Jim McAllister was certain that whatever it was had been living in Bannock forest for years.

Perhaps this beast was bred and contained in the forest by a handler and eventually turned against them. A famous example being when magician, Roy Horn of Siegfried and Roy was attacked by his white tiger in front of a live audience, having previously performed hundreds of shows with the animal. This scenario was unlikely, however, as the Wildlife Rescue's blacklist had not produced a single credible lead.

Achebe's phone buzzed again, a shy grin forming on her face in anticipation of another witty message from Ash. She glanced at her mother to make sure her smitten smile had gone undetected, grateful to avoid an interrogation on who she was messaging.

Achebe's grin flopped as her phone notified her of a missed call from High Constable Gardyne. She had not heard it ring. She stepped into the kitchen.

'GG, you called.'

'Nikki.' he shouted.

The low grumble in the background told her Gio was in the car.

'There's been another attack. It's the cryptozoologists. Several are reported dead, and many injured. I'm heading there now.'

*

Dargo hovered his fork mid-flight as he read the message on his phone. Steam effused from the broccoli that was held in limbo.

'I'm gonna have to go,' Dargo said to his wife, Sally.

'This is the first time we've sat down for dinner together in weeks, Tom.'

'I know. I'm sorry, but I need to help Nikki. There's been another attack. She needs my support.'

'Can't Xander help this time?'

'Yes, I think we both need to go.'

Sally nodded, annoyed but understanding of the situation. It was not the first time she had made sacrifices due to Dargo's occupation.

He hopped around the kitchen, shovelling keys and police identification into his pockets. He kissed Sally on the forehead.

'Thank you. We'll go out for dinner soon. I might even pay for it.'

'McDonald's then.'

'Hmm, I was thinking a KFC bucket would suffice.' Dargo said with a cheeky smile.

'Away you go werewolf hunting.' Sally said, withholding a smile of her own.

CHAPTER 22

Achebe arrived upon a war zone. The homely campfire had transformed into a panicked blaze. Screams of physical and emotional pain blended with the whirring helicopter to overwhelm Achebe's senses, making logical thoughts difficult to keep a hold of.

General Maynard's muscles rippled as he slammed the jeep door, causing Achebe to flinch. He passed her a handgun while staring at the flaming mess. It had been a while since she had visited the gun range, but she felt safer with the firearm in her possession.

'My men will position themselves around the perimeter of the campsite. If there's any deceased or injured beyond our perimeter, we cannot get to them immediately. I want to scope the scene and see if this bastard is still here.'

'Understood.'

Maynard's unit began running in formation around the outside of the burning blaze. Achebe followed in Maynard's slipstream. As well as the fire, mini floodlights designed to capture better images of the beast illuminated the campsite. Against the backdrop of thick darkness, the camp looked like a stage show, playing out the final act of a Shakespearean nightmare.

Blood-soaked, the grass wore a brown hue in the unnatural light. Several bodies lay strewn in odd places. One was wrapped around the wheel of a camper van. Another was sprawled at the foot of a tent, causing

116

the structure to sag on its left side. A further body was next to the original campfire, the legs of which were alight. They all had visible gashes, some still haemorrhaging as the blood poured over the curves of their bodies like lava flows. Two severely injured individuals had loved ones kneeling by their side, holding their hands, attempting to squeeze life back into them. Their love superseded any fear that the beast was nearby.

Most of the group sought refuge by huddling into the camper vans. Achebe raised her palm to indicate they should remain inside the vehicles, although their petrified faces never looked inclined to exit.

As she turned away from the vans, Achebe almost tripped over a fourth body. Most of the victims had gashes to their stomach, puncturing their vital organs. This was an intelligent animal. One which had learned to kill in a more cultured manner than the erratic slashes at the caravan park.

The smell of metallic blood stewed in the hot air, thick like a viscous medicine sticking in the roof of her mouth. Achebe gargled sick before forcing it back down. This was not a crime scene. This was a massacre.

The light from the camp never travelled far until it was engulfed by the night. Achebe stared into obscurity, wondering if the beast was ready to pounce from mere metres away. She recalled the techniques of her youth in Botswana. If they had to wander out of the house after dark, they would shine a torch into the night to detect which animals lurked nearby. White eyes were harmless impalas. Red eyes were lions. Tonight, nothing reflected back, but this did not stop Achebe's imagination playing devilish tricks. Every breath of wind that flapped the tent doors morphed into the sound of a heavy-breathing beast, and every flicker of the waving fire altered the composition of light and dark to form energetic apparitions of a blood-hungry monster.

Achebe opened the door of the first campervan. She asked if anyone in the vehicle was injured and informed them that the ambulances were on their way. Her attention then turned to the main tent, the door of which clapped furiously in the wind. She realised then that no one had actually confirmed the beast had even left the campsite.

Achebe approached the door from the side, crouching and edging nearer with the gun pointed at the entrance. Her palms began to sweat and her legs turned numb, but somehow kept moving. She waited for the wind to blow the flap open so she could slink inside with both hands still holding the gun. Her movement was swift, her eyes darting to the only target in the dishevelled tent.

Achebe lowered the gun from Meldrew, who was unscathed and undeterred by the chaos. Instead, he was untangling electric cables.

'Mr Meldrew. Are you okay?'

'Perfectly fine, detective. You just missed the action.'

'Action?'

'Follow me.'

Meldrew brushed past Achebe, who could do nothing but follow him to the back of a van which contained a setup akin to a TV news network. Achebe stood with her back against one of the open doors so she could speak with Meldrew while staying alert to any wandering danger.

Meldrew pushed a cable into a laptop. His ignorance of the surroundings mystified Achebe.

'Mr Meldrew, members of your group are dead.'

'How many?'

'I was going to ask you the same.'

'I don't know what happened. The werewolf attacked someone, and then everyone else went crazy. Typical! If you aren't ready for an attack, then what are you even doing here?'

Not only was Meldrew ignorantly calm, he was an impenitent leader, unequivocally remorseless at the loss of life. Questioning his behaviour was not Achebe's priority, however.

'Do you know if anyone ran from the campsite? Do we need to send a rescue team to find them?'

'I have no idea, detective.' he said without looking away from his laptop. Achebe was unconvinced he even registered her question.

'Did you manage to shoot the beast at all?'

'Not with a gun,' he sniggered. 'Most of us were having a nightcap. Even the people on guard duty left their posts. Not to worry though, detective. I think we should have some footage of the werewolf.'

'That doesn't matter just now. I need to know if anyone is injured outside of the camp area?'

'Everyone was in the camp,' he said while continuing to click the mouse and tap at the keyboard. 'The beast attacked from the east side, so that is camera five.'

Achebe threw her hands in the air despairingly. Commander Maynard approached.

'The perimeter is manned. No sign of the animal, but I don't want to stay here any longer than we have to.'

'Okay. No one was outside the camp at the time of the attack, according to him.' Achebe said, tilting her head towards Meldrew. 'Is it safe enough to bring the ambulances over?'

'Yes. In and out. If they're dead, we're shoving them all in one ambulance and getting the fuck out of here.'

Achebe did not know whether to agree or disagree with Maynard's approach, but she was quickly distracted by Meldrew's cursing. He was not looking at Achebe, but he began talking on the assumption that she was still listening.

'Camera five was knocked over. Camera four might have picked up something, though.'

Blue lights flashed between the tents as four ambulances bobbled to the camp. Achebe spotted two more fallen bodies she had not seen before. She kneeled to check for signs of life, but recoiled upon viewing the laceration on a victim's face. It sliced through their left eye, across their nose and pierced their lips. A single talon sheared them unrecognisable. The second body had two tram track lines across the torso. A pile of innards sat atop the body as if the beast clawed into the victim as if scooping a pumpkin's interior. There was no way only one animal caused all this destruction, she thought.

Achebe dropped her gun as, for the second time that week, she projected a bitter-tasting version of her mum's cooking. Her mouth remained agape as she continued to wretch.

A cry came from the van.

Achebe wiped her mouth and took a deep breath of hot air to compose herself, although this only intensified the fresh halitosis.

Meldrew saw Achebe return to the van in his peripheral vision.

'Come see, detective. We've got the werewolf on camera.'

June 10th

CHAPTER 23

'What the fuck is that?' Bullock said, slapping a palm off his desk. 'How come these clowns never manage to capture a clear image of whatever they are trying to find?'

Bullock supplemented his scathing assessment of the still image on the screen with an agitated flick of his hand, as if dismissing the sham out of his office. Achebe had been running on adrenaline through the small hours of the morning, but as they watched Meldrew's footage in Dargo and Bullock's office, disappointment flushed away her final reserves. The pathetic black splodge resembled the traditional paucity of evidence cryptozoologists are renowned for.

'It looks like a bird's-eye view of a stingray. It's just a black smudge,' said Dargo. 'How he can seriously think that's a werewolf is beyond me.'

'I think it is more hope than belief,' said Achebe. 'He's seeking validation for the expedition. Especially now several members are dead, some of whom funded the hunt.'

Achebe screwed her face and massaged her eyebrows as she fended off visions of the deceased. Exposed intestines, burst eye sockets, and the rusty smell of spilt blood still attacked her senses.

'He's off his nut,' said Dargo.

'He certainly handled the situation in a unique manner. He showed no remorse for the victims,' said Achebe.

'He'll be thinking about the fame and money this photo will bring him.' Bullock said. 'Even though this image resembles nothing more than a coffee stain, there will be thousands of paying degenerates eager to hear him speak about the night he went toe-to-toe with the werewolf.'

'I should have arrested him and prevented the attack.' Achebe said.

'On what grounds?' asked Bullock.

Achebe shrugged.

'Every crime affects you differently,' said Dargo. 'You need to learn which ones to allow into your headspace and which don't warrant dwelling on. The caravan park was the first we learned of this beast. It is unfortunate it happened, but we could do nothing about it because we never knew the threat existed before that attack. The incident at the forestry plant hurts more because we knew of the threat, and those guys were just getting on with their job. However, on the night of the first attack, you sent officers to the forestry plant to warn them of the potential danger. They decided to continue working. As for the attack last night, it was out of your control. Those people placed themselves near the beast's known location and were actively trying to lure the animal to them. So, when they were attacked, as horrific as the incident was, you should not hold any guilt.'

'The key thing is to focus on what's next.' Bullock said. 'Keep moving the case forward. Keep ploughing on. What's on your agenda today?'

'I'm going to get out of these stale clothes, maybe sleep for a few hours, then I'll see if I can catch Angus Mintoff at his solar panel launch event. I spoke to Sam a couple of days ago and she is convinced Strathaven's Sector Five bred the animal causing these attacks. She also mentioned that Mintoff fled his role in the government abruptly, and Sam thinks something about Sector Five spooked him into doing so. Given the Chief has yet to approve my request to visit Sector Five, I'll speak to Mintoff first. He might give me an insight as to what goes on inside that place.'

'You should stay close to Sam. Her nose is normally correct.'

'Well, she's relying heavily on her instinct, because she's going to break into Strathaven.'

'What?' Dargo shouted like a concerned father.

'She told me she has someone on the inside who's going to help her gain access to Sector Five.'

'She's mad,' Bullock said. 'If Rockwell finds out.'

Bullock left the consequences unspoken. Dargo looked more ashen than normal.

'We need to protect her in any way we can.'

'She gave me this burner phone. If she gets into any trouble, she'll message me.'

'Who else knows about this?'

'Only her boss, I think.'

'Leigh.' Dargo said. 'Okay, good. You've not told Jen or Gio, or anyone else?'

'No, I wouldn't do that. The fewer people that know, the better. I'm telling you in confidence because you've worked with her before.'

'She's mad,' Dargo said, a grin now forming at Sam's deviousness. 'Keep me updated on her progress, please.'

Their conversation was interrupted by Viti knocking and entering.

'Oh, I wasn't expecting all three of you to be here, but I do need to speak to you all. I'll start with you, Nikki, and I'm afraid it's not such great news. Quite baffling, actually.'

'Hit me.' Achebe said, a hot flush rushing over her body with anxious anticipation.

'The fur samples found at the forestry plant do not match to a timber wolf. They belong to a black wolf, such as those found in the Romanian mountains.'

'I knew there were two animals causing the attacks.'

'Well, the fur samples from last night's attack, while not having been tested yet, are grey, and I would say very similar to the grey wolves that inhabit Caledonia.'

Achebe's shoulders slumped as she stroked her temples in an effort to relax her scrambled mind.

'What the fuck is going on? Caledonian wolves don't attack humans at all, never mind as violently as last night's attack. Do the paw prints match those of a black or grey wolf?'

'Nope. The paw prints of all three attacks are consistent, although the ones from last night appear slightly bigger. And they do not belong to the maned wolf, as Gio suggested. I've had confirmation from the zoologists on that.'

'Three attacks. Three different types of wolf fur, only one of which is found in Caledonia. All paw prints are similar. The only explanation I have is that someone has imported wolves and they've become diseased, possibly rabid, or deformed due to inbreeding, hence the paw anomalies. But that sounds so implausible and given we have already investigated everyone on the Wildlife Rescue's blacklist and ruled them out, I think this scenario is unlikely. Still no nail fragments that could offer another genetic clue?'

'None. I'm sorry, Nikki. Normally I have answers for you, but on this occasion I'm baffled.'

'Ask Jen to run checks on the Wildlife Rescue blacklist again,' said Dargo. 'But it sounds like you already know what your next line of inquiry is.' Dargo said, nodding to the burner phone in Achebe's hand.

Achebe nodded. Viti was keen to move on, pivoting onto Dargo and Bullock's case.

'Am I able to talk about your case in front of Nikki?'

'No, she's a gabshite.' Bullock said. 'The entire office will know what you're about to tell us if she stays.'

Bullock gave Achebe a playful nudge, who responded by pinching the skin on the underside of his arm, causing him to jump.

'I'm leaving, anyway. I need to get some sleep.'

Viti moved closer to the centre of the office once Achebe left. Dargo yawned like a puppy.

'I have more positive news for the two of you. Well, it's at least a lead to explore. I got a call from one of my contacts at Edin hospital. They've helped me understand unusual anatomical quirks or diseases during many post-mortems over the years, so we are in regular contact. Anyway, a student admitted themselves to the hospital because of infected cuts across their body. Now, these cuts are not your average injuries. They are severe lacerations. The student also has a huge rash covering his upper left thigh and left buttock. The doctors ran comprehensive blood tests to understand the extent of the infection and the cause of the rash. In doing so, they encountered a chemical they could not immediately identify. After further tests, they eventually found the chemical to be formaldehyde. And what is one use of formaldehyde?'

'Dead bodies.' said Bullock.

'Well, preserving dead bodies, to be exact. I'll caveat by saying that formaldehyde is also used in many cosmetic and household products, but not to the extent that it should give you a rash. My friend at the hospital is very astute, so she identified the potential connection between the student's test results to the stories of the missing teenagers she's seen on the news, two of which are students. I've seen pictures of the cuts. They are not self-inflicted.'

'You think he's a victim?' said Bullock.

'Or an accomplice.' Dargo said. 'Who is he? And did he give any details on how he got the wounds or the rash?'

'We always keep our discussions on a no-names basis. But if you believe disclosure of personal information can help assist a criminal investigation, we can request his personal details. As for an explanation for the cuts, he told the doctors they occurred during a rugby initiation event at university. They didn't buy that story, though.'

'You have my approval to request the boy's personal information.' said Dargo. 'Please get his name and address as soon as you can. We need to speak to this guy today.'

CHAPTER 24

It took three pronounced doorbell rings to wake Darren, despite the morning drawing to a close. Bullock led the inquiry, since Dargo's lack of sleep left him looking like a zombie on smack. Although, compared to the bleary student, he looked pretty chipper.

The boy wore an off-white t-shirt and red boxer shorts, the pungency of alcohol indicating a heavy night. He was the antithesis of the criminal they sought, the two detectives as good as ruling him out as a suspect based on first impressions.

'We're here to see your bum rash.' Bullock said, holding up his identification while staring at the ugly red gashes across Darren's shin bones.

Darren blushed.

'What?'

'You have a rash on your bum. I'm guessing a similar colour to your face at this very moment. We want to know how you got the rash. Shall we come in?'

The question was rhetorical as Bullock placed the toe of his boot in the doorframe.

Inside, Bullock flicked away a garment draped on the sofa so he could find a spot to sit down. The flat was the typical lazy tip to be expected from a languorous student. Darren surveyed his surroundings as if just

126

noticing the mess, but he showed no signs of tidying up as the two detectives made themselves comfortable in his living room.

'We'll let you get back to your chores when you tell us how you got the rash.'

'I can't say for certain, but I think it was caused after I fell into some water. Well, I suppose it wasn't water.'

'Where?'

'At this girl's flat.'

Dargo sat forward, suddenly alive at the prospect that the culprit was female. Bullock stopped teasing, which was a telltale sign that he too was intrigued and wanted answers, answers that he would have to work hard to extract from the hungover human.

'Who is the girl?'

'I don't know her name.'

'You were in the flat of a person whose name you did not know?'

'Yes.'

'You're going to try really hard to remember her name before the end of our conversation.'

Bullock's steely stare wiped the sleep from the boy's eyes.

'What age was she?'

'About my age.'

'Which is?'

'Twenty.'

'What happened at the girl's flat?'

'It was weird.'

Darren glanced at the detectives as if considering whether to tell them everything.

'Trust me, son, we've seen and heard a lot of weird shit before. I'm guessing if you don't know her name, this was a one-night stand?'

'Yes.'

'We've been called out many a time to bad one-night stands over the years. Just take your time and tell us all you can remember. Start with how you met the girl.'

'I met her at Colony, the nightclub.'

'We might be auld duffers, but we know what Colony is.'

'Right, yes. We went back to hers after that.'

'Did you instigate the interaction in Colony, or did she?'

'I did.'

'Was she with anyone?'

'Now that you ask, I think she was on her own. She wasn't dancing with anyone else and never spoke to anyone before we left. I suppose that's quite strange because you don't often find girls on their own, not in a nightclub anyway. We danced for a bit, just the two of us, had a drink and left.'

'Where to?'

'Her flat.'

'Which is where?'

'I don't know.'

'You're going to try much harder for me on that one. You must have an inkling.'

'I was fucked, I mean drunk. I can't really remember. The whole night is a blur.'

'Did you take a taxi?'

'Yes.'

'Using a taxi app? We can obtain the route and address from the cab company if so.'

'No, she insisted on using a black cab.'

'Which general direction did you travel in when you left Colony?'

'Down the Bridges, I think.'

'North, towards the sea?'

'Yes.'

The boy leaned forward as he pieced the evening together. His biceps rippled as he scratched his head.

'It was near the sea, right on the edge. I remember hearing waves.'

'At the complex near the docks or the shopping centre?'

'The docks.'

'Which block?'

'I don't know. I was drunk, mate.'

'We're not your mates. We're here regarding a serious investigation and believe you have been in the presence of someone who may have kidnapped the teenagers that have been going missing of late. I'm sure being a student yourself, you will be well aware of the missing boys.'

Bullock thought it would be impossible for Darren's face to look sicklier, but his complexion paled further after hearing Bullock's words.

'Honestly, I wasn't paying attention. I was just thinking about, you know?'

'What?'

'Sex.'

'I see. Was there foreplay or straight to it?'

The boy checked the detective's face to see if the question was serious, but Bullock's hardened expression was carved in stone.

'Pretty much straight to it.'

'I'm struggling to establish a storyboard of events that led you to fall arse-first into formaldehyde. That's the substance that caused that rash down your side.'

The boy brushed the cracked skin on his left thigh. Bullock waited to be asked how the detectives knew he had a rash caused by formaldehyde, but the boy was too hungover to think of such a basic question. Bullock continued to probe.

'So, you're both butt-naked, getting the groove on, have sex and then what? When did you fall into the liquid that gave you that rash?'

The boy looked edgy.

'We never had sex in the end. She didn't fancy it?'

'Why?'

'Dunno. She changed her mind.'

'Just on a whim? There must have been a reason.'

'No reason, she just changed her mind.'

'Bollocks! What happened?'

'She just decided against it.'

'Look, whatever the story is, our attention is focused on this girl and how you managed to get formaldehyde, a substance used to preserve dead bodies, on your arse.'

The boy flinched. The reality of his lucky escape suddenly dawned on him. He stroked his wounds anxiously.

'She said she was too tired.'

Bullock knew the answer was bullshit. Impatient with the boy's lies, he perched himself next to Darren, who tilted his body away from Bullock's intimidating frame.

'Listen, whatever the story is, even if you did something embarrassing or wrong, this is a safe space for you to speak about it. We are investigating something far bigger than your ego.'

'I'm telling you, she was tired.'

Bullock grabbed the boy's neck with his right hand, digging his beefy fingers into the pressure points under Darren's earlobes. This steadied the boy while Bullock used a finger on his left hand to pierce through the boy's fungal-ridden lash mark on his shin, burrowing deeper into the cut while holding the writhing, screaming macho man in his grasp.

'Okay, okay. Fuck!'

Bullock released Darren, who stumbled off the sofa, hovering his hands over his bleeding wound, too scared to agitate it further. He turned away from the detectives, too embarrassed to tell the truth to their faces.

'She wasn't turned on by my body.'

'You look in good shape. What was the issue?'

'She thought my p...'. The boy's words faded to an inaudible whisper.

'I didn't catch the end of that.'

'She thought my penis was too small.'

Bullock turned to Dargo with a top lip smirk filled with genuine joy.

'Well, your bulge isn't that big, to be fair.' Bullock said, pointing to the boy's boxer shorts.

Darren sat back down with his arms crossed over his crotch.

'So, she doesn't like your tadger and calls off the sex. How did you react to that? Pretty miffed, I imagine.'

'A little.'

'Did you get violent?'

'No.'

Bullock squinted sharp eyes as he detected dishonesty.

'Lies!' he said, raising his finger to indicate he would press it into Darren's wound again.

'Okay, I grabbed her, or at least tried to. She pulled out a whip and started smacking me with it.'

'Kinky. So that is why you have lacerations on your legs.'

'Yes, and here as well.'

The boy lifted his shirt to reveal two lashes protruding like puff pastries an inch off his chest. Blotchy green and blue fungi were starting to infect the interior of the wound, like mould solidifying on the top layer of strawberry jam.

'Shouldn't that be covered up?' asked Bullock.

'Yes, the hospital treated it, but I must've taken all the dressings off when I was drunk last night.'

'Very clever. So, what happened once she started whipping you?'

'I ran out of the room, but I didn't know where to go, so I stumbled into a dark room. I couldn't see anything, and I fell backwards into what felt like an industrial drum of liquid.'

'Did you escape, or did the girl let you leave?'

'She ordered me out and smashed my phone by chucking it off the balcony. I had to convince a bus driver to let me ride for free in the skud.'

'Did the balcony face the sea or the courtyard of the complex?' Dargo asked.

'The courtyard.'

'How many stories?'

'I don't know exactly. Maybe three or four, definitely not the bottom or the top floor.'

Dargo used the map application on his phone to display the flat complex he thought Darren was describing.

'This block of flats?'

'Yes,' Darren said, pointing to where he fled from.

'Okay, if you think of anything else once you've sobered up, phone me.' Bullock said, ending the conversation and leaving his card on a small, litterless section of the coffee table. He turned back to the senseless student.

'Get your clothes on. We'll drop you off at the hospital to get your wounds treated again. Maybe avoid any wild nights out for a while after this visit, yeah?'

*

After taking Darren to the hospital, Bullock drove to the apartment blocks. Dargo counted four bookies within a two-minute drive of their location. He was yet to place his bets on the football that evening. Even though he could use a betting app, he enjoyed entering the bookies to assess all his options and watch a couple of horse races. As they entered the courtyard, it was as if Bullock was reading his thoughts.

'Got your bets on yet?'

'Nope. Will do it after our visit here.'

'I might do the same, haven't bet for a few weeks. Won anything big recently?'

'Not really, going through a bit of a barren spell.'

Dargo found plastic fragments of Darren's phone in the grass of the courtyard. He scooped some into an evidence bag.

'The boy reckons level three or higher, but not the top floor, that being floor six,' said Bullock.

'It's the middle of the working day, so I doubt many people will be around to help us.'

'Don't sound too defeatist, Tom. Plenty of people skive from home these days.'

They approached the main door. There were three flats on each floor and they pressed the buzzer of each. Eventually, a man on the sixth floor let them in after introducing themselves over the intercom. The man had no information about any of his neighbours on the lower floors, so the detectives filtered down each storey, knocking on each door of levels five, four, and three, but no one was home.

'Typical modern flats. There's no sense of community,' said Bullock.

'Coming from the man who planted an eight-foot hedge on all sides of his front garden to block off the neighbours.'

'Aye.' he laughed. 'Amy is the same. She hates all the neighbourly niceties.'

'Stuff this, Xander. Let's hit the bookies. We can come back tonight or tomorrow.'

CHAPTER 25

Leigh Rocastle slumped in her swivel chair to create an artificially bloated belly. She placed her hands over the curve and yawned, looking down upon an array of delis frantically serving the lunchtime traffic.

'Y'know, I used to be the hotshot journalist, full of stamina and skill. Then I turned chubby. It's the late nights that kill you. Broken sleep cycles, poor rest, erratic eating schedules. It'll come for you one day, Sam.'

Leigh turned away from the window wall to face her protégé. Rather than listening, Sam was hunched over a desk, studying blueprints.

'Do you think my office needs a makeover?' Leigh asked. 'It's a tad bookish. Like I'm trying too hard to show I'm well read. Meanwhile, the office floor out there is full of beanbags and hammocks. My office should reflect the culture out there. I'll put a sofa here. Oh, and a coffee machine.'

Sam groaned a response that neither agreed nor disagreed, but indicated to Leigh that she was not paying attention. Leigh wore a mischievous grin as she continued.

'I've been experiencing some feelings I've never felt before, or at least never allowed myself to fully accept.'

Leigh paused, hoping Sam would probe, but she was not forthcoming. Leigh continued.

'I've come to realise that I'm much more sexually attracted to women. I'm a lesbian, Sam, and I want to fuck you on my desk right now.'

'What?' Sam said.

'Hurrah, now I have your attention. Put those blueprints away. You already know your plan. Staring aimlessly at them isn't going to improve anything.'

Having spent her younger years as an adventurous, controversial journalist, Leigh now prided herself on supporting the rising stars in journalism to reach their potential, even if that support meant abetting Sam's attempt to break into Sector Five at Strathaven Science Centre.

'We need to uglify you.' Leigh said. 'You're far too gorgeous to be breaking into Strathaven. Someone will recognise you. Rockwell will recognise you.'

'Don't be daft.'

'I mean it, Sam. Uglify yourself.'

Leigh rolled up the blueprints so that Sam's sole focus was on her.

'You know this animal isn't a bloody werewolf?'

'Of course, but it's an animal which is alien to the Caledonian landscape, and there's only one place I know that has a history of genetically modifying animals.'

'Those experiments were only conducted on rats and rabbits, and all in the interest of national security.' Leigh glowered, doing her best impression of the Head of Strathaven, Dr Torion Rockwell.

'If you wore a pair of orange specs, that would've been uncanny.'

'Yes, but as much as we ridicule this man, he's a powerful cunt.'

Leigh sunk back into her chair.

'Please take a seat, Sam. It's unsettling having you stand over me for this long. Let's go over your plan one more time. I need to get as comfortable as possible about your safety while you're in Strathaven. This friend you have on the inside, why is she helping you, and how can she help you?'

'Her name is Elodie Ricard. She is a scientist in Sector Four, the biological disease facility. When I was at university, I worked for A Fling Too Far.'

'Ah yes, the company which uncovers affairs on behalf of their suspicious spouses.'

'The very one. I was instructed by Elodie to investigate her husband, Jeremy. I found that not only was he cheating on her, but he had impregnated another woman. Elodie was relieved rather than angry, took custody of her daughter and moved on. She tried to pay me more than the fee quote, but I knew she worked at Strathaven, so I refused the money and told her I may need a favour one day. I don't know how to describe it, but I just knew her job would become useful at some point.'

'Good instinct.'

'Like so many other employees at Strathaven, Elodie operates in her own silo, and while she finds her work valuable, groundbreaking even, she is extremely suspicious of what goes on behind the sealed doors of Sector Five and is becoming disillusioned as to what the purpose of the facility is for. Elodie's work could be conducted in a city centre lab. There is no reason to commute to the wilderness to do her job. She fears her work is a façade, giving legitimate justification to fund, build and conduct morbid experiments within Sector Five, all under the guise of…'

'National security.'

'I trust her, Leigh. She only wanted to know the truth when her husband was cheating on her. She wasn't angry. She didn't regress within herself. She just needed to know, and then she moved on. This is the same. Elodie wants the truth as much as we do. Well, maybe a little less than I do.'

'I don't think there's anyone in the world who wants to disrupt Rockwell as much as you. So how is she helping you get in there?'

'She knows someone inside Sector Five.'

'The insider of the insider.'

'Yip. Her insider has obtained an access card that gets me into the main building, as well as Sector Five. I guess that means I'm not really breaking in, since I'll be walking right through the front door.'

'What about Strathaven's security team and cameras? What if a staff member in Sector Five sees you?'

'Well, I don't know if I'm going to uglify myself, but I am going to wear a dark wig and non-prescription glasses. I'll wear professional clothes so they think I'm part of a management team working late. You know how it is in these places, the security personnel are older men who want to earn a few merks during their retirement. They're not thorough with their work and have become careless after endless uneventful shifts.'

Leigh nodded. Back in her prime, she had burrowed her way into many buildings due to failures in security, almost always because of human complacency. Scaling skyscrapers with suction pads, jumping through windows on a zip wire, and wading through sewage tunnels to come up through the toilets seat were the stuff of movies. In reality, people can walk through any door with enough confidence and the ability to blag.

'Who is the dissident from Sector Five?'

'I don't know. They didn't want to give their name.'

'That doesn't sit well with me, Sam. We can't trust this person. What if they've fucked up? What if they are luring you in there? What if they've changed their mind at the last minute and revoked the access? If we have access to a dissident from Sector Five, why do we even need to enter Sector Five? Why can't we ask this person for pictures, recordings, or give an anonymous interview? Why do you have to endanger yourself if this contact can already provide what we need?'

'That's the thing, they aren't a contact. I don't know who they are. They won't reveal themselves. But they fear Rockwell enough that they don't want to be the ones leaking information.'

'They are right to fear him. God knows what spooked Mintoff when he was in government. Trust me, I've spent many a gala dinner supplying him with enough alcohol to coax out the real reason he abruptly scuttled back to the private sector. But what I do know is that if someone as wealthy, intelligent and powerful as Mintoff is scared into silence by Rockwell, then his employees will be scared stiff of the man.'

The notion of Rockwell percolated into a pregnant pause between the two women. Sam mustered images of Rockwell's masterful squint, staring anxiety into journalists when defending Sector Five's activities; their courage dissipating mid-question. Sam likened him to an evil surgeon, a person of authority who operates with a charming smile while secretly killing the very patients he was meant to heal.

'I know you know this already, Sam, but it's worth saying again. You need to be careful in there. I know you have this lovely plan, and it sounds good in the safety of my office, but once you are in there, it's a different prospect entirely. If Rockwell catches you.' Leigh paused. 'Just tell me you have a communication plan?'

Sam slapped two burner phones on Leigh's desk.

'These are the burners.'

'I didn't know smartphones could act as burners. I thought Nokia bricks were the phone of choice in that regard.'

'These have been encrypted to act as a burner. I can't use an old phone because I need the camera and video capabilities to snap photographic evidence of anything I find.'

'Indeed. Am I the only one with a burner?'

'You and Detective Nikki Achebe.'

'Nikki Achebe. I saw Tom and Xander were not on this case. I found that a bit strange given the high-profile nature of it.'

'It was meant to be a straightforward capture of an escaped animal. Obviously, it has exploded into something greater. Plus, Tom and Xander were preoccupied with Bob Huskins.'

'Sick fucker.'

'And now there's the missing teenagers taking up their time. Nikki seems to have potential, though. I've been impressed in the few dealings

I've had with her, both as a high constable and when I spoke with her a few days ago. She's definitely up for the fight.'

'We've been lucky in the past to work closely with Tom and Xander who are willing to turn a blind eye to some of our truth-seeking methods. Is Achebe cut from the same cloth?'

'I think initially she's battled with her morals. It must be tough turning detective and within a matter of weeks you have me turning up and openly disclosing my intentions to commit a criminal act, asking that she be okay with it. At the very least, she accepted the burner I gave her. She'll consult Tom and come round to their way of thinking.'

'Let's hope so. So, you are only going to communicate with those two numbers, none of which can be traced back to us?'

'Correct.'

'And you still want me to drive you there?'

'Yes.'

'Last time I attended Strathaven, there was a security barrier to get into the carpark. If we are going full incognito, then we can't rock up to that carpark. There will be cameras and my registration number will be clocked.'

'You can drop me here.' Sam said while zooming into the maps on her phone. 'There's a small clearing in the woods next to the road leading to Strathaven. From there, I can walk.'

'What happens when you walk up to the security barrier? The operator will wonder where the hell you've come from on foot in the middle of the night. There's nothing for miles, and any buses taking commuters there stop on the grounds within the security barriers.'

'I'm hoping to sneak up on the booth without the security personnel realising. I'll knock on the window and ask something trivial, making it look like I've come from within the facility to ask a question, rather than from the preceding road.'

Leigh tilted her head to the floor as she contemplated Sam's plan. As basic as it sounded, Leigh knew the less elaborate plans were often the most successful.

'Okay, I'll hang fire in the clearing for fifteen minutes or so and you can message me if there are any issues getting past the first few hurdles. How long do you intend to be inside?'

'An hour, maybe a bit more. I'm not sure what I'll find.'

'In that case, after I've waited fifteen minutes, I'll drive to Banff and back. That should be roughly an hour. If I don't hear from you after two hours, I'm going straight to Tom.'

Sam nodded.

'And if you get into any trouble, The Thistle will protect you. I will protect you. I own the most impactful media company on the planet. When I kick up shit, the world will know about it. If you go radio silent, I'll have the police, politicians, celebrities, sport stars, and the fucking army barging into Strathaven before Rockwell can say *in the interests of national security.*'

'Thanks. I'm ready to go tonight.'

'Right, let's go for his fucking throat.'

CHAPTER 26

Achebe flashed her police badge to the stern security guards, who duly let her enter the backstage area. Angus Mintoff, founder and CEO of Pangea International, was on stage launching the latest innovation within the company's solar panel division. From the side of the stage, Achebe watched Mintoff speak passionately about how the company had developed technology which can store and control more energy than ever before. Mintoff was also promoting a new non-profit subsidiary, which aimed to deliver the solar panels to every residential home on three Caribbean islands who had volunteered to the plan. Part of Pangea International's global vision is to provide affordable, clean energy to everyone, and success in the Caribbean would be the evidence needed for major nations to buy into that vision.

'Who the fuck are you?'

The question was punched at Achebe from a visibly stressed woman wearing a headset.

'I'm the fucking police. Who the fuck are you?' Achebe replied in a soft but authoritative manner.

'What are you doing here?'

'I'm here to speak to Mr Mintoff.'

'You can't. He's busy. Security to stage left please.'

'Did you really just call security on the police, as if I haven't just walked past them on my way here?'

'I don't have proof that you are who you say you are.'

Achebe showed her badge.

'I need to speak with Mr Mintoff once he's finished his presentation. It shouldn't take long.'

'As soon as he's finished, he has another meeting scheduled.'

'I'm sure it won't be the first time he's been late for a meeting.'

'I'm sorry, to arrange a meeting with Mr Mintoff, please email me at...'

'I'll stop you there,' Achebe said, doing her best to remain calm.

'Have you got the car ready?' the woman said.

'What?' Achebe replied.

'Good, see you there in eight minutes. Eight minutes exactly, okay?'

The mousy woman was talking into the headset while constantly jerking her neck like a meerkat on the lookout. Achebe clenched her jaw, deliberately displaying her agitation towards Mintoff's irritating personal assistant.

'If you don't let me speak to him after the show, I will wait until he's leaving for his car and then I'll approach him. No doubt there're reporters out there waiting to snap a shot of him, so how do you think it will look when I approach him, flash my police badge and start conversing with him in a serious manner? The media know I'm the detective in charge of the *werewolf* case, so it won't take long for rumours to spread of how Angus Mintoff is connected to a savage beast.'

The personal assistant stopped twitching as she assessed the detective. Achebe continued.

'We live in the age of speculation. Truth goes out the window for more sensational theories when images and videos, like the scenario I just described, make their way on social media.'

'You wouldn't do that,' the assistant said, calling Achebe's bluff.

Achebe snatched the cordless headset, tossing it onto the stage like a frisbee before the assistant could react. The headset landed in between two armchairs on the stage, interrupting the post presentation question-and-answer session taking place between Mintoff, a presenter, and a now murmuring media audience.

Mintoff's chair was already facing stage left, his expression subtly glowering towards his assistant.

'He's probably wondering if that's an emergency signal you're giving him.' Achebe said. 'Look, he doesn't know how to react. You've stalled the rhythm of the product launch. I think you've really fucked up here.' Achebe said mischievously.

140

The woman made two paces towards the stage but cowered back in fear that she would make the situation worse. The presenter held the unforeseen object to his ear.

'And our next question comes from the phantom headset,'

The audience laughed, and Mintoff smiled, moving quickly onto the next question.

'I like to play fair.' Achebe said. 'But I'm not scared of theatrics, either. You'll give me five minutes with Mr Mintoff or I'll make an even bigger scene outside.'

The woman let out a squeak of frustration, then used her phone to tell the driver to have the car ready in twenty minutes.

After the product launch was over, Mintoff entered his designated dressing room alone, his assistant squirrelling off as he shut the door.

'What was all that about?' he asked Achebe with a calm smile.

'Your assistant wasn't playing ball, so I had to show her the lengths I'd go to get five minutes of your attention.'

'I'm sorry. She's a great assistant, but she has a tendency to become blinkered when I'm on a tight schedule. I'm happy to talk with you, although I do only have ten minutes before I need to shoot off.'

Mintoff's presence was warm. He was not the tallest, but his charisma made him seem so. His body shape was athletic, but there was a layer of chubbiness preventing an impressive physique, as if he enjoyed working out but never had the time to do it enough given his business commitments.

Achebe explained the case she was working on and the fact she was hoping to visit Sector Five. Mintoff wore a curious expression as he took a seat.

'You realise I need to be very careful about what I say in relation to my time in government, especially anything related to Sector Five?'

'I do, but if I'm honest, this case is not making a lot of sense. There's been three attacks now, and the beast is proving elusive. This is not a time for worrying about the legal consequences of breaching an NDA. This is about saving lives.'

Achebe could not believe she had been so open about her struggles with Mintoff, but he was magnetic. He had just spent an hour on stage launching a new product, subsequently answering challenging questions from a media audience, and had another important meeting to attend. But there were no signs of tiredness, no agitated gestures signalling he was on a tight schedule and needed to leave soon. He was present. He was listening, and his position in society meant he operated at a level where he appreciated secrecy, all of which disarmed Achebe's normally guarded approach when speaking to members of the public.

'There's been a lot of speculation about my time in government. People say I regret it, but I don't. There was always going to be an economic blip after Caledonia gained independence. The country was always going to need time to find its feet. When I was Minister of Business and Trade, it was my job to lay the foundations for an independent Caledonia, and me and my team worked tirelessly to achieve that. We introduced the Merk, a whole new currency which is now trading strongly alongside the traditional major currencies. We are now world leaders in renewable energy, although I'd say we have a bit of catching up to do on the Scandinavian countries. We are less reliant on other countries for food and we are exporting at levels we've never experienced before, so I am proud of my time in government.'

'So why leave so abruptly?'

'To focus on Pangea International.'

'Bullshit!'

Mintoff grinned, knowing his answer was the same throwaway line he gave the media when he left the government.

'This is where I need to be careful about what I say. I want to help you, Detective Achebe. I really do. So, here's what I'll tell you. I visited Strathaven a lot, but my exposure to Sector Five was very limited. As I say, I was Minister of Business and Trade, so I'd visit the biological disease, renewable energy, transportation and cultured meats departments if they had any innovations that were ready to be brought to market. I would advise on how to commercialise these innovations and build a team to help with that process, using anyone in my business network to give each product the best chance of success in the open market. Whatever projects were happening in Sector Five largely remained a secret to me, however. I only visited that area of Strathaven three times, as far as I can remember. I can't say I saw any evidence of a beast or have any insight into what might be running around in Bannock forest. But what I do know is there are projects conducted in Sector Five that go beyond the boundaries of national security, far beyond those boundaries, in my opinion.'

'What kind of projects?'

'The kind that would shatter your belief in humanity.'

Achebe saw a tortured soul in the eyes of Mintoff; a desperation to reveal the true nature of Sector Five while also conscious of what the consequences of doing so would be.

'And what about Dr Torion Rockwell?'

Mintoff's eyes narrowed, the warmth draining from him. Even mentioning Rockwell's name wrangled him.

'It's no secret I despise the man.'

'You must've had some sort of working relationship since you worked closely with the various divisions in Strathaven, and he invited you to Sector Five on three occasions?'

'He thought I was someone worth having onside. Given my business connections, I could be a useful asset to him and Sector Five, the same way I was proving useful to the other sectors in Strathaven. He misjudged me, though, and when I voiced my concerns about what goes on in Sector Five, concerns which led to my eventual departure from the government, he turned against me. He would love nothing more than for Strathaven to out-muscle Pangea International. It seems that every time we launch a new R&D project, one of Strathaven's departments launches a similar project. He wants Pangea to go bust.'

'Could your relationship really be that bad after three visits to Sector Five?'

'Sorry, I've misled you. We met many times, and got along well on the whole, I might add. But in terms of physically being in Sector Five, I was only there three times. But what I saw on one of those occasions has Torion Rockwell terrified.'

'Terrified that you'll go public.'

Mintoff nodded.

'I'm his biggest threat because he knows I have the financial capabilities to hire the best lawyers should I decide to breach any nondisclosure agreement. I am a powerful whistle-blower, and let me tell you, I've come very close to revealing what goes on in Sector Five.'

'Why haven't you?'

'I'm not sure the public could handle it. I'm not sure it would help society for people to know what goes on there.'

'You're not giving me anything to work with here. Could Sector Five have created a mutant beast capable of these attacks, the same way it created Alba the glow-in-the-dark rabbit?'

'I want to make it clear that I saw no evidence of any beast during my visits. However, do I believe Sector Five has the capabilities to produce a lab-created beast? Possibly. But, I think it's more likely that this creature is something we have not discovered before. I thought you might be coming to ask me about my research funding, but since you haven't mentioned it, I assume you are not aware that I finance lots of biological research expeditions. A lot are marine biology expeditions. Most people are aware that there are thousands upon thousands of species in the oceans we are yet to discover. What people don't tend to believe, and what biologists struggle to gain funding for, are expeditions to discover new species on land.'

'Like the cryptozoologists?'

'I saw what happened to them, tragic. But unfortunately, it is groups like them that create a stigma around land-based expeditions to find new species. The media and public automatically think any biologist exploring our lands in search of new large species is crazy. The fact is, we know so little about our earth. We haven't explored every corner of every jungle. One expedition I funded was the search for the Zanzibar leopard. It was declared extinct. No one had seen one for twenty-five years. For context, Zanzibar island is smaller than Bannock forest and has a population of roughly a million. On this expedition, a biologist caught a leopard on camera for the first time in over two decades. Remarkable. So, if the people of Zanzibar island hadn't spotted a leopard for that length of time on that small island, imagine what could've been in Bannock forest for all these years.'

'You think this creature could have been around for a while?'

'It wouldn't completely shock me. Given the climate in Caledonia, Bannock forest is only really used in the summer months, and even in those months there are vast areas that are untouched. If you need help identifying scat samples, paw prints, or would like a team of experts to explore certain areas of Bannock forest, then let me know. There are more than a few biologists who would do me a favour.'

'Thanks, I might take you up on that. So, you don't believe Rockwell could be behind these attacks?'

The room fell quiet as Mintoff stewed on the question.

'Let's say this animal was born and bred in Sector Five. What does Rockwell have to gain by letting it attack Caledonian civilians, with all the media and public spotlight that could bring on him and the Strathaven facility if it was ever traced back to him?'

'Maybe it escaped. Maybe they can't control what they've bred.'

'That's the part I struggle with. For as horrible a man as Rockwell is, he isn't stupid. He rarely makes mistakes. If an animal escaped Sector Five, he would deal with it swiftly.'

Mintoff pouted with stern contemplation.

'But,' he said. 'While I can't think of a reason, it doesn't mean there isn't one. Torion Rockwell is a psychopath, a ruthless psychopath. If you are visiting Sector Five, you should be very careful. Rockwell does not operate within the law.'

CHAPTER 27

All bouncers have tiny dicks. That is the only logical hypothesis Dargo could muster to account for the tiresome, inflated machismo he tolerated every time he set foot in a nightclub. They would flex their biceps and puff their chest upon seeing Dargo and Bullock trespass on their territory and wipe out their authority.

'Have you seen this kid?'

Bullock flashed the image of Ryan Etherington, who was reported missing the day before and was now the fourth teenager to disappear. His last known appearance was at the trendy Macau nightclub, but trying to trace the teenager's last movements was proving difficult due to the two lumbering obstacles who were assiduous in their efforts to protect Macau from any adverse publicity.

'No.' replied the bouncers.

'You barely looked.'

'I've never seen him before.'

'Can you at least take a better look at the photo?'

'I looked. I've never seen him.'

'Can I get a copy of the CCTV footage on the night of...'

'Our cameras don't work. They're just for show. Saves on the leccy bill.'

'Look, there are young males going missing. This is an important investigation, and we need your help.'

Six silver filings smiled back at the detectives. 'If it's sympathy yer after, you'll find it in the dictionary between shite and syphilis.'

Both bouncers sniggered like immature children, irking Bullock to his mischievous best.

'Well, you cock-rockets have been as useful as two balls on a dildo.' Bullock said while pointing to the bald bouncer. 'That slaphead of yours makes you look like a dildo actually, except you wouldn't be rammed up a fanny. You'd be the type of dildo that gets rammed up a bloke's hairy arse with dangleberries flicking off you as you move in. And as for H. Samuel over here, you've got a face like a slow-motion sneeze.'

Baldy stepped closer with clenched fists. Bullock's grin danced with glee.

'Let me just remind you two boggin' bastards that it's illegal to hit a police officer. A shame, isn't it? You've traded erections for steroid muscles, and you can't even use them against me. That's a new level of sexual frustration.'

*

Midnight loomed when Dargo dropped Bullock off at his house. He contemplated returning home himself to curl up next to Sally in bed. Heck, he may even get lucky. But she'll be tired as well, he thought. Going home to eat the dinner she had left in the fridge alone didn't seem so appealing. He would only wake Sally up. Plus, she knew he was working late on the case, so his presence was not expected.

Dargo took the drive back across town to meet the Midnight Club. His eyelids slipped shut at a traffic light junction, his neck jarring as it dropped before bungee jumping back to its default position. He tried to calculate how long his current period of sleeplessness had endured, but the days and weeks blended into each other, creating a misty timeline that was not worth clearing.

The red casino lights rosied Dargo's cheeks, and the summer air dampened his forehead with sweat. The receptionist recognised the regular guest.

'Warm outside, isn't it, Mr Dargo?' she said.

'Hopefully, the table is hot tonight as well.'

'Good luck!'

Dargo approached the familiar table which was occupied by Bert and a red-eyed Connor; the preceding hours had evidently been heavy with drugs.

'Alright, chaps?'

Bert kept his nose pointing down to his fidgeting hands.

'He's not heard the news.' Connor said.

'What news?'

Only now did Dargo realise that Connor's eyes were not reddened by excessive drug-taking, but from sustained tears.

'What's wrong, Connor?'

Dargo regretted asking the question as it came out of his mouth, preparing himself for a story about gang fights. A drug deal that went wrong and now Connor was in hot water with some madman who wanted his head on a spike.

'It's Ronan. He killed himself.'

Dargo opened his mouth, but the sucker punch sentence suppressed his speech. His mind wanted to ask five questions at once, but instead, only one word emanated.

'When?'

'Last night. I've been supplying him with a bit of gear, y'know, to take his mind off the divorce and not seeing his kids as much. He asked me to come to the house and promised we'd hit up the casino after a couple of spliffs. I went to his house and when he never answered, I walked round the back. He's got these big bastard patio doors.'

Connor slavered as he cried. He composed himself in between hiccups to tell the rest of the story.

'That's when I saw him... sitting on the sofa with his brains splattered all over the wall.'

Connor leaned over the table, crying hysterically. The croupier dare not intervene, despite Connor moving several chips on the table. Dargo had seen many dead bodies over the years, but he never forgot how the first corpse gave him restless nights, constantly itching with discomfort. He empathised with the boy. The traumatic experience would live with him forever.

'That's hard for anyone to see,' Dargo said.

'I thought I could come back here and get on with life, but I canny. I canny unsee it. It's been in my heed the whole time.'

'I'm sorry, Connor. Trust me, you'll learn to live with it.'

'I dinny want to live with it.'

'Did he leave a note?' Dargo asked.

'Fuck knows. I never went into the house. I just came here last night hoping to find you.'

'Why me?'

'To make the police aware.'

'Wait, you haven't called the police?'

'How could I? I had gear on me. I was there to dish out drugs. My head wasn't switched on right to make up an alternative story.'

'It was me that told him to wait until you were next here rather than go to the police.' Bert said, shuffling in his seat before speaking. 'Didn't want the boy getting into trouble. He's been through enough.'

Dargo was trying to understand the rationale behind not reporting Ronan's suicide. The police would turn a blind eye to a bit of gear when there's a dead body in the lounge, but he supposed Conor would not know this.

Their expectant gazes told Dargo it was up to him to sort out the mess, but all he could think was how pathetic, rather than tragic, Ronan's death was. Slouched on the sofa with half a head in a cold, gloomy room of an empty house. His death went unreported even after being found. Lonely in life and even lonelier in death.

Dargo racked his brain to think of a night shift officer who could attend the scene without asking too many questions about how Dargo knew of the death. The Midnight Club was not a subject he wanted to become office gossip.

'Okay. I'll call it in. Are you going to be okay, Connor?'

'No. I just need to go home. I can't get Ronan out of my head when I'm here.'

'Okay. Phone me if you are struggling.'

Connor ran to the toilet as Dargo walked and talked to call-in the suicide. Bert threw twenty quid on red.

CHAPTER 28

I know for a fact Rockwell is working late tonight. Good luck!

Sam considered telling Leigh to stop the car upon reading the chilling message from her insider, Elodie. They could return another night when Rockwell was not working. Breaking into Sector Five while he was there intensified her nerves, certain that Rockwell would recognise her underneath the dark wig, fake glasses, brown contact lenses, and jet-black mascara.

Sam convinced herself to plough ahead with her plan. Rockwell's presence was both a threat and an opportunity. The public was in danger from a killer beast, and she was convinced it was bred in Sector Five. If she could find evidence of it, and that evidence also incriminated Rockwell, then she could terminate the most dangerous man in Caledonia, potentially the world.

As they drove past the cosmos black farm fields, the eyes of curious sheep leered into the car's full beams. Leigh noticed Sam's fidgeting increase as they drew closer to Strathaven Science Centre.

'Remember your safeguards,' Leigh said. 'You have your burner phone. I'll be right by mine the whole time you are in there and you know Tom and Xander will look after you if you are arrested. The Thistle will cover any subsequent fine or lawsuit. The worst-case scenario is you are caught and banged up in a cell for a few nights.'

Sam did not believe a slap on the wrist was the worst-case scenario, but she still took comfort knowing Leigh and the police were on hand should anything go wrong.

Sam pulled down the passenger visor flap and started adjusting her wig so the long fringe sat as naturally as possible. After applying the non-prescription glasses, she was surprised how corporate and studious the transformation made her. As the car oscillated on the fractured country road, a brown contact lens wobbled on her finger.

'Best do that part when I stop.' Leigh suggested.

A few minutes later, Sam directed Leigh to the hidden clearing in the woods she had identified half-a-mile short of the facility. Sam used a two-finger brace to expose each eyeball to the incoming brown lenses. She leant back against the seat to view as much of her Cleopatran disguise as possible.

'Not quite the uglification I had in mind, but it'll do.' Leigh said.

The nerves kicked inside Sam's stomach like she was pregnant with a dozen babies. She paused, wondering if she was going to be sick. Leigh sensed her anxiety.

'Sam, you can pull out now if you want to. There will be no issues with that whatsoever. But I know you, and I know if you pull out, you'll be kicking yourself. If you try and fail, so be it. We move onto the next strategy.'

'I'm okay to go. I used to get nervous before netball games, but once the whistle blew and the match started, the nerves went away. It will be the same here. I just need to get out of the car and get moving.'

Leigh hugged her over the handbrake.

'You don't need luck. Just go do your thing.'

The valley basin contained its own climate. Edin's summer air had been warm, but the valley nipped at Sam's earlobes and the tip of her nose. As she approached the facility, her first obstacle came into view. The barriers to the car park were manned by a watchman in a security kiosk.

Sam assessed the situation from behind a tree. The light within the kiosk sat bright against the dark backdrop of the car park. Strathaven sat dimly beyond, as if on standby.

The watchman was an elderly gentleman, the exact type of individual Sam knew would be working the night shift at an isolated science centre, earning a leisurely wage to top-up his pension.

Sam considered running past the kiosk and ducking under the barrier without the watchman noticing. Whilst it was possible, if she were caught, it would be game over at the first hurdle. Instead, she stuck to her plan, waiting for her opportunity, and when the watchman turned around to fill his kettle by the sink, Sam took her chance.

She briskly approached the kiosk, praying the watchman remained facing in the opposite direction. When she got there, she wrapped her knuckles against the window. The man jumped, placing a hand over his chest. Once he recovered from the heart scare, he pulled across a glass panel to speak to Sam.

'You gave me a fright there, love.'

'So sorry. I've never worked this late before, so I thought I would come out and make sure the barriers are always in operation?'

'Aye, love. Twenty-four-seven. You could've just asked reception.'

'I know. I needed some fresh, though. It gets a bit stuffy when you've been in that place all day.'

'I know what you mean. Try being in here all shift.'

'When did your shift start?'

'Four hours ago. Still got another six to go.'

'Aw, well, I hope you have enough supplies to keep you going?'

'Coffee, digestive biscuits, and the radio. What more does a man need?'

'Good stuff. Well, I better head back in and crack on. Nice speaking to you.'

Sam walked by the small gap next to the barriers to enter the car park. Passing the first obstacle induced somersaulting nerves. She faced the facility, taking a deep breath as she entered the stem of the leaf-shaped building, the tip of which extended up the ridge of the mountain.

At the glass entrance, Sam swiped the keycard Elodie had smuggled for her. The doors opened to an expansive hollow foyer. The tiled flooring glistened with cleanliness and Sam had to restrain herself from marvelling at her surroundings like a tourist staring at the artistry of the Sistine Chapel. Instead, she feigned casualness, as if her presence in Strathaven was normal. She waved at two security guards lounging in front of an impressive water wall at the reception desk.

'Evening boys, can I come hang out with you when I get bored with work?'

The two burly men looked flattered to receive attention from a female half their age. The small talk gave Sam time to glance at the signage, ensuring she was heading to the correct door.

'Of course, any time.'

'I'll be five minutes then.'

Sam laughed nonchalantly as she swiped her keycard. To her relief, the door clicked open, meaning she had successfully hurdled the second obstacle on route to Sector Five.

Dim energy-saving lights cloaked an endless corridor in a grey hue. Four electric vehicles, like golf buggies, sat charging to her left. She was now in the leaf's midrib. It contained four lanes for the vehicles to drive on, two on each side of the corridor, separated by a central walkway so vast that it housed market stalls selling food, gifts, books, and coffee. There was a barbershop, a beauty salon, a massage parlour, yoga zone, and a gym area. It was a mini village designed to meet the needs of the staff who worked at the science centre. But tonight, it was a ghost town.

The hum from the electric vehicle was almost imperceptible, maintaining a silent science centre as Sam drove along the midrib, passing veins which split off to the cultured meat and biological disease sectors. The transport and renewable energy sectors stemmed from the other side of the corridor.

Just as Sam had studied in the Strathaven blueprints, the doors to Sector Five were enclosed within a bullet-proof glass security chamber. X-ray machines and radiation body scanners were stationed like a row of soldiers, ready to block her path. But it was on the frontline where the toughest obstacle was situated. Sam glanced apprehensively at the machine designed to scan her keycard and face, corroborating the facial scan with the profile assigned to the keycard. Sam's disguise was not accidental. The brown hair and contact lenses mimicked Elodie's look, whose profile was designated to the keycard.

In a separate security room within the glass chamber, a lonesome security guard slouched in his seat with his feet brazenly resting on the desk. He sipped from a Strathaven branded mug while watching a video on his phone, earphones blocking any outside noise. He was oblivious to Sam parking the electric vehicle in a charging bay.

'Walk with confidence,' she whispered.

Sam knew two key pieces of information she could use to her advantage to bypass the pot-bellied guard with minimal questioning: all Strathaven staff feared Rockwell, and the man himself was in the building.

Sam thumped the glass next to the security guard. Startled, he spilt coffee down his jumper as he swivelled his neck to see who was there.

'I take it Dr Rockwell is already inside?' Sam said with a frown.

'Yes, do you need me to ring his assistant to inform him you've arrived?'

'You mean Elle?' Sam said, having been supplied with knowledge of Rockwell's assistant by Elodie. 'No. I work here. I'm late, so he'll be angry. Maybe I'll deflect attention away from myself by telling him his security prefers to chillax rather than act professionally.' Sam said, glaring sternly at his feet, which were still on the desk.

The guard fumbled his legs off the table, his face burning red like a spot ready to pop.

'So sorry, madam.'

'Yes, let's hope for your sake I don't need to disclose my observations. Now, you'll need to help me with this keycard. This fucking machine never reads my face properly.'

Sam swiped her keycard. The anxiety inside her sloshed around in a violent eddy as a red "X" appeared on the machine's monitor. Red lights flashed above the scanner.

Unable to verify. Report sent to security.

'Told you.' Sam said, attempting to remain authoritative. 'Now approve my access. I can't be delayed any longer. Dr Rockwell is waiting.'

The security guard analysed Elodie's mugshot on his screen and looked back towards Sam. Her heart was pumping hard against her breast. He squinted at her, then again at the screen. Sam tapped her foot as if impatient, but in reality, she was releasing nervous energy.

The guard pressed a button. A green tick appeared on the machine's monitor and the doors opened, allowing Sam to move onto the line of body scanners and x-ray machines.

'I need to take all phones and devices off you,' said the guard, as he began hobbling out of his security booth.

Sam was prepared for this, removing the burner phone from her pocket and sliding it in the gap between two body scanners with the gentle accuracy of a bowls player. Her heart fluttered with success as the phone stopped just beyond the scanners. The security guard, who was hobbling out of his booth, was momentarily blind to her motion. Remaining crouched, Sam untied the laces on her left shoe.

'I've worked here long enough to know not to bring a phone.'

The guard appeared suspicious. Everyone has a phone on them.

'Backpack through the x-ray please and stand in the scanner with your hands up until the machine flashes green.'

Sam placed her bag on a conveyor belt and stood within the body scanner, arms raised. She took a deep breath. The scanner flashed green, and she was able to proceed. As she did, her phone lay to the left while her bag was scanned on the right. She bent down to tie her lace, subtly snatching the phone into her pocket before standing to attention, waiting as her bag drifted to her

With no further obstacles in Sam's way, she strode to the tip of the leaf; the entrance to Sector Five. Opening the double doors was like opening the windows of a butterfly sanctuary in Sam's stomach. Goosebumps rose underneath her clothes. She was always confident of gaining access to Sector Five, but the expectation did not make the achievement any less thrilling.

Her accomplishment, though, was humbled by the monotonous grey corridor evoking the headache-inducing lethargy of a doctor's surgery. There were two doors on either side of the corridor and two elevators hummed dramatically at the end of the underwhelming hallway. No blueprints existed for this part of the facility, meaning there was no specific plan to execute. Sam was operating purely on instinct.

An acidic smell nipped at her nostrils as she approached the first door on the left. Lights sparkled into life and Sam's skin tightened under the vulnerability. Her movements were known, and she expected Sector Five personnel to walk through the elevators at any moment to remove her. She exhaled slowly to calm her nerves. She had only triggered the motion sensor lights. Still, she needed to get out of the spotlight.

Moving towards the first door on the left, Sam immediately retreated as if it were radioactive. Rockwell's name was emblazoned on a golden plaque. She bypassed his office, fearing Rockwell was on the other side, and noticed the corridor lights from the gaps around the edges of his door. The next door was labelled a conference room, which was hardly inspiring. She rotated to the other side. A lab room. This could be of interest, but Sam reckoned employees could be working late within.

The pores on Sam's neck oozed salty droplets as she panicked. The next room was titled the archive room. Sam swiped herself into the room, believing it would be unattended and she could catch her breath. She was right.

The room was the size of a large classroom. Shelving units stacked with boxes lined up parallel to each other in the centre of the room. The boxes were sorted chronologically, starting when Strathaven opened at the turn of the century. Each had mysterious titles such as Operation Taboo, Project Cipher, and The Octopus Trials.

Sam had struck gold. Too prosperous even. The number of top-secret documents was endless, and she only had the capacity of her backpack to transport anything out of the facility. There was no computer available to send or save files to a hard drive, only old-fashioned paper filing.

'Paper can't be hacked, I suppose,' Sam whispered.

Sam started shifting boxes of intrigue to the empty desks pushed against the wall. She could not believe her luck in finding a panoply of classified Sector Five information. She had to let Leigh know.

'Fuck!'

No signal. She was cut off from Leigh and Detective Achebe.

Sam froze when the elevator doors pinged. A collection of brogues and high heels clip-clopped across the linoleum floor like cantering horses. The authoritative steps were heading to the archive room. There was no time to hide. Instead, she would be caught standing in the middle of all the files like a guilty puppy amongst burst cushion fluff.

To her relief, the feet shuffled into the conference room. Her watch ticked towards half-past eleven. The only meetings taking place at this time were crisis meetings, and there was no bigger crisis than losing control of a carnivorous animal.

Sam had to observe the meeting.

CHAPTER 29

Simply placing an ear to the conference room door was not an option. Sam had to be smarter, more covert, to hear the dialogue of Sector Five's top secret meeting.

She looked to the ceiling. It was made of square plastic tiles placed on top of a sturdy metal lattice. Sam stood on a table and pushed open a tile, exposing the pipe works. Using the metal lattice for leverage, she pulled herself up, her hips lightly grazing the edges of the square gap.

Inside the ceiling, the distance between the metal lattice and the piping was no more than half a metre, meaning she had to lie flat on her front and crawl like a gecko. Her movements were deliberate, careful not to place any body part on the flimsy ceiling tiles which would not hold her weight.

Sam stopped moving when the voices were within earshot.

'Thank you for the demonstration on Project Metazoa. Some of the hybrids seem close to being field-ready.'

The man talking was not Rockwell. The voice was deeper and agitated.

'And in terms of your other projects,' the man continued. 'Everything is in hand, I imagine?'

The room fell silent. There was no verbal response, but someone must have nodded because the same voice continued.

'Good. I just wanted to make sure you are in control and that none of us at this table will become exposed?'

There was another pause in the conversation. Then Sam's spine tingled with fear.

'You are everything I despise about modern politics, Terry.'

The second voice carried the unmistakably harsh resonance of Dr Torion Rockwell. His tone stabbed the statement towards the recipient. Without seeing him, Sam imagined his cool posture, slicing his counterpart to shreds with his cutlass tongue and scything stare.

Sam racked her brains to think of the only Terry she knew who could be involved in a top secret meeting; Terry Halkett, the newly appointed Head of Caledonian Secret Service.

'People like you, career politicians, are the blockages to progress. You have sucked the cocks of your superiors and made deals with the most abhorrent high-net worth individuals to get where you are today. You have lied to the public and media about your capabilities. All for your own gain, and at the expense of anyone who couldn't help propel you up the career ladder. Your ego sought the title you now have. Not talent. Not experience. Not intelligence. Ego. And as you wiped wealthy semen from the edges of your mouth, you carefully curated narcissistic social media posts boasting about your new role. You held celebratory drinks with friends, colleagues and family, wanking at their congratulations. Because it's all about wee, odious, Terry. But do you know what all your self-centred brown-nosing and bullshitting means? It means that I now have to deal with someone who has bent over their whole life, achieving nothing but getting fucked. I have to work with someone who is weak. Someone who has never truly put their neck on the line. Someone who has never actually achieved anything. Someone so dispensable they could be replaced tomorrow with no impact, and trust me, Terry, I could have you replaced tomorrow. Now take a good look around. You're at the table of influence now. This is real work. This is not political posturing. This is about protecting Caledonia, no matter the cost. You've lied and cheated your talentless little being to where you sit now. You are already morally corrupt, and yet now you are worried about a public backlash if they learn of your involvement with Sector Five experiments. If you are embarrassed to be connected with our activities, why not quit? Follow your moral compass and walk out those doors now.'

Nobody breathed a muscle.

'I'll tell you why you'll stay seated. Because despite Sector Five activities not conforming with the fabricated morals your friends and family believe you hold, you get hard rolling around in the phony power

157

you have, and you won't let that go for anything. And so what if the public found out about your involvement here? What would really happen? Inflict reputational damage to an inconsequential career built on a mountain of deceit and spunk? If you are going to place your own selfish motives before the success of a Sector Five project, leave now.'

The monologue shrouded the room in shadow. Rockwell's words lingered hauntingly over the meeting.

'So, what's the plan?'

The eventual question came from a female voice. Sam recognised it. She had interviewed this person before. It was Hilary Vox, Head of the National Defence unit.

'The plan does not change.' Rockwell said.

'Is that it?'

The question came from a fresh voice, one that Sam did not know. Male, but lower and solemn in tone.

'What do you mean, *is that it*? I never arranged this bloody meeting. If you feel it's been a waste of time, then believe me when I say the feeling is mutual.'

Each sentence Rockwell uttered was like a bite from a viper, methodically considered and struck with pace and precision.

'I hear the police have requested a visit. Should we be worried?' asked Vox.

'The police. The fucking police. Look around this table. We hold the power in Caledonia. The power of the police and politicians is for commoners to be fearful of. If they request a visit, I will allow them in, but they will only see what I want them to see. The hybrids will be hidden. Plus, if I ask Chief Vincent Thorne to dance for me, he will jig in the corner like a court jester. You cannot seriously be fearing the fucking police.'

Silence settled in the meeting.

'I think we are done here,' Rockwell declared, ushering a rush of creaking chairs as each individual rose from their seats and left Sector Five.

Sam waited in the safety of prolonged silence before pivoting on her belly to head back to the archive room.

'Can you hear me?'

Goosebumps erupted on Sam's skin, and her breathing felt like it was projected through a megaphone. Her insulated hiding place had morphed into a position of vulnerability. She braced for a weapon: a gun, a blade, a fist, to puncture the brittle ceiling tiles and expose her.

'Can you hear me now? The signal is shit in here.'

Sam exhaled slowly in the relief that Rockwell was talking on the phone.

'Come to my office, now.'

Sam assessed her position in relation to Rockwell's office and began carefully crawling in its direction. She pried open a tile with her fingertips and peered through the slit, but she was positioned over the corridor outside. As she crawled further, she became cognisant of her loud breathing. One incongruent decibel could alert Rockwell to her presence. She stopped crawling when she felt she was above Rockwell's office, regulating her breathing before pulling a tile away a millimetre at a time.

All Sam could see was the first few metres from Rockwell's door, an area doused in a haunting gloom. Beyond her blinkered view, streaks of moonlight suggested the office opened up, but the crawlspace in the roof ended, meaning Sam could not see the main part of the office, an office which sounded absent of Rockwell.

A vibration caused Sam's body to shudder. It was her phone. She had signal and received a message from Leigh. She tilted her head awkwardly towards her pocket so she could read the message which was asking for an update.

Sam heard a cough from the room. Rockwell was suddenly there. She heard no movement, no door opening or closing. Then she heard a knock.

'Enter!' Rockwell answered.

Two people edged into the room. One was a young female conforming to the personal assistant stereotype by wearing smart, tight-fitting clothes holding an iPad. The other was a middle-aged man, bald, with a ginger goatee. His face was dimpled from acne scarring, and his skin was translucent from a lack of sunlight. They stood within Sam's view, but Rockwell remained deeper within his sanctum.

'The police have requested access to Sector Five on account of these animal attacks that you've probably seen in the news. A werewolf, the witnesses say. Ludicrous, it really is, but we need to figure out how we are going to facilitate this visit?'

The two individuals looked like scared school children standing in front of the headmaster's desk.

'Say nothing, then. I'll do all the thinking.'

'Do they know we have the hybrids?' the ginger goateed man asked nervously.

'No.'

'Are we sure that is the case?'

'Yes, because I have spoken with the Chief of Police. The man is an idiot. If they knew about the hybrids, he would have blabbed that piece of information to me. Anyway, it's not a hybrid that's causing these attacks.

God knows what it is. In any case, by the time the police arrive, I want the hybrids gone from the main floor. That project is of the highest secrecy. We can let them see some of our weapons research and development projects instead.'

'Can't we just reject the police's request?'

A paperweight flew inches past the man's temple, chipping the thick mahogany door.

'I know how to handle the fucking police. If we don't let them in, it looks as if we have something to hide, and the last thing I need are any media reports about how we rejected a police visit during an active investigation, especially one as public as this werewolf nonsense. We will invite them in and show them nothing. Use the mountain storage to house the hybrids temporarily. Remove all traces of their existence from the main floor. Start now.'

'Yes, sir.'

The scientist's words wobbled as he left the room, petrified. Rockwell turned to the assistant, who, despite her baby-faced image, appeared unfazed by Rockwell's violent tantrum.

'Elle, I have a task for you. Billy seems shifty. Keep an eye on him. Report back to me if you find anything suspicious.'

'Yes, sir.'

The ceiling tiles oscillated as the door closed behind Elle.

Sam's phone buzzed again.

If you don't respond in twenty minutes, I'm phoning Tom.

Sam used her thumb to type out a response from the rim of her pocket. She paused before sending, but she had made her decision. She was not leaving Strathaven. The archive room was too rich with information to abandon this early. Although Rockwell had dismissed the notion of a werewolf to the two employees in his office, Sam reckoned he could be hiding the truth, with each Sector Five project managed on a need-to-know basis.

References to hybrids and Project Metazoa indicated animals existed in Sector Five, and the archive room was where she could find the details. She sent Leigh a message stating her intention to stay.

Returning her attention to the office, she listened for any sign of movement, but there was nothing. No shuffling, no sniffing, no coughs, no breathing. No one can remain so silent for so long. Rockwell was gone. But how? When his assistant left the room, the thick door caused the roof to vibrate. But there had been no vibration since then. Sam would have felt it. There must be another exit from Rockwell's office.

Sam's thoughts were disturbed by another vibration, localised to her leg. It was Leigh.

You're a fucking crazy bitch, but I love it. Be careful and stay in touch.

June 11th

CHAPTER 30

The firm breeze wafted a pungent smell of seaweed from the docks into the courtyard. Dargo and Bullock were peering at the windows on floors three, four and five of the apartment block, monitoring for any signs of life.

'The blinds on floor three are closed, as they were yesterday.' Dargo said.

'Let's go for it.' Bullock replied.

A resident on the fourth floor buzzed them into the building and after several unanswered knocks on all three doors on level three, Dargo gave his partner a nod of approval. Bullock chapped a final cursory knock on the middle flat door. He adjusted his leather jacket as he took preparatory steps back. He kicked the door ajar, the lock hanging on by a whisker. A light shoulder barge opened the door fully.

'Frightening how easy it is to enter a home.' Bullock said.

'Just as well, because now we can investigate the loud screams we heard coming from inside.'

'Exactly.'

Bullock stepped gingerly into the flat, calling out to make his presence known. The flat was unresponsive.

The short hall led to a gloomy living room where the smell of incense clung to the furniture. Dargo opened the curtains covering the patio doors to the balcony, bringing light to the tidy living space. Bullock inspected the bedroom while Dargo explored the pokey kitchen, but nothing untoward was immediately apparent.

'We might have fucked it here,' said Dargo.

'Nothing a new door, an apology and dinner vouchers can't fix.'

Dargo slid open the balcony doors. The wind growled past him into the living space, adding kelp to the multifarious scents of incense.

'Everything seems normal enough.' Bullock said.

Dargo stepped back inside.

'Except for that.'

Dargo pointed to the bottom corner of the rug on the wall, which now fluttered in the wind, each flap indicating a thick darkness lay beyond.

Dargo threw Bullock a pair of latex gloves. Instinct told them it was time to prevent contaminating any evidence. Bullock lifted the rug to reveal the hole it was covering, allowing Dargo to step into the unknown.

'This goes into the next flat.' Bullock said as he flipped open his pocketknife and stepped through the hole.

Using the torch feature on his phone, Dargo scanned the walls for a light switch. Flicking them on revealed three steel drums containing formaldehyde sitting idle in the middle of the room. The walls were decorated with whips and bondage, resting on hooks like a sex armoury. Dargo felt uneasy in their presence. Like medieval weaponry, the items did not need to be in someone's grasp to illustrate their viciousness.

'It's like a sadist museum.' Bullock said.

A stench resembling raw chicken rotting in the baking sun halted Bullock on his way to the bedroom.

'Fuck sake.' Bullock said, fully aware of what awaited him behind the bedroom door. Pulling his shirt over his nose, he turned on the bedroom light to illuminate a face as grey as stone.

'Tom. Body in here. Been dead for days, maybe a week or two. Looks like Jason Manson, the first boy to go missing.'

Dargo covered his nose. The victim lay on a bloody mattress with his hands and feet bound to each wooden bedpost. Infected lacerations covered his body like mouldy tributaries of a vine. His throat was a deep purple after extreme and repeated strangulations. Painkillers and Viagra pills were scattered over the sink of the accompanying toilet and a heap of bloody towels lay in the bath.

Dargo entered the second bedroom. Another body, this time face down and bound. The obvious murder weapon was the spiked dog collar around the victim's neck. It had a leash attached to it, which the killer pulled to suffocate the boy. The considerable reduction in stench led Dargo to conclude the boy was freshly killed. His skin was red around his buttocks, with dried blood crusting on both cheeks. Dargo checked the identification in his wallet on the bedside table as Bullock arrived in the room.

'Alex McCray, another of our missing boys,' said Dargo.

'How undignified. Facedown and raped with a strap-on, or strap-ons, I should say. What sort of monster are we dealing with here?'

'A murderous sadomasochist.'

'She was keeping them alive to perform violent sexual acts,' said Bullock. 'The necks look too badly bruised for a single strangulation. I reckon she got a kick out of choking them to near death then releasing to let them breathe again. She fed them Viagra if she wanted intercourse and, at other times, raped them using the strap-ons.'

'I agree, but I don't think she necessarily needed them to be alive. The formaldehyde was keeping the dead ones supple for posthumous abuse.'

Bullock paused as he processed Dargo's vulgar summation.

'Check the girth of these things.' Bullock said, pointing to the strap-ons. 'Everything in here is designed for pain. That one has spikes.'

They both winced at the equipment's functionality, their anuses hot with unwelcome imagination. They ventured back to the centre flat, keen to leave the corpse smell.

'Three flats on this floor, Tom.'

Dargo was already thinking along the same lines as he entered the kitchen.

'It's drafty in here.'

Bullock opened his palms to feel where the cold air emanated from. He shuffled the thick fridge freezer with his muckle paws to reveal an archway entrance into the third and final flat on the floor.

'Darren told us he ran through the kitchen and past these beads to try to escape. The fridge freezer must not have been covering this gap that night,' said Dargo.

More weapons of eroticism littered the coffee table and the floor in no discernible order. A drum of formaldehyde was leaning against the sofa, a puddle soaked into the carpet. It was a stark contrast to the other neat living rooms.

Bullock entered the first bedroom. The cadaver was four days dead, his face squished into the pillow and his rear end raised in the air, humiliatingly exposed, primed for penetration.

Dargo entered the second bedroom. The indigo veins of the victim's face were fresh. He was not a forensic pathologist, but Dargo had seen enough strangulations to know that two of the victims were killed within the last twenty-four hours. He hovered over the body. The victim's face was so blue it almost obscured him beyond recognition, but Dargo

165

was certain it was Ryan Etherington, the latest to go missing. Killed mere hours ago.

Dargo's stomach erupted without any tremor warnings. He retched in the bedroom doorway, but nothing surfaced.

'You alright, Tom?' Bullock said, perplexed by the frailty of his normally steely partner. Neither of them had ever been squeamish.

'He was alive when we were here yesterday.'

Dargo moved past Bullock into the middle flat.

'We were right out there. Two of them could have been saved, should have been saved.'

'We don't know that for certain.'

Dargo's face was translucent.

'The girl was here yesterday. She must have heard us press the buzzer and seen us lingering around, then she killed them before she fled.'

Bullock went to speak, but his words were caught by the smack of reality from his partner's analysis. Dargo leaned on the arm of a sofa to compose himself. There was something deeper than the boys' deaths causing his nausea. The deaths were preventable, but why were they not prevented? What was the root cause? He instinctively knew there was an issue, but his mind struggled to structure it.

'I'll call it in.' Bullock said, as he dialled a number on his phone.

Dargo fled for the balcony in search of fresh air. Instead, he inhaled the rotting kelp which rocked him forward in disgust, his hands gripping the corpse cold metal railing.

He looked down at where they stood the day before. They were looking up at a flat that still contained life. If they had kicked the door down, two boys would still be alive.

'We always kick the fucking door down.' Dargo whispered.

The meaning of his words was as metaphorical as they were physical. No matter the situation, he and Bullock never took a closed-door or a rejection at face value. They always ploughed on, smashing any door and banging heads together to make progress.

Dargo's tormented mind now understood why the deaths were not prevented. The blame rested firmly on him. They never kicked down the door because his insatiable desire had shifted, shifted from a need to stop criminals, and superseded by a gambling addiction in which he valued attending the bookies over two boys' lives.

CHAPTER 31

The office rumbled with an energetic bustle. Achebe overheard a peace officer claim Dargo and Bullock had found the killer's flat. For Achebe, the hysteria was distracting. Her superiors' success only emphasised how little progress she had made with her own case, one that was supposed to be a straightforward animal capture; a confidence-boosting introduction into life as a detective. She was embarrassed to be slumped in her chair seven days deep into the investigation and the animal remained unidentifiable.

Amid the chaotic office, she studied photographs taken by Viti and her team at Bannock Manor. One in particular caught her attention. Before collapsing through the flooring in the manor's master bedroom, Achebe's attention had been drawn to an exposed bottom corner of the bedroom wall. Geometrically accurate etchings suggested a grander image lay beneath the plasterboard. She rotated the photograph and raised it to her eye line for closer inspection, but she could not discern the drawings' significance. She grabbed her coat and dragged High Constable Gardyne away from the restless officers. Her desire to leave the office was driven by her need to block out the distractions rather than the urgency of the lead. Tom and Xander were right, she needed her own private office.

*

Far from the choking city walls, the expansive green hills dispelled all junk from Achebe's headspace. Caledonia's scenery had a soothing charm, especially given High Constable Gardyne was navigating the serpentine roads, allowing Achebe to stare out the window and lose herself in its beauty.

'So, what is the sketch on the wall you want us to look at?'

'I don't know. A drawing of some sort. I saw it the last time I was there, but then the floor caved in and I fell through it. We had to leave because of the asbestos risk. I thought I'd bring you along in case a similar incident occurs.'

'So, we are risking our lives for some sketch that is most likely irrelevant?' Gardyne said, protracting his sarcasm.

'Yes. I've brought masks, don't worry.'

'I'm keen to visit the manor for myself if I'm honest. I need to see those scratch marks to believe them. Are the Special Response Unit still there?'

'No. Resources are spread pretty thin at the moment. They remain patrolling Dalmally caravan park given people are still living there, and some are set up at the cryptozoologist camp, using bait to lure the animals there again. Unfortunately, they haven't witnessed anything more dangerous than a fox.'

Gardyne enjoyed the challenge of shifting gears around the bends of the dirt track road towards Bannock Manor. He used the handbrake to drift the rear of the car around the tighter corners.

'Someone's been on the advanced driver's course.'

'Passed three weeks ago.'

'You passed! Well done. Why did you not mention that to me?'

'You're a hotshot detective now. I didn't think you'd be interested in a lowly high constable like me.'

'Fuck off.' Achebe said, slapping Gardyne's arm playfully.

Gardyne avoided the driveway's tyre-popping potholes and parked on the gravel within the crumbling stone wall encircling the mansion. Without the small hubbub of Viti's forensic team and Maynard's armed unit, the place felt colder, as if the house itself was telling visitors it was no longer capable of welcoming guests.

Achebe held a mask in an outstretched hand, waiting for Gardyne to collect it. She remained focused on the manor, entranced by its mystique. Two sharp shrieks caused her to jump. It was only Gardyne's car, releasing its antiquated double beep as he pressed the lock button.

'That sounds like my dad's car from the turn of the century, back when it was a sign of wealth that your car locked without a silver key,' said Achebe.

'I love it. A wee blurt of energy to help you along with your day.'

Gardyne's energy halted when he saw the claw marks on the stairway wall.

'It's one thing calling the witnesses crackpots from the comfort of the office. It changes your outlook when you see the evidence in the flesh, doesn't it?' Achebe said.

'You've got that right.'

Gardyne placed a finger into a talon-carved groove and followed it as they climbed the stairs and stood outside the master bedroom, staring at the gaping hole in the middle of the room. Gardyne muffled through his mask.

'How come no one mentioned you fell through the floor? I would've thought the office banter would have been rife with that chat.'

'I'm all for office banter, but I also realise many of you don't think I should have got this job, so I wasn't going to offer up easy ammunition.'

Gardyne tilted his head back. The face-covering enhanced the emotion in his eyes. They evoked an incredulity that Achebe read as genuine.

'Nikki, it's no secret that a few of us went for the detective role, myself included. Yes, we had our noses put out of joint by the rejection, but please don't mistake our personal disappointment for animosity towards you, and if it has come across like that, then I can only apologise.'

'It's not so much you or Jen. It's the judgement from the peace officers. I can feel their appraisals of unworthiness when I walk into the room.'

'Nikki, I'm twenty-nine, same as you.'

'You've added a year onto me, but who's counting?'

'Whatever, my point is that I was promoted to high constable ahead of officers who were in their mid-thirties, or even older. I felt the exact same as you, still do to a degree. You feel like people are waiting, or rather hoping, you make a mistake, just so they can vindicate their jealous-ridden opinion of you. What you are feeling is normal.'

'How did you get over that? I arrived as a high constable externally, so I never felt the same pressure of being promoted ahead of other officers I had worked with.'

'You just learn to live with it. It drives you forward, pushes you. Do your job diligently, as you are already doing, by the way, and you'll gain their respect eventually. It's not something that you need to focus on. It will come naturally by doing your job well. Plus, you have the respect of Tom and Xander. That's worth more than any envious officer, or high constable.' Gardyne said with a wink.

'Cheers, GG, that means a lot.'

Achebe patted Gardyne on the arm. She disliked being judged, but she also cringed when anyone praised her, always moving quickly to brush it off. This time, however, she was grateful for it.

'Right, what is it you want to show me?' asked Gardyne.

Achebe pointed to a scabby area of plastering at the bottom right of the far wall.

'See that blue marking on the white wall underneath the first layer of plastering?'

'Barely.'

'It's got to be a sketch of some sort. We need to rip off the rest of the plaster.'

Achebe handed Gardyne thick garden gloves.

'Let's get it done.'

As they shimmied around the edge of the room, the gaping hole stared at them. The jagged, splintered wood was like teeth awaiting an unsuspecting victim. They took each step as if walking the plank, tentatively tapping their foot on the floor before committing their full weight.

When they arrived at the wall, Achebe was the first to start tearing away the plaster. The physical labour proved therapeutic, taking her mind off the case, for ten minutes at least. Gardyne tore away the plaster high above Achebe's reach. The markings stretched across the entire wall in varying degrees of faintness. When they finished, they both felt the urge to step backwards to take it all in. Achebe saw Gardyne's leg move.

'Stop! You'll fall down the hole. Shuffle back round to the door.'

From the doorway, they viewed the entire wall, but the diagrams, measurements and scribblings were still unintelligible. Achebe took photos with her phone. She zoomed in on various sections.

'What is it?' asked Gardyne.

'I can't say for certain, but I think it might be sketches of the escapology trick that led to the owner of Bannock Manor's death.'

'This is how he was meant to do it.'

'Well, if you look at this section.' Achebe pointed to a close-up photo of the left side of the wall. 'This looks like the box he would be locked in and the various methods of escape.'

They continued studying the pictures on Achebe's phone. Gardyne crouched, zooming in on the bottom sections of the wall. He stood, looking at Achebe as if to speak, but his intentions were halted by a sound resonating through the bedroom's glassless window.

Crisp footsteps and scraping gravel tightened their bones as if listening to nails down a blackboard. So incongruent to the usual sounds of the forest, the atmosphere was gripped by a sinister aura.

Achebe put a finger over her masked lips. She lightly dabbed her feet as she moved towards the shoogly bannister, conscious not to force the floorboards to creak. As she delicately planked across the top of the stairs to peer around the thick bannister stanchion, the floorboards exerted an imperceptible groan.

Staring through the vacant doorway, Achebe's skin turned to frost. An invisible hand grabbed her heart to prevent the sound of the beat.

Taller than any human, it stood at an intimidating eight feet.

Dirty brown fur.

Tangerine eyes.

Ears perked up as if listening for radio signals.

A radar snout capable of scenting prey from miles away.

Rippling muscles.

Bulbous thighs.

Talons sharper than carving knives.

A claw that could kill with a single swipe.

It was a fucking werewolf.

Achebe shuddered uncontrollably. She wanted to move, but she also wanted to savour the moment, if savour was the right term for embracing this incredible, jaw-dropping, reality-bursting creature.

Dragging a dead sheep by the brain, mutton blood dripped from the hairs of its chin; snarling teeth stained with death. It stopped at the three stone steps outside the front door. The sheep dropped with a thud, and the beast began tearing at the lifeless mutton, growling as it wrestled with each limb.

Although blind to the werewolf, Gardyne's chest began oscillating faster when he heard bone-crunching chews. Their wafer-thin protective masks felt pathetic in the presence of a far greater threat. Achebe removed hers as she moved back across the landing.

'Stay calm,' she whispered. 'We need to go out the bedroom window, onto the ledge and jump at an opportune moment.'

Thud!

The bannister shuddered.

Thud!

The beast took another slow, monstrous step.

Thud!

It was ascending the stairs.

Achebe and Gardyne grabbed each other's arms. They were mere seconds from its view. It can smell us, Achebe thought as she ushered Gardyne into the bedroom and shuffled towards the glassless window.

'We can't jump that, Nikki.' Gardyne whispered.

Achebe looked out the window. The height was greater than she had initially eyeballed when entering the building. A suboptimal landing could cause a broken leg or twisted ankle, and then they really were at the mercy of the beast.

Thud!

The top of the stairs was visible from their position in the bedroom. They clung to the wall as if trying to camouflage against the paintwork. Heavy thuds continued ascending. Pointed ears and thick chestnut fur appeared through the slats of the bannister.

Thud!

Gardyne began hyperventilating. His efforts to reduce the sound of his breathing made the flow of air through his body erratic. Achebe's heart was pumping against the edges of her skin and her breathing quickly fell out of sequence, gulping as she struggled to regain rhythm. Gardyne's body gyrated. The fear was taking control, rendering him useless to Achebe. They had to brave the jump onto the uneven stones below. There was no other option.

Achebe stepped up to the window, assessing their distance to the car. Then an idea sparked in her mind like lightning splitting dark clouds. She stood back in the room and plunged her hands deep into Gardyne's trouser pockets. He was too terrified to notice as she pulled out his car keys and pressed the button to unlock the car. It responded with the irritating beep she had mocked him for.

The werewolf collapsed on all fours once it heard the noise. It spun and stared down the stairs, prowling with uncertainty. Achebe pressed the button to lock the car. A double beep followed, luring the werewolf towards the sound. Achebe watched from the window as the werewolf bound to the car, growling and scratching at its veneer.

Achebe grabbed Gardyne's hand to peel him off the wall.

'Downstairs now.' Achebe whispered.

'No chance.'

'Fucking move.'

Achebe ran down the stairs, clicking the lock and unlock buttons as many times as she could to keep the werewolf distracted. Through the door frame, Gardyne caught his first glimpse of the beast slashing at his car. Achebe dragged him into the front room, next to the pile of broken wood from the collapsed ceiling. They had their backs to the wall, unable to see the beast.

'Now what? That thing will smell us.'

'More likely to hear us if you don't control your breathing.'

Achebe picked up a thick piece of wood, half a metre long. She pressed the lock button one more time to ensure the werewolf was adequately occupied as she moved into the hall and threw the wood towards the top of the stairs.

It landed with a thump and was answered by a growl as the beast hunted the noise. A backdraft of air funnelled into the front room as the beast rushed through the hallway.

Achebe's breathing wobbled. Gardyne closed his eyes. Death never felt so close. Life never felt so terminal.

The werewolf climbed the stairs and sniffed at the disturbance. Achebe and Gardyne were frozen against the wall. They were sitting ducks should the creature turn around. She knew they should move, but her body would not shift. Despite its horror, an untimely fascination struck Achebe as she examined its extraordinary height and rippling muscles. She likened it to being in Chobe national park. There was no substitute, not even a zoo or safari park, for seeing a lion in the wild. Its breathtaking presence left everyone awestruck. The creature before her was no less magnificent.

Achebe knew the creature would soon become bored with the piece of wood, so they had to move. She glanced at Gardyne. His eyes were still shut, and he was mouthing something in Italian. He was preparing for death.

The creature's hip leaned into the bannister as it examined the piece of wood with its snout. Unbeknown to the beast, the bannister wilted under its weight, creaking in pain as it fell with a crash. The werewolf jolted in shock. Enraged, it exhaled a deep, disturbing growl of discontent. The noise pinned Achebe and Gardyne so ferociously against the wall it could have swallowed them.

Achebe tried to regain focus as the werewolf clawed its way upstairs, out of their line of sight. Its departure sparked Achebe's mind into action.

'We have to go now. You are driving.'

Achebe placed the car keys in Gardyne's hands. They needed a speedy getaway and, as Gardyne had driven to the manor, the seat was too far back for her to reach the pedals. Every second counted, so adjusting the seat was not a luxury she would have if the werewolf attacked the car.

'Run.'

Achebe ran so fast she forgot to breathe, gasping as the humid air turned her mouth into an oven. She felt sick, but her legs kept running. Her ears were open, but she refused to look back. Gardyne forked away towards the driver's seat. He clicked the unlock button. No! It's too early, Achebe thought.

The car beep was followed by an agitated growl. At the passenger door, Achebe granted herself a millisecond glance behind, enough to witness the werewolf jump from the bedroom window. Its shock-absorbent feet landed on the gravel with ease and the eyes of death lay upon her as the creature bound towards the car.

Achebe shut the car door so fast she almost caught her trailing leg. The beast jumped on the boot. Each toenail cracked the windscreen like darts. Its claws punctured the roof of the car, the end of one talon inches from Gardyne's crown.

'Start the car.'

The rumble of the engine scared the beast enough to jump off. Achebe tracked the creature as it ran away from Gardyne's window, perhaps too scared of the engine to continue its attack.

Achebe was wrong.

The werewolf charged just as Gardyne pulled away. Its head smashed into the driver's door. Achebe heard a crack, like a twig snapping underfoot. Gardyne wailed. The dent in the door had crushed his leg, causing a clean break above his ankle. His foot was now limp and useless, and the car stalled as his other foot came off the clutch. They were a sitting feast.

'Restart the car.'

'I can't. My leg is broken.'

Achebe did not have time to assess the situation before the passenger window smashed and an intrusive clump of brown fuzz brushed against her left cheek. The werewolf's head was above her lap. The jaws popped as it tried to wriggle its head into a biting position, but it could not manoeuvre its neck successfully.

Achebe punched the snout, causing various bones in her fingers to shatter. The beast was solid, undeterred by the impact. She slipped onto Gardyne's lap, careful to manoeuvre away from the beast's snapping jaws. Gardyne howled due to Achebe's weight pressing on his broken leg.

Placing one hand on the dashboard and the other around Gardyne's headrest, Achebe leveraged her legs in midair and kicked the werewolf on the tip of the nose, causing it to recoil. Its head scraped against the edges of the window frame as it retreated.

Achebe fiddled the gearstick and restarted the engine. Gardyne's teeth were grinding in pain as Achebe sat on the edge of his thigh and pressed the accelerator. She checked the wing mirror to witness an increasingly distant werewolf on all fours, shaking the pain away from her kick. She kept checking her mirrors, conscious that such a fast-moving creature could easily catch up with a car that was meandering across a driveway that had more craters than the surface of the moon.

Despite Gardyne's constant wailing, she refused to stop until she was sure the creature was not following them. She repositioned herself further back onto Gardyne's thigh to take the pressure off his broken limb.

'I'd stick to the girls at the titty bar if you want a less painful lap dance.'

CHAPTER 32

Dargo sat at the now permanently reduced Midnight Club. Bert's posture was more sombre than usual as he placed chips on his favoured numbers. Connor rested his head in his left hand. He was present in body, but not in spirit. Ronan's death toyed with him, manipulating his thoughts as candidly as Bert was clinking his chips.

Dargo was agitated. His mind was on Ronan, but not specifically about Ronan. It was his own life projected on top of Ronan's that caused his leg to bounce anxiously. A family man with an accomplished career and multiple properties. All lost. Lost to an addiction which sought an implausibly fleeting winner's thrill versus a dishonourable list of far greater losses. Ronan might be dead, but his presence haunted the table.

Connor cracked the silence first.

'Can we please stop pretending?'

Bert blinked a second too long. He showed flickers of sorrow for the man he shared a table with for years, but dissecting Ronan's demise was not something he wanted to address. In the absence of an answer, Connor tried again.

'Can we stop fuckin' pretending?'

His chips fell out of his hands. A few rolled across the roulette table.

'Game in play. No more bets, sir,' said the croupier, unaware of the trauma Connor was alluding to.

'Is that right? No more bets?'

Connor grabbed the ball out of the spinning wheel.

'See this, this wee pearl of misery. It should be called peril, P-E-R-I-L, cause that's all it fucking brings. That's all this whole fucking place brings.'

'Sir, please. Put the pill back, or I will call security.'

'A pill? A fucking pill. This wee thing is called a pill. What joker came up with that name? Did you know the ball was called a pill?' Connor asked the Midnight Club.

Neither Dargo nor Bert reacted. Connor continued.

'How very apt. Just another addictive pill. Take one of these and I'll escape all my troubles, will I?'

To the disbelief of Connor's newly acquired audience from the other tables, he swallowed the pill with five gulps of his beer.

'No more fucking bets,' he declared.

Security was running down the stairs from the entrance. Connor looked at Dargo with watering eyes.

'Why are we fucking pretending like nothing's happened?'

The security guards flung their arms under Connor's armpits and dragged him out without a struggle. His despondent stare rested on Dargo until the automatic exit doors closed.

Dargo knew he was right. The drug-dealing teenager was the only one with the clarity to realise how absurd their decision to return to the casino was. Ronan's death was a poignant warning to them all, and yet here they were, jumping into the same turbulent waters their friend just drowned in. Dargo felt queasy, the same nauseous feeling he felt upon finding the four dead boys tied to the bedposts. His body shivered with sickening guilt.

'Gentlemen, if you would like to move to the other table, you can continue playing.'

'We are not moving tables. Fetch another pill.'

Bert's words were definite. The croupier obsequiously scurried off.

'You've gone white.' Bert remarked.

'I feel sick.'

Bert never responded as he watched the detective struggle to compose himself. If Dargo were not sitting down, he would have fainted. He leaned forward to avoid swaying over the edge of the backless stool. He opened his mouth, but he was too scared to utter the question, and even more terrified to hear the answer.

'Bert.'

His voice wobbled. Bert glanced up at him. Despite sitting at the table for almost three years with the man, Dargo realised he had rarely looked his hunched, insular companion in the eyes. His grey pupils evoked a man weathered by enduring pain. They made Dargo feel ordinary. He was merely a human stencil that Bert had seen drawn too many times in all his years of gambling. Dargo was not a Jovial, or a Blunder, or even a Habitual. He did not levitate above the categories, as he once thought. He was in a fourth category. A category oblivious to those who are in it. The Deluded category.

'I need you to be honest. Do I have a gambling problem?'

'That's a question only you can answer.'

'But you know the signs.'

'So do you.'

'But you can see them, see them in me, can't you?'

'You have to look at yourself.'

'For fuck's sake, Bert. Will you just answer me?'

Dargo's raised voice darkened Bert's pupils, as if possessed by a demon. He hunched over the table and played with his chips again. A tired wave of his hand signalled the approaching croupier to leave them alone.

'You want my analysis?'

'Yes.'

'My analysis is you walked through those doors seeking a small relief from your normal life, like so many others who join this place. Ronan was the same. He also started off playing paltry sums just for fun. But slowly, his stakes grew, and so did his aversion to risk, so he lost his gains and chased his losses. You bet between twenty to fifty per spin?'

Dargo nodded, although the question was rhetorical.

'Ronan was betting at that level two years ago, if you remember. Like the frog that doesn't realise it's boiling alive as the temperature slowly rises, you don't realise you are becoming more and more addicted with every play. Do you know how much you've spent since joining?'

Dargo knew roughly.

'Between forty to fifty grand.'

'Forgive me as I venture into hard-hitting territory here, but you asked for my analysis. I don't know what a detective earns, but I know it won't be staggering. I know you have a wife, a kid with university aspirations, and probably a mortgage. So, for you to have spent fifty grand, and the rest,...' Bert supplemented the damning words with a glare. '...with all your other living expenses, you can't sustain that without compromising other funds. What's your source? Credit cards? Payday loans? Savings?'

'I intend to pay it back.'

Bert snorted and shook his head.

'Your job is to snuff out people's lies, but you don't notice the lies you're telling yourself.'

It was Dargo's turn to hunch over the table as the reality grew heavier.

'I borrowed money from my son's university fund.'

'There you go again. Borrowed. You borrowed nothing. You took it.'

'I will pay it back.'

'How much?'

'Twenty thousand.'

Bert shut his eyes in despair.

'Ronan fell over the edge of the waterfall, but don't for a minute believe you are on dry land. You are sitting in the rubber dinghy with your back to the danger, and you're in for a nasty fall. If you really want my advice, you find a way to return that money to the savings account. Never tell your wife or son you took it in the first place. You have to admit your addiction, but do not admit you took the money. It's the mistrust that kills the family, not the addiction. You still have a chance of recovery. Don't become Ronan. And when you walk out those doors tonight, don't come back.'

Dargo rose to leave. He wanted to thank Bert, but knew his gratitude was unwanted. Bert was a lost soul, and Dargo suspected if he had the mental capacity to turn a gun on himself, as Ronan had, he would have pulled the trigger many years ago.

'See you at Ronan's funeral,' was all Dargo could muster to an unresponsive Bert.

CHAPTER 33

Sam operated like a mouse nibbling on leftover food as she silently sifted through the multitude of boxes in the archive room, struggling to digest all the information in one sitting. Most of the files she read that day focused on military weapons and stealth vehicle designs. Others contained information on anthrax and other crippling nerve agents. None of it was revelatory. It was common knowledge that while politicians smiled, shook hands and signed peace treaties, they were all preparing weaponry that could inflict maximum pain.

Having napped surprisingly well underneath the desks in the archive room, Sam started the day cautiously, meticulously repacking and returning each file on the shelves. But, given her fingertips blackened upon touching each dust-covered box, she deduced the archive room was barely used, and as she became more relaxed in her new surroundings, she removed the wig and brown contact lenses and shortlisted the more intriguing projects on the desks. Despite her efforts, she was unable to locate a box labelled Project Metazoa, or find anything related to a carnivorous beast.

As midnight approached, Sam cast her mind to the previous evening, when Rockwell had vanished from his office using an exit other than his front door. A murmuration of starlings burst inside her stomach as the mischievous part of her brain told her that sneaking into his room was imperative. He can't be working this late two nights in a row, she thought. The excitement agitated her heavy bladder, having drank her solitary bottle of water down to its final drips. Her belly also rumbled with discontent. Getting into Rockwell's office was not just about uncovering Sector Five's secrets, it was about finding food.

Sam delicately crawled across the roof's metal lattice to Rockwell's office, judging the direction perfectly. Prying open a roof tile by an inch, she waited for five minutes. No one was in the gloomy office. She removed the roof tile and slowly lowered into the room. After a quick scan for life, she used an umbrella leaning by the door to move the roof tile back into place.

Sam gasped as she turned. Rockwell's office opened up, just as she guessed. What she did not expect was to be stepping into an observatory. The stars sparkled magical dust through the fenestrated dome ceiling. At ground level, glass doors placed within a white marble viaduct provided a view of the moonlit valley, and thick mahogany bookshelves lined the other half of the circular office.

A robust wooden desk with meandering carvings sat pride of place in the centre of the room. Sam began opening the heavy drawers. The top one was locked. Another contained stationery. The next stored an abundance of fudge. Sam ate a cube and stowed some in her backpack for later.

As Sam reached down to open the bottom drawer, she froze. A figure lingered in her peripheral vision. Their face was obscured. Their arms outstretched. A menacing scythe raised above their heads. Sam spun around, throwing a stapler from Rockwell's desk at the assailant. But they were unmoved. Luckily for Sam, white marble sculptures had a habit of standing still. She exhaled relief, a detailed outline of the sculpture forming as her eyes adjusted to the darkness. Curiously unnerved by its presence, she edged closer. The cloaked figure was ten feet tall with huge wings spread intimidatingly behind its back. It was an angel of death.

'What sort of freak keeps this in their office?' she whispered.

The angel's disturbing aura followed Sam as she inspected a whisky decanter sparkling on a bookshelf. Not her first choice, but she would drink it if nothing else was forthcoming. Then a whimsical idea squiggled out from the most mischievous depths of her mind once again. She grabbed the decanter, popped the glass top, and placed it on the floor. After a deep breath, Sam performed the garland pose to release a liquid similar in colour to the murky orange whisky.

'Wet your whistle with this, dickhead.'

Droplets of urine dribbled down the glass and blotched the lush carpet, but not significant enough for Rockwell to notice.

181

Feeling five stone lighter, Sam scavenged the cupboards along the bottom of the bookshelves. One contained a tin of shortbread. Even this ravenous, the bland biscuit was unappealing. Opening the next cupboard door sent a chill across her shins as a blue light escaped into the room.

'Jackpot!'

The mini-fridge was filled with water, chocolate, chicken Caesar salad and sandwiches. Sam stashed some supplies into her backpack for later, excited that her time in Sector Five was no longer dictated by her need for nourishment.

Sam pulled on the last cupboard door.

'Shit!'

Sam covered her head, bracing for impact as the top of the bookshelf shifted, ready to topple on top of her. She cowered, but there was no impact. The top of the bookshelf moved, not because it was loose, but because it was not a cupboard at all. The entire unit was a door.

'You sly bastard, Rockwell.'

A frightening draft shivered Sam's bone as she pulled the rest of the bookcase open. Stone stairs spiralled downwards into an abyss. The passage was cavernous with damp walls and slippery steps. As Sam descended, the path remained dark and unwelcoming.

At the bottom of the steps, filament lighting emitted a stinging indigo into the grey corridor. Huge glass panels embedded into the rocky structure lined each side of the corridor, like the reptile house at the zoo.

Sam's ears tuned into a faint nursery rhyme; a chilling instrumental of Pop Goes the Weasel. Her teeth chattered under the cold, then clenched in reaction to an anguished wail. Human or animal, she did not know.

Peering in the first window, Sam shrieked. A person stared back. Her presence in Sector Five was known, but her safety was still intact. The face looking back was blackened and bloodied from radiation exposure. The figure of indeterminable gender lay on a bed. Their arms and legs moved slowly, like a creaky animatronic whose power was waning. Their mouth was constantly agape under the enduring torture, but their brain still longed for oxygen. The eyes staring at Sam were desperate; kill me.

Sam felt nauseous. She never knew a living person could look so ravished.

In the next window, a man lay twitching and jerking unpredictably, protruding bones threatening to pierce their skin with each jolt. The man exhaled short whimpers each time his body convulsed. Sam looked for an entry point into the room. She pressed the glass at various points and checked the rock walls on each side of the window, but there was nothing. She looked away, ashamed to walk on, leaving the man to suffer.

Sam's shoulders rolled as she hyperventilated to stop herself from bawling at the sight in the next window. She composed herself to a murmuring sob as she pressed a soothing hand on the unbreachable window to comfort the dying soul on the other side. Fixed to a sloping bed, the woman's veins were a mixture of deep purple and ivy green as multiple intravenous drips pumped noxious liquid into her. Sam could not decipher the chemical symbols labelled on the canisters of liquid, but it did not take a scientist to see the effect was killing the human test subject at an agonisingly slow rate.

Sam bowed her head as she continued down the corridor. She felt useless, unable to support the human lab rats. There was no entry into any room, and even if she found an access point, there was no way of knowing if it was safe to expose herself to the chemicals present in each cell. Even if it were safe, the only help she could realistically provide would be to end their already terminal existence.

The sickening feeling tightened in Sam's chest as she observed the next victim lying motionless with an uncountable number of needles pierced into their skin. The only sign of life was the movement of his left index finger, twitching with each wave of pain.

Tears blurred Sam's vision. She rested her back against the rocky support in between two windows. She needed to compose herself before carrying on. The pause allowed a moment of mental clarity to squeeze through. The barbaric corridor was mere feet away from Rockwell's private office, his en suite of personal experiments. Very few scientists would ever be allowed in the secret hallway. Only those Rockwell could trust, or rather, control, would interact with the human subjects. The arrogant megalomaniac saw himself as the angel of death.

Sam continued down the tunnel. It was nearing an end, with another set of stone stairs winding up to the left. Two more windows remained. The perpetual nursery rhyme grew louder.

Sam stepped back from the glass, aghast. The tears started again, and this time there was no composing herself. Behind both panes were twelve cots, each containing babies with significant disfigurements: extra fingers and toes, missing limbs, deformed facial features. Sam observed twenty-four heart-wrenching images. Some babies were standing in their cots, others lay staring at the ceiling, some slept still, so still that Sam believed they were dead.

A baby with a swollen, oblong head stood at the foot of their cot. They pointed a hand with six fingers towards Sam before slumping back into the cushioned cot as it struggled under its own weight.

Sam broke down in tears in the centre of the dungeon. The secret passage was a gateway to Hell, where torture was delivered morning, noon, and night. The victims' pain was unrelenting, each praying they would not wake up the next time they blinked. From the opposite chamber, a baby cried over the nursery rhyme. Sam turned but was startled by a sudden, tormented wail from one of the preceding rooms. She crouched to the floor, holding her head to block out the horror she stood within.

Eventually, smearing tears away from her glistening cheeks, she held her phone up to the glass.

'I'm so sorry, but I need to take these pictures so I can put a stop to all of this. I can't help you now, but I promise to help you soon.'

June 12th

CHAPTER 34

'Nikki's here.'

Achebe stopped sooking the residual coffee on the disposable cup lid. Her smiling colleagues formed a guard of honour at the front of the office and began a greenside applause. High Constable Robinson whistled, and some male officers began howling like wolves. Achebe winced as Robinson squeezed her tight, unperturbed by the steaming hot coffee. Or the fact Achebe's right hand was bandaged after punching the beast's solid snout.

'I'm so glad you're safe, Nikki. Gio told us all about it.'

High Constable Gardyne waved from a swivel chair; his broken leg stretched out in a moon boot cast. Achebe weaved amongst the applause and adulations to reach him.

'You should be at home resting.' she said.

'So should you.'

Achebe hugged Gardyne.

'I'm sorry, Gio.'

'Sorry?'

'For your leg. If I hadn't asked you to join me....'

'Steady on, boss. You asked me to follow up with a lead, as any diligent detective would do.' he winked. 'You saved my life. You have nothing to be sorry about.'

Gardyne's eyes glowed with emotional gratitude.

'We saved each other. If it wasn't for your beeping car, I'm not sure how we would've escaped.'

A fresh-faced officer punched an excitable question into the air.

'Go on, tell us what animal it was, then?'

Achebe and Gardyne shared a hesitant look. Both had tortured themselves since the incident, replaying the scene over and over in desperate and unsuccessful attempts to comprehend the alien creature they had confronted.

'It certainly appeared to be a new species of wolf. If I'm honest, I'm struggling to fathom what we saw.'

Achebe's words sobered the room. Hearing one of their own confirm an unidentifiable beast was alive and killing was not something they could shrug off as shocked witness testimony. The paw prints, the claw marks at Bannock Manor, the fatal gashes to the dead victims. All had been rationalised to conclude the beast was a figment of the witness' imagination, or an imported predator, or a hoax. But that merely deluded them into the reality they wanted, a reality in which a rational explanation for the flesh-hungry creature existed. Yet, it was the impossible, the incredulous, that was the reality.

Chief Thorne's head almost brushed the doorframe of his office. He was on the phone but glared in Achebe's direction. He pointed his bony finger towards her to remove all doubt whose attention he sought. Achebe sidestepped past him into his office.

'I'll phone you back in ten,' Thorne said, as he hung up the phone. 'Take a seat, Nikki.'

Even after previously glimpsing the Chief's frailties as a leader, his stature and seniority still held enough gravitas that Achebe felt duty bound to impress him.

'How are you doing?' he asked.

'I'm good, sir. Thanks for asking. We got lucky yesterday. I'm relieved Gio is okay.'

'Yes, I spoke to him this morning. It sounds like you did a stellar job.'

The Chief paused, staring at the ground with his chin resting on his knuckle.

'So, this beast. What is it?'

'I'm honestly not sure, sir. If I can speak candidly away from the officers. Based on its appearance, I can understand why the witnesses described it as a werewolf.'

'But it can't be a werewolf. They don't exist.'

'Yes, but I can understand why. It was a wolf that could walk on its hind legs.'

The Chief nodded.

'I've been on the phone to Maynard's unit. He says you've requested they set up around Bannock Manor.'

'Yes, I think it is our best shot of catching the beast. Setting traps at the other attack sites has not proved effective. The beast may have only stumbled across those areas, but it appears to have visited the manor on more than one occasion.'

'Good. Just catch this bloody thing, Nikki. We can't have any more incidents.'

'Yes, sir. Did you get a chance to approve my visit to Strathaven's Sector Five?'

'Yes, I was going to speak to you about that. I don't think it is an avenue worth pursuing.'

'But, sir. I...'

The Chief raised a hand, signalling Achebe to stop talking.

'However, I have spoken to Dr Rockwell, and he has agreed to welcome you, and you only, to Sector Five. He will personally show you around.'

'Thank you, sir.'

'You will be entering a top-secret facility. You cannot disclose anything you see there to anyone, and as such, you must sign this non-disclosure agreement before entering.'

The Chief slid a multi-page document across his desk, folded over so the signature page was on top.

'Can I read it first?'

'It's standard stuff. I sign them all the time.'

Nikki flicked the stapled document to the first page, scanning through four pages within seconds. The words *sworn to silence, criminal offence, imprisonment, and life sentence* jumped from the paper. She got the gist and scribbled an unintelligible name on the dotted line as she struggled to grip the pen in her bandaged hand.

'Might have to learn to write with my left.'

The Chief showed little sympathy, sliding the document back towards him.

'One last thing. Rockwell is a friend of mine, and he is doing you a favour by giving you special access to Sector Five. Don't go pissing him off.'

'Yes, sir.'

Achebe left the Chief's office, making a beeline for Dargo and Bullock's room, muttering angrily in her mind. People have lost their lives. It was not a privilege to gain access to Sector Five. It was a fucking necessity.

As Achebe entered, she sensed Dargo and Bullock were in the midst of bouncing ideas off each other, unpicking their own case. Bullock was pacing widths while Dargo was slumped in his chair with unkempt hair and dark rings around his eyes. Sleep had evaded him for a further night.

'Sorry. I can come back....'

Bullock grabbed Achebe by the shoulder of her suit before she could finish, holding her as if she were a t-shirt in a retail store he wanted Dargo's opinion on.

'Didn't we say Nikki had the, the, how do I say in a politically correct manner?'

'You can say balls, sir. You don't have to be PC around me.'

'Minerals. Didn't we say Nikki had the minerals for this job, Tom?'

Dargo smiled, but Achebe detected his affable gesture was struggling through more important matters that were occupying his mind.

'It's good to see you looking well, Nikki.' said Dargo.

Achebe wished she could reciprocate with candour.

Bullock let go of her as he perched in his usual position atop the filing cabinets.

'So, what was the animal?' asked Bullock.

'I hate to say it, but it looked like your classic depiction of a werewolf. It could walk on two legs, run on four, was over eight feet tall, large snout, teeth and claws sharp enough to rip the car roof open.'

Dargo and Bullock watched Achebe as she lost herself to mental replays of the werewolf.

'Whatever this creature is,' Bullock said, 'it's not just magically appeared after years of living in Bannock forest. We would have known about it by now if it was.'

'I wouldn't be so sure. I was doing more research on rare creatures while I was getting bandaged up in the hospital. There are regions of the Mongolian desert where the locals don't venture because they are convinced, no, they know, that a bipedal man-like creature exists. Almas, they are called. They do not fear this creature. They respect it and its environment, allowing almas to have their own space.'

'You really went down the conspiracy rabbit hole, Nikki.' Bullock said.

'I have to. Nothing about these attacks makes sense. The creature I saw did not make sense. It was not from the same world I grew up in. To be clear, I'm not being drawn in by the ludicrous bigfoot sightings in North America. I'm aware all those claims are hoaxes created by sad individuals seeking attention, money, and fame. But, even taking it down a level from

189

almas. There are reports of the thylacine in Australia's outback, a creature believed to be extinct since the nineteen-thirties. Who's to say that within the hundreds of miles of Bannock forest, this creature has not been happily evading humans until eventually, over time, the caravan sites, the forestry plants, the hamlets crept further within the forest's boundaries?'

Achebe cut a tortured figure.

'Keep pushing on your instincts, Nikki,' said Dargo. 'On a more positive note, Gio could not speak highly enough of you earlier. I don't think you need to worry about endearing yourself to the officers anymore. You not only have their respect, they are in awe of you.'

'You'll go down in folklore.' Bullock said. 'The werewolf slayer.'

Achebe smiled, but it was too soon for praise so quickly after flirting with death. She was acutely aware of how lucky she and Gardyne had been, and it made living feel uncomfortable, as if she had cheated death. Her mum had thanked god when she visited the hospital, a gesture she would normally scoff at, and yet she felt someone needed to be thanked for keeping her alive. It was not all her own doing.

Achebe directed the conversation back to the encounter. Talking about it helped process the harrowing experience.

'What struck me most about the beast was how strong it was physically. I've witnessed lions charging safari trucks in Botswana. They can make a fair dent in the vehicle, but they normally back off after one charge against a relatively unforgiving surface. This wolf thing was on a different level, though. It jumped out a top-floor window and charged twice without showing any signs of injury. Only when I kicked it in the snout did it retreat.'

'Like tapping a dog on the nose.' Bullock said.

'Exactly.'

'Every creature has its weakness.'

'What's your next plan of action?' Dargo asked.

'I've spoken with Maynard. I want the Special Response Unit surrounding the manor for the next few days, starting tonight. We know it, or perhaps more accurately, they have visited the manor many times before. The one we saw was dragging a sheep into the manor as if finding a quiet spot to eat. I'm guessing the wolf, or at least this particular wolf, uses the house as some sort of den or sanctuary.'

'Hopefully often enough for Maynard's unit to be there when it returns. Sounds like a good plan, Nikki.'

'Thanks. I'm also heading up to Morven Asylum.'

'Checking yourself into the madhouse?' Bullock asked.

'Would be a nice holiday from all this. In truth, I'm following up on Jen's background research into the manor. I have a hunch about these wolf creatures and I'm wondering if the former Bannock Manor groundsman can help we with it.'

'Does he work at the asylum now?'

'No, he is a resident of the asylum. He has permanent brain damage after a lawnmower propeller spun off and sliced his head, so I'm not sure how useful the trip is going to be, but I can only try. The Chief has also approved my visit to Sector Five. I just signed the NDA.'

'Has Sam done her visit yet?'

'She's still in there. It's been two nights now.'

Dargo and Bullock looked at each other and laughed.

'She's fucking mental.' Bullock said.

'Is she okay?' Dargo asked, simultaneously impressed and concerned.

'She messaged the burner phone saying she doesn't have much signal, but she had found an archive room containing thousands of files on Sector Five's projects. She's working her way through them, trying to find something that could relate to these attacks.'

'Sounds like she's hit the jackpot. Let us know if she comes into any trouble.' Dargo said. 'We'll protect her if she's caught.'

Bullock nodded in agreement, still grinning at Sam's brazenness.

'How's your case going?' Achebe asked.

Achebe noticed Dargo slump deeper into his chair. Bullock ran his hands through his soft hair before he spoke.

'We have four dead boys in their late teens, early twenties. All were killed after being tortured and raped by the killer, a female killer.'

'I heard the scene was pretty gruesome. Rare to come across a female killer, let alone one that tortures and rapes male victims.'

'Caledonia seems to be a breeding ground for killers these days: Bob Huskins, a female sadist, and your unidentifiable beast. It's a dangerous auld time.'

'She's extremely methodical and calculated in her approach,' said Dargo. 'Which makes the fact she released a potential victim so strange.'

'She's a psychopath, Tom. Her victims need to meet certain criteria, and Darren didn't.'

'What criteria is that?' Achebe asked.

'His dick was too small,' Bullock said. 'All four victims were strong, muscular individuals, and were well-hung, I suppose. It's as if she got a thrill from taking down the most macho guys possible.'

'Even so, letting Darren go was an erratic move.' Dargo said. 'But at the same time, her relative comfort in releasing him makes me think she will have planned for a scenario where the flats become compromised. She will have a place, or places, to escape to.'

'Do you think she's still in the city?' asked Bullock.

'No. She will leave the city to regroup. She will kill again, though. It's just a case of when and where.'

'Do you think she could go abroad?' Achebe asked.

'No. She'll avoid high-security areas like airports and ferry terminals. She'll go rural. Highlands or the Borders. I don't know which.'

Achebe marvelled at Dargo's assuredness in his character analysis. He might be off-kilter in terms of mood, but his criminal profiling was as shrewd as ever.

'All security footage from the city centre bus stations has to be checked to see if we can spot her and find out where she is going. She will have taken a bus. Train stations have more security, and the bus is cheaper, easier to pay in cash. She won't be using a bank card that can be traced back to her.'

'No name?' Achebe asked.

'The flats are registered to a Ms Liv Sibine, but that doesn't match anyone on our systems. We need to get a team to find out where she sourced the sex equipment.' Dargo reminded Bullock.

'Oh, could you maybe give that work to Constable Edmunds? I had a conciliatory chat with him after his outburst at my first meeting. I said if he apologised for his behaviour in front of everyone, then I'd give him more responsibility, but I have had nothing substantial to give him.'

'Has he apologised?' Dargo asked.

'Now that you ask, I'm not sure.'

'Fuck him.' Bullock said. 'I'll ask him, and if he hasn't, he's getting a transfer. We are not putting up with that sort of behaviour. You've given him a second chance, and if he's not apologised, then he's blown it.'

'Fair enough.'

Achebe backed up towards the door. As fascinating as it would be to stay and watch the famous detective duo bat ideas like an investigative tennis match, her presence was no longer required.

'I'll leave you two to it.'

As Achebe walked out of the main office, High Constable Robinson interlocked their arms.

'Fancy lunch?'

'Oh, I'm already heading out for lunch, sorry.'

'Plans, huh? Who with?'

'Just a friend,' Achebe said, not disclosing to Robinson that it was with Ash, the mysterious man she had met in the jazz bar.

Robinson placed the back of her hand on Achebe's cheek.

'Check you getting all hot and flustered. You can tell me about him later. Here's a mint for after you've eaten. Don't want your breath to be all smelly for the post-lunch smooch.'

'That's not going to happen.'

Achebe took the mint, but Robinson had freshened more than just her breath. An idea was spinning like an eddy in her mind with no purpose or endpoint until eventually it was sucked away, leaving just the niggling feeling of a missed opportunity. Whatever the notion was, Achebe hoped it was bubbling away in her semi-conscious, ready to reappear.

CHAPTER 35

The anxious moisture on Dargo's fingertips made it impossible for his phone to accept his biometrics. Instead, he unlocked his phone by typing his passcode. His stomach grumbled in anger. He had not eaten for over a day, but the thought of eating also made him nauseous. The sickening realisation of his addiction had suppressed any desire for nourishment.

He opened FootyBet, one of seven gambling apps he held accounts with. But when searching the frequently asked questions for an option to delete the account, he did not find one. Dargo clicked the vague "account management" heading, hoping some support on how to delete his account was contained within. He was right.

An in-app advert dominated the screen. Favourable odds for the evening's big football match were being offered for a limited time only. Three-to-one for the in-form team was just giving money away, Dargo thought. He could place one last bet, a parting gift to himself, a farewell gamble, recouping some of his debt back.

He shuddered out his musings and slammed a palm off the dashboard as his betting analysis infected his mind like a parasite.

'Fuck off!'

He left the app, which took him back to his phone's home screen. His wallpaper was a picture of him, Sally, Fin and Rosie by the marina in Monaco, a day trip from their holiday in Nice. He and Fin were pretending to be big-timers with cheap cigars in their mouths. Sally's hair was golden, her smile radiant. She did not need to pretend to be glamorous. He stared at her twinkling eyes as they burst with happiness, love, and trust. Confessing to Sally that he gambled with money from Fin's university fund would crush her, and permanently damage the foundation of their relationship. Dargo's job was to serve and protect, but at home, as well as protection, it was his duty to ensure his family thrived. He wanted to reveal everything to Sally, but he was not prepared to assassinate his own marriage and watch from the sidelines as Sally raised his two children, both of whom would learn that their father jeopardised their future to fund his selfish, irrelevant habit.

'That's who you're quitting for,' he whispered through gritted teeth.

He unlocked his phone, flicked the gambling advert off the screen and continued on his quest to delete his betting account. After fifteen minutes of reading through corporate bullshit, he discovered he could not delete his account via the app. He had to call FootyBet's customer service number.

'They don't make it fucking easy,' he mumbled.

Dargo phoned the number, which was answered by an automated voice asking Dargo to press one on the keypad if his request related to deposits and withdrawals, two for general customer queries, three for account closures. Dargo pushed three for account closures, cognisant that FootyBet is now aware of his intentions and would likely keep him on hold. He put the phone on speaker and rested into his seat, watching the cars whip past him from his static position in the lay-by.

The same automated voice told Dargo that FootyBet's staff were busy with other calls, his patience was appreciated, and a staff member would be with him shortly.

Soothing music rolled frustratingly on a thirty-second loop, then it suddenly stopped. Dargo sat upright in anticipation to speak, but the automated voice returned to remind him that FootyBet's staff were busy with other calls, his patience was appreciated, and a staff member would be with him shortly. Dargo cursed as he sat back into his seat again.

He turned the radio on a whisper.

Ten minutes passed.

Twenty minutes passed.

Dargo fell out of a daydream.

'Shit!'

He had forgotten about the FootyBet call as his ears tuned in to the radio DJ. He tapped his phone with his finger, panicking that he had missed the opportunity to speak with a human, but the same monotone voice spoke back to him, reminding him again that FootyBet's staff were busy with other calls, his patience was appreciated, and a staff member would be with him shortly. Infuriating choir voices played after the message. He was relieved that he had not missed a chance to speak to FootyBet, but frustrated that the call had lasted twenty-five minutes. He stared out the window at the weed-ridden lay-by.

Thirty minutes passed.

Dargo considered redialing and pressing one for deposit requests, pretending he wanted to put cash into his account until he got hold of a human and would then reveal his true intentions. He reckoned it would incite a quicker response, but after waiting for thirty-one minutes already, he was too invested to change strategy now.

The call time ticked to the forty-three-minute mark when a person answered, startling Dargo and causing his mind to scramble to remember why he had phoned in the first place.

'James from FootyBet. How can I help?'

'You could have helped forty minutes ago when I first phoned. I've been waiting ages.'

'I'm sorry, sir, we are short on staff today. How can I help you?' James asked, brushing the wait time off as if it were as common as a lost bet.

'Whatever, I want to cancel my betting account.'

'I'm sorry to hear that. Can I ask why you want to leave us?'

'I just want to leave.'

'Okay, sir. If the reason is that you have found better odds elsewhere, then let us know, and we will match them.'

'No! Just delete the account.'

'Okay. Can you tell me your account ID number?'

'I have no idea what that is.'

'It's the unique account number we assign to each customer.'

'I know what an account ID is, but I don't know what my number is for this account.'

'Oh, I see. Well, in that case, can I take your name and email address then?'

Dargo gave the details, wondering why the fuck the handler had not initially asked for the simpler information.

'Oh, I can see that your account is due a fifty-pound free bet. Are you sure you don't want to use this before closing the account?'

Dargo let his mind drift back to the advert that had popped on his screen. He could combine the fifty-pound free bet with some of his own money, place it all on the three-to-one odds and earn enough to repay one of the payday loans he had taken out. Free bets, free money, low risk, less debt. He paused, staring out the window. He gripped the steering wheel until his knuckles turned white.

'No. Just fucking cancel the account. I have a bloody addiction.'

'I'm sorry, sir, but I must put the phone down if any profanity is directed towards me. If you still wish to cancel your account, then please call back once you have calmed down.'

The line went dead.

Dargo stared at his phone, aghast, wishing he could teleport through the phone line and kick the prick's head in. His skin became irritable. The car felt like a snare. Tears of frustration blurred his vision. He smashed his phone off the dashboard. The screen cracked and blood trickled from where miniscule shards of glass had wedged into his fingers.

He watched the cars race past at sixty miles an hour, imagining the consequences of diving headfirst at one. His troubles would be over. His shame would evaporate in an instant.

Dargo opened the door and got out of the car.

CHAPTER 36

Achebe relished the meditative solitude of navigating the tree-lined roads towards Morven Asylum. The visit was an escape from the chaotic office, and with each revolution of the wheels, her shoulders relaxed into the seat as the wilderness felt distant and superior to the world in which she was attacked by an unfathomable beast.

The guarded gates of Morven Asylum were a sight she had only ever seen on the news whenever a deranged criminal was being admitted; camera lights flashing across their face at rapid speed so the editor could pick the most serial-killer looking image.

The asylum was a rectangular horseshoe, split into three grey brick buildings which were as unwelcoming as the summer rain which spat over the facility. It was dubbed a place of rehabilitation, but to Achebe, the asylum appeared to be habitual barracks to suppress the residents' personalities rather than nurture them.

As Achebe approached the building, a woman jogged out from the main entrance. She was keen to greet Achebe and retreat from the swirling wind blowing loose petals like confetti. Her suit was the same colour as the buildings and her brown hair was untidily tied in a bun. She approached with a smile and a cold handshake.

'Detective Achebe?'

'Yes.'

'Doctor Fliss Baxter.'

'Nice to meet you.'

'Welcome. Hope the drive wasn't too strenuous in this weather.'

'I quite enjoyed it.'

'It can be lovely commuting on these roads in proper summer weather. None of that today, though, let's get inside. Mr Lundstrom is in the main room playing draughts.'

'He has the ability to do so? I was told....'

'Playing *with* a draughts set is perhaps a more appropriate description.'

'I see.'

Inside, the building was slightly more inspiring. The walls were a calming shade of blue and the temperature was set to cosy. Staff buzzed through the corridors, ushering patients from room to room for exercise and entertainment.

Dr Baxter stopped at the doorway of the main communal room, where two dozen patients were huddled around the television or playing board games. Achebe noticed a collection of younger, more able individuals studying textbooks with two staff members supervising.

'That's Mr Lundstrom there.'

Achebe had only seen a grainy picture of Ulrich Lundstrom. He was a traditional burly groundsman with hands the size of shovels and muscles naturally defined from years of manual labour. The hunched man she looked at now was a skeletal imp, his body shrivelled as if slowly imploding. His black hair had deserted him to leave a shiny bald scalp. In every visual sense, the man was depleting.

'As I told you over the phone.' Dr Baxter said. 'I don't think your journey here will be very useful. He doesn't engage in conversation. I'm not sure if he has the ability to speak or chooses not to. His injury has left him with severe brain damage, so I suspect the former. You might want to move the draught board, otherwise he'll just play with the pieces and not even look at you.'

'Thanks. I shouldn't be long.'

'You're free to head over and speak with him.'

When Dr Baxter left Achebe on her own, she was overcome with a rush of foolishness. Her attendance was a departure from her normally assured visits to suspects or witnesses. In those scenarios, she always knew what she wanted to ask and had expectations of learning something new. Now she was walking towards the incapacitated former groundsman of Bannock Manor; a house only involved in the attacks because a wild animal had lain down there for a while. She knew her journey would be fruitless, but now, standing in the asylum, the idiocy of her attendance was emphasised.

Achebe sat across from Mr Lundstrom and introduced herself. His colourless eyes lifted briefly, but there was no emotion, no sense of welcome.

'I'm hoping you can help me, Mr Lundstrom.'

Examining the man up close, Achebe realised he was not bald by choice. The skin on his head gleamed from scar tissue where the lawnmower blade had ripped through his flesh. It was long, venturing from his left cheek to a central position at the back of his scalp.

'I want to know about your time at Bannock Manor working for Hamish Stewart.'

There was a flicker of cognition in his eyes, but he remained clinking draught pieces together. You seem to understand what I'm saying at least, Achebe thought.

'How long did you work at Bannock Manor?'

There was no answer. Achebe let the next minute go unspoken.

'Do you enjoy it here?'

Lundstrom shifted a white draught piece but showed no signs of answering the question. Achebe surveyed the other patients. Some were skin and bone without a soul, crawling to death, craving to get there faster than their tickers would allow. She was surprised that the asylum blended them with a lot of younger individuals, as if a care home had collided with a youth centre. Achebe surmised that perhaps seeing how terrible life can get gave the younger ones a kick up the arse to make the most of their lives, away from the criminal world.

Achebe decided to just sit with Lundstrom for a while, believing that company must be in short supply for the man with no family.

'I saw pictures of Bannock Manor when you were working there. You did a fantastic job. The plants were beautiful. You seemed to take great pride in your work. You must have enjoyed living there.'

Lundstrom moved a black draught piece. Achebe picked up a white piece, but Lundstrom swept her hand away before she could blink.

'Oh, sorry. I was going to play a game with you if you wanted?'

You're pissing him off, she thought.

'I must be annoying you. I'll leave.'

Lundstrom fiddled with another white piece as Achebe rose to her feet. A notion barged through her weariness. She sat back down.

'Do you enjoy living here?'

Lundstrom moved the white piece.

'Did you enjoy living on the Bannock estate?'

Lundstrom moved the black piece.

'Black is yes, white is no? Were you with Hamish Stewart on the day he died?'

Lundstrum moved a black and a white piece. Achebe questioned her logic. She was seeing patterns where none existed, but she kept trying.

'Was Hamish's death an accident?'

There was hesitation before the white piece moved.

'Who killed him?'

'Shit! Yes and no questions only. Can you write the name of the person who killed him?'

The white piece moved.

Achebe contemplated what had been answered in the quick-fire round of questioning. Lundstrom's answers suggested Hamish Stewart's death was no accident. Perhaps Lundstrom himself took the opportunity of the escapology trick to kill Hamish. After all, he was to inherit the Bannock estate.

'Did you kill Hamish Stewart?'

Lundstrom moved the white piece to indicate a negative answer.

Achebe paused as she assessed the man across from her. His hopelessness overwhelmed her with pity. He was similar ages to her dad, and during all his years as a ranger in Chobe national park, or in his current job as a zookeeper, she worried he would be left disfigured, disabled, or worse, at the hands of one of the wild animals. She opened her mouth to ask another question, but halted. Thinking of her dad while staring at the ghastly sheen of Lundstrom's scar reflected a familiar nightmare on a different individual.

'Did you get your injury from a lawnmower blade?'

The white piece moved.

'Did a werewolf give you that injury?'

Achebe could scarcely believe she asked the question. It was a stupid question. It was absurd, naïve, desperate, but it was vindicated as Lundstrom moved the black piece to indicate an affirmative answer. This time, however, he let the piece drift off the table. It bounced off the floor, which distracted Achebe as she reached down to grab it. When she rose, Lundstrom's body flinched. His mouth was wide open as if to scream, exhaling air like a dragon without fire. His eyes rolled behind his head. Achebe stood frozen, terrified, as Lundstrom's body contorted in stiff and painful movements. The tension in his bones was like elastic bands threatening to snap.

Four staff members rushed to the table, laid Lundstrom on the floor, and began coddling him while muttering soothing words.

Dr Baxter ran to Achebe.

'Are you okay?'

'Yes, I'm fine. Is he okay?'

'Don't worry. This is not unusual. He goes into a state of shock sometimes.'

'Does it happen around Halloween?'

'I'm sorry.'

'Perhaps when a werewolf appears on that television?'

Dr Baxter's eyes narrowed.

'I'm sorry, I don't follow you.'

'I mentioned a werewolf to him, and this is the reaction I got. How long has Lundstrom been admitted here?' Achebe asked to confirm her timeline was correct.

'He was admitted around the same time I took on this role. He arrived with a fair few other patients about fifteen years ago. They were kept at Strathaven back when they were conducting studies on degenerative brain diseases. They hoped for a cure, but after a while, it became too expensive to continue the program.'

'Who were the others? Are they here?'

'They are all dead, I'm afraid.'

'All of them? Is it normal to have such a high death rate among your patients?'

Dr Baxter looked to the ground in shame.

'Not particularly, but we had a few incidents with the patients that came from Strathaven. They were very troubled individuals. One of them killed another patient, and a few others attacked the staff. It was tough to manage. The facility became a far more dangerous place to work after the Strathaven patients arrived. Despite our best efforts, they were, unfortunately, put to sleep.'

'That's a worrying new definition of end-of-life care. I heard you euthanize people here, but was never sure if it was true.'

'Since independence, there's barely any money to keep this place running. A lot of those patients were causing staff to leave. Overheads increased because we had to improve security and hire temp staff. Let me be clear, euthanizing patients is always a last resort.'

'That's a lot of death for one person to deal with if this all happened during your tenure. Who decides on which patients to put to sleep, as you say?'

'You're right, it does affect me at times, but it's not my decision. It comes from the government.'

'They approve each death based on your recommendation as head of this facility, though, right?'

A layer of sweat formed on Dr Baxter's top lip. Her face blushed red as she cupped a hand round the back of a rapidly perspiring neck. The questioning was making her uncomfortable.

'I'm sorry. I am not allowed to divulge any more. I've probably said too much already.'

Dr Baxter went to move away, but Achebe grabbed her arm.

'I understand you're conflicted between your morals and the orders from the government. No patient should be put to sleep without their consent. Each one should be supported right to the end, no matter how deranged or disabled, and that's why I want to help you with Mr Lundstrom. I was able to communicate with him via the draught pieces. If he moves the black piece, it means yes. The white piece means no.'

'Oh, my.' Dr Baxter recoiled in shock. 'What did he say?'

'Like you, I can't divulge that.'

'We have tried various methods of cognitive communication. Nothing seemed to work.'

'He's definitely going to be okay?'

'Yes, yes. It was just another fit. He gets them occasionally. Please don't feel responsible. I would love to answer your questions, detective, but I'm going to have to help out here. Give me a call or email me. I'll happily answer any of your queries. Was lovely meeting you.'

Achebe jogged back to the car. Lundstrom had confirmed her hunch. She messaged Sam immediately.

Check files from Sector Five's inception. These beasts are a lot older than we think.

CHAPTER 37

Sam winced as her tongue bobbled across her sticky, plaque-ridden teeth. The notion of hot water and soap seemed fanciful from the confines of the stuffy archive room. Her hair was dry spaghetti, brittle under her touch, and the sweat under her armpits chafed, wet like the damp walls of Rockwell's dungeon. A dungeon that had latched onto Sam's mind, lingering no matter how hard she tried to immerse herself in Sector Five's archives.

Checking files from Strathaven's inception, as Detective Achebe requested, had garnered nothing of note thus far. Therefore, around noon, Sam recalibrated her objective, intent on discovering files linked to the human experiments in Rockwell's dungeon. She had the photos - of which poor reception had foiled her attempts to send on to Leigh - but Rockwell would toss any photo or video evidence aside as doctored nonsense, heralding the dangers of artificial intelligence to purport fake news. She needed the project files to supplement her evidence, and she was not leaving without them.

Sam's progress halted when she heard high heels in the corridor. She leaned her ear against the archive room door.

'What the fuck do they want this time?' asked a stern Rockwell. 'Never mind. After tonight, we'll have a good reason to postpone another meeting. Is our guest coming to Sector Five?'

'Billy is already down there and Elodie is on her way. Shall I show her to your office?' asked Rockwell's assistant, Elle.

'No, bring her to the bunker.'

'She's not cleared for Sector Five.'

'Do you not think I bloody know that?' Rockwell snapped.

Sam imagined Rockwell's steely stare spreading hot nerves across Elle.

'Yes, no problem, sir. I'll bring her down when she arrives.'

Sam shuddered. What did Rockwell want with Elodie, an employee of the biological disease department? And why did he want her to come to the bunker? Sam feared her source was compromised. Ominous nausea threatened to resurface the chicken caesar salad she had eaten that day.

Sam took a deep breath, shaking on the exhale as she became agitated with questions. If Elodie was compromised, was she compromised as well? Did Rockwell know she was in the building? Sam suddenly felt vulnerable, but she had to figure out what was going on. She had to get to the bunker.

Sam waited for the elevators to ping closed before she poked her head out of the archive room. Two murky elevators rested at the end of the silent corridor, but Sam dare not use them. The stairwell to the right was a more appropriate option.

Sam tiptoed down the dizzying steps descending deep into the ridge of the mountain. Two flights down, she faced a door labelled the viewing platform. The stairs continued on, but she decided the viewing platform might not be utilised late at night. The card reader lit green and Sam pushed the door to a barely ajar position, peering through the slit to ensure no one was on the platform.

Sam crouched on the enclosed gangway raised high above a bunker floor. Her eye-line poked just above the windowsill of the viewing platform's glass panels, allowing her to see a plethora of wild animals below, all stationed around a polygon walkway marked onto the floor.

Her heart hiccupped upon seeing Rockwell, his slender frame talking down to the ginger-bearded scientist. The orange lenses of his glasses reflected his fiery mood. His blue shirt with a white collar was patchy with indigo sweat, and black garters wrapped around his rolled-up sleeves exposed the definition of his biceps. His ego negated the need for the safety attire the rest of the employees were wearing. The only downside of her vantage point was that she could not hear what Rockwell was saying through the thick blast-proof windows.

So focused on the personnel, only now did Sam see there was something bizarre about the animals at each station. These were the hybrids Rockwell had discussed with Terry Halkett during the covert meeting.

Starting from the left side of the polygon, a caged animal possessed the claws and face of a bear, but tough and impenetrable skin like a hippo. It chewed playfully on a thick branch while a technician fired a bullet through the metal bars into its gut. The bear-hippo growled in mild discomfort, then continued biting into the bark with no apparent injuries.

A second cage contained the body of a snake with an alligator's head. The animal was twitching, as if malfunctioning.

A lion prowled in the third cage. The wall at the back of its cage displayed varying landscapes: golden Sahara sands, volcanic rock, green meadows, and underwater coral. Meat was thrown into the cage to force the lion to move. As it languidly pawed towards the food, Sam gasped as its skin colour shifted with kaleidoscopic majesty, blending into each new scene on the back wall. An apex predator with deadly camouflage.

Thousands of rats clambered over one another in the next cage. Even from Sam's distant vantage point, she could tell their teeth were slightly too large for their bodies. Some fell on their faces under the weight.

The production line of barbaric creations continued, with rhinos, Komodo dragons, reptiles and more big cats being examined by attentive technicians.

Sam struggled to process the scene in front of her. She took out her phone and began snapping away. Her belief that Sector Five created the beast returned. The bear-hippo being the prime suspect. But again, she needed the box files to prove it, not just the photographic evidence. She knew these images, with suboptimal sharpness because of the glass panel, would be discounted as attention-seeking, photoshopped nonsense.

The elevator doors opened. Elodie's confident first steps were quickly curtailed by an aghast expression that told Sam she was witnessing the horrors of Sector Five for the first time. Her instinct, suspicions, and distrust were all vindicated in too short a time to comprehend. She was ushered by Elle, who quickly returned to the elevator, terrified.

Sam wished she could hear what Rockwell was saying as he greeted Elodie. Like the hybrid crocodile-anaconda in the corner, his insincere smile fronted the stranglehold with which he controlled Strathaven.

Rockwell pointed and steered Elodie's eye-line in various directions as he began a tour around the floor. They stopped at the hybrid bear-hippo. Rockwell became animated as he described the specimen to Elodie. He instructed another employee, who walked to the back of the cage, opened a flap and threw in a piece of meat. The excitable cross-species bound to claim their feast.

Elodie was remonstrating back at Rockwell.

'You tell him, El.' Sam whispered.

Rockwell shook his head calmly, a condescending smile pointing down at her. He motioned to another hybrid, but Elodie had turned away toward the elevators. Her defiance ended Rockwell's accommodating facade. In one movement, he lunged and grabbed a fistful of Elodie's hair, yanking her head back so she was staring at the ceiling. He whispered in her ear as Elodie grappled to get him off. Rockwell spun her around and punched her in the gut, causing Elodie to crumble in a heap on the floor.

Sam rose from her crouched position. She was leaning against the glass as she urged one of the dozen onlooking employees to step in. They all watched as cowardly cooperators.

Elodie was only semi-conscious after Rockwell kicked her in the chin while on the floor. Her hands were flailing of their own accord, grasping thin air as she battled for the world to stop spinning.

Rockwell shouted something to the room, which sparked all the scientists to exit via mouse holes carved into the rocky walls. Billy, the ginger scientist, moved with them but froze as Rockwell pointed at him, his hands fidgeting nervously as he reluctantly remained in situ.

Rockwell threw Elodie over his shoulder like a rag doll. The bear-hippo hybrid was content with the meat at the far end of the cage. Rockwell opened the cage door and threw Elodie in.

'NO!'

Sam slammed her fist against the glass, but it was too thick for the sound to be heard in a room full of noisy animals.

Adrenaline rose Elodie from her semi-conscious state upon realising she was sharing a pen with a monstrous beast. Rockwell stood unmoved.

'Rockwell, you fuck.'

No one could hear Sam shouting. Her movement high above in the shadowy terracing went unnoticed as Rockwell and the scientist's gazes remained on the trapped victim. The ginger-bearded man shook. He shifted towards Rockwell as if to ask him to stop, but Rockwell's palm told him to go no further. He obeyed, fearing he was as dispensable as the terrified Elodie.

With the hybrid too distracted for Rockwell's liking, he grabbed a gun from the centre of the polygon and fired at the bear-hippo, causing it to turn in anger. Now Elodie's presence was known.

The beast charged at Elodie and swiped her with its claw. Her punctured body fell to the ground, and for a morbid millisecond, Sam hoped the blow had killed her to avoid any further suffering.

But Elodie was still alive. The beast hovered its snout over Elodie's bloody torso, digging deeper before resurfacing while chewing on flesh. Sam was only privy to the visuals, but her brain mimicked the screams of anguish for her. She smashed the fleshy end of her fist against the glass as she cried.

'Elodie!'

Her call was more of a whimper.

Elodie's limbs twitched until her death. The scientists re-entered from their burrows. Their expressions no longer looked conspiratorial. Fear was Rockwell's foundation for control, but this was even more ruthless than Sam had imagined.

Rockwell watched until there was no life in Elodie. His attention then turned to the scientist with the ginger goatee. The man cowered under Rockwell's stare. His ember eyes glowed a demonic dance as he pressed a hand on the scientist's shoulder, causing his knees to buckle. Rockwell delighted over the man's limp body while fiddling with the ring on his finger, which had caused the electrifying damage.

The man was not yet dead, but Sam wondered why he had shown no desire to fight back. There was no panicked run to the elevators or attempts to arm himself with a weapon. He accepted his fate like an obsequious servant indoctrinated to believe their life is worth less than the master in front of them. Sam realised this must have been Elodie's contact within Sector Five. He helped her obtain the Sector Five keycard, and Rockwell had found out Elodie's profile was linked to it.

Hungry for retribution, Rockwell dragged the scientist to the rats in the centre of the bunker, strapping sensors around the man's limbs, torso and neck before throwing the paralysed scientist into the cage. The rats spread to the corners of the enclosure, frightened of the new specimen invading their space. After a few tentative seconds, some crawled across the man's body, but none appeared interested in treating their uninvited guest with any malice.

Rockwell paused outside the cage with a remote control in his hand. He was waiting for the man's body and mind to regain full functionality. Sam felt like a rat was gnawing inside her stomach as it curdled vomit. Rockwell was gesticulating to petrified staff members as if he were a circus ringmaster. Sam guessed he was issuing a warning: comply or die.

The groggy scientist knelt while rubbing his eyes. Upon realising he was wearing the sensors, he panicked, frantically pulling at the straps. He spun on his knees to face Rockwell, pleading for mercy with an outstretched arm.

Rockwell held the remote control in the air for dramatic effect, arching a finger towards the device with suspenseful showmanship. He pushed a button, causing each sensor around the scientist's body to emit a frequency that sent the rats into a crazed frenzy. Each jumped as if the floor gave them an electric shock, and as they each landed, they had transformed into rabid vermin, their heads jerking and teeth gnashing as they became compelled to attack the source of their distress. A heap of filthy brown smothered the scientist as the rats burrowed their enlarged teeth into the scientist's flesh like piranhas.

Sam crouched behind the frosted lower section of the glass, shaking. Her mind flicked to Elodie's daughter. When would she find out about her mother's death? What fucked up story would Rockwell create to cover it up?

Sam's teeth chattered amid the sobs, realising she was in far greater danger than she imagined. She had become too comfortable in the archive room. Her phone had no signal to plea for Leigh to pick her up, but she had to escape.

As Rockwell gesticulated passionately at the rest of the scientists, Sam took the opportunity to run back to the archive room. The pile of documents she had earmarked to escape with was small. She found no documents related to the human experiments or to a flesh-hungry beast, but some still warranted further inspection for her personal investigation into Sector Five's activities. Remembering Achebe's message, Sam lifted the lid on boxes she had not reviewed from Sector Five's infant years, stashing a modest number of documents into her bag without inspection. She then tidied up, only small clusters of sandwich crumbs indicating anyone had been in the room.

Sam's primary exit plan was to simply walk out Sector Five's doors as confidently as she had walked in. However, witnessing a murderous Rockwell meant this idea was unviable. If Rockwell found her, she was dead.

Instead, Sam devised a contingency plan. From studying the blueprints of Strathaven prior to her arrival, she knew there was a storage room next to the entrance of Sector Four. With her newfound ability to move undetected in the ceiling, Sam decided she would crawl and drop into the storage room, then exit into the midrib of the building.

With a bulbous cyst of a backpack, she gently crawled towards the storage room. At the border of Sector Five, her thigh buzzed as her phone signal returned. Sam craned her neck awkwardly towards her pocket, typing with her thumb.

Leaving tonight. Pick me up asap.

Leigh's response was instant, confirming the pickup, which Sam estimated would arrive in roughly an hour.

Complicating her movements further was the fact her backpack kept running off the sides of her back as the loose shoulder straps slipped out of position. She tightened each strap, so the bag clung to her back like a leech. Droplets of sweat dripped from the tips of her dangling hair as Sam continued to take slow, deliberate movements across the metal lattice. Any sound, any broken tile, any commotion would alert the security guards, and Rockwell, of her presence.

After several peeks under the roof tiles, and over an hour of crawling, Sam reached the storage room. She opened a roof tile and dropped her bag into the empty room, slowly lowering herself onto a metal shelving unit, and steadying herself enough to put the tile back in place.

Sam sat on the floor, giving her shaking arms and legs time to recover after the strain, grateful she could move as a biped once again. Leigh messaged to inform her she was parked at the hidden drop-off point where she left Sam three nights ago. Sam reinstated her disguise, but it felt transparent against the imminent danger she was in.

Outside, the corridor was lifeless. Only the hum of the electric car was heard as she steered it around the curvature of the leaf, her body odour wafting a rancid trail like a bin lorry. Tears began kayaking down the contours of her face. The closer she got to freedom, the more her mind pondered what she was leaving behind. She had investigated human trafficking, war, and the corrupt power of egomaniacs. She thought she had already ventured to the depths of human depravity, but Sector Five usurped everything. The human experiments were more vile and more inhumane than anything she had observed before, and Rockwell's propensity to eliminate people as candidly as swatting a fly cloaked her with a vulnerability she had not even experienced when interviewing soldiers on the frontline.

Sam waved to the security guard in the foyer, having wiped her cheeks dry before exiting the midrib.

'Get yourself home, love, too late to be working here.'

Once outside, Sam inhaled, accepting the fresh oxygen with the gratitude of a trapped miner who thought they would never feel the air again. It partially soothed her anxiety as she walked briskly under the barriers of the car park where the same security guard was pouring a cup of coffee for himself with his back to the entrance.

Sam took her chance, running within the shadowy trees which lined the country road away from Strathaven.

As she approached Leigh's car, the emotion condensed in her throat. She puffed into the air to clear the blockage, but the build-up of everything she had witnessed filled her throat again. Her survival instinct had dropped, and the emotions were free to tamper with her body.

Sam's hand quivered as she opened the passenger door. She tried to control herself, but as soon as she felt Leigh's embrace, her wobbling lip surrendered.

'She's dead, Leigh.'

'Who?'

'Elodie. My contact.'

'How did she....'

'Rockwell, fucking Rockwell.'

'Let's go to the police.'

'He controls the police. He controls the Chief. He controls the government. I witnessed it all.'

Sam took a moment to compose herself.

'They are experimenting with animals, creating hybrids between two or three species. The beast definitely came from here.' Sam paused. 'But worst of all, they are experimenting on people. Horrible, fatal experiments.'

Leigh's hand hovered over the gearstick as if wanting to drive off, but she was struggling to process what Sam was saying.

'Please, just drive.' Sam said. 'I want to get as far away from here as possible.'

June 13th

CHAPTER 38

Dargo shuddered under the wail of anguish. The father ran to the bathroom to vomit a violent, vulgar version of vindaloo. The mother's face turned gaunt instantly. She knelt down from the sofa, trying to physically hit rock bottom. She reached out as if snatching at her son's apparition, but he was gone, straddled and raped to death by a sadistic killer.

Four boys murdered, and at least two were preventable had Dargo's addiction not distracted them from the investigation. They kicked the killer's door down a day too late. If they had broken into the flat on their first visit, two lives would have been saved, including Ryan Etherington, whose mother was now crumpled into the crumby carpet, inconsolable; her soul shattered into a million irremediable shards.

'Once again, I'm very sorry for your loss, Mrs Etherington. We will leave you alone for now, but the support liaison officer is outside and will provide further assistance.' Bullock said.

They let themselves out. Dargo placed a hand on the pebbledash exterior as he staved off a moment of dizziness. He had informed families of lost loved ones too many times to count. His actions after each deliverance were ritualistic. He would return home to tell Sally he loved her and spend time with Fin and Rosie with a renewed appreciation for his stable life. On this occasion, however, he could not return to play happy families. He could not tell Sally that he tried to save the boys with the sincerity of a detective who had done his best. Going home to have dinner and watch the football with Fin would laugh in the face of the mother inside whose life he helped obliterate.

'Pull in here.'

Bullock obeyed, bemused at the request to stop in the scabby lay-by.

'What's up?'

Dargo never answered.

'Tom, what's wrong? You look like a ghost.'

'I've not been sleeping of late.'

'Because of the case? We're getting closer. Don't you feel it?'

Dargo stared out the passenger seat window towards the overgrown bushes. He could not look at his partner. He did not know how to say what he needed to say, but he knew he could not look Bullock in the eye when he did.

'I contemplated what it would be like to commit suicide here yesterday.'

Bullock stuttered a breath, Dargo's words stabbing him mute. He could not envisage a life without his partner, his confidant, his friend.

Dargo stumbled out another sentence.

'I've been gambling.'

Bullock frowned.

'I know you have. We both love a wee flutter on the footie.'

'I love it a little bit more than you, mate.'

'I see.'

'I've got an addiction.'

There was a quiver in Dargo's voice. Bullock put his hand on his partner's shoulders in an attempt at solidarity, but Dargo flinched as if he was unworthy of being consoled.

'Whatever the extent of the addiction, we will get through it. Don't you worry.'

'All I do is worry. I've got debt, Xander. Lots of it, to lots of parties.'

After lingering silence, the clouds parted, and the sun's glare fell perfectly to reflect Bullock's face in the window. Dargo diverted his focus away from his partner's reflection to the weeds below. The shame was crippling, but at the same time, he felt the boot against his neck release slowly as he made his admission.

'I've been going to the casino till four, five, six in the morning. I tell Sally I'm working late on a case. She never asks any questions. That's how much she trusts me. Yes, I bet on the football, but what you see is about ten percent of my gambling.'

Bullock was stunned. They had both leaned on each other over the years, Bullock many more times than Dargo ever needed him. He was a mentor, the leader, the man who had taken him under his wing when he was a cantankerous high constable always looking for fights. He owed him everything, and now it was his turn to step up.

'How much debt?'

The question crawled over Dargo's skin like cockroaches.

'I'm not sure exactly. I think I've frittered away over fifty, sixty thousand in three or four years.'

Bullock remained silent.

'Most of it has come from my salary, but Sally thinks some of that was going into our savings. But the worst part.' Dargo paused. 'I've used money from a fund we set up to support Fin's university ambitions.'

'How much of the fund?'

'Twenty thousand.'

'Fucking hell, Tom.'

'Sally could forgive the addiction, but she will never forgive the lies. She will never forgive the fact that I jeopardised our son's future. What sort of father does that to their kid?'

'You've not told her yet?'

'No. I don't know how.'

'You've made an important step, Tom. You've told me about your addiction before it really gets out of hand.'

'It's already out of hand.'

'No, it's not. I promise you we'll sort this together.'

The windows steamed up to squeeze the detectives deeper into the awkward realm of money-talk. Bullock removed any embarrassment of having to ask for financial assistance.

'Let's go to the bank now. I'll transfer twenty thousand and you can replace Fin's university pot. No one needs to find out about that.'

'No, Xander. I can't ask for money. You've saved that up.'

'You've not asked. I'm offering. Amy and I live modest lives. We have no children, and ain't planning on having any. Trust me when I say that I have no qualms about lending you this money. This situation you've got yourself in is bigger than money. This is about saving your marriage and keeping your family together.'

Dargo looked at Bullock for the first time, but it was only fleeting.

'I wouldn't accept it unless I was desperate, and I'll pay you back as soon as I can.'

'I know you will. It's honestly not a problem, so don't feel, you know, embarrassed or anything soppy like that. We'll work out a plan to repay the rest. Who else do you owe money to?'

'Banks. Payday loan companies.'

'Let's deal with the payday loans today as well. They charge exorbitant interest so let's get them off the table. The banks show a bit more leniency, so we can work a plan around that debt.'

'I'm sorry, Xander.'

'Don't be sorry. The situation is what it is. You've made a big step owning up to me. Now we have an opportunity to deal with it. But what I'm really hoping is that any fleeting notions of suicide were just that, fleeting notions with no genuine desire.'

'Yes, yes. Of course.'

'Cause if you ever fucking do that, you'll hurt your family far more than any money troubles will. They can deal with some family austerity, but they will never get over the loss of their husband, the loss of their dad.'

Bullock began driving to the nearest bank branch

'So, when did all this start?'

'About four years ago, during the "bloody rose" case. Wee Rosie was only two years old at the time, and seeing those young, innocent girls murdered affected me more than any other case. I just needed a release from work, and my home life wasn't enough because when I returned home and looked at Rosie, I saw those dead girls. I wanted to escape any world in which my wee Rosie could become one of them. So, I started off betting for fun, gambling pennies. But then the stakes gradually grew and grew over time. I met a bunch of guys at the casino, and we became an informal club that gathered there late at night. It got to the point where I couldn't wait to get to the roulette table with a beer and chat away with them while we gambled into the early hours.'

'What led you to realise a change was needed? Why are you only opening up to me now?'

'One of the members of the club took his own life last week. I knew gambling had ruined his life, but I didn't think it would end it. He was divorced, only seeing his kids fortnightly and verging on bankruptcy. Arrogantly, I thought I was above all that.'

The moving car acted like a dynamo, winding up Dargo's tongue.

'I guess I always knew deep down that I have a gambling problem, but I always thought it was under control. I thought I could repay Fin's university fund, top up the joint savings account with Sally, but I had no plan on how to do so. I just ignorantly believed I would somehow manage it with a big win.'

'Sounds more stressful than the job you were trying to escape from in the first place.'

Dargo nodded.

'Then there're the boys, Xander. We left the killer's flat unexplored during our first visit because I wanted to put a coupon on and watch a couple of horse races. Two kids died in the time it took for us to return the next day. All for what? A fleeting rush of enjoyment if I win a few merks. How pathetic is that? The boys in those rooms, not much older than Fin, were terrified. They were in pain, staring at the ceiling, wondering, praying that they would be spared of any more torture. We always kick the fucking door down. We always kick it down. When our gut instincts are telling us to act, we act. But this time we didn't act, and it was because of me, because of my addiction. When all is said and done, I valued a two hundred merk gambling fix over the lives of Jason Manson and Ryan Etherington. I'm not fit to be a detective, not in this state.'

Bullock spotted a sign stating *world's best coffee, half a mile*. Dargo continued.

'Gambling erodes the life and soul of good people. The worst part is no one in the industry cares. No one at the casino ever intervenes and asks if you are okay. I tried to cancel one of my accounts with a betting company. They made it so difficult that I failed to close it. It made me feel like trying to quit wasn't worth the hassle, that I'm never going to escape.'

They approached the lay-by where the tired-looking coffee stand was situated.

'Let's get some coffee and fresh air. You've disclosed a lot of information and I think it will do you good to get out of the car for five minutes. Trust me, we are going to phone each betting company and cancel every account you have, no matter how long it takes or how difficult they make it.'

'Thanks, mate.'

'And I disagree that we would've kicked the killer's door down on our first visit. The only reason we did so on our second visit was that the curtains were still drawn from the day before, and after no answer from any flat on the third floor, then, and only then, did our gut instinct kick in. So, you are fit to be a detective. Get any notion otherwise out of your head. Let's take five minutes to get some air and then we'll sort out your debt. In the meantime, let's taunt these idiots with false advertising charges.'

CHAPTER 39

Strathaven sat powerfully in the crevice of the valley, vast and domineering amongst a multitude of greens. Rays reflected off its wooden veneer as if the facility was designed to suck in the sunshine.

The smile on the security guard's face tightened after Achebe flashed her badge and name-dropped Rockwell. She was carted along the perpetual corridor to Sector Five on an electric vehicle.

'Wait here. Dr Rockwell will be with you soon,' said the overweight guard in the security booth next to Sector Five.

Rockwell kept her waiting for thirty minutes. A cheap tactic, but it still irked Achebe.

'Detective Nikki Achebe.'

Rockwell's voice was soft but commanding. He wore a blue shirt with the sleeves rolled up and the top two buttons undone. The tips of his white collar were doused with neck sweat, and his hair was matted as if he had been up all night. Despite a slightly dishevelled appearance, power emanated from his presence, a magnetic force that could attract who he wanted, but rebuff those he did not have time for. Achebe had only ever seen video clips of him wearing his iconic, orange-tinted glasses. Now, without them, he looked younger, but the calculating severity of his stare remained hostile.

'Dr Rockwell.' Achebe answered, offering a hand for him to shake. His grip was intentionally firm while squinting a crocodile smile.

'I'm impressed with the facility, both exterior and interior.' Achebe said, pointing to the bustling inner village within the building's midrib.

'Twenty-five thousand people work here, doing hard graft and innovative work.'

'Impressive that everyone commutes from afar.'

'Most teams operate a shift pattern, which means people work longer hours but fewer days than the conventional five-day week. Each team starts work at different times, so we can manage traffic in and out of the facility. Unfortunately, the road to and from Strathaven only has one lane in each direction until the motorway, but we are working on plans to improve the transport links.'

'Given a fair portion of the twenty-five thousand employees work for a division called Transportation, that shouldn't be too difficult.'

'Trust me, that department has far bigger problems to solve. Shall we start the tour then?' Rockwell said, bypassing the body scanners and x-ray machines toward the Sector Five doors. 'This is the hallowed door, detective. This is where we experiment on aliens and store their aircraft, talk to ghosts, resurrect the dead, and maybe even create mythical monsters to roam Bannock forest.'

Rockwell's grin flopped off his face.

'I think you'll find your visit here extremely underwhelming. Your boss informed me that this was merely an avenue you had to tick off in your hunt for the alleged werewolf, so I provided you with access to Sector Five as a favour. You've already signed a non-disclosure agreement, but allow me to reiterate that if you disclose anything beyond these doors, there will be major consequences. Is that clear?'

The threat of imprisonment included in the non-disclosure agreement appeared a desirable consequence compared to the peril evoked in Rockwell's stare.

'Crystal.'

After entering the drab corridor of Sector Five, Rockwell beelined to his office, inviting Achebe inside.

'This is where I reside most of the day.'

'Wow!' Achebe said, taking in the observatory roof and the view of the valley. 'Now I see where all the taxpayers' money went.'

'I spend most of my life here, so I created a space that was enjoyable to work in. I'd offer you a dram of whisky, but I doubt you'll accept since you're on duty.'

'Tastes like piss anyway.'

Rockwell opened a set of patio doors to the shimmering valley.

'The office may seem grandiose, but I mean it when I say I live most of my life here. I have to make a lot of unpopular decisions, some more difficult on the conscious than others. This valley is my escape. At night, I sit here and watch the stars. The cosmos lures me in and makes anything I do on earth feel wonderfully insignificant. That does not depress me though, it liberates me. Why not take a chance, grasp an opportunity, make the tough decisions when, in the context of the universe, it really doesn't matter?'

'I'm not sure what type of decisions you are referring to, but what you justify as insignificant might be very significant to someone else. You don't have the right to decide how others should feel about a decision you make.'

'It's not me that makes the decision insignificant. It's the cosmos.'

Achebe stepped back into the office, keen to move on from Rockwell's celestial musings.

'And what is that?' Achebe asked, screwing her face towards the white marble sculpture.

'A marvellous piece. I saw it and just had to have it, not at the taxpayers' expense, I might add.'

'Who pays your wages?'

Rockwell ignored the comment.

'It's a soul collector.'

'And you think having it in your office is conducive to a positive working environment?'

'Similar to the cosmos, it reminds me how finite our time is, and liberates me even more to take risks, a trait that is of the utmost importance in this role.'

Rockwell's speech faded towards the end of the sentence. His eyes trained on part of the sculpture. He moved forward, caressing his fingers along the contours of chipped marble at the hip of the figure. He frowned towards a stapler on the floor behind the sculpture, his mind trying to piece together the scene that led to the defacement of his prized possession.

'Well, as impressive as this office is, I was hoping to see more of what goes on in Sector Five.'

Rockwell remained analysing the sculpture for any other imperfections as he answered.

'Too boring for you. Did you expect a secret passage to a lair of aliens?'

Rockwell read Achebe's face for a reaction, but when none was forthcoming, he smiled and walked Achebe towards the door.

'Come on, detective. I'm trying to lighten the mood a bit. No need to be so rigid.'

'I don't smile much when members of the public are being slashed to death by a killer beast.'

'Ah yes, and I heard you had personal experience with it.' Rockwell said, nodding towards Achebe's bandaged hand.

'Is there anything my boss didn't tell you?'

'He told me the beast is an oversized wolf. Is that what you saw?'

'I was hoping you were going to tell me. Any more lab-generated animals like Alba, the glow-in-the-dark rabbit?'

'Ah!' Rockwell said. 'That's what led you here. I was wondering why you thought Sector Five might be linked to these beasts.'

'I never said there was more than one, but it's interesting that you seem to think so.'

Rockwell paused, staring out the glass doors to the valley.

'Again, my wee friend Vinnie told me there was more than one.'

Achebe internalised her frustration. Even away from the office, the Chief was proving obstructive.

'Alba was a long time ago.' Rockwell continued, 'And if people knew how difficult it was to genetically modify animals, they would know that little Alba was an exceptional case and the chances of creating anything larger than Alba are the stuff of fantasy.'

'So, you don't experiment with any animals?'

'We do, but it's more analysing animal behaviour than genetic modification. Let's continue.' Rockwell said while walking out of his office. 'We have a couple of lab rooms for low-risk experiments on the right here.'

'What does low risk mean?'

'Experiments which present little danger. In other words, experiments which are not required to be contained in the bunker?'

'And what goes on in the bunker?'

'Patience, Nikki. I'm about to show you. There are lots of rumours about Sector Five, but the only one that is somewhat true is that we are a research and development facility to enhance Caledonia's national security. Sometimes that requires working with hazardous materials.'

'And developing nuclear weapons?'

Rockwell coughed a laugh.

'We have dabbled in such experiments, yes. But that doesn't touch the surface when it comes to the dangers we deal with on a daily basis.'

Rockwell continued walking.

'We have a conference room there and an archive room there.'

Achebe glanced at the archive room. She had not spoken to Sam since she left the facility.

'Not much to see in either, so we will continue to the bunker, which is what you'll want to see.'

Rockwell led Achebe down the stairwell, humming a tune as they descended. She thought it was a nursery rhyme, but she could not name it. What she did recognise was Rockwell's charm. Superficial though it may be, she knew it was a key component of his sustained prosperity.

Rockwell opened the door to the viewing platform and produced a wry smile as Achebe looked in wonder at the buzzing bunker floor. Scientists and technicians operated in small silos at various stations around the polygonal walkway. She could scarcely believe it all existed deep within the mountain.

'That is one of our more interesting projects.'

Rockwell pointed to a boulder at the bottom right of the pathway. Three men were huddled around the large rock wearing earmuffs. The boulder shot rapid gunfire at a target fifty metres away. After the gunfire was over, a woman appeared from a lid on the rock surface.

'We are attempting to build mini-tanks that are only operated by one individual. This one is designed to camouflage in the Zagros mountains. It's just a trial, for now.'

Achebe pointed to a glass room in the centre of the floor.

'What's in there?'

'That room contains nerve agents. If a chemical is spilled in there, we can seal that room to contain it.'

'And those who work in there?'

'They are well compensated for the dangers of the job.'

'Money isn't worth shit if you're dead.' Achebe remarked.

'We take safety really seriously. Every experiment is carefully planned and developed with staff safety in mind.'

'What happened over there?' Achebe asked, pointing to the far corner where a burly man held a weak hose over a smouldering pile of charred clutter.

'Ah, that is what happens when employees ignore our safety procedures. We had an extremely unfortunate accident last night. Sadly, two staff members perished in a fire. The lady, Elodie, I think her name was, thought she could get away with having a cigarette in the bunker rather than make the long journey outside to the designated smoking area. Despite our safety protocols, we cannot legislate for reckless rogue employees.'

Rockwell leaned his forehead on the glass as if succumbed to the devastating loss of life.

'Typical French, though. They can never contain their nicotine cravings.'

Achebe let the viewing platform fall silent. Their meeting had been too nice thus far.

'I'm glad you share a similar aversion to unnecessary loss of life.' Achebe said, not trying to hide the sarcasm in her tone. 'My only aim is to stop whatever animal has killed a dozen people and caused so much grief and loss to many more. My question is simple, do you, or did you hold an animal, lab-created or not, here at Strathaven, and has it escaped?'

Rockwell remained calm, opening his mouth to speak, but Achebe cut him off.

'And I don't want a diplomatic answer, cause frankly, I don't give a shit about potentially exposing what goes on in Sector Five. I don't care if we capture a mutant beast and tell the public it was a big cat. All I care about is stopping a savage animal from killing more people. So, if it's your reputation or public backlash you're worried about, then don't. I just want to know what we are dealing with so we can capture it and stop the casualties. Surely you can get on board with that?'

'I would love to help you, detective, but I can't. No such animal exists here.'

'That's interesting, because I know for a fact that's not true.'

Achebe flashed a photo of the hybrid animals Sam had sent her using the burner phones.

'From the angle of the photograph, it seems it was taken from this very viewing platform.'

Rockwell removed his orange glasses from his top pocket at a deliberately glacial pace; a tactic used to compose himself in unpredictable or difficult moments. He took the phone from Achebe to inspect the photo. He did not flinch. Instead, his stare bore through Achebe like a flaming screwdriver.

'Who sent you these fakes?'

'Fakes?'

Rockwell chuckled.

'These aren't even convincing. Sent to you by some crackpot conspiracy theorist.' Rockwell said, examining Achebe's expression. 'Or a smear campaign from a disgruntled employee?'

Rockwell grinned.

'That's it, isn't it? I thought detectives were good at identifying people's motives. This is just another crank trying to discredit me and

Sector Five. There's plenty of them out there. None have succeeded to date, and none ever will.'

'Well, I may not see any animals or hear any animals, but I am definitely getting a whiff of them. Can't you smell that? You can shovel shite, but you can't mask the smell. I know animals have been in that lab recently, and I know you are hiding something, so I'll give you one last chance to tell me what's going on.'

'Listen, detective. I know you're frothing at the mouth like the proverbial werewolf to solve your first big case, but you won't solve it by drooling around here. First, no such animal exists. Second, I allowed you in here willingly. I could easily have denied you access, and you should be mindful that you are standing in territory that is way above your pay grade and well above your infantile comprehension. You should be very careful before pointing an accusatory finger at me. You might think you hold all the power, being a snooty wee detective, but I'm the omnipotent, all-seeing being. I am everywhere. I am at your work. I am at the Jazz bar when you sing. I am at your parent's house when you scurry back to safety after a tough day at work.'

Achebe froze.

'Now you have me wondering how desperate, how guilty you have to be to try to discomfort me by mentioning my family.'

Achebe was studying Rockwell for any twitch of emotion, but he remained stoic. Like coming face to face with a tiger in the reeds, she knew she was staring at an apex predator in their own kingdom.

'I won't give up, you know. You may as well tell me now and help me save lives.'

'I admire your tenacity, detective, and I wish you well. The attacks are awful, and if there is any way I can help, I will. The tour is now over. I'll show you out. And remember, detective, you are bound by Caledonian law never to speak of what you witnessed or experienced here in Sector Five. Poor judgement could lead to life-altering consequences.'

CHAPTER 40

The boy, wide-mouthed, desperately fought for air, but the choker around his neck meant he only produced gargled gasps.

The cabin lay deep within the hamlet of chalets; expensive tourist accommodation for those looking to walk the scenic trails and kayak the rivers of the Borders. The girl had long identified a specific chalet surrounded by Caledonian pines, capturing the noise of her midnight slaughter within their needles.

The girl selected the writhing teenager from a nearby pub. It was all too easy in these small towns. The locals are always desperate for fresh meat compared to the stale offerings that normally frequent the boozers.

Sitting atop the boy's naked back, she yanked the dog leash choker, grinning as the boy's neck turned pink, then red, then purple. She released her grip. The boy's head fell into the pillow. She could hear his muffled groans as he frantically inhaled.

The girl strapped a dildo around her waist. Pink and ten inches long, it wobbled like a raw ham joint. As the boy gasped for air, she strapped a bite-down gag into his mouth and slowly inserted the strap-on into the boy's anus. The boy bit down on the gag, bubbling saliva spitting from the sides of his mouth. His tethered arms thrashed within their shackles. The girl pressed her body down, the sex apparatus pushing slowly into the boy's body like a human fist punching through soft clay. She savoured each painful inch.

She snatched a controller with an ominous red button. Her eyes were closed as she continued to grind into the boy with greater force. Her body tingled with excitement, the electrifying anticipation of what was to come causing the hairs on her body to rise like thrilled colosseum spectators.

She pressed the button.

A dozen two-inch spikes protruded from the stem of the dildo rupturing flesh and tissue. The boy's body jerked as he tried to wriggle away from the pain, but his squirming caused the blades to cut through fresh flesh. He wailed underneath his muzzle.

The girl unclipped the strap-on. Blood trickled from the boy's rear like a pitiful water fountain on a dry day. The girl licked the air with a hideous smile, reaching for the wicked whip to fatally wound her victim to a slow and torturous death.

CHAPTER 41

Commander Maynard marched towards Achebe, his skull-crushing boots crunching into the stones of Bannock Manor's driveway. He sported a short-sleeved top that exposed his rippling arm muscles; the humidity causing angry beads of sweat to drip from him like a melting waxwork.

'Warm one tonight, Commander.'

'We've battled through far worse.'

'You seem to have the place well secured. I'm guessing there were no signs of any predator last night?'

'Did you receive an update from me today?'

'No.'

'Then obviously there was no news to speak of,' Maynard snapped.

'I was only asking.'

'What are you even doing here? Are you serving a purpose?'

Achebe was taken aback. She knew Maynard was a bit of a prick, but he seemed unusually tetchy.

'I have twenty armed soldiers around the perimeter wall, three scaffold lookout towers with two men on each, four men on the roof, a helicopter surveying the area, live sheep tied to the trees as bait. You say there are three of these predators. We have three distinct groups of soldiers within the perimeter. When one predator comes, one group moves in to take it out. If more than one attack, then one of the other two groups is ready to support the perimeter soldiers in taking it down as well. So, with all that in mind, what is your purpose here?'

'I'm here to support in any way.'

Even to Achebe, the words felt pathetic as she said them.

'You're a liability.'

Achebe readjusted her stance, straightening her posture.

'I'm the only one here who has seen what we are dealing with. That has to be of some value.'

'You would think.' Maynard scoffed, looking over Achebe's shoulder as if her presence was not worth acknowledging. 'You can't even confirm the identity of the animal. This is the most ill-informed operation I've ever had to manage. We know nothing about our enemy. What is its preferred method of attack? How does it behave? What are its weaknesses? We are totally blind.'

Getting the excuses in early, Achebe thought.

Achebe moved away from the fizzing Maynard. She stood next to the bulletproof jeep by the front door of the manor. An ominous mist filled the gaps between the trees, suffocating a dozen floodlights attempting to illuminate the darkness. For the soldiers stationed at the wall, visibility into the forest was as low as a few metres, or as Achebe calculated, one leap of the werewolf's stride.

Maynard was pacing, unable to stop fidgeting within the endless anticipation. The atmosphere was tense, the surroundings still. The forest breathed calmly. Until a piercing howl from an unworldly creature reverberated an echo of death between the trees.

The soldiers shuffled.

Safety caps clicked off.

Postures braced.

Achebe pulled the gun from her holster.

Maynard was talking into his headset as he reached for his gun.

'Where's the helicopter? Refuelling! You've got impeccable timing, you fucking moron.'

He ripped the headset off while marching to address his unit, raising his voice so the soldiers on the other side of the house could hear his battle cry.

'Right, team, we're on our own. Towers on guard. Shoot on sight.'

Maynard turned to the right of the house.

'The howl came from the west.'

An officer kept his eyes fixed on the forest as he replied.

'The mist has thickened. No sign of movement, sir.'

Achebe's heart was pumping harder, combining with the warm temperature to cover her body with a sticky heat. A dampness, like wet socks, overwhelmed her sinuses. She retreated until her back pressed against the cool surface of the van. She had her gun, and the soldiers had theirs, but if things went completely awry, she could swivel into the relative safety of the vehicle.

Achebe scanned the obscurity of the mist, duped into thinking each gentle waft of wind was the murky movements of the beast.

The air hummed in anticipation.

Then a wail came from her left.

It was not a sound of pain, but the sound of hopeless anguish. It started loud, then cut off as if a vocal cord snapped under a sharp pluck.

The fright caused Achebe to hit the back of her head off the van.

'Stay in position.' shouted Maynard as he ran east of the house.

A team of six soldiers on standby in the centre of the perimeter wall moved towards the scream with him. As they approached, they were distracted by another scream from the back of the manor.

All Achebe could do was listen to the audio of panicked gunfire, followed by an ugly clatter of metal as a scaffold lookout tower toppled.

There were more high-pitched screams and quick-fire shots.

'No-kill. No-kill.' was the cry.

The demoralising words told Achebe all she needed to know, that even the Special Response Unit, after all their great preparation, were going to struggle to stop the beasts. She moved gingerly from the safety of the van along the gable end of the house to the back. There were still dozens of armed soldiers holding position, but the sight of the fallen tower was unsettling. One officer was unmoving beneath the structure while another screamed in pain, clutching his folded leg.

There was a dart of movement to the left of Achebe's peripheral vision.

Teeth, claws and a growl. The motion was instantaneous as the werewolf snatched a soldier's legs and dragged him within the cover of the mist, his gun left agonisingly behind. His scream was limited to a millisecond before he was sliced into silence.

There was another spray of gunfire from the soldiers in front of Achebe, but they were hopeful bullets as the beasts remained elusive behind the fog curtain.

Achebe counted at least four soldiers who had been killed or wounded. She met Maynard outside the manor entrance.

'Sir, I recommend pulling your team back ten yards to draw the animal further out of the mist so we can get a better shot. I can't tell if there's more than one yet.'

Maynard shot a beady stare in Achebe's direction, offended by the strategy recommendation; an intelligent suggestion he failed to think of in the heat of the moment. He toyed with the idea, not because it was a tough choice to make, but because to agree with Achebe would mean admitting she added value, but to dismiss the idea would leave his troops in a dangerous formation. He had no choice.

'Everyone step back, at least fifteen yards.'

'Add an extra five yards to make yourself feel better,' Achebe muttered.

The armed unit obeyed, but the new human perimeter was too claustrophobic for Achebe's liking. She went from sitting in the royal box to being courtside, in danger of catching a rogue ballistic.

The night turned deathly quiet. Every rustle of branches taunted the troops into thinking the werewolf was brushing against them. Each second of inactivity endured sickeningly in Achebe's stomach, but eventually, the tension calmed. The final act of the theatre display had finished. The werewolf was content with their performance, off to eat human flesh at the private afterparty.

Maynard ordered four soldiers to enter the mist where a soldier had been taken, in the hope, dead or alive, that his body was on the very fringes of the forest.

Ten uninterrupted minutes lingered as the soldiers composed themselves.

Then came the gunfire.

The shots from deep in the forest were sporadic, rushed, and desperate.

Then came the screams. The varying tones of the four soldiers resonated as if the beasts were playing a human xylophone.

Maynard's complexion was translucent. His shell-shocked eyes betrayed the steely expression.

'No one else is dying. Everyone back.'

The soldiers reluctantly retreated to the armoured vehicles, while the wails of their colleagues were left trapped in the forest of damned souls.

From the passenger seat in the van, Achebe watched Maynard stand alone outside the vehicles, listening for any hint of life. The soldiers whispered in the back.

'I can't believe we're leaving them. Commander Maynard won't survive this.'

Achebe thought it strange that respecting hierarchy was valued over the soldiers' moral compass. She contemplated what she would do in their shoes. If she were trained to hunt, capture, shoot and kill to their standard, would she leave her colleagues behind? If it was Tom, Xander, Jen or Gio, there's no way she could simply drive away.

When the night fell silent again, Maynard returned to the van, slamming the door as he barged into the seat next to Achebe. He ordered the driver to move it while he stared out the window into the deadly abyss.

June 14th

CHAPTER 42

'Achebe!'

The shout from the Chief was ominous. He hung his lanky figure in the door frame before turning back inside, a signal for Achebe to follow. It was seven in the morning, so there were barely any peace officers to witness Achebe's bashful walk to the Chief's private office.

Achebe shut the door as she entered, pausing when she saw Commander Maynard sitting in a chair that was too small for him. His face was stone, fixed in a scowl aimed in her direction. What the fuck is this, she thought.

'Sit, Nikki.' the Chief said, pointing to a vacant chair next to Maynard.

The Chief walked behind his desk. His glare drilled down at them from an uncomfortably steep angle.

'Last night was a disaster, a complete disaster. Seven men died. Three more seriously injured. One is in intensive care and will most likely be dead by the end of today. What happened?'

Achebe shifted in her seat. The attack was so harrowing she had not slept. Her mind was tortured by the images of the werewolf dragging soldiers off to feast. Even worse was her imagination taunting her with reels of the soldier's last moments. Her mind constructed slashes to the face, internal organs punctured by a claw, a bite to the throat. She imagined how they must have felt in those final moments, knowing their lives had mere seconds remaining. The number of family members and friends mourning their deaths was too nauseating to think about. She spent the early hours of the morning twisting in her bed, her body gyrating with anxiety as every shadow in the room formed into a lupine-shaped monster.

Despite her torment, guilt was not an emotion she burdened herself with on this occasion. It was Maynard's job to form the strategy. He had the expertise to station his unit as safely as possible.

Achebe opened her mouth to speak, but Maynard nipped in front of her.

'Detective Achebe failed to accurately describe the extent of the threat prior to our setup. I was unaware of the animal's speed, which would have drastically altered where I positioned my unit around the manor. If I had done so, many lives, if not all lives, would have been saved.'

'That is ludicrous.' Achebe said, her face burning a temperature close to lava. 'I gave you a detailed brief of the threat to the best of my knowledge, having only been in its presence for the best part of fifteen terrifying minutes before last night. How dare you lay the blame on me. Setting the position of your soldiers is literally your job, so do not....'

'Prior to last night, you were the most senior officer to witness the animal. If you had told me it could leap that high, be strong enough to take down a robust lookout tower, and move faster than a bear, then I would have set up differently, and lives would have been saved.'

'If it weren't for me telling you to retreat your soldiers back....'

'Chief, this was an unknown enemy. The only information I had to work with was what High Constable Achebe told us prior to setting up my unit. Information that has, unfortunately, proven faulty. This is what ultimately led to the loss of life.'

Achebe's cheeks burned with a fiery rage. Maynard calling her a high constable was no slip of the tongue. She turned to the Chief, disgusted, hoping he might side with her, but his support was not forthcoming. Nor did he correct Maynard's misrepresentation. Instead, he stared at the floor with his hand under his chin as if doing mental arithmetic.

'The death toll would have vastly reduced had you not sent those four....'

Achebe was cut off by Maynard once again.

'As you know, Chief, we agree to help the police force on a case-by-case basis. Our cooperation is not guaranteed if I'm not comfortable with the job description.'

'Will you stop interrupting me when I'm speaking?' Achebe snapped.

The Chief looked uninterested, as if his mind was already made up. Maynard looked too comfortable. Achebe scolded internally; you bastards agreed I would take the blame before I even entered the room.

The Chief waggled his finger towards Achebe.

'I'm sorry, Nikki. Since the initial attack at the Dalmally caravan site, little progress has been made to stop this threat. As well as last night, there have been two further attacks at the forestry plant and the campsite.'

'The cryptozoologists placed themselves in the middle....'

'I. Am. Speaking.' The Chief stared down at her. 'Requesting that the Special Response Unit set up at Bannock Manor was your decision, and based on what Commander Maynard has told me, you have failed to describe the threat sufficiently. Seven lives were lost, Nikki. This cannot be brushed under the carpet. You have to take responsibility for these decisions. Regrettably, I am pulling you off the investigation with immediate effect. You will take two weeks' paid leave to rest, regroup, and come back ready to support Tom and Xander who will pick up this case. Perhaps this was too much for you too soon.'

'No, sir. You can't. Last night was not my fault. There was a clear opportunity to stop the beasts.'

Achebe's heart was pounding with fury. Her jaw muscles wrangled. She resisted the urge to lamp a cheap shot on Maynard's cheekbone.

'I've given you an order, Detective Achebe. I don't think you want to protest too much and turn this into a disciplinary. Commander Maynard and I will handle this in a manner that we hope will prevent an inquest, something that would not reflect well on you at all.'

Achebe stood.

'So that's it. You're dressing this up as if you're doing me a favour. I'll leave you to enjoy your little boys' club. Maybe I'll request for an internal inquiry of my own.'

'That would be career-ending, for you,' said the Chief, his voice deep with warning.

Achebe slammed the door behind her, stunning the early-rising officers, who looked at her like terrified meerkats. The hurt, the shame, the rage caused her body to shake. She wanted relief from standing, but she was too agitated to sit down. High Constable Robinson approached, still wearing her jacket as she had only just arrived.

'Nikki, what's wrong?'

Achebe opened her mouth, but the frenzy scrambled her words to nothing. She had to leave. She could not be in the office when her team started their day. She could not face the humiliation of seeing their *I knew it* expressions as she explained she was off the case.

235

A panicked young officer shouted to Robinson after coming off the phone.

'There's been a murder in the Borders. Same style as the murders at the Edin flat.'

CHAPTER 43

The corpse was bloodier than the four bodies in the Edin apartments. The gashes in the victim's back were deep with rage as the whip was thrown with greater intensity. As the blood greased the leather, each flick of the girl's wrist sprayed the walls with red zebra stripes. The cadaver lay blood-soaked, like a hunted carcass.

Dargo stood next to the deathbed. He could almost hear the whistle and crack that accompanied each laceration. The girl's attacks were no longer meticulous. She would claim each victim as if it was her last kill, squeezing every last tingle of enjoyment.

Bullock was doing all the verbal deduction, hypothesising the girl's next move, but Dargo's sharp mind was blunted by his guilt. There was no escaping his culpability in the lives lost, despite Bullock's best efforts to tell him otherwise. His personal and professional lives were cloaked in shame.

Bullock spoke with the proactive local officer from the Borders police unit.

'I was called here this morning,' the junior officer said. 'One of the owners saw blood on the walls when she was emptying the outside bins of each cabin. She went to explore further, and that's when she found him. She's really shaken up.'

'I can imagine.' Bullock said. 'So, who's the boy?'

'Mark Severin, a local lad. I've already informed his parents and spoken to some of his friends. Hope I haven't overstepped my rank in doing so. I just knew as soon as I saw the body that it was similar to your ongoing investigation and we would have to move fast to catch the killer.'

'Yes, your boss spoke to us and we approved your actions. You've done really well.'

'The victim was with friends at the pub last night. They said he started chatting up a girl, no name, and then they left soon after he approached her.'

'Any CCTV at the pub?'

'Only at the back door, but not at the front.'

'Any here?'

'None here. The only witness of the girl leaving was the owner's husband. He's elderly and gets up to pee five times a night. He said he spotted a girl leaving while on one of his journeys to the toilet at five a.m. She was heading toward the bus station.'

'She must have used a name to book the accommodation?'

'Liv Sibine was the name she gave, but the owners don't hold copies of any identification.'

'Thanks. That name matches the owner of the flat where we found the other victims.'

'Oh, by the way,' the junior officer said nervously. 'nice work on stopping that other murderer last week. I heard you beat him to death.'

'He actually fell to his death, but I landed a few blows before he did. So did he, though,' Bullock said, pointing to his soft purple cheek.

As they examined the crime scene, Bullock noticed the young officer glancing several times at Dargo. It was not uncommon for officers outside of the city to become awestruck by his presence, such was his legendary status within the force. Today, however, he was not living up to his reputation.

'Forgive him, we've not had much sleep since this case started,' whispered Bullock to the junior officer.

Bullock did not have to make excuses, however. The junior officer would confuse Dargo's vacant shell for being the detective's quirky, deep-thinking style. It would only add to Dargo's reputation.

What the young officer failed to realise was that guilt was peeling Dargo's confident persona. Another victim was dead, and it could have been prevented if gambling did not consume his life. Football, horses, casino, golf, tennis, rugby, boxing. He bet on them all; the options flicking through his mind like categories on a slot machine. Wherever it landed, he bet on it.

238

Back in the car, the rain battered off the windscreen to obscure their view of the outside world.

'Don't do that again,' Dargo said.

'Do what?'

'Make excuses for me in front of other people like I'm some puppy that's shat on their carpet. It's humiliating.'

Bullock frowned as he suppressed a bitterness in his mouth.

'You're a walking zombie, Tom. You never said a word in there. You just stared at the body like it was the first time you've seen a corpse.'

'This is the first time there's been bodies because of me. It's already humiliating enough that it's my fault. I don't need you dishing out pity as well.'

Bullock's jaw clenched as he withheld his anger.

'Pity? Fucking pity. I've just given you the best part of twenty-five grand to pay off some of your debt and save your family from falling apart, and now you're giving me shit because I told a junior officer you were tired. These people idolise you, Tom. Behaving like you did in there means they'll know something is off. I'm deflecting them from probing further because I'm guessing you'll want to keep this addiction a secret. I didn't do that because I pity you. I think you've behaved like an idiot, a complete fucking idiot. Luckily for you, I know you are more intelligent than your addiction suggests, and that's why I know that this addiction is serious. But don't for one minute think I pity you, because I don't.'

Dargo wiped his face with his hands, as if scrubbing off his rudeness.

'I'm sorry, Xander. I'm a fucking mess.'

'The only person feeling pity for you is yourself. You are not responsible for anyone's death. There was no way we were kicking that flat door down on our first visit. I can guarantee you that. You need to snap out of this mindset. Stop feeling sorry for yourself, because we've got a killer to catch, and we're fucking close. In the next twenty-four hours, we're gonna have her.'

CHAPTER 44

'Fucking dickheads.'

Achebe shouted through the phone with the same temper she had displayed in Chief Thorne's office. She thought her anger had settled, but the emotions lay dormant, waiting for an opportunity to erupt. The call to Tom and Xander triggered the explosion. Every cell in her body burned with rage, and her speech was impassioned with involuntary spit.

'He threw me off the fucking case. I can't believe....'

'Hold on, Nikki. The Chief has taken you off the case? Why?' asked Bullock via the speakerphone in the car.

Dargo straightened his miserable posture in the passenger seat when he heard Achebe's outcry.

'It was that fucking twat, Maynard. He blamed the deaths of his team on me. He blamed the whole attack on me, and of course, the Chief protected his fellow frat boy. How can a plan devised by Maynard be my fault?'

'Nikki, take a deep breath and tell us exactly what happened,' Dargo said.

Achebe stopped pacing her living room and sat on the sofa to compose herself. She described the previous night's attack at Bannock Manor and explained that Maynard had deflected the blame onto her.

'I can't be taken off the case. I'm finished as a detective if I am.'

'Listen to me, Nikki.' Dargo said. 'You will not like what I'm about to say, but there's nothing you can do at the moment. We will have a word with the Chief and try to straighten things out once we are back at the office.'

'Where are you now?'

'We are heading up to the Highlands. We believe the killer took a bus there after the murder in the Borders. With the help of local police, we are checking every bus stop, hoping to locate her.'

'Sounds like you are closing in on her.'

'It feels like it, but it means we won't be back in the office for a few days, so we won't be able to speak to the Chief about your situation until later in the week.'

'He's such a dickhead. Is this what I have to endure the further up the chain I go, cronyism?'

No one spoke. Achebe could only hear the hum of the car on the other end of the line.

'Are you still there?' she asked.

'Yes.' Bullock replied. 'There's not much more we can say on the matter other than we will do our best to convince the Chief that you should be reinstated as lead on the case. You know our thoughts on him, and you know highly we think of you. Do not worry about your career as a detective. This case seemed like a straightforward, escaped animal scenario that turned out to be far more insidious and peculiar than anyone foresaw. You should still be on the case, and, on reflection, we should have supported you better on your first outing as lead detective. Whatever has happened does not reflect on your ability to perform in the role.'

'Yeah, right. It's good to see life had a little more room for irony today as well. I am currently staring at my detective trilby, which has just arrived in the post. I've not taken it out of the box yet, I don't want to touch it. I may as well send it back.'

Dargo leaned forward. He empathised with Achebe, and he admired her uncompromising desire to succeed. She had been unfairly treated, so he decided to throw her a bone.

'What are you going to do with yourself today?'

Achebe was preparing to release her rage on phony targets at the gun range. She had asked Ash to join her, but that piece of information could be left unsaid.

'I'm heading to the range.'

'Golf?'

'Gun.'

'Perfect.' said Dargo. 'Go there and let off some steam, but pay heed to my next words. I was removed as lead detective from my second case because my superiors felt I was focusing the investigation on one suspect rather than considering other options. I had found no incriminating evidence on this individual and my boss saw an unsuccessful raid on the guy's premises as proof of my narrow-mindedness. I was given a week's leave to refocus, but, of course, I could not sit still or relax. You can get taken off a case, but the case does not leave you. As it happened, that week off was a blessing in disguise. It gave me the freedom to personally, but unofficially, conduct surveillance on this individual. That surveillance led me to discover that he was using an alternative building to produce the drugs I suspected he was selling. It took a few photographs and a lot of persuasion to convince my superiors to approve another raid. They were incensed that I had continued to work the case, but when we caught the culprit in that second raid, my misbehaviour was forgiven and forgotten.'

Achebe knew what Dargo was alluding to, but she wanted him to confirm.

'So, what you mean is?'

'What I mean is you might be officially off the case, but you are unofficially still on it so long as the motivation lives inside you.'

'Cheers, Tom.'

'Have fun at the range.'

*

Achebe smiled at Ash's bowed head in the driver's seat of the tiny, three-door car. It was not designed to accommodate a man of his height. He parked next to her outside the unassuming exterior of the gun range. She felt his nervousness as she embraced his muscular arms, and when he reciprocated, Achebe melted into his chest.

'Everything okay? Your message seemed quite abrupt,' he asked.

'Tough morning at work. I'm here to let off some steam, and I knew you would have plenty of time on your hands to join me, given you are a PhD student.'

'Oh really, you think important research involves sitting around watching Netflix all day?'

'That's exactly how I imagine it being.'

'You're not completely wrong. There are actually some superb, well-researched documentaries on cognitive diseases on these platforms.'

Ash said this with the sincerity of a nerd.

'Remind me to choose what we watch on movie night.'

Once inside, Ash shifted uncomfortably when asked which gun he wanted to shoot. He stared aghast at the firepower on display behind the counter, glancing to Achebe for help.

'He's new to this, Bill,' Achebe said. 'A small handgun will do.'

'And for you, Nikki?'

'Automatic rifle.'

'Someone's feeling feisty this morning.'

'After the week I've had, you'll have to order new targets by the time I'm done.'

The range was perched on the lip of a valley. Descending to the basement, the sheltered shooting booths faced a dirt field with metal targets placed sporadically at various distances.

Achebe gave Ash a tutorial on how to handle the gun and watched him miss the target with his first six shots. She took quiet satisfaction at his misfortune, her innate competitiveness knowing no boundaries. Not quiet enough to keep the smile off her face, however.

'What are you laughing at?' Ash asked with a grin.

'I'm sorry. It's just that most people at least hit the target once with their first round of bullets. That was pretty pathetic.'

'Thanks.' Ash smiled.

'Don't worry, you'll hit the target before we leave.'

Achebe went into her booth. She pressed a button underneath the waist-high shelf which triggered the targets to move horizontally along a girder; others poked their heads from behind brick walls, giving the shooter fleeting moments to make their shot.

There was a clamour of noise as the bullets came into contact with the metal figures, like hard rain pounding off a conservatory roof. She barely paused for a second as she realigned her aim to new targets. The spray of bullets was powerful and accurate, transforming the unassuming five-foot-five detective into a deadly assassin. She laid the gun down, removed her earmuffs, and turned, expecting Ash to be impressed.

'Not bad, I suppose, but even I could hit something with that gun. It fires a hundred bullets per minute.'

Achebe raised an offended eyebrow, keeping the fact it was something closer to five hundred bullets per minute to herself.

'Well, look at you being ballsy despite never hitting a target.'

Achebe picked up Ash's gun, loaded it and fired five headshots on five different targets, the other round skimming a metal shoulder. She turned to face him. This time, he was impressed.

'I think I've underestimated the girl with the beautiful voice at the jazz bar.'

'Don't mess with me.'

Achebe continued tutoring Ash, who hit the target on his ninth attempt. They high-fived and embraced as Achebe enjoyed a mental reprieve from the investigation, at least until they settled in at the cosy coffee shop afterwards. Ash went to the toilet, and in that window of isolation, Achebe's thoughts were consumed by the case once more.

'We can talk about your work. I really don't mind.'

Achebe had failed to notice Ash returning to the table. She surveyed the tranquil restaurant. No one was paying attention to anything other than their own company.

'I'm sorry, it's not that I don't want to be here, it's just that the last week has been incredibly tough, and it's very hard just to put it all aside, even when I'm not at work.'

'Let's talk about it then. I'm interested.'

'Most of it is confidential, so I can't.'

'In that case, we can eat in silence while I stare at you as if admiring a painting in an art gallery.'

'An awful abstract piece, no doubt.'

'A beautiful portrait.'

'Oh please, I'm already on the date. You don't have to flatter me anymore.'

They welcomed the hot drinks the barista brought to the table.

'Maybe you can help me with my case.' Achebe said, withholding the fact she had been removed from the investigation that morning. 'You do research and development as part of your PhD, right?'

'That is what a PhD is.' Ash said with a smile.

'Have you ever conducted an experiment where the result was unexpected? More than unexpected, it was completely bonkers, defying the laws of the science underpinning the experiment. Defying what anyone believes is true.'

'Yes, a lot more frequently than you might think.'

'What do you do in that situation? How do you go about understanding something you didn't even know was possible?'

'Well, the basic rule of science is to run the experiment multiple times to eke out any erroneous results. The bonkers results are often an error in one of the variables used in the experiment, often a human error of some sort. So, I guess the result is not truly bonkers in that respect because we would then re-run the experiment correctly.'

'Let's assume the bonkers results keep on coming. How do you figure out what's going on?'

'Lots of brainstorming, and lots of reading to understand scientific theories that both support and oppose what we are trying to prove and the results we have generated.'

'And what if none of that gives you the answer that you want?'

'That normally works, to be honest.'

Achebe sat back in her chair, uninspired, sipping from the coffee mug. Ash sensed his answer had not been the advice Achebe was seeking.

'Sometimes, when everything is pointing in one direction, it is hard not to follow the path it leads you down. We tend to focus on the key elements of an experiment, which might be true of your case. But, by focusing our attention on the key components of an experiment, we can overlook the finer details that could explain or gazump the entire study. It sometimes takes a person removed from the whole experiment or an incredibly analytical mind to identify the issue or the cause of the results.'

'Don't let the main act distract you from logical reasoning.'

'Exactly, and it helps to not completely disregard a theory you've previously dismissed. Keep going over old ground. You never know when it might prove important.'

Achebe pondered this thought. The werewolf was the main act. It was the bonkers result that defied logic, and so far, any theory to explain its presence fell short. No attempt to ensnare the beast had been successful. Traps of raw and live meat, an armed tactical unit, cryptozoologists with cameras, anaesthetic darts and impediments from old fables. All had fallen short. Achebe believed it was a new species of animal. As preposterous as it sounded, Komodo dragons and okapis were designated to myth until the early twentieth century. A giant squid was only captured live on camera for the first time in the twenty-first century. A new species of snake was discovered in Vietnam as recently as two-thousand-and-twenty, its skin so iridescent it is hard to believe it was not conceptualised by science fiction writers. The animal kingdom is littered with creatures that humans would regard as fiction if it were not for photographic evidence: two-headed vipers, mantis shrimp, shoebills, narwhals, star-nosed moles, pangolins, sunda colugos, leafy sea dragons, gerenuk, Venezuelan poodle moth, Japanese spider crabs, matamata, sea pigs, leaf-tailed geckos, pink fairy armadillo, goblin sharks. Achebe had researched them all, seeking inspiration.

The barista brought their food. Achebe ordered a bacon roll while Ash went for an egg sandwich.

'I'm glad I brought mints with me. My breath will be sour after eggs and coffee.'

Achebe shot a dead stare towards Ash, who thought he had spoken out of turn.

'I never meant that to sound forward. I'm not assuming I need fresh breath for any particular reason. I just....'

'No, I don't care about that. I mean, I do care, but that's not what I'm thinking about. You've just made me realise something. The mints. Jen said the same thing to me the other day, and I couldn't think why it bothered me, but now I do. Don't disregard old theories, you say. I knew something wasn't right. We've been using the wrong methods to hunt this creature.'

Ash sat like a brick wall to Achebe's ramblings.

'I need to leave.' she said. 'I need to follow this up while it's in my head. Do you mind if we end this here? I'm so sorry. I promise we will meet again. If you want to, that is.'

Achebe rose to her feet. Her mug clanged off the saucer, causing a small splash of coffee to tsunami over the rim.

'Of course, I want to meet again,' said Ash in a confused tone, still unsure whether he had spooked or supported Achebe.

'I promise I'll call you.'

'Okay.'

Achebe stepped a few paces past Ash. Before leaving, she turned, placed a gentle hand on Ash's cheek and kissed his smooth head.

In the car park outside, Achebe checked her phone. There were four missed calls from Sam and a message in capital letters telling her to get in touch straight away. Sam answered on the second ring.

'Nikki, I'm so glad you phoned. I know what the animal is.'

'So do I.'

CHAPTER 45

Dargo almost heeded Bert's advice and concealed from Sally the fact he had used Fin's university money to fund his gambling. But when he opened up to his wife about his addiction, he could do nothing but confess the full extent of his behaviour to the person he had loved for over two decades.

Dargo gave up hope that his call would be answered on the fifth ring. He visualised her curled on the sofa, a crumpled tissue dabbing runny eyes, fractured by betrayal, their relationship permanently scarred by disloyalty. She would analyse snippets of Dargo's behaviour from the last four years. His schedule, his excuses, his lies, even his truths warped to become lies; past conversations exhumed and reassessed for deceitful intent.

'Hello.'

Dargo was taken aback by the voice.

'Hello, Fin?'

'Dad. Where are you? What's going on? Mum's been crying.'

Dargo looked to the heavens as he controlled the urge to cry himself. He had not told Fin about his addiction.

'Everything is fine. Can you get mum for me?'

'Not until you tell me what's going on.'

'Mum is upset because I am currently closing-in on a killer and she is worried. You've probably seen it on the news. I phoned just to say I'm not coming home, but not to worry about me.'

'Okay.'

Fin appeared to believe the tale. Lying again, Dargo thought to himself. When will the lies stop?

'Why did you not phone her mobile?'

Dargo had called Sally's mobile several times, with no response. The landline was his last resort.

'You know what she's like, she puts her phone on silent after a certain time. I couldn't get through to her.'

More lies.

'I'll get her.'

Nerves were meant to be reserved for job interviews, raids on a killer's home, public speaking, penalty shoot-outs. Not in the lead up to speaking to your wife of seventeen years. Yet here he was, sick with anxiety. The next voice he heard was Sally's.

'What do you want?'

'Sally, it's good to hear from you. I just wanted to say sorry again, and that I won't make it home tonight. Xander and I are in the Highlands. We think we're close to catching this killer. We are staying at a hotel in….'

'Is that the excuse tonight? It's gone up a level from pretending you are working late in the office or touring the nightclubs as part of an investigation. Is there a casino up there that you fancy spending the rest of your son's money in?'

Slumped against the wall of his hotel room, Dargo partially regretted confessing all to his wife. This was his reality now. A life of lying meant he was no longer trusted. An addiction can be overcome, but the lies are tougher to forgive. Their relationship would be contaminated with mind games, second-guessing, and doubt. It was a baseless foundation to continue their marriage.

'Sally, I'm telling the truth.'

'Whatever.'

Dargo suspected she knew he was telling the truth, but wanted him to know that her trust was gone.

'I just wanted to speak with you.'

'I don't want to speak with you. I don't know who you are. You're certainly not the husband and father I thought you were.'

'I'm still me, Sally.'

Dargo closed his eyes in frustration. He sounded pathetic, desperate, just as desperate as Ronan sounded when detailing his family misfortunes at the casino.

'Don't plead your case to me, Tom. I'm glad you're not coming home tonight. I was going to ask you to stay at a hotel, anyway. You can't be around the house right now. When you're finished in the Highlands, come and collect some clothes and whatever you need to live somewhere else for a while.'

'I'm going to get help, Sally. Fin's money and a large portion of the loans have been repaid already. I'm going to fix this mess.'

Dargo looked at his phone. The call had already ended. This was his new life, a life without family.

CHAPTER 46

The girl sat in the corner of the bustling pub, deflecting the usual glances that came her way. The men were drinking her in more than their beer, downloading memories for their midnight masturbation, chugging in the bathroom while their wife slept in the adjoining bedroom. Several oglers vanished to the toilets, a little too long for a piss, and with the bogs hardly welcoming anyone to squat, the girl bet the toilets were more likely clogged with semen than shit.

The pub would be described as cosy if it were not for the cool breeze whistling into the main seating area every time a smoker bundled through the front door. Most guests had their jackets on, making it harder for the girl to judge who had the best physique. Her options were limited. Even in dog years, the tail-wagging mutts by the bar were younger than most of the punters.

The only viable option was one of three young guys standing at the bar. They were in their late teens, and each took turns to glance in the girl's direction. One stared while sipping his beer as if his glass was disguising his true intentions. They were not the bonniest boys in the land, but two more vodkas and one might become bearable.

The hottest, or least ugly, was Babyface in the checkered shirt. Blondie was second, and Tattoo was by far the ugliest of the trio, his neck art unable to overshadow his plooky face. None were overly muscly. None looked particularly athletic, but they were available and, with slim pickings within their small Highland town population, they would be pathetically horny. She would not have to work hard to lure one back to the hotel. In fact, all it would take is a raise of her eyebrow and a shy smile the next time Babyface looked in her direction. She may even waggle a discreet finger as she leaves the pub.

It duly worked.

The girl wore a lilac jacket with a deep purple feather boa at the collar. It swung behind her as she strode up the cobbled road towards her hotel. Behind her, she heard the hinges of the pub door squeak open. Not one, but three whispering boys piled outside. Babyface was goaded by the other two to join her, but he was hesitant to interact with the girl. Pathetic, she thought, before her body tingled upon realising the major opportunity presented to her.

'No need to decide who is walking me home, boys. You all can, and you'll all be rewarded.'

An excitable murmur emanated from the boys, who hastened the pace to catch up with her.

'You're not from around here,' said Tattoo.

Despite his facial misgivings, he was the most confident of the group. His red raw acne was even more vicious up close.

'How very astute of you,' the girl replied.

'So, where are you from?'

'Edin.'

'You just visiting?'

'Just passing through and looking for a good time. I think you guys can help with that, can't you?'

The boys exchanged feverish yet nervous smiles at each other. Babyface and Blondie were virgin shy, but Tattoo had no doubt shagged someone equally repulsive to shake off the virgin title.

'I think we can.' Tattoo said. 'Where are you staying?'

'Lochside Hotel.'

'Not far then.'

The boys hugged the stone wall lining the narrow road leading to the hotel. The girl walked in the centre of the empty road. Her gait was more of a stroll, dictating the boys' pace. She discreetly assessed each of them. Height, strength, estimated penis size.

At the entrance of the hotel, the girl turned to the nervous herd. She handed the keys to Babyface.

'If we all go piling into the room at the same time, it might look a bit suspicious to any onlooking guests or the hotel owners.'

The girl pointed to Babyface and Blondie.

251

'You go to room twenty-three, first floor.'

The girl turned to Tattoo while biting her lip.

'You and I will have a little adventure in the linen cupboard.'

Tattoo turned to his mates wearing a smile as discreet as a fire alarm. Babyface and Blondie walked in gingerly while the girl rested on the metal awning pillar as if she were bored waiting in a queue.

'What's your name?' Tattoo asked.

'Let's not ruin tonight with names?'

'You're very forward.'

'There's no point wasting time.'

Tattoo opened his mouth to speak again, but the girl interrupted him.

'Let's go in.'

The girl led him by the hand, past the deserted reception area to the linen cupboard, which would not be used until morning when the owners replenished each room with fresh towels.

The girl loathed the boy's desperation as she led him into the cupboard. In this world they claim belongs to the men, there is one glaring weakness giving girls the upper hand; men can be lured into any situation on the premise of sex. This boy was walking into a dark cupboard with a stranger who was on her own and refused to give her name. If the sexes were reversed, the decision to follow would be deemed ludicrous, but for a guy, this situation was all too comfortable. The girl watched the boy swagger into the cupboard. The arrogance, she thought. Not a single fibre of his being was the least bit concerned about his own safety. Like an impala drinking from a muddy, crocodile-infested river, he could not see the danger loitering within.

In the cupboard, the girl wasted no time, pressing the boy against the wall, kissing him on his disgusting, inky neck before leaving teeth marks on his skin.

The boy released a deep but fleeting scream.

'We can't make too much noise,' the girl said.

The girl lowered Tattoo to the floor and pressed her palms against his chest until he was lying on his back. She grabbed a facecloth from the shelves and sat on top of him, feeling a hardened lump through his jeans. She gagged him with the face cloth while caressing his crotch, causing him to squirm and moan into the towel.

'That should keep the noise down.' she whispered.

Tattoo arched his back, allowing the girl to rip off his jeans. His boxers followed shortly after.

Unbeknown to the squirming boy, the girl winced as she pulled back the foreskin of his chubby penis. The boy writhed under her touch. She scowled in disgust at the boy on his back, powerless from the gentlest rub from her hand.

Lowering herself over his body, she began kissing his abdomen, then licked a slug line down to his penis, where she sucked on five inches of pathetic skin. Muffled moans were caught in the fibres of the towel. Pressing firmly on the gag, the girl bared her teeth and clamped her mouth into his erection, biting through the shaft and ripping at the skin like wrestling with the fatty section of a steak.

The boy sat up; his screams muted by the towel wedged into his mouth. His hands clutched the bloody hole previously occupied by his penis as the girl spat a flesh pile on the carpet. Blood stained the crevices of her smile.

The boy spat the face cloth from his mouth, but he had no time to shout as the girl twisted him onto his front and looped a towel around his neck. She sat on his back and gripped both ends of the towel, pulling on them as if attempting to tie a bow. The boy pushed in a press-up position to knock the girl off his back, but she squeezed harder to impede any energising oxygen. His cheeks turned purple. The girl pulled harder, so hard she heard something pop in the boy's neck. A vein, a bone? She did not care as her body burned with fiery eroticism.

The boy stopped wriggling, and the girl exhaled a breath of elation. She had only been hunting for one victim, but the prospect of killing another two stoked the fire even more. She cleaned all the visible blood from her body with other towels and wiped her teeth with a small face cloth.

In the bedroom, the two bashful boys looked up from the bed like nesting chicks waiting for their mother to bring them some food.

'Which one of you wants to take me in the shower, and which one wants me when I come out all dripping wet?'

The two boys looked dumbstruck. One, if not both, was definitely about to experience their first, and last, sexual encounter.

Before either could answer, the girl took Blondie by the hand and pulled him into the bathroom. Babyface, the least offensive looking of the group, sat patiently on the bed.

The girl tied her hair up with a thick metal hairpin. Keeping her bloody teeth concealed, she undressed and entered the power shower. The water crashed off the plastic flooring, creating enough noise to drown out any commotion.

The boy tentatively followed her into the shower, uncomfortable with his skinny nakedness. The girl led proceedings, pushing Blondie's head down between her legs, where he tentatively licked her vagina like a cat drinking milk, unsure how to handle the new experience.

The girl smiled into the water and used a finger to brush more blood from her teeth. Keeping the boy's head wedged in between her legs, she squeezed her thighs tighter, and like a boa constrictor wrapping around its prey, her stranglehold strengthened every time the boy exhaled, his head jammed in between her glistening quad muscles. Blondie clawed at her thighs as he struggled to free himself. Air burst onto her vagina as the boy gasped for breath.

When the girl released her leggy grip, the boy fell onto the shower floor, holding his jaw. The girl sat atop his chest and began strangling him underneath the onrushing shower. He was not strong, and his reactions were stunted by the shock of the abuse. The girl pressed her knee against his throat and slipped a bar of soap into his gaping mouth, wedging it at his uvula, causing him to convulse.

With a firm knee squeezing the boy's neck and a bar of soap gargling in his throat, the girl removed the sharp, metal hairpin, letting her hair fall like a lion's mane. The stabs were slow, careful incisions into his protruding neck veins. Soapy red froth spluttered from Blondie's mouth as if he had bitten into a cyanide capsule, and blood poured from each stab like weaknesses in a dam. Between the strangulation and the blood loss, the boy's eyes wilted until there was no life left in his body.

Standing over his corpse, the girl washed the blood off her body, the soap eventually returning to its natural milky complexion. She left the shower running as she exited.

'He's just cleaning himself up in there. Things got rather messy. Perhaps not as messy as they will get in here, though.'

Babyface was not fully listening as he gawked at her twinkling body. She began undressing him until his pasty white figure was sprawled on the bed like a salamander.

'How about a little foreplay? I'm going to tie you up, then suck you off.'

Babyface nodded. He was concentrating on his breathing, praying his penis would work properly.

The girl removed leather straps from her bag and tied all four of his limbs to the bed. She decided against the blindfold. Seeing the pain in his eyes when he died was what she craved, but only after she was satisfied.

She slipped the boy's mediocre penis inside her and rode him fast. He ejaculated within twenty seconds, but she continued riding to maintain his erection. She was done in under two minutes.

'You enjoy that?'

The boy did not speak. His euphoria was so great that he did not even open his eyes as he nodded. Nor did he react when the girl gagged him with his rolled-up boxer shorts.

Retrieving the whip from her bag, she began lashing him before he had recovered from the sex.

Ten lashes.

Twenty lashes.

Thirty lashes.

Her appetite for pain was insatiable. Each remorseless infliction was more ferocious than the last, causing the bloody canyon in the boy's chest to gouge deeper to the bones. She was not sure which crack of the whip killed the boy, but she did not stop just because his breathing did. The tingle inside her grew. Her smile widened. Her grip tightened.

Crack!

Blood sprayed off the whip like a snake spitting poison.

Crack!

The girl bared red teeth as she pulled the whip over her head.

Knock! Knock!

Someone was at the door.

June 15th

CHAPTER 47

Bullock never refused an opportunity for a high-speed chase, the blue light trivially flashing atop his car despite the empty Highland roads. Dargo tried to wipe the sleep from his eyes but poked his eyeball as Bullock swerved round a tight corner. His hair swayed erratically, but Dargo knew he was in control.

The Lochside Hotel shimmered in the dawn sunlight. Police had cordoned off the front entrance and all the guests were huddled in the conservatory dining area at the side of the building. Some wore their bath robes while smoking outside.

'We're here for five minutes max,' Dargo said.

They knew the killer was nearby, so they agreed their goal was to establish which direction she went and by which mode of transport so they could pursue her rather than hang around the crime scene.

They flashed their badges to access the hotel. Dargo told Bullock to check the victims. He did not want to view the deceased, fearing he would turn motionless again. The guilt of his malfeasance still lived with him and seeing what he was guilty for was unnecessary at the present moment. He would have plenty of time to reflect on his actions once the girl was caught.

Dargo introduced himself to the hotel owners. The elderly couple were perched on stone steps with blankets wrapped around them. Both were visibly shocked that such an abominable crime had happened on their premises.

'Can you explain what happened?' Dargo asked brusquely.

'Yes.' It was the husband who spoke. 'We received a noise complaint from a guest. They said they could hear banging and whipping sounds coming from the next room. When Vera went to investigate, she also heard whipping noises. She knocked on the door, but no one answered. By this time, I was in my dressing gown and wondering what was going on. I went outside to see if a light was on in the bedroom. That's when I saw the window wide open. We used the master key to open the door, and that's when we found the body. When the police arrived, they found another in the shower and the cupboard where we keep the towels.'

Vera shut her eyes as if trying to blink away the images in her head. Her husband wrapped his arms around her.

'Did you see the killer jump from the window?'

'No.'

'Which room was it?'

'Room twenty-three.'

'First floor?'

'Yes, they jumped into those bushes. They were lucky to avoid breaking an ankle.'

'How much time passed between you first knocking on the door and then using the master key to get into the room?'

'I'm not sure. It could only have been five minutes at most.'

'Did anyone see which direction she went?'

'One resident said they saw someone running out of the driveway and turn left as if going out of the town.'

Dargo confirmed the killer's direction of travel with the eyewitness, who was wrapped in her dressing gown and huddled with the other guests, boastfully broadcasting that she had seen the killer.

Bullock exited the property, and Dargo signalled to get back in the car.

'She's moving on foot, heading out of town. Take a left out of the drive.'

'Could she have got a bus or train?' Bullock asked.

'At that time in the morning, nothing is operating out of here. She's travelling light as well. The owner entered the room five minutes after knocking. Their statement suggests the girl was whipping the victim when they interrupted her. I reckon she would have been naked, or close to it, so when she heard the knock, she had to scramble to get dressed, collect a few important things and escape out the window.'

'The room is a mess. All the sex equipment is still there.'

'She must literally have the clothes on her back and some hard cash, then.'

'Do you think she would go into hiding in the town?'

'No. This town will be a hotbed of activity today. It's not that big, so she'll risk being sighted if she stays.'

'Where is she heading then?'

'No idea. I'm not convinced she's planned for this. She seems more erratic, more ferocious, don't you think?'

'You can say that again. She's munched one of their dicks off.'

Dargo looked to Bullock, incredulous.

'It's been roughly two hours since she left the hotel.' Bullock said. 'If she's on foot, she could have travelled what, five, six miles? What's the next town, and how far away is it?'

'The next town is Tongue.' Dargo said, scrolling the map on his phone. 'Four miles away.'

'But when we get there, we don't really know who we are looking for. What the hell does she look like? We know it's a young girl with brown hair, but that hardly narrows the scope.'

'She has Adidas trainers on. There was an imprint in the soil beneath the window she jumped out of.'

Bullock screeched round a tight chicane. Dargo eyed the landscape with binoculars. Apart from the occasional fluttering birds and grazing deer, there was no movement.

'Pull in here.' Dargo said, pointing to the public toilets at the ramblers' rest stop on the way to Tongue. 'You're walking in the dark, your bearings are poor, and it's cold. I don't care who you are. You would seek shelter and respite, even if only for a moment.'

With no obvious sounds of movement from within the women's toilet, Dargo entered unannounced while Bullock quickly confirmed nothing untoward in the men's. The lukewarm lighting was not conducive to forensic inspection, so Dargo used his phone torch. The sink itself was clean, but there were dark patches on the metal taps.

'There's blood here. The smudges would be hard to notice under the toilet light, which is probably why she hasn't cleaned the place properly. She must've washed the victim's blood off her so that she doesn't raise suspicions when walking into the next town.'

Bullock stepped past a mushy trail of toilet roll emanating from a cold cubicle.

'I think she's wearing a purple garment. I'm no fashionista, but I reckon it's fluffy.'

Bullock pointed at loose threads soaked onto the toilet roll holder.

'She's in a frenzy.' Dargo said. 'How far to the next town?'

'Roughly two miles.'

'She'll be there by now, or at least close. I'll phone the police in Tongue and update them about the purple clothing and Adidas trainers,' said Dargo as he ran back to the car, punching a number on his phone. 'Then I'll phone Viti and tell her to get a couple of personnel to examine this toilet, as well as the hotel.'

Bullock slowed the pace to below twenty miles per hour in Tongue's sleepy town centre. Footfall was low as the clouds spat an early morning warning. After scanning the high street like owls, there was no sign of the girl, so they headed to the police station, which was nothing more than a house with a police plaque on its exterior. As they approached, the door barged open. A policeman, with his mobile wedged between his ear and shoulder, was pulling his trousers up while fumbling with his belt.

'You'll definitely want to tuck your tackle away with this girl roaming the streets.' Bullock said.

'Oh, I'm phoning you right now,' the policeman said hysterically.

'Well, you've got the next best thing. We're here. What's the rush, Davey?' Dargo asked.

'The girl's been spotted.'

'That was fast.'

'When you phoned, I sent a bulletin on the local Facebook page. Normally it's full of folk moaning about bin collections and people not picking up dog shit, so as you can imagine, a message about a fleeing murderer captured the whole town's attention pretty quickly.'

'Where is she?'

'Mr Galloway spotted a girl he didn't recognise with a purple coat. He started chasing her with a garden fork, so she fled towards the Ben Hope trail.'

'Can a car get up there?'

'Only so far.'

'Does it lead anywhere?'

'Aye. Up the Munro. The trail runs for miles.'

'Which direction is the start of the walk?'

'The other side of town. Drive as if you're leaving and take the first left. You'll get as far as the car park, and then it's a foot chase if she's there. Do you need me to come with you?'

'Yes, but first, can you update Major Crimes HQ that we are in pursuit and request helicopter assistance so we can scan a larger area? Send for backup as well.'

The car park was exposed to the elements as the earth opened up at the mouth of the Ben Hope Munro trail. The rain fell in greater volume and the vortex wind made sure they were hit from every direction.

'There she is.' Dargo said.

The girl was a couple of hundred metres above them on the gentle slope at the start of the trail. She wore a lilac jacket with a purple frilly section on the collar. The sound of the car doors slamming caused her to turn. Her open jacket swayed in the wind like a magician's cape. Her gaze was dark, squinting a tenacious scowl.

Not even the rush of adrenaline could overcome Dargo's lack of sleep.

'I can barely run a bath, Xander. You're up.'

'Lazy bastard.'

'I'll be closely following, don't worry.'

Bullock started jogging, pacing himself for the cross-country chase. The girl started running.

'Just keep her in sight.' Dargo shouted over the wind.

The subdued morning temperature shifted into a thick brunch heat, causing Bullock's sweat to stick to his skin like honey. He hung his leather jacket on a fencepost. Even in a foot chase, he would not discard his precious garment to the ground. His jumper, however, was thrown on the muddy terrain while running, leaving him to chase in a tight white t-shirt. Dargo was in close pursuit. He too had removed his jacket because of prickly heat.

The girl bound like a rabbit over the mountain's stone steps. Bullock shouted something, but between the wind and the gushing ravine to their right, Dargo could not hear the message.

Fifteen minutes elapsed, and Bullock was gaining ground. The girl was athletic, but Bullock had stamina.

Dargo stopped at the embankment, put his hands behind his head, and inhaled heavily to restore some energy. There was a sheer drop to the ravine ten metres below where the river forked in two directions, one towards the sea via a majestic waterfall, and the other flowed towards Tongue in a far calmer fashion. Despite the precarious white rapids, the river maintained an inviting allure to wash away his sticky perspiration.

Dargo trundled on. The next time he looked up, Bullock was no more the fifty yards behind the girl. She approached a wooden bridge; a necessary passage for any ramblers seeking to summit Ben Hope.

At the bridge, the girl removed her purple jacket, an undergarment of lycra exposing her athletic physique. She climbed the bridge's frame and balanced on the wooden ledge above the aggressive waves which clapped against the sides of the ravine, applauding her into its control.

Dargo could not hear Bullock, but witnessed him plead for the girl to come down. Before he could reach her, she jumped feet first into the ravine while squeezing her nose.

With the girl now flowing in Dargo's direction, he found a thin, muddy trough leading from the ravine edge to a slippery boulder that jutted into the river. He knelt down, holding his hand out in anticipation for the struggling girl who would be battling for survival amongst the rapids. As he saw her neck barely holding above the water, he shouted for her to grab his hand, but his voice was feeble against the slosh of the waves and the cry of the wind.

As the girl got closer, Dargo saw she was not struggling at all. She swam with the tide, smiling as she grabbed Dargo's hand and yanked him into the water with her.

Dargo's world spiralled from murky waters to cold air as the rapids spun him like damp clothes in a washing machine. His jumper was instantly saturated, weighing his arms down beneath the waterline. He gasped for breath, but all he felt was pain as two hands squeezed his neck while forcing his head underwater.

His back smashed against a rock.

The grasp on his neck released.

His body spun again, but he could not determine which direction he was facing.

A gasp towards the sky brought him much needed oxygen.

His ribs hit an undercurrent boulder, and his knees scraped against a jagged rock.

He gasped again for more air, his body twirling so he now faced downstream.

The girl clawed his face and pushed his head under once more.

The water was murky, but there was enough visibility to see the girl's legs scissor around his neck, constricting like an anaconda.

Dargo grabbed the girl's legs, but in trying to separate them, he swallowed water.

Panic.

His body twisted.

They both smashed into a boulder.

The girl's legs separated, and Dargo's head rose above the waterline, but he was still choking, his gasps desperate and loud.

He eventually caught his breath, but his energy was stilted. The world around him moved at a furious tempo, but his mind was suddenly tranquil in the middle of it all. His struggle to breathe was rendered meaningless. What was he fighting for? Why did he want to survive when

262

his future included estrangement from his wife and children? Did he really care if he lived?

The girl was ahead of him, battling against the tide to get closer to him like a crocodile drifting in for the kill. Dargo saw the fork in the river appear behind her. They were approaching the waterfall, but the girl was oblivious to its presence.

With survival no longer imperative, Dargo swam towards the girl rather than seeking safety. Her two hands limply gripped onto Dargo's clothing giving him an opportunity, with a fierce surge of energy, to grab the girl's arms and spin her so his chest pressed against her back, gripping in a bear hug which caused her to scream and writhe in his hold.

Their shins smashed against underlying rocks, but Dargo's arms remained locked around her.

Their bodies capsized under the water, resurfacing seconds later.

The girl screamed and wriggled as the rapids spun them in a waltz towards the waterfall. Jagged rocks awaited them at the bottom of the deadly drop.

Dargo closed his eyes, preparing for whichever form death came: a sharp collision with a rock or the serene silence of drowning. He did not care which.

They approached the fork in the river.

The girl smashed knee-first into a boulder that was obscured under the sprinting river.

Dargo's grip loosened, releasing the girl.

He was then propelled to the right-hand side of the fork which flowed down to the town.

The girl continued towards the waterfall.

Dargo heard a scream, which was quickly drowned out by the gushing waves.

The river was gentler on its route to Tongue and Dargo only travelled a few metres before becoming caught in a crevice within the ravine wall. He raised his arms over two rocks as if chilling on the sofa, but he did not have enough strength to pull himself out of the water.

Despite the disregard for his own life, Dargo's survival instincts still begged for air. Oxygen never felt so critical as his body cherished each molecule.

His sense of time was lost, so he was unsure how long it took for Bullock to reach him, but his breathing had not yet recovered when his partner ripped him from the water as easily as picking a baby out of the bath.

'The girl.' Dargo spluttered.

'Forget that bitch.'

'Is she alive?'

'Down that waterfall. No chance.'

They both lay exposed to the elements on the embankment as they regained their energy. Initial investigations showed no sign of the girl's body at the bottom of the waterfall. Instead, she was dragged down the river into the mouth of the sea where her body would meander until eventually washing up on a nearby beach.

CHAPTER 48

Achebe intended to detail everything to Dargo and Bullock, but the phone line was crackly, and she was too excitable to explain the situation coherently. The dodgy connection was a blessing, as Tom and Xander would have numerous questions as to why she was standing outside Bannock Manor with Sam Stone, requesting their assistance. It would be easier to discuss in person when they arrived.

'What's their ETA?' Sam asked.

'Half an hour.'

'Should we wait for them?'

'No, let's try to find something to show them.'

Having been removed from the case, Achebe could not request any support from the Chief or Maynard's Special Response Unit. Sam was comfortable with this. She would be ushered away from the scene immediately if the police hierarchy were present, denying her the opportunity to follow through on what she had discovered in Sector Five.

Achebe flicked the safety cap off as they entered the fringes of the watchful forest. She paused a few steps into the gorse to study a map taken from an old archive file from Sector Five, labelled Project Volcano.

The manor was of no interest to them. It was the forest that offered the chance of discovery. As they studied the bark on several tree trunks, a squawk echoed between the forestation, causing Achebe to flinch with her gun outstretched. The harmless pheasant fluttered away into the distance, but as its fleeting remark faded into obscurity, the subsequent chilling silence was emphasised. Both women shared anxious looks before continuing their search in an area dictated by the map.

'Over here.' Sam shouted.

Achebe hopped over a fallen tree to reach Sam. She flicked open a barky flap on one of the tree trunks. It concealed a showerhead, ready to exhale whatever contents flew up the piping, camouflaged beneath a layer of bark.

'You found one,' Achebe said. 'It was unusually misty the night Maynard's unit was attacked. The ravers mentioned poor visibility in their testimonies as well. This pipe system has been here for years.'

A brown pipe, hidden by carefully placed bark, slithered down the tree trunk and trailed underneath damp foliage to a point where the roots of two trees entangled above the ground.

Achebe started clambering over the roots, squealing as her leg fell with an unnerving snap, grateful it was a branch and not her ankle. Her forehead wore worried furrows as she became trapped in the root structure. Her leg dangled into an abyss while the rest of her body sat awkwardly in the network of branches. She tried to push herself up, but brittle branches snapped under her weight and she fell further in.

'Grab my hand.' Sam said.

Their hands clasped and Sam dragged Achebe from the forest snare, sharp twigs puncturing small holes across her sweatshirt.

As Achebe dusted flakes of the forest from her midriff, a clang of metal emanated from beneath the roots, incongruent to any woodland sound. They shared ominous glances before Achebe started pulling away the loose roots to reveal a dark hole underneath the strategically positioned undergrowth.

'The den,' Sam whispered.

Another clang of metal hissed out of the hole. They stared at its unwelcoming entrance, both recounting occasions when curiosity almost killed them, and once again, the absurdity of their decision to enter the den was superseded by an insatiable desire to discover the mystery of the werewolf.

The entrance descended at a steep angle to a flat tunnel formed with thick-set soil walls. The air inside was trapped in a hot vacuum. A rich earth smell blended with an off-meat stench migrating deep from within. A waving light dimly lit their path forward. Whether it was a candle or a fire, they could not tell, as the light source was tucked within a chamber at the end of the tunnel.

Achebe held out her firearm as they edged across the untidy floor, where loose clumps of soil had fallen from the ceiling. A fleeting shadow on the wall at the end of the tunnel stunted their movements. The gun wobbled in Achebe's hand.

Sam pinched her nose as the smell of the earth dissipated and the odour of rotting flesh stunned their sinuses. Achebe halted too, but Sam nudged the detective, urging her to keep moving.

The clang of metal and shadows became more frequent. As they approached the chamber at the end of the tunnel, they could hear a voice, or rather, voices, deep in discussion. Achebe slowed, tentatively planting her foot to peer in.

Werewolf!

A hungry mouth, covered in a mane of brown fur, stared at Achebe with jaundice eyes. Her finger almost pulled the trigger as she backed onto Sam's toes, who puffed her cheeks to contain a squeal.

Achebe took another step towards the unwavering werewolf. She pointed the gun at its head, but the werewolf was not disturbed by her presence. It was fixed on a podium, arms outstretched, mouth agape, and its back ripped open. It was not alive.

Keeping her back against the soil wall, Achebe entered the room, sweeping the barrel of the gun for any signs of movement. Sam followed, their jaws becoming as slack as the werewolf upon observing the room.

Candles poked into the soil walls provided enough dim visibility to see that the odour of rotting flesh emanated from a pile of soldier's limbs in the far left corner, like logs ready to go on the fire. Most of the light, however, came from the fire underneath a cauldron of boiling liquid bubbling insidiously in the centre of the room. Not one, but three werewolves surrounded it. One silver, one black, one brown, all with their spines ripped apart as they rested on podiums as if displayed in a museum.

A large cog, shaped like a pirate's wheel, was embedded into a concrete wall at the back of the room. Hissing voices emanated from another tunnel to the right of it.

'This is creepier than I expected,' Sam whispered.

The voices stopped abruptly. A ghostly human hand gripped the earthy edges of the far side doorway before a scabby, bald head peered around the soil wall. Bloodshot eyes looked incredulously upon the unexpected arrivals. Cheekbones protruded from a malnourished face, and their skin was pulled back like stretched leather. They walked with a hunch, but their naked frame stood taller than Achebe and Sam. There was no fat on the body, only natural muscle mass bulging through marble flesh, blotched with purple and blue bruising.

267

Duncan Weir was not dying of cancer, as Achebe once thought. His pallor was due to years of sun deprivation living beneath the earth; his blotchy skin a result of dieting on human flesh; his name, an alias to hide his true identity.

'Mr Lundstrom.' Achebe said. 'We're here to help you.'

The human creature did not react to the name. Instead, he assessed Sam and Achebe, possessed by evil.

'Mr Lundstrom, we know everything that's happened. We know you suffer from a rare and terrible case of lycanthropic schizophrenia. We know that Rockwell brought you to Strathaven, not to heal you from your demons, but to leverage on them so you can inflict violence. You need to come with us. We can help you. These attacks need to stop.'

Lundstrom hopped in front of the brown werewolf like an ape. He spoke in a devilish tone.

'Looks like we don't need to hunt for a while.'

The man hopped around the cauldron to the black werewolf and rolled on the floor laughing, soil sticking to his elbows and heels. His voice turned childish.

'Our easiest kill yet. I want the black one,'

Licking chapped lips, the man hobbled in front of the brown werewolf. His voice deepened once more.

'That's not up to us. Fenris decides.'

A hop back to the black werewolf meant a return to the high-pitched voice. He stared at the grey werewolf in fear.

'Yes, Fenris can decide,' he said with his head bowed.

Lundstrom's antics were so ungodly, Achebe and Sam were stunned into silence. Eventually, Achebe regained her composure and began talking, slowly and calmly, hoping her words would bring Lundstrom out of his schizophrenic episode long enough to arrest him.

'Mr Lundstrom, these werewolves are not real. They were built for you in Strathaven's Sector Five to nurture your lycanthropy. You can fight against your disease. We can help you so that you never hurt anyone again. Please come with us, Mr Lundstrom. We can end all this suffering.'

Sam's breathing became more pronounced upon realising that nothing Achebe said was going to seduce the Lundstrom's mind into a compliant, human state. Instead, the pale man wriggled across the floor in front of the black werewolf, his teeth chattering feverishly. Saliva slithered down his chin as he hopped between the black and brown werewolves.

'Let's just finish them now, so tasty.'

'No, wait for Fenris.'

'When is he…'

The man's neck cracked, and he coughed onto all fours.

'Mr Lundstrom, you're under arrest.'

Achebe's words were pathetic in a den that was far from the world of law and order. Lundstrom became more animated.

'Let's go, Nikki. Shoot him or run.' Sam said, tugging at Achebe's free arm.

Achebe's gun was raised, but she hesitated, wanting to give Lundstrom every chance to snap out of his delusion and surrender. She fired a warning shot into the soil wall next to him. He snarled yellow teeth and his spinal cord wriggled like a dragon swimming underneath his translucent skin.

'You've woken the boss.'

'You're in trouble, you're in trouble, you're in trouble.'

The man started giggling underneath the black werewolf while pointing at Achebe, but sharp kinks in his neck began triggering a change. High-pitched laughs were interrupted by intermittent growls as gloopy spit sprayed with each erratic movement.

'Shoot him, Nikki.'

Nikki obeyed without thinking, firing a bullet into the Lundstrom's leg to maim him. The ballistic was like a shot of adrenaline to the growling creature. He rolled under the brown werewolf, crouching as he spoke with his cold eyes examining Achebe.

'Fenris is here.'

'Ooooooooooo, bye bye tasties.'

Lundstrom growled, then chuckled, then growled. His muscles rippled, and the hunch he carried cracked straight. His neck rolled, and he convulsed as if coughing up a fur ball. He stood tall, stretching his arms up so his fists brushed the soil ceiling. He began turning the metal cog, causing steam to hiss through the pipe system. He then climbed atop the silver werewolf, frothing at the mouth like a rabid dog while straddling into the werewolf's back.

Unnerving amazement stupefied Achebe and Sam; horrified as the werewolf's back creaked shut like elevator doors.

'It's a fucking metal suit, Nikki. You should have shot him dead when you had the chance.'

The dead eyes of the werewolf glowed with a flicker of life. Its jaw clenched and its body clicked with each jerky movement as it adjusted to living once again.

Achebe fired several rounds, but they bounced off the werewolf's metal shell, which was buried beneath dense wolf fur. Their own mortality was more at risk from a ricocheting bullet.

The werewolf fell from its podium, moving ungainly as the man inside adjusted to the suit. Its growl was deep, divergent from the man's intonations because of a voice modulator projecting from the beast's throat.

'Fucking leg it.' Achebe shouted.

The tunnel felt eternal, but before exiting, Achebe turned. The werewolf was only just entering the soil corridor, rearing its head, grunting, snorting, and stumbling like a newborn giraffe. Its body covered any light from the room behind, shrouding the tunnel in a black shadow apart from two devilish red eyes poised for carnage.

A silhouette of the beast returned as it crouched on all fours, readying the springs in its feet, which gave it extra running and jumping power. Its growls and snarls were short and frequent, and rather than echoing off the walls, the sounds died as quickly as a victim of the werewolf's talon.

By the time Achebe exited the tunnel, Sam was hurdling over felled tree trunks to get back to the car. The fake mist was not yet thick enough to obscure Achebe's view, allowing her to dart quickly through the trees and have the engine running and wheels spinning as she prepared to flee.

Metal toenails smashed through the rear windscreen.

A claw pierced the roof as the werewolf anchored itself to the car.

Sam screamed.

The back right tyre punctured under a talon swipe.

The car diverted off the dirt road driveway.

Tree trunks loomed.

Achebe wrestled the steering wheel to veer back onto the road.

Dusty dirt from screeching tyres powdered the vehicle.

The left tyre bumped into a deep pothole.

Achebe and Sam smacked their crowns off the roof, but the werewolf clung on.

An outstretched talon burst the front right tyre.

Sam braced against the dashboard as the car squirmed uncontrollably.

'We're fucked.' Achebe shouted.

The bonnet crashed into a tree. The sound of grinding metal slithered down the spine of the two passengers as the werewolf's momentum scraped its holstered paw along the roof, smashing into the tree trunk with a thud.

'Get ready to run.' Achebe said as she opened the door.

The werewolf cumbersomely flailed its limbs. The suit was not designed for its user to be on their back too often. Achebe remembered her last experience with the creature. Her kick to its face had stunted its attack, something she assumed was because of its sensitive nose, but since realised must have compromised the integrity of the suit.

Achebe stamped on the werewolf's snout three times, the nose and jaw now askew, the modulated growl fading as the voice box altered position within the suit.

'Run!'

Achebe's chest was burning. Her legs were not long or fast enough to match the horrific, and yet euphoric, adrenaline surge coursing through her body.

The werewolf struggled to readjust its crooked snout, presenting Achebe and Sam with valuable seconds to form a plan of action. Their breaths were loud, their hearts pumping too much blood to their brains to think clearly.

'To the house.' Sam puffed, edging in its direction.

'There's nowhere to hide,' Achebe replied. 'It's too open and dilapidated.'

'Could we get to the roof?'

'Doubt it.'

The werewolf stood on its hind legs, its claws still scrambling to mend its snout.

The sound of tyres crunching into stones sparked hope in both women as a vehicle approached. Achebe waved a desperate plea. The car sped up, charging at pace and colliding into the back of the werewolf. The bonnet buckled within itself and the windshield shattered as the beast rolled over the roof of Bullock's car. Smoke billowed from the vehicle as the two passengers swiftly exited, jogging next to Achebe.

'What the fuck is that thing? I thought I was going to kill it, but now my car's fucked and it's still alive.' Bullock said, exasperated.

'It's a man in a very sophisticated metal suit. No time to explain. We need to leg it.'

'In the house.' Dargo said.

'No, there's no hiding from it in there.' Achebe said, while processing Dargo's scraggly clothing and bedraggled expression. Something had happened to him, but she did not have time to dwell on it. 'We're going to have to scatter in the woods and hope we reach the lodges by the loch. It's our best chance.'

'Which direction?' Sam asked while rubbing the dull pain in her arm from the crash into the tree.

'Behind the house.' Achebe said. 'About a mile or so.'

'Leg it.' Bullock shouted, looking back at the werewolf. The voice box was back in place. It discharged ungodly growls of frustration as a lack of dexterity meant it remained struggling to fully realign its snout.

Achebe could hear Dargo shouting for backup into his phone, but his voice was soon lost as they spread farther apart within the woods. The treetop ceiling consumed the daylight, and the unnatural mist fogged their vision, meaning all was dark as they attempted to escape from the werewolf within the forest of damned souls.

CHAPTER 49

Achebe's route forward only became visible milliseconds before she planted her feet, such was the thickness of the man-made mist. Her cheeks were flushed and her thighs radiated heat. The pace at which she ran overwhelmed her sense of hearing, so she slowed to listen for any sound of the werewolf. At least they did not have to worry about an impressive sense of smell sniffing them out.

A piercing howl of terror echoed through the woods.

The beast was back in action.

As Achebe ran, her eardrums pulsated a ferocious drumbeat. But the faint sound grew in fervour and emanated from her left. Then she saw a shadow accompanying the drumbeat, a drumbeat caused by the bounding paws of the werewolf slapping the ground on all-fours.

Achebe clung to a tree trunk.

Sharp, vicious panting weaved in between the drumbeat as the crescendo reached Achebe.

She closed her eyes.

The beast was upon her.

The breeze of its backdraft wafted cold air across her face as it whistled through the mist, passing her on the blind side of the tree.

Achebe inhaled a breath that was stuck in her throat.

Then Dargo screamed; not in pain, but in a manner which goaded the beast in his direction.

Achebe started running again.

From the opposite direction, Bullock shouted profanities at the beast.

The drumbeat returned.

Achebe stiffened.

A few yards ahead, the galloping beast punctured a tunnel of clarity through the swirling mist, unaware of Achebe's presence once again.

'Clever bastards,' Achebe spluttered under heavy breaths.

Dargo and Bullock kept provoking the beast in the hope the werewolf zigzagged between them until they reached the lake.

After a few hundred metres, the air cleared as Achebe breached the border of the manufactured mist. She could see Sam darting ahead like a gazelle, her blonde ponytail swishing from the back of her cap. She was safe, for now at least.

The brighter surroundings generated an illusory sense of safety until the werewolf's howl of death pumped extra adrenaline into Achebe's legs.

Dargo shouted from her left.

Achebe remained focused on her running lane.

Trees rustled to her right.

Frightened birds flapped from their branches.

The hairs sharpened on Achebe's neck.

A feeling, an aura, an instinct told her death was near.

The grunts became louder, triggering a flood of survival information to the forefront of her mind, reminding her of the day the lions infiltrated her family's land in Botswana. She was miles from her house, and as the lions approached from afar, knowing they are notoriously poor climbers, she found refuge high in the trees.

Achebe scanned her surroundings for a climbable tree trunk, evaluating each one in a nanosecond as she continued darting towards Loch Bannock.

The growls were louder, closer.

She did not turn round. She did not want to see her killer. If death was her fate, she wanted it to be sudden.

A tree with a low fork in its structure grabbed Achebe's eye. She wedged her foot in the groove to leverage herself up the tree, climbing to the third layer of branches, too brittle and small for the werewolf to scale, if it could even climb at all.

Hugging the branch while facing the undergrowth, the beast slowly emerged through the trees, kinking its neck as if cracking it to a more comfortable position. The snout was realigned, but its sense of smell was non-existent. Instead, it was listening and observing. Its silvery fur wafted in the forest chill as it traced Achebe's muddy footprints with its snout.

Stopping at the foot of the tree on its hind legs, the beast slowly tilted its head upwards until its blood-red eyes fixed upon Achebe, teeth bared. It clawed at the bark before pacing backwards, poised for a leap towards her, but its movement was halted by a shout amongst the trees. It was Bullock.

The werewolf scampered towards the more accessible target.

Achebe turned to assess whether there was a tree-lined route she could swing across rather than risk the forest floor again. You're not bloody Tarzan, she thought.

Achebe abseiled down the tree, jumping the last few metres. The adrenaline started pumping again as the claustrophobic forest exposed her vulnerability once more.

Running hard, she glanced to her right as a shout from Dargo was followed by a clatter of paws flowing past behind her. Without consciously making a definitive decision on whether to take part in their strategy, Achebe expelled an angry shout of her own. The reality of her action pushed her pace a little faster. Glimmers of white sky appeared through the trees in the distance. She estimated they were three-quarters of a mile in. Only a few hundred metres more until the loch.

Birds flapped to her right.

The beast was running towards her.

Panic flushed heat through her veins.

She was scanning for another climbable tree, but none were forthcoming.

The war drums returned.

The grunts even angrier than before.

The forest was endless.

Tree after tree laid out in organised chaos.

An inescapable labyrinth.

Death was the only exit.

She felt the beast's eyes locked onto her.

Bullock shouted from somewhere to her right, but the beast ignored him.

She used a barky node jutting out from a tree trunk to propel her arms around a thick branch.

Dangling, she tried to pull herself onto the tree.

The werewolf swiped.

The claws ripped the skin around her ribcage.

She lost her grip, somersaulting to the ground, unleashing a howl of her own as the bottom of her spine landed firmly on the tree roots.

The werewolf's momentum meant it ran past the tree and was now circling back towards her. It howled in celebration, standing on its hind legs as it strode the last few steps towards the fearful detective.

Achebe braced herself for the impact of its claw. During the case, she had tormented herself, wondering how the victims felt during their last moments. Now she knew. She was petrified. Pained by the notion that she would never see her parents again. Love possessed her final thoughts as the werewolf's right arm prepared a fatal swipe. She closed her eyes in anticipation of the blow, but too many seconds passed without impact.

When she opened her eyes, Dargo was hanging on the beast's right arm. The werewolf swiped at him with its left claw, but he swivelled onto its back with his arms wrapped around its neck. Crouching on all fours, the werewolf writhed viciously to dismount Dargo, but his grip was too strong.

Achebe rose to her feet. The werewolf stood as Dargo yanked on its head with his arms around its neck. Only now, up close, could Achebe hear the strain of the metal suit as Dargo tested the robustness of the engineering.

The beast rolled across the dirt.

Dargo lost his grip.

Achebe froze.

The beast snarled over Dargo, slamming a claw towards his head. He rolled to evade its impact, but the beast slapped another claw at the detective. A talon sliced through his shoulder, sinking deep into the tissue and snapping the nerve.

This time, Dargo did shout in anguish.

The werewolf went down on all fours, hunched over Dargo.

Achebe uncocked her gun.

The werewolf growled before gritting its teeth. Its head lowering to Dargo's neck.

An idea exploded in Achebe's mind.

Pressing the barrel of the gun into the werewolf's eye, she pulled the trigger.

The eye smashed like glass. It was glass. Achebe ducked in anticipation of the bullet ricocheting off the creature's metal structure, but the bullet had penetrated the suit and rebounded internally, maiming the man inside.

The werewolf retreated six steps, wailing more than Dargo, who was now breathing in short bursts. The beast fell into the dirt at the foot of a tree as it struggled to recover.

Achebe lifted Dargo to his feet. Blood spurted from his shoulder, which rested limply by his side. He was not moving anywhere swiftly.

'The loch is just there, Tom.'

They scampered through the remaining trees to a cliff edge that overlooked the shimmering loch, meditating amongst the chaos.

Achebe could see the lodges dotted sporadically at the fringes of the loch, but they would have to venture down a sloping footpath to get there. Sam was already halfway down, but it would take them at least twenty minutes to descend to relative safety.

There was a howl from within the woods. Dargo lay down, gritting his teeth in pain while clutching his injured shoulder.

'You go.' Dargo said. 'I can stall it while you go to the lodges and get help.'

'No chance.'

Achebe could not see the werewolf, but she could hear its modulated panting, like the low spooks of a ghost before it properly frights.

The pants were louder, angrier, and as it emerged from the trees, the cycloptic beast looked even more sinister with just one blood-soaked eye.

The werewolf charged at them.

There was no time for Achebe to reach for her gun.

The beast leapt in the air with its arm raised to slash the two detectives.

Achebe and Dargo cradled each other as they braced for impact.

The werewolf howled.

Achebe looked up just in time to see the creature bundle off the edge of the cliff, Bullock clinging to its fur, having tackled the beast mid-flight.

'No!' Achebe shouted as Bullock cannoned off the cliff with the werewolf.

Achebe let go of Dargo and ran to the cliff edge.

Dargo rolled onto his front and used his good arm to drag his body, peering at the loch below.

Bullock's head rose to the surface. He lay on his back and started kicking his feet towards the shore, his arms motionless by his side.

'He's injured.' Dargo said. 'But at least he's alive.'

277

Achebe never answered as she watched for the werewolf, terrified Bullock would be clawed under by the beast.

A swirl of desperate, hopeless splashes spouted next to Bullock as the werewolf floundered to tread water in the heavy metal suit, unable to generate any momentum or movement. Eventually, the ripples faded into calm waters as the beast was devoured by the twinkling loch.

June 17th

CHAPTER 50

Bullock leaned into the cushion of his leather chair, letting out a sigh as it reclined. His feet rested on the radiator and his dislocated shoulder hung in a sling. His midriff was mummified, having fractured several ribs when tackling the werewolf; an injury exacerbated when he skelped the loch waters. The swelling of his left cheek from his encounter with Bob Huskins still lingered amongst the assortment of wounds.

Dargo, sitting at his own desk, was in no better shape. He also wore a sling on his left shoulder, sporting an injury far more serious than his counterpart. The beast's talon had punctured his skin, scraped away tissue, and caused serious nerve damage. It would take months of rehabilitation to restore any sort of functionality. When he walked, he did so with a limp after his knees smashed off the jagged rocks during his river rapids duel with the female killer, Liv Sibine; injuries he inflamed during the foot chase through the forest of damned souls.

'How're things with Sally?' Bullock asked, facing the ceiling with his eyes closed as he succumbed to his physical discomfort.

Dargo gave a tentative nod before he spoke.

'Thankfully, the prospect of me dead is a far worse notion than the reality of my gambling addiction. She's still angry, of course, but I don't think divorce is imminent anymore. I used my time in the hospital wisely. I closed all my betting accounts. Sitting on hold for forty minutes isn't so bad when you physically can't do anything else. I even phoned the casino and told them to refuse me entry if I ever turn up again. Sally and I agreed I need professional help, though. All these actions feel effective today, but it's tomorrow when I'm bored at home and the football is on the telly, that's when the addiction becomes dangerous. That's when I'll think about re-downloading the betting apps and setting up new accounts.'

'I'm glad to hear you're working things out with Sally. Almost drowned by one killer, then almost killed by a mechanical werewolf. It doesn't take much to keep a marriage together these days.'

Dargo smiled.

'I can't thank you enough for the money, Xander.'

Bullock waved his hand, eyes still shut.

'Don't mention it. You would've done the same for me.'

'I know, but.'

'Tom, I said don't mention it.' Bullock shooed away the comment, too stubborn to accept gratitude.

'Okay!' Dargo said with a chuckle. 'But I will never forget the support you've given me.'

The office floor exploded with noise.

'Nikki's arrived.' Bullock said while swivelling in his chair to look through the blinds into the main office of Major Crimes.

Achebe walked through a guard of honour from the clapping officers as she made her way to Dargo and Bullock's private office.

'Is this the orthopaedic ward?' she asked while readjusting a backpack over her shoulder.

Due to their respective hospital treatments, it was the first time they had been in the same room since the werewolf chase. Had they met earlier, the events would have been too raw to fully comprehend, but now, after two days, a few dozen painkillers and several stitches, their spiralling minds had settled, and it was time for Achebe to explain everything.

'I wish I could hug you both, but I'm guessing you are too fragile for that,' Achebe asked.

'I'm already broken, so I'll take one.' Dargo said.

Achebe delicately embraced Dargo.

'Xander?'

'Quickly, before someone else sees,' said Bullock, throwing out his good arm. 'And how come I didn't get an ovation like that? It was me that bloody killed the thing.'

'Aww, feeling underappreciated?'

Achebe ruffled Bullock's hair to supplement the feigned pity.

'I spoke to Sam earlier. We both can't thank you enough.' Achebe said. 'Without you two shouting to distract the werewolf in the woods, Sam and I would be carved up right now.'

281

'Bollocks!' Bullock said. 'You would have found a way out of there. It was you that made sure we didn't become stuck in the manor. Directing us to the lodges by the loch was a brilliant plan in the heat of the moment.'

'And shooting the beast in the eye when I was on the deck. Excellent stuff, Nikki.' Dargo said.

'You saved my life first,' Achebe replied.

'Okay, let's stop blowing smoke up each other's arses,' Bullock said. 'Has the Chief spoken to you?'

'Yes, he visited me in the hospital. He didn't mention the fact that I had disobeyed his order to take time away from the case. He just wanted to make sure I was okay. Although, I think he was being overly sympathetic so I would sign a non-disclosure agreement regarding the werewolf. Looks like our exploits will never be truly known. That lot in there.' Achebe said, nodding to the peace officers in the main office. 'They've been told by the Chief we encountered an oversized grey wolf.'

'Not sure they will believe that,' Bullock said. 'But what can they do? They've no proof otherwise. Any stories of anything other than a giant grey wolf will just be rumour, and the government, the Chief, and Rockwell are well accustomed to assuaging rumours.'

'I also never mentioned Sam was with us in Bannock forest.' Achebe said.

'Good, neither did we.' Dargo smiled. 'Best to keep her involvement quiet. I spoke with her yesterday and she was singing your praises. But it sounds like without her, we may never have found the werewolf's den.'

'Correct. She was really shaken up when I met her after she left Sector Five. She was keeping her cards close to her chest, but I think she saw more than she bargained for.'

'Please talk us through everything that happened before we were chased by a giant grey wolf in Bannock forest. I've not quite pieced everything together.' Dargo said.

'Well, on reflection, there were signs that a human was behind the beast. The werewolf attacked one victim at Dalmally caravan park while he was reloading his shotgun, which could have been fortuitous timing for the beast. But I should've identified that human knowledge of a shotgun's reload time was vital for that attack, something Ulrich Lundstrom possessed given the shooting parties on the Bannock estate. Then at the cryptozoologist camp, the place was surrounded by cameras and yet none caught a clear picture. Most had been knocked over, which at the time I shrugged off as a consequence of a reckless beast, but again, because there was a person behind the werewolf, they knew how to evade any exposure.

282

Similarly, with the helicopters, the beast only attacked Maynard's unit when it heard it fly away from the area to refuel.'

Dargo squinted, unconvinced by Achebe's analysis.

'You're seeing signs that weren't really there, Nikki. We hear this all the time about murderers, don't we? At first, people are shocked when they find out someone is a killer. But afterwards, they make past incidents fit the murderer narrative. "He's not sociable in the community. They were a loner at school eighteen years ago." None of it means the person is a murderer, but people make it fit, and that's what you are doing now. You're trying to fit pieces of the jigsaw in the wrong place. Don't let these thoughts prey on your mind.'

'Well, if not those signs, then the lack of DNA found in the scratch marks at Bannock Manor should've made it obvious something other than an animal was at play.'

'But the fur samples belonged to species of wolf. Viti and her network of zoologists were baffled by the mismatch between the fur and the paw prints, but at no point did they say there wasn't an animal at play. Also, there are a lot of surviving witnesses to this beast, and not one of them had any notion that the animal wasn't real, such was the sophistication of the suit's technology. Even you and Gio witnessed it and didn't conclude it was anything other than a beast.'

'Ah, but this is the point I am most annoyed with myself about. A peculiarity from the day Gio and I were attacked bothered me. There was a moment when the werewolf's head was effectively in my lap because it smashed through the passenger window and was chomping away, trying to bite me. There was one thing missing from that whole scene, and I couldn't identify it, but it threatened to surface when Jen offered me a mint the next day, and only when talking to my friend over an egg sandwich a few days ago, did I realise what it was.'

Achebe paused for dramatic effect.

'I couldn't smell its breath.'

Achebe let the sentence hang, but the two detectives appeared bemused.

'You would understand if you worked with animals. When my dad was a ranger in Botswana, we would visit the veterinary clinic all the time and watch the vets attend to wounded sanctuary animals. Sometimes, as a treat, I was let into see the animal while it was anaesthetised. I got to touch lions, hippos, giraffes, zebras. The most vivid part of those memories, though, is the boggin' breath of the animals. It was always horrifyingly foul. If this werewolf was real, the halitosis would've been horrific.'

Bullock stroked his goatee with a grin, which told Achebe he was impressed.

'Soon after realising this, Sam phoned me. She was out of Sector Five and we met up so she could show me this.'

Achebe pulled a folder from her backpack and thumped it on Bullock's desk. He groaned as he sat upright in his chair.

'My visit to Morven Asylum confirmed that the werewolf was much older than we first thought, so I asked Sam to check any files in the Sector Five archive room from around the time Strathaven first opened. This is Project Volcano; a human experiment conducted in Sector Five almost two decades ago. The experiment operated under the guise of attempting to cure mental disorders such as bipolar disease and paranoid schizophrenia. What they were actually doing was cultivating killers. The same way football teams scout young talent with the goal of nurturing them over several years in preparation for first-team action, Strathaven was recruiting what they termed the criminally ill; people that have a mental disorder combined with a history of violence. The aim was to harness this violence and teach them the trait that makes serial killers so effective; their ability to blend into society unnoticed. This experiment developed a new breed of agents to be deployed in enemy territories. Ulrich Lundstrom was their star player. Turn to page seven, Xander.'

Bullock flicked through the file and began reading from the synopsis of Lundstrom's profile.

'Ulrich Lundstrom suffers from a rare psychosis known as lycanthropy. Furthermore, the subject has split his lycanthropic tendencies into three personalities. One vicious persona, known as Fenris, appears to dominate the other two, although all three personalities are capable of dangerous and fatal behaviour.'

'The profile outlines the mechanics of the suits they built for him.' Achebe said. 'That fed into his lycanthropy. It's an extremely rare disease. Less than fifty people have ever been diagnosed with such. By building a suit for each personality, Lundstrom succumbed deeper into his delusion. The immediate vicinity of Bannock Manor has purpose-built piping which dispenses mist, allowing the werewolf to attack unnoticed, as was the case when the ravers went missing. I believe Lundstrom was responsible for those deaths.'

'Fucking hell.' Bullock said, while studying the engineering diagrams of the suits.

'Also, the man reported to be Lundstrom at Morven Asylum is Hamish Stewart, the heir of Bannock Manor. Stewart was part of the initial intake of the *criminally ill* at Strathaven after years of drug abuse caused him

284

to become erratic, even shooting at some guests at Bannock estate. When he didn't quite make the grade as a master criminal, Strathaven released him, eventually faking his death knowing that Hamish had left the Bannock estate to Lundstrom, which they turned into a secret training ground for the werewolves. I believe Strathaven organised the raves to train Lundstrom and get him accustomed to different iterations of the suits, although I have no proof of this last point.'

'The kids were fucking guinea pigs.' Bullock said, clenching his fist at the injustice.

'But the raves were over ten years ago. Why the long absence of activity?' asked Dargo.

'Each subject is trained to be deployed in enemy territories. They would become sleeper agents, lying dormant, ready to erupt and kill at any moment, like a volcano. Each killer has to prove they can switch off their bloodthirst and live, for lack of a better term, normally. Lundstrom had a job working at another estate under the name Duncan Weir, proving he could be useful to society in some capacity. Jen and I went to interview him at the estate. I thought he was ill, in the late stages of cancer. He even referenced as much. But his complexion was not chalk white because of any disease; it was a lack of sunlight coupled with a diet that included cannibalism.'

'I still find it hard to believe they kept this beast away from civilians for all this time.'

'Who's to say they didn't deploy them in the field already? The document doesn't reveal any past missions the killers may have been on, but it does outline several versions of the werewolf suits. I think Lundstrom and his werewolves have already been out in the world. Sector Five then redesign and perfect the suits, Lundstrom has another trial run on Caledonian soil, albeit a bit more public this time, and then is sent back out into the field somewhere. The file does reference a potential mission for Lundstrom near an enemy army base in Siberia.'

Dargo shook his head before speaking.

'If this beast has been in Bannock forest for a while, intermittently or otherwise, it might be worth checking to see how many missing persons reports there have been in the area in the last two decades, most likely concluded as hikers who took a wrong turn and whose bodies were never recoverable.'

'It's worth checking.' Achebe said. '

Dargo puffed his cheeks as he struggled to comprehend what Achebe was presenting.

'All I keep thinking is how would I react if you were explaining MK Ultra to me for the first time, or the Holmesburg experiments, or operation Top Hat, or even the animal experiments at Porton Down? I'd be in disbelief of all those as well.'

'Rockwell is a sick fuck.' Bullock said. 'He's a terrorist, and yet we have signed NDAs to keep all this quiet. We are complicit.'

'He doesn't know we have this project file, though.' Achebe said.

'But it's admissible in court because Sam obtained it illegally, so the bastard will still get away with it.'

*

Rockwell rubbed his forehead as he listened to Caledonia's Head of Secret Service, Terry Halkett, vent his frustrations on the video call. Rockwell watched his pale complexion burn red, hoping it would pop like a squashed cherry.

'Terry, I'm going to stop you there. All you have cared about from day one is making sure your name is not associated with Project Volcano. Well, let me appease your irritating small-mindedness.'

'Rockwell, you…'

Rockwell muted Terry on the call. The other four attendees, including the Head of National Defence, Hilary Vox, dare not interrupt the man whose orange lenses shone just as intimidating a glare on screen as they did in person.

'I've always had an exit plan for this particular subject. I attended Morven Asylum today and personally saw to it that Hamish Stewart was put to sleep forever. To the outside world, Ulrich Lundstrom has now died there, and Bannock Manor will be transferred to the hands of the state. They won't do anything with the land for a while, so this gives us time to clear any evidence. You won't see it in the news, but there's been an unfortunate fire at Bannock Manor caused by some inconsiderate campers. The whole manor and surrounding trees have been destroyed. I have a team clearing the aftermath as we speak. This draws a line under this subject.'

Rockwell smirked as Halkett started talking, unaware that his microphone was silenced. Rockwell unmuted him.

'Go on, Terry, we can hear you now.'

'This is exactly the sort of poor planning I was talking about. If the land was going to be state-owned after Hamish's death, we would have full control, anyway. We are the state. So why did we keep Hamish alive until now? It's an unnecessary risk. This entire project has been littered with them.'

Rockwell exhaled an exaggerated sigh to let everyone on the call know he was not amused.

'Now that the Bannock estate is available, the public-facing part of the Caledonian government will come under pressure from both the citizens and businesses to open up the area for commercial activity and tourism. This was always a risk if we killed the Lundstrom name too early. It is my job to assess the risks and understand the motivations of external parties. It's your job, Terry, to toe the fucking line.'

'Then why do we have to do trial runs on our own people? Look at the lives its cost.'

'You are as thick as your career in politics suggests, Terry. If we do the trial runs abroad, on enemy shores, and they are caught, can you imagine the international scandal it would cause? Caledonian spies captured by our greatest foes because they have not been trained properly. The mess would be far greater than what I am dealing with now.'

This time, Halkett was not silenced by Rockwell's tinkering with technology. He went mute because he had to bow to a superior mind, one that had mapped out all potential scenarios and was already covering his tracks.

'There's no doubt that losing our biggest asset in this experiment is a sore loss. This subject was frequently successful in the field, but we must move on. Project Volcano continues.'

'What's the party line in the press on the attacks?' asked Hilary Vox.

'The attacks were conducted by an abnormally large grey wolf. Chief Thorne has already given a statement to this effect. I've procured the biggest grey wolf I can find from Canada, which we will shoot in Bannock forest. We will take photos, using optical illusions to make the wolf seem bigger, and then we will share these with the press.'

'What about Thorne's subordinates? They know all this is lies.'

'Thorne will make them cooperate. What good does it do to tell the public the truth? People want a story which conforms to their reality. In any case, Detectives Nikki Achebe, Tom Dargo and Xander Bullock have all signed NDAs. I will, of course, be keeping a very close eye on them. There will be a few unfortunate car accidents should any of them step out of line.'

There was a pause in the meeting. The attendees' shoulders sunk further back in their posture. They were appalled by Rockwell's callous disregard for human life, but simultaneously grateful he would conduct the necessary dirty work to keep the experiment forever silent.

'We are done here.'

The attendees were poised to say goodbyes, but Rockwell ended the call without another word spoken. He leaned back in his chair, opening the bottom drawer of his desk for a block of fudge. As he chewed the sugary delight, he poured himself a dram from the decanter, sitting back at his desk to savour the smoky Lagavulin liquid.

His phone buzzed. A message from a withheld number contained a video. He clicked to download it, watching as his phone struggled to load the content. When it did, he played it, his heart sinking into his stomach as he watched a replay of him punching and kicking Elodie Ricard before feeding her to the bear-hippo cross-species. His mind spiralled with possibilities of who could be the sender. The video continued to show him killing the scientist informant. He had helped Elodie obtain the Sector Five keycard, but only now did Rockwell realise the keycard was not for Elodie to use. It was for someone else entirely, the cameraman. He assessed who it could be. One of Terry Halkett's spies, or another disgruntled employee. Did he have to display yet another act of strength in front of them? Or could it be someone external? A detective, a private investigator, a journalist. The possibilities were not endless, but the scope was far too wide.

A text message pinged underneath the video.

You are finished.

Rockwell's nostrils flared, and his jaw muscles roiled with agitation. A doctored video, fake news, a pathetic smear campaign; the defence tactics were already spinning in his mind.

He put the phone down, composing himself through a series of deep breaths with his eyes closed. He took a sip from his dram, swirling the golden contents in his mouth before spitting in revulsion due to a concoction of whisky and Sam Stone's urine.

*

'So, I mentioned Lundstrom was part of a group of *criminally ill* subjects recruited by Sector Five.' Achebe said. 'Turn to page forty-seven.'

Bullock thumbed through the file.

'No fucking way,' he said.

288

Dargo used his feet to push his wheeled chair round the office to Bullock's desk. He gritted his teeth as his ravaged knees creaked with each exertion, but as he stared at a mugshot of Liv Sibine, his jaw became slack. Bullock read the synopsis under her name.

'The subject is a paranoid schizophrenic. Abused by her father as a child, we have been successful in leveraging on her natural tendency to become violent towards men, especially those with muscular physiques like her father. Asphyxiation is her chosen method to kill, evoking a sense of control over her victims.'

Bullock scanned the body of the file, speaking again when he spotted a point of particular interest.

'The subject struggles to control her urges, often inflicting overly gruesome and exorbitant violence, even post-mortem. If not controlled, this can lead to erratic behaviour which draws unwanted attention and could compromise any mission. We have developed a control method using probability wheels to dictate how violently she can behave and what weapons she is permitted to use for each kill. This has been successful in early trials and will continue to be monitored.'

'What was it you said about all the recent murders, Xander; Caledonia feels like a breeding ground for killers. That's because it has been. Liv Sibine was a fairly new addition to the Project Volcano programme. As was Bob Huskins.'

'Fuck off!' Bullock said.

Dargo appeared less shocked by Achebe's revelation. Instead, his mind battled with an unnerving notion.

'Given there's a fair number of profiles in this file, that means there are more sleepers out there, either lying low and waiting to attack when Rockwell instructs them, or maybe killing right now without us knowing.'

'It appears that way, and one of them is Dr Fliss Baxter, Head of Morven Asylum. I met her when I visited who I thought was Ulrich Lundstrom, but was actually Hamish Stewart. Morven Asylum took in many of the early participants of Project Volcano after Sector Five deemed them obsolete. With an array of mental health issues and violent tendencies, society was not missing them. So, over the years, Dr Baxter killed them; all controlled, measured deaths in their sleep via poison. Some deaths were even sanctioned by the government when a patient's behaviour became problematic in the asylum, but it's Dr Baxter who recommends each execution. You don't need to be a detective to deduce she's been falsifying those recommendations so the government would sanction a kill. She might not be a murderer in the conventional sense, but she's a murderer all the same.'

'We have to locate these individuals before they kill again,' Dargo said.

'We can locate them.' Bullock said. 'But how can we get clearance from the Chief to start an investigation when our only piece of evidence is this document, which was obtained illegally, and incriminates his chum, Rockwell? We would have to investigate this on our own. Go rogue.'

Bullock said this with mischievous delight.

'We might not have to do that.' Achebe said. 'Sam has copies of every page of this file. She's going to write an article exposing various experiments in Sector Five, this being one of them. She will say the files were delivered by a whistleblower called Elodie, who was killed by Rockwell, according to Sam.'

'Does she have evidence of that?' asked Dargo.

'Not sure.'

'If Sam writes an expose, Rockwell will know Project Volcano is compromised. And what do you bet the individuals in these files start dying off or go mysteriously missing as Rockwell covers his tracks? Our predicament is, when is Sam going to publish that article? These stories take time. A lot of lives could be lost between now and publication.'

'I'm not sure what her timescale is,' Achebe said, watching the cogs of Dargo's mind play out in real time.

'This could get messy really quickly. The three of us need to come up with a plan to apprehend or conduct surveillance on the remaining individuals of this project, and we need to do that without the Chief or Rockwell finding out.'

Each detective fell silent, letting the information settle in their minds.

'There is one thing that's bugging me,' said Achebe.

'What's that?' Bullock asked.

'These murderers are trained to kill, then lie low and blend into society. So, bearing that in mind, have you found Liv Sibine's body?'

Dargo exhaled as he stood next to the whiteboard with Liv Sibine written in marker pen at the top.

'You think she's in hiding?' Bullock asked.

'Could she have survived the rapids?'

'I mean, potentially.' Bullock said, reluctantly.

Dargo began drawing lines from each letter of Liv Sibine's name, rearranging the order to spell the word; *invisible*.

The End